# Homosexuality in Renaissance and Enlightenment England: Literary Representations in Historical Context

# Homosexuality in Renaissance and Enlightenment England: Literary Representations in Historical Context

OCT 1993

Claude J. Summers, PhD
Editor

*Homosexuality in Renaissance and Enlightenment England: Literary Representations in Historical Context*, edited by Claude J. Summers, was simultaneously issued by The Haworth Press, Inc., under the same title, as a special issue of *Journal of Homosexuality*, Volume 23, Numbers 1/2, 1992, John DeCecco Editor.

Harrington Park Press
An Imprint of
The Haworth Press, Inc.
New York • London • Norwood (Australia)

ISBN 1-56023-019-3

Published by

Harrington Park Press, 10 Alice Street, Binghamton, NY 13904-1580 USA

Harrington Park Press is an imprint of The Haworth Press, Inc., 10 Alice Street, Binghamton, NY 13904-1580 USA.

*Homosexuality in Renaissance and Enlightenment England: Literary Representations in Historical Context* was originally published as *Journal of Homosexuality,* Volume 23, Numbers 1/2, 1992.

**Library of Congress Cataloging-in-Publication Data**

Homosexuality in renaissance and enlightenment England : literary representations in historical context / Claude J. Summers, editor.
 p. cm.
 Includes bibliographical references and index.
 ISBN 1-56024-295-7 (acid-free paper). – ISBN 1-56023-019-3 (acid-free paper)
 1. English literature – Early modern, 1500-1700 – History and criticism. 2. Homosexuality and literature – England – History – 16th century. 3. Homosexuality and literature – England – History – 17th century. 4. Homosexuality and literature – England – History – 18th century. 5. English literature – 18th century – History and criticism. 6. Erotic literature, English – History and criticism. 7. Enlightenment – England. 8. Renaissance – England. 9. Sex in literature. I. Summers, Claude J.
PR428.H66H65 1992
820.9'353 – dc20
                 92-10394
                  CIP

# Homosexuality in Renaissance and Enlightenment England: Literary Representations in Historical Context

# ABOUT THE EDITOR

**Claude J. Summers, PhD,** is William E. Stirton Professor in the Humanities and Professor of English at the University of Michigan at Dearborn. The co-editor of collections of essays on a variety of subjects in seventeenth-century English literature, Dr. Summers is the author of book-length critical studies of Christopher Marlowe, Christopher Isherwood, and E.M. Forster, and of numerous essays on Renaissance and twentieth-century literature. His most recent books include *Gay Fictions: Wilde to Stonewall: Studies in a Homosexual Literary Tradition* and *E.M. Forster: A Guide to Research*. Dr. Summers is a recipient of the Crompton-Noll Award in gay studies and is former chair of the Modern Language Association's Division on Gay Studies in Language and Literature.

# CONTENTS

ALL HARRINGTON PARK PRESS BOOKS
ARE PRINTED ON CERTIFIED
ACID-FREE PAPER

# Introduction

Over the past two decades, gay studies has emerged as a distinct, though somewhat amorphous and necessarily interdisciplinary, field of intellectual inquiry, characterized by a particular subject matter—the study of gay male and lesbian experience, broadly defined—and by a sympathetic and supportive attitude toward that subject matter. That is, the term *gay studies* signifies not merely the study of an issue associated with homosexuality, but also a positive attitude toward homosexuality, an appreciation of the complexity and variety of gay and lesbian experience, and an awareness of the difficulties involved in approaching homosexuality historically and transculturally. As a field gay studies embraces an extraordinarily wide range of issues and methodologies, welcoming—often demanding—historical, psychological, sociological, anthropological, biological, medical, legal, political, philosophical, aesthetic, cultural, and literary perspectives, among others. The very breadth of the topic means, of course, not only that gay studies is perforce interdisciplinary, but also that in practice it is always pursued partially and narrowly, roughly aligning along familiar disciplinary divisions, such as gay studies in history or gay studies in sociology. Perhaps because literary studies have traditionally adapted the paradigms and insights of other disciplines, especially those of the behavioral and social sciences, the practice of gay studies in literature has been especially amenable to a multidisciplinary approach.

The present volume focuses on the literature of Renaissance and Enlightenment England, but as a contribution to gay studies it is multidisciplinary in both practice and theory. It aims to illuminate particular works of literature in which homosexuality is represented or encoded and, by means of exploring that literature, also to elucidate the status and shape of same-sex desire in a circumscribed era, roughly the period from Marlowe to Gray. These two goals are not only naturally complementary, they are also reflexive and reciprocal, for literature is at once a reflection and an expression of social attitudes. Insofar as literature documents (or challenges) its period's sexual beliefs and prohibitions, it is an extraordinarily valuable resource for concretizing and charting the outlines of sexual ideology at any particular time. More than any other kind of discourse, literature expresses desire and gives us access to the subjectivity and complexity of sexuality, depicting the nuances and ambivalences of desire from the inside. Conversely, the interpretive constructs of reality that constitute our notion of history provide indispensable contexts in which to locate and probe texts, as well as important new lenses through which to view and anatomize both neglected and overly familiar works.

Homosexuality, and even homosexual subjectivity, is writ large in the literature of the English Renaissance and Enlightenment, but its inscription in this varied discourse is only rarely direct and unambiguous. In studying the literary representations of homosexuality in the English Renaissance and Enlightenment, the essays collected here are engaged in a vital and necessary process of rehistoricizing and re-contextualizing literature. Utilizing a variety of critical methods and proceeding from several different theoretical and ideological presuppositions, these essays raise important questions about the methodology of gay studies, about the conception of same-sex desire, about the depiction of homoerotics, and about the relationship of sexuality and textuality in a demarcated period, even as they also bring to new light or reconsider the homosexual import of a number of significant works of literature. Some of the texts considered here are quite familiar and expected, part of the small, generally accepted canon of gay literature in English; while others are more surprising, either because they are obscure or because they are not usually discussed in the sexual contexts provided here. In establishing new contexts for this literature, these essays ask fresh questions and elicit striking — and sometimes unanticipated — answers.

What is perhaps most noticeable about the essays as a group is their authors' consciousness of the problems of discerning and defining homosexuality in texts of earlier ages. The difficulty arises in the first instance from the historical pressures against writing openly about same-sex emotions and relationships, and it is compounded by an entrenched scholarly tradition that has denied and obfuscated the homosexual presence in English literature. But discerning homosexuality in the literature of the Renaissance and Enlightenment is also rendered problematic as a result of our sometimes paralyzing awareness that while homosexual behavior and feelings are universal, homosexual identity and roles are culturally and historically specific. Hence, the essayists here, like most gay studies practitioners, are sensitive to the dangers of anachronism and feel compelled to locate their texts in carefully delineated cultural and historical milieux. Yet they by no means agree as to the precise nature of homosexuality as a historical construct, nor are they unduly constrained by the tyranny of theory or the anxieties of anachronism. For most of the contributors to this collection, theories of sexuality are still in process, subject to the empirical evidence to be gained from literature and other documents of the past. That is, rather than proceeding from hidebound or fashionably current ideologies, they sift the texts they study for the concrete — if not always obvious — evidence from which theories might be constructed or modified.

The historical conception of same-sex attraction is at issue in Joseph Cady's lead essay on Renaissance language. Forcefully challenging the idea that homosexuality is a new historical "invention," it disputes the currently prevalent notion that the Renaissance had no definite awareness of or language for homosexuality as a distinct category of experience or person. Cady focuses on the term "masculine love" as used in such different works as Bacon's *New Atlantis* and Heywood's *Pleasant Dialogues and Dramas*, and concludes that it was but one of several public languages that acknowledged homosexuality as a distinct category in the Renaissance. Cady's essay is important not only for its close analysis and thoughtful interpretation of primary texts, but also for its trenchant critique of the methodology of gay studies in Renaissance history, especially the excessive reliance on ecclesiastical and civil laws and police and trial records and the concomitant neglect of other sources, including literary ones.

Gay studies methodology is also at the fore in Gregory Bredbeck's densely argued but fascinating study of the sonnet sequences of Barnfield and Shakespeare. A meditation on critical theory,

Bredbeck's essay explores the relationship of textual and social subjectivity, particularly in reference to the difficulties of finding within the discursive practices of Renaissance literature a place for those whose subjectivity is defined by their male-male sexual preferences. In the process, the essay offers carefully modulated readings of poetic sequences whose homoeroticism inscribes the sodomite for different rhetorical purposes.

In contrast to Cady and Bredbeck, Gregory Woods is less interested in theoretical issues than in practical criticism. Exploring the depiction of homoerotic desire in the poetry and plays of Christopher Marlowe, Woods concentrates on such motifs as clothing and the body and offers valuable insights into a number of works, including *Dr. Faustus* as well as *Edward II*. In his lively and accessible essay, Woods reveals the Marlovian world as one in which most desirers are mature men in the prime of manhood while most of the desired are adolescent boys or very young men. He concludes that in Marlowe's arena of the erotic every embrace involves an assertion or adjustment of power relations.

If Marlowe, Barnfield, and Shakespeare are authors whom one might anticipate as the subjects of essays on the literary representation of homosexuality in the English Renaissance, John Donne emphatically is not. The witty and passionate, alternately cynical and idealistic, author of *Songs and Sonets* and the love elegies is widely recognized as the late Renaissance's supreme poet of heterosexual love in all its variety. Yet, as the two essays devoted to him in this collection attest, Donne is also a powerful — if hitherto unrecognized — poet of homosexual love and experience. The surprising example of Donne is yet another reminder of the fluidity of sexual and emotional response, in literature as well as in life.

In the first sustained and serious consideration of four verse letters that the youthful Donne addressed to a younger male friend, probably Thomas Woodward, George Klawitter finds in them a highly charged homoeroticism. Placing the individual poems (including Woodward's response) in their correct order and analyzing their patterns of imagery and allusions, Klawitter demonstrates that the poems constitute a sequence that records, first, Donne's infatuation for his friend and, then, his disappointment with the friend's failure to respond with a like ardor. Klawitter's work is important not merely—or even primarily—for its biographical implications, but also for focusing fresh attention on these neglected verse letters, which deserve recognition as significant documents in the Renaissance literature of homoeroticism.

In a notably erudite essay, Janel Mueller turns her attention to another neglected work by Donne, the extraordinary dramatic monologue entitled "Sapho to Philaenis." Placing the poem within a rich context of humanist scholarship about Sappho, and comparing it both with other Renaissance poetic representations of lesbianism and with the discourse of modern lesbian feminism, Mueller finds "Sapho to Philaenis" a remarkable achievement. Unlike his contemporary poets and scholars, Donne portrays lesbianism positively. More than that, his sympathetic depiction of lesbianism questions the conventions of heterosexuality that dominated his age's literature and society. Not only does Donne make lesbianism a master trope for utopian sexuality, but, Mueller argues, he also configures lesbian self-sufficiency onto the economic plane as well. Although "Sapho to Philaenis" has until recently been largely ignored by Donne scholars and critics, it is here rehabilitated as a visionary poem that projects lesbianism "into a fully utopian moment for human possibility."

The subject of Ellis Hanson's essay is the relationship of sodomy to the Jacobean conception of monarchy, especially as illustrated by Lady Mary Wroth's prose romance *Urania* and Shakespeare's *Antony and Cleopatra*, both of which may refer to King James's infatuation with his favorite Robert Carr. The age's widespread anxiety about the King's "erotic doubleness" is reflected in Wroth's disguised account of James's relationship to Carr in *Urania*, as well as in the comments of a number of Puritan memoirists who treat the King and his favorites much less sympathetically. In contrast, Shakespeare, in *Antony and Cleopatra*, reproduces the conventional sexual narrative favored by the Puritans, but complicates it by evincing and eliciting sympathy for the illicit sexuality of the title pair. Hanson suggests that in the polarities of *Antony and Cleopatra*, especially its contrast between duty and pleasure, Shakespeare may obliquely represent the division in James's own life, torn as he was between duty to his wife and pleasure in his favorites.

Protesting against a tradition that denies the sexual content of lesbian literature, Arlene Stiebel examines masking techniques in the poetry of Katherine Philips and Aphra Behn. Both poets employ traditional literary conventions — including the courtly love address to the beloved and her response, the idealized pattern of Platonic same-sex friendship, and the hermaphroditic perfection of the beloved who incorporates the best of both sexes — but the voice of the lover is not disguised as a male. The reliance on familiar conventions helps make the representation of a woman's desire for a female lover seem as innocuous as literary exercises, but even as the poems mask the reality of sexual desire, they simultaneously reveal it as well. As Stiebel demonstrates, the apparent "innocence" of lesbian love in Renaissance poetry is itself an ironic mask.

Two essays are devoted to Cleland's *Fanny Hill*. Kevin Kopelson analyzes the famous scene in which Fanny spies on two young men making love. This scene, Kopelson argues, disturbs the representational framework of the novel, and, in its erotic transgression, transcends significance. The sodomitical passage is also crucial to Donald Mengay's essay on the rhetoric of cross-dressing in *Fanny Hill*, which views Fanny as a female drag persona for a decidedly male implied narrator. In Mengay's reading, the sodomitical scene is structurally and thematically central to a pervasive homoerotic subtext. Emphasizing the phallocentrism of the text, its homoerotic classical allusions, Fanny's self-referential phallic rhetoric, and the work's anxiety over anal penetration, Mengay interprets *Fanny Hill* as subversive of the code of bourgeois heterosexuality that it ostensibly celebrates.

In his contribution, George E. Haggerty deals not with the explicit depictions of sexual activity characteristic of *Fanny Hill* but with the indirect and subtle effects of Thomas Gray's sexual frustration and internalized homophobia in his masterpiece, "Elegy Written in a Country Churchyard." Examining as well Gray's moving sonnet on the death of his beloved friend Richard West, Haggerty draws particular attention to the poet's hardwon recovery discernible in the differences between the original and revised versions of the "Elegy." Especially in its treatment of the personified figure of Death, the original version expresses Gray's fear of his own sexuality. In the revision, however, the poet confronts more directly his tormented sensibility and finally embraces the possibility of intimacy in the world.

These thoughtful essays are shaped as responses to narrowly defined and specific literary and cultural topics. Each significantly illuminates the subject that it carves out as its own. But the collection as a whole is valuable for more than the sum of its parts. In addition to the numerous local insights provided by each essay, the collection illustrates the vitality and variety of gay studies in literature, especially as applied to works of earlier ages. Some of the essays are self-conscious in their theoretical approaches, while others are primarily interested in practical criticism; some use the texts they discuss as evidence for formulating broad statements about homosexuality in the period, while others apply cultural generalizations to particular texts; some discover homoeroticism in hitherto unknown places, while others meditate on the significance of works that are obviously but problematically homoerotic; some of the essays proceed from biographical knowledge to textual illumination, while others reverse the process. For all their diversity of method and goal, however, taken together these essays achieve coherence by virtue of their focus on a single period and their shared commitment to a historical understanding of the gay and lesbian experience in literature. The collection attests both the current intellectual ferment of gay studies and the richness of English Renaissance and eighteenth-century literary representations of homosexuality.

*Claude J. Summers, PhD*

# "Masculine Love," Renaissance Writing, and the "New Invention" of Homosexuality

Joseph Cady, PhD

University of Rochester Medical School

**SUMMARY.** Contrary to the dominant claim in gay studies now that homosexuality is a relatively new historical "invention," the Renaissance had a definite recognition of a distinct homosexuality, acknowledged at least by those who were willing to face and discuss the subject frankly. A key example of that awareness is the earlier term "masculine love," which seems to have been particularly prominent in the Renaissance as a language for a male homosexual orientation. Significant differences have clearly occurred in the homosexual situation over time, and homosexuality can never be discussed totally independent of historical and social conditions, but the "new-inventionism" currently prevailing in gay studies has serious problems of concept and method and needs careful examining.

---

Joseph Cady teaches literature and medicine at the University of Rochester Medical School and gay and lesbian literature at the New School for Social Research. Correspondence may be addressed to Division of the Medical Humanities, Box 676, University of Rochester Medical School, Rochester, NY 14642.

Research on this article was begun while on a fellowship from the American Council for Learned Societies. The author would like to thank the ACLS for its invaluable assistance and for its willingness to support a gay-identified project when it was largely unheard of to do so. A partial version of this article was delivered as a paper at the 1990 annual meeting of the Renaissance Society of America.

For their special help and encouragement with this project, the author would like to thank Annette Kolodny, Judith Lowder Newton, the late Richard Newton, John Richetti, James M. Saslow, Paul Strohm, and Claude J. Summers. This article is dedicated to the late Richard Newton.

9

## *1.*

The notion that homosexuality is a relatively new historical "invention," which I shall refer to here as "new-inventionism," has become, at least in tone, the vanguard position among academics and intellectuals interested in gay studies now. Before that "invention," this outlook implies, sexuality took, or was understood to take, one of two forms of what was in effect a kind of bisexuality (although without any such label of course being applied then). To commentators like Alan Bray and Jeffrey Weeks, what might be called the "pre-homosexuality" era was marked by an "undivided sexuality" (Bray 25), or a generalized "flux of sexualities" (Weeks, "Havelock Ellis" 33), in which a person's erotic attractedness followed no predominating or predictable pattern, including direction toward one sex or the other. To others like Randolph Trumbach, there prevailed then a more regularized and differentiated bisexuality, whose homosexual component was always age-asymmetrical, an "older pattern [in which] the debauchee or libertine who denied the relegation of sexuality to marriage [could] find . . . women and boys with whom he might indifferently . . . enact his desires" ("Sodomitical" 118). In any case, both groups agree that in that earlier era sexuality was understood only as discrete "acts" or "behavior" that people performed and not, for example, as the expression of any inner inclination or directionality (see, especially, the introductory sections in Katz, *Gay/Lesbian Almanac*).

There is disagreement among new-inventionists about exactly when "the invention of homosexuality" took place. Most favor the late nineteenth century, when laws directed specifically against homosexuality (instead of against a more broadly defined "sodomy") appeared in the West for the first time and when our contemporary terms "homosexual" and "heterosexual" first came into being and were later promulgated by the new medical and social sciences.[1] This position owes much to the pioneering work of Michel Foucault and Jeffrey Weeks, and spokespersons for it maintain, for example, that "As defined by the ancient civil or canonical codes, sodomy was a category of forbidden acts; . . . the nineteenth-century homosexual became a personage, . . . a species" (Foucault 43), "From the mid nineteenth century . . . homosexuality gradually emerges as a separate category'' (Weeks, *Coming Out* 25), and ''[Before the time of Oscar Wilde there was an] *absence of* any felt specificity of male homosexual desire in the culture at large'' (Sedgwick, ''Comments'' 108).[2] Other commentators shift ''the invention of homosexuality'' back to the start of the eighteenth century, with what they see as the first appearance of identifiable male homosexual subcultures in major Western European cities at that time. Advocates of this date hold, for example, that ''A distinct, separate . . . 'homosexual' emerged in England at the end of the seventeenth century'' (McIntosh 188) and that ''[In the] late seventeenth century . . . homosexuality began to be conceived of as a characteristic of certain individuals only and not of others'' (Bray 108).[3] In addition, it is not always clear what new-inventionism means by ''the invention of homosexuality.'' As reflected in the quotations above and to follow, commentators sometimes seem to be discussing de facto homosexuality/homosexuals, sometimes broad cultural awareness of the subject, sometimes individual homosexual self-consciousness, and sometimes organized homosexual subcultures.

However, at least two clear points emerge in new-inventionism, despite these differences and fluctuations. One is that, whenever ''the invention of homosexuality'' occurred, it had not yet happened by the time of the Renaissance. This view is clearly implied by the comments above and explicitly stated in remarks like Alan Bray's that ''Homosexuality . . . was not a sexuality in its own right'' in the age (25). The second is that, whatever other dimensions of the subject may or may not have ''existed'' at that time, before ''the invention of homosexuality'' there existed no significant conception of, nor language for, homosexuality as a distinct, categorical, sexual orientation (i.e., as an ongoing, predominant or exclusive, erotic attraction, in someone or some persons, to the broad category of their own sex, especially an attraction chiefly toward adult age-peers). This perspective is reflected in such various remarks as Foucault's comment that ''The sensuality of those who did not like the opposite sex [was] hardly noticed in the past'' (38-39) and Jonathan Goldberg's assertion that ''There were no discrete terms for homosexual behavior in the [Renaissance]'' (371).

My main purpose in this essay is to propose a markedly different view of the Renaissance as an era in which a definite awareness and language for a distinct homosexuality existed, at least among those who were willing to face and discuss the subject frankly. My example is the phrase "masculine love," a term that seems to have been particularly prominent as a language for a male homosexual orientation in the Renaissance but that has never been the subject of study before.[4] "Masculine love" was by no means the Renaissance's only language for male homosexuality, but it is a particularly revealing one since it exists totally outside the disputed and occasionally ambiguous terminology of "sodomy."[5] I shall discuss it here through a detailed analysis of two English Renaissance texts in which the phrase appears, followed by a shorter mention of some continental Renaissance materials that also use the term and reflect the same recognition. To be sure, "masculine love" is a term for male homosexuality only, but I believe the point I draw from it can apply to homosexuality as a whole, since it does not seem likely that a culture would be aware of one kind of homosexuality without a corresponding broader recognition that such a thing as same-sex attraction in general also existed.

My other purpose is to call for a substantial examination of new-inventionism through my discussion here. Some scholars associated with new-inventionism, like Jonathan Katz, John D'Emilio, and Judith Brown, have done crucial work in uncovering new primary sources about pre-contemporary homosexuality. Furthermore, significant differences have clearly occurred in the homosexual situation over time, and homosexuality can never be discussed totally independent of historical and social conditions. In addition, I do not even mean to object in principle to the ultimate new-inventionist idea that a de facto homosexual orientation might itself be a historical "invention." However, as presently practiced new-inventionism is a problem-ridden enterprise lacking in careful attention to its methods and concepts.

Two clarifications need to be established before turning to my specific materials. The first is an explicit definition of what a distinct language or term for homosexuality would be, in any time or place. Such language would clearly be a crucial, though not indispensable, index of earlier awareness of homosexuality, but the scholarship on this subject has not yet provided a clear guideline for identifying it. I would propose that a "language" about homosexuality (either as a sexual orientation or as a universal occasional feeling) is any kind of verbal construct that, according to the particular modes of denoting reality that were characteristic of the age or culture in question, sufficiently differentiates same-sex attraction (again, either as an orientation or as an occasional feeling) as a distinct category of experience; this same formulation could of course also apply to the denotation of homosexuals as individuals or as a group. As my words "any kind" stress, no arbitrary restrictions of texture or length should be placed on what could be called a "language for homosexuality"—i.e., it could include a spectrum of designations, ranging from focused categorical terms (either literal or figurative), to terms that have different technical meanings but that are effectively used to denote only homosexuality, to extended descriptive or generic phrases that amount to de facto recognitions of the subject.[6] This purposely broad range gives us the widest possible net within which to catch designations of same-sex eroticism in any one period. In addition, by accounting for the fact that different eras can denote reality quite differently (a point that under other circumstances would, I know, be a truism not needing mention), it also gives us a way to chart this subject across periods, to identify, for example, terms that might seem totally foreign to us, or totally unrelated to each other, as equivalent languages for homosexuality within the frameworks of their times.

Secondly, I should explain my particular critical vocabulary in this essay. Most readers in this field would probably identify the position I am questioning here by the more familiar label of "social constructionism." However, there is often an obscurity about what advocates actually mean when they refer to "social constructionism" and its opposite term "essentialism" in discussions of homosexuality (just as there frequently is to the phrase "invention of homosexuality").[7] In addition, the language of the "social constructionism" label could create the mistaken impression that anyone questioning it is also critical of the idea that social conditions can have a profound influence on homosexuality. For these reasons, I prefer my term "new-inventionism" here instead. Though, as I have mentioned, it is often unclear what proponents mean by "the invention of homosexuality," "new-inventionism" at least has the virtue of evoking specifically and concretely the basic issue in this debate in gay studies — i.e., is or is not homosexuality a new historical "invention"? It also more sharply highlights some of the possible broader social consequences of this outlook — e.g., new-inventionism's apparent concern with eliminating homosexuality from the earlier historical map can, if unintentionally, give implicit support to opponents of contemporary gay rights.

## 2.

One of the most notable uses of "masculine love" in English Renaissance writing occurs in the "feast of the family" section of Francis Bacon's *New Atlantis*, the unfinished utopian work about the ideal land of Bensalem that Bacon wrote in 1610 and that was posthumously published in 1627. It seems clear that Bacon himself was chiefly or exclusively attracted to other males, and he is one of the few figures from periods as distant as the Renaissance for whom we have significant supporting evidence for his homosexuality from sources outside of his work, in this case from comments by contemporaries and family members. For example, in his *Autobiography* Sir Simonds D'Ewes, a younger contemporary, refers to Bacon's attraction to other males as his "most abominable . . . sin [that] I should rather bury in silence than mention" (192).[8] The somewhat later and less prudish chronicler, John Aubrey, states flatly in his *Brief Lives* that Bacon "was a pederast," using that term in the sense of "a male homosexual" (11).[9] (Even Aubrey's discussion of the subject is somewhat censored, however; while the rest of his account of Bacon's life is in English, he leaves the word "pederast" in the original Greek.) In addition, a letter of 17 April 1593 from Bacon's mother to his brother Anthony survives (Anthony Bacon apparently also was homosexual), in which she accuses Bacon of keeping a certain "bloody Percy" as a "bed companion — a proud profane costly fellow, whose being about him I fear the Lord God doth mislike" (Spedding 244).[10] Since the practice of sharing a bed non-sexually with someone of the same sex was so common in earlier periods like the Renaissance, Lady Bacon's alarm here clearly seems to be about a likely sexual relation between Percy and her son.

Bacon himself hints at his attraction to other males in some of his writings, most strongly in his essays — in "Of Friendship," where, like other homosexual/bisexual male writers of his time and later, he uses the language of "friendship" to allude to homosexuality;[11] in "Of Marriage and the Single Life," with its praise of "unmarried and childless men" as the "best friends, best masters, best servants" and as the sources of "the best works, . . . of greatest merit for the public" (29-30); and most especially in "Of Beauty," which discusses examples of male beauty only, a startling focus given what my materials here suggest was the intense hostility to male-male attraction in his age. (As is well-known, Bacon was married, but his omission of women from his pantheon of beauty should of course caution us against seeing him as confirmation of the "bisexuality" that new-inventionism implies was universal in earlier periods; it is also relevant here that Bacon did not marry until the late age of 45, that his wife is barely mentioned in his biography, and that he had no children.) In addition, there is a marked suggestion of homosexuality in Bacon's interestingly-titled *The Masculine Birth of Time*, an unfinished short polemic against the prevailing Western philosophical and educational traditions that he composed around 1603 and that scholars have called "from the personal angle, one of the most illuminating of all [Bacon's] works" (Farrington 17). A monologue by an older man in authority to a younger man whom he is setting out to instruct and whom he calls his "son," *The Masculine Birth of Time* ends with a plea by the speaker to "my dear, dear boy . . . from my inmost heart" to "give yourself to me so that I may restore you to yourself" and "secure [you] an increase beyond all the hopes and prayers of ordinary marriages" (Farrington 72).

Bacon's reference to male homosexuality in the *New Atlantis* contrasts markedly with these veiled praises of the subject in his other works; constructed to give the clear impression of coming from outside the phenomenon, it is much more in keeping with his age's prevailing opposition to male-male attraction. Scholars have usually emphasized the educational and scientific aspects of the *New Atlantis*, seeing it as a complement to Bacon's earlier *Advancement of Learning* (1605) and, in its delineation of the agricultural and scientific experiment center known as Solomon's House, as a direct inspiration for the founding of the Royal Society a generation later (1660). Indeed, much of the *New Atlantis* is devoted to such concerns. The opening half of the work is dominated by the Governor of the Strangers' House and his explanation of Bensalem's history, survival, and manner of dealing with the outside world, and the last third is largely devoted to a description of the purposes and characters of Solomon's House by one of its "fathers." But in between these two parts is a shorter section that, though not overlooked by commentators, needs to be emphasized more for the extremely valuable information it imparts about Renaissance attitudes toward the family, gender, and sexuality. This section, in which the narrator and his shipmates leave the Strangers' House and explore the city, is devoted to a delineation of a ceremony that Bensalem calls "the feast of the family," and it amounts to an extended paean to what in contemporary terms we would call the heterosexual/patriarchal nuclear family and its values – e.g., the centrality and primacy of the (preferably married) male and father; the exaltation of biological procreation (and an ideally abundant procreation); the auxiliary/secondary status of women; and the strict division of gender roles.

The "feast of the family" section falls into two parts. In the first the narrator describes the feast itself. A ceremony held in honor of any father of a family who has lived "to see thirty persons descended from his body" and who is accordingly given the honorific title of "Tirsan," it signifies, we are told, the ultimate moral ideal – "a most natural, pious, and reverend custom it is, showing the nation to be compounded of all goodness" (274). The patriarchal assumptions and values I mentioned above are clearly implied in the characterization of the Tirsan and are echoed throughout the ceremony itself, chiefly in the paramount role played by men and the subordinate, and sometimes invisible, position of women. For instance, in the opening procession the Tirsan is preceded by his male offspring and followed by his female line, while the mother of the family, "if there be [one] from whose body the whole lineage is descended," is seated in an enclosed balcony compartment where she can view the ceremony but cannot be seen (276). In the same spirit, the embroidery decorating the Tirsan's throne is always the responsibility of "the daughters of the family," while the special child the Tirsan chooses during the ceremony "to live in house with him" is always a son (275). Relatedly, in the hymn sung at the end of the feast "the subject . . . is always the praises of Adam, and Noah, and Abraham, whereof the former two peopled the world and the last was the father of the faithful" (278).

Bacon's mention of "masculine love" occurs in the second part of the section, which consists of a conversation between the narrator and a merchant named Joabin several days later. Declaring that he had been "Much affected [by] their custom in holding the feast of the family, . . . I had never heard of a solemnity wherein nature did so much preside," the narrator pursues the subject by asking Joabin "what laws and customs [Bensalem] had concerning marriage" (281). There follows a long passage contrasting Bensalem's virtues in this regard with the sexual "foulness" of Europe, a passage seemingly aimed at Bacon's contemporary English audience and perhaps also recalling the two-and-a-half years Bacon spent at the French court during Henri III's reign, where the homosexuality of the king and his "mignons" was rampant and much discussed.[12] (Bacon was a member of the staff of Sir Amias Paulet, the English ambassador to the French crown, from September 1576 to February 1579 and would thus have had ample opportunity to observe the homosexual milieu of Henri III and his entourage.) "There is not under the heavens so chaste a nation as this of Bensalem; nor so free from all pollutions or foulness," Joabin proudly begins. "With them there are no stews, no dissolute houses, no courtesans, nor anything of that kind. Nay they wonder (with detestation) at you in Europe, which permit such things . . . [that] remain . . . as a very affront to marriage." Joabin then elaborates on this charge: "There are with you seen infinite men that marry not, but chuse rather a libertine and impure single life, than to be yoked in marriage; and many that do marry, marry late, when the prime and strength of their years is past. And when they do marry, what is marriage to them but a very bargain; wherein is sought alliance, or portion, or reputation, with some desire (almost indifferent) of issue; and not the faithful nuptial union of man and wife that was first instituted." These married men, he asserts, continue to haunt "those dissolute places, or resort to courtesans," where they "delight in meretricious embracements, (where sin is turned into art)," and this "depraved custom" is "no more punished in married men than in bachelors" (281-83).

Next, near the end of his speech, Joabin turns to the subject of what he calls "masculine love." One of his final recommendations of Bensalem over Europe is that, "As for masculine love, they have no touch of it; and yet there are not as faithful and inviolate friendships in the world again as are there" (283). Then, after a few brief references to more of Bensalem's customs concerning marriage (e.g., its outlawing of polygamy), the "feast of the family" section ends, and the *New Atlantis* turns to its final focus on the character and activities of Solomon's House. Given the profound tension between homosexuality and the values of patriarchy (for example, the tendencies within homosexuality toward autonomy of being and equality/"symmetry" in relationships), it is not surprising that here, in what is in effect an exalting of patriarchy, the characterization of male same-sex love would be totally negative. Still, it may have been at some emotional cost, or at least significant personal compromise, that Bacon—involved in a "late," childless, and pro forma marriage himself and attracted predominantly or exclusively to his own sex—composed this paean to marriage, the patriarchal family, and biological procreation and depicted his ideal commonwealth as having absolutely "no touch" of "masculine love."

This long passage tells us in several ways that "masculine love" here refers to what we would now call a male homosexual orientation. In the first place, and most broadly, the context indicates that "masculine love" must refer directly and frankly to some aspect of male sexuality. As is obvious, all the other examples of European sexual "foulness" that Joabin mentions earlier concern male eroticism only, and by moving from them to "masculine love" in effortless sequence the passage unmistakably portrays it as a male sexual phenomenon as well. This aspect of the passage, by the way, clearly indicates that for the Renaissance audience "masculine love" was not a euphemism or otherwise ambiguous term, a misconception that could easily arise for readers conditioned to our modern terminology of "homosexuality" and to the entire abstract/ "scientistic" mode of denoting reality out of which that vocabulary comes (a mode that of course did not yet exist in the Renaissance). Rather, the term "masculine love" derived from one of the Renaissance's characteristically different ways of denoting reality, one that seems to have been second nature to the period but that has largely disappeared in the twentieth century. This was the practice of "naming" reality in what I would call an "affective" way, in which the emotion involved in or pertaining to a subject was directly stated.[13] "Masculine love" exemplifies this procedure in its frank conjoining of a reference to erotic desire ("love," clearly used in the sexual sense here) with a reference to the male-male ("masculine") nature of that desire. Furthermore, because it could be so easily misread from a contemporary perspective, I want to underscore here that for the Renaissance audience the qualifier "masculine" in "masculine love" had no connotation of male-supremacy—i.e., rather than meant to imply that there is something "more manly" or "better" about this love than about male attraction to women, "masculine" here is simply a neutral, descriptive term to denote the male-male content of this love.[14]

As for the aspect of male sexuality that "masculine love" refers to, which would be the only substantial question readers still might have here, the structure and style of the passage, I believe, define the term unmistakably as male homosexuality, and, more importantly, as a male homosexual orientation (and not, as new-inventionism would have it, as just one "act" or component of a form of bisexuality). This point is first suggested by the bipartite structure of the passage. The first, longer, part of the passage implicitly registers an awareness of a separate, distinct, male-to-female sexuality, if only of a transgressing, "libertine," variety in this case. All of Joabin's language here belongs to the universe of what we would now call "heterosexuality"—e.g., "married men," "bachelors," "courtesans," and "stews," a late Medieval and Renaissance term for a male-female brothel.[15] The "masculine love" that Joabin then mentions in a separate sentence is, simply by the very separateness of the reference, established to be a different, male-to-male, sexuality. And it is this structure of separate sentences that implicitly portrays those two kinds of sexuality as two different sexual orientations. Had Bacon on the contrary perceived in his contemporaries the kind of "fluctuating" bisexuality that new-inventionism implies predominated in the period, he surely would have linked all the male sexual traits he discusses in the passage in one section or sentence, which would seem to be the logical structural expression of a belief that all those traits overlap or are co-equal within the same persons. For example, he would have included "masculine love" in his opening inventory of "libertinage," referring to those men who haunt "those dissolute places, or resort to courtesans, *or* pursue masculine love." Instead, he breaks up those references here, *first* discussing male-female "libertinage" and *then* moving to a separate mention of "masculine love." In so doing Bacon clearly implies that, sexually speaking at least, there are two separate kinds of men, identifiable by the pursuit of male-female pleasure on the one hand or by "masculine love" (i.e., the pursuit of other males) on the other. This distinction is of course tantamount to our modern understanding of "heterosexual" and "homosexual" orientations, if phrased inevitably in different, though characteristic, Renaissance terms.

Bacon's mention of "masculine love" in the same sentence with "friendship," especially his implicit paralleling of it with friendships of the most "faithful and inviolate" kind, only cements this implication of the passage's two-part structure. On the manifest level, Joabin's assurance that Bensalem has "no touch" of "masculine love . . . and yet there are not as faithful and inviolate friendships . . . as are there" clearly distinguishes between "masculine love" and "friendship," i.e., seeing one as sexual and the other not.[16] But the sentence also implies that "masculine love" and "friendship" have enough similarities to be easily mistaken for each other were the observer not careful (else why go out of the way to differentiate them, as Joabin does here?), and this implicit paralleling is the remark's more important feature for our purposes. Most obviously, it further defines "masculine love" as a male-male phenomenon only, since the period did not customarily apply the language and framework of "friendship" to male-female relationships.[17] More crucially, the particular quality of the friendships Joabin invokes here seems to certify "masculine love" as a sexual orientation, for the implicit logic of his remark is that it, like them, is "faithful and inviolate," i.e., it has the depth and persistence of what we would now call a "sexual orientation." (Another relevant feature of this passage for students of sexual history is its implication that the Renaissance understood sexuality to be fundamentally an internal, emotional, phenomenon and not the abstracted "act" or "behavior" that new-inventionism argues it was in earlier eras. Otherwise, this sexual "masculine love" would not be paralleled with a phenomenon like friendship, which is defined chiefly as a state of feeling. Similarly pertinent is the passage's implication that the Renaissance saw homosexuality as usually a peer relationship and not as the exclusively age-asymmetrical phenomenon new-inventionism argues it was then. Otherwise, again, "masculine love" would not be paralleled with a phenomenon like friendship here, which is usually understood as a bond between people who are in some sense peers or "sames" — i.e., of similar ages, in similar situations, with similar interests.)

My second example of "masculine love" in English Renaissance writing is from Thomas Heywood (c. 1575-1641), the prolific playwright whose long career extended from the end of Elizabeth's reign well into the time of Charles I and who is chiefly remembered today for his dramas of middle-class realism like *A Woman Killed with Kindness* (1603). "Masculine love" appears twice and prominently in a late work by Heywood, a 1637 miscellany entitled *Pleasant Dialogues and Dramas* consisting of free translations from classical and contemporary European writers (Lucian, Ovid, Erasmus, various Italian poets) and diverse other offerings that Heywood labeled "emblems, . . . elegies, epitaphs, . . . epithalamiums, . . . anagrams and acrostics, . . . [and] other fancies" (unnumbered title page).[18] There were pronounced differences between Heywood and Bacon. For instance, the "common" features of Heywood's career and writings contrast markedly with Bacon's aristocratic status and "philosophical" reputation (a difference represented in microcosm by the contrast between the loose and now-forgotten *Pleasant Dialogues and Dramas* and the pointed and continuously-influential *New Atlantis*). Heywood was born a gentleman and later studied at Cambridge, but was chiefly associated with the middle and lower classes throughout his career. The acting company he most frequently wrote for, the Queen's, was considered the least distinguished of the three that regularly performed in London, with what has been described as "a rather low-class clientele" for its audience (Brooke 544).

Also unlike Bacon, Heywood became known in his time as a

champion of women, through a long and hastily-executed prose work he published in 1624, entitled *Gunaikeion, or Nine Books of Various History Concerning Women*. The appearance in 1615 of Joseph Swetnam's *The Arraignment of Lewd, Idle, Froward, and Unconstant Women* sparked a controversy in England about the nature and proper role of women that produced quantities of commentary about the subject for at least the next ten years, and Heywood's encyclopedic *Gunaikeion* was considered a major defense of women in the debate.[19] In a further contrast, Heywood seems definitely to have been heterosexual. Though little information survives about his private life, Heywood seems to have been married twice and to have had six or seven children. Despite these several crucial differences between Bacon and Heywood, "masculine love" appears as a subject in the work of both authors and is judged in the same manifestly negative way, suggesting how widespread the concept and terminology of "masculine love" were in English Renaissance culture and how thoroughly hostile that culture was toward homosexuality.

Heywood includes loose translations of fourteen of Lucian's *Dialogues of the Gods* in the *Pleasant Dialogues and Dramas*, and his mentions of "masculine love" appear in two of these concerned with the Jupiter-Ganymede relationship, one between Jupiter and Ganymede themselves and another dramatizing Juno's anger at the situation. Heywood's use of this particular classical material to portray "masculine love" continues an earlier historical convention and is also consistent with currents within his own culture. John Boswell has documented the pervasive use in the Middle Ages of Ganymede as a symbol of male homosexuality/homosexuals, a tradition Heywood seems clearly to be carrying on in these dialogues; Heywood's practice here also parallels the use of "ganymede" terminology in other Renaissance writing about homosexuality, such as in the Pierre de L'Estoile *Mémoires-Journaux* that I discuss below.[20] In addition, Heywood's portrait pointedly echoes a use by Marlowe of the same situation (though with a very different purpose), a source that Heywood, as a younger fellow playwright, may well have been familiar with and perhaps was even directly borrowing from here. Marlowe's play *Dido, Queen of Carthage* (written c. 1587, published 1594) is a loose adaptation of *Aeneid* I, II, and IV, and it opens with an approving love scene between Jupiter and Ganymede and a subsequent outburst by Juno about their relationship. Since the scene is not in Virgil and also plays no role in the rest of Marlowe's text, it seems a clear example of the homosexual Marlowe taking an opportunity to present a rare frank literary image of male-male romantic attachment. Heywood's representations of the homosexuality between Jupiter and Ganymede in his *Pleasant Dialogues and Dramas* are as blunt as Marlowe's portrayal, but, in contrast, are thoroughly disapproving.

Heywood introduces his translation of each dialogue with a short verse "argument" of his own devising, a combination summary-and-moral that does not appear in the Lucian original. Heywood's first mention of "masculine love" occurs in the one of these that precedes the *Jupiter and Ganymede* dialogue, which portrays Jupiter's attempt to get Ganymede into bed immediately after their arrival on Olympus. Here a smitten Jupiter is ironically counterpointed with an innocent, country bumpkin-like Ganymede, in a tension in which Jupiter's homosexual attraction is made quite clear. Jupiter coaxes, "Now kiss me, lovely Ganymede . . . / . . . I from thy sheep / Of purpose stole thee, by my side to sleep" (96); and at Ganymede's balking reply, "But my father every morn would chide, And say . . . / I much disturbed his rest; tumbling and tossing / Athwart the bed," the god persists, "In that the greater pleasure I shall take, / Because I love still to be kept awake. / I shall embrace and kiss thee then the ofter, / And by that means my bed seem much the softer" (99-100). Heywood describes the desire driving Jupiter here as "masculine love" — in his opening argument to the dialogue Heywood states censoriously, "Jove's masculine love this fable reprehends, / And wanton dotage on the Trojan boy" (96).

Heywood's other mention of "masculine love" is in a *Jupiter and Juno* dialogue concerned with Juno's jealousy of Ganymede (the *Pleasant Dialogues and Dramas* also contains another *Jupiter and Juno* dialogue on an unrelated matter). Here Juno repeatedly condemns Jupiter's attraction to Ganymede while Jupiter repeatedly counters with passionate praise of him. Juno protests that, whereas Jupiter had previously strayed only with female "prostitutes below" (an arrangement she implies was acceptable to her), he now is "inflam'd with an unheard desire," having "set'st thy wife at nought / . . . Since this young Trojan swain to heav'n thou hast brought'' (102, 101). Positing what in modern terms amounts to an exclusively heterosexual Golden Age, Juno adds, ''In times past, / None of this foul deformity was seen'' (104). Jupiter returns with remarks like ''his kiss / Many degrees more sweet than nectar is . . . / . . . Shoulds't thou but taste those lips (which I am loth) / Thou wouldst not blame me to prefer them'' and ''Pray . . . do not so deprave / Those loves and pleasures I am pleased to have: / This pretty sweet effeminate lad to me / Is dearer far—but I'll not anger thee'' (103). Here ''masculine love'' is the term Heywood applies to Jupiter's romantic gushings—in the midst of Jupiter's just-quoted remarks about Ganymede's being ''sweeter,'' ''dearer,'' and ''preferable'' to him, Juno explodes, ''These are the words of masculine love, much hated'' (103). (Three years after this dialogue, in 1640, the first editor of Shakespeare's poems, John Benson, altered the original male-male passionateness of the *Sonnets* to make the sequence appear heterosexual instead. This falsified version of Shakespeare's text remained until the eighteenth century, and, if contemporary literary evidence were needed to explain Benson's bowdlerizing, a remark like Juno's here certainly helps to predict it.)[21]

The broad fact that ''masculine love'' is a sexual, and homosexual, phenomenon is evident much more immediately in Heywood than in Bacon. No reasoning from context is needed to establish that meaning here, which instead jumps out at the reader from each dialogue's action (here again we have excellent support for the fact that ''masculine love'' cannot have been an ambiguous term to the Renaissance audience). But the fact that ''masculine love'' here also has the same specific meaning of ''male homosexual orientation'' as in Bacon is not at all as obvious. Indeed, a quick look at these dialogues might seem to support new-inventionist claims about earlier sexuality instead, with Jupiter here an apparent example of bisexuality and homosexual attraction imagined only as an occasional age-asymmetrical phenomenon. A closer reading, however, suggests that Heywood's ''masculine love'' refers to a categorical male-male erotic orientation that he and his audience were well aware of, though he reveals that awareness more implicitly than explicitly here.

For instance, the Jupiter of these dialogues cannot, with scrutiny, really be called "bisexual," in either of the senses employed in new-inventionism. His present eroticism is neither in an untrackable "flux," nor is it divided more or less equally between women and "boys." Instead the text is studded with terms suggesting that Jupiter's interest in women is a thing of the past (see Juno's remarks above and his own comment that "I was in hope thou only hadst a spleen / To women, such as I before have been / Familiar with" — 101) and indicating that he is attracted only to Ganymede now ("prefer . . . those lips"). This situation would still give a "bisexual" arc to Jupiter's sexual history as a whole (i.e., from a heterosexual past to a homosexual present), but it also implicitly recognizes that there can be such a thing as an ongoing homosexual inclination in some people. The fact that Heywood has Juno demonstrate such outrage at the situation implies the same point. If the issue here were simply a homosexual addition to an "undivided" or comfortably differentiated bisexuality, rather than a homosexual orientation she fears he may now be set in, Jupiter's "masculine love" would have been no calamity to Juno, and Heywood would not have made her so livid about it.

True, Jupiter is now in a homosexual relationship that is not entirely equivalent to "masculine love" as it is implicitly defined in Bacon — instead of being directed potentially at all other males and envisioned usually as a peer relationship, Jupiter's "masculine love" mimics the traditional polarities of heterosexuality in being both age-asymmetrical and based in opposite gender traits (i.e., a "masculine" man attracted to an "effeminate lad"). But the text directs us not to define "masculine love" by this specific situation alone. Juno's reference to Jupiter's "words *of* masculine love" (emphasis mine) tells us to define "masculine love" in these dialogues ultimately by language rather than by action — i.e., "masculine love" here must finally be the way Jupiter talks rather than what he specifically does. And since Jupiter's "words" at the time of Juno's outburst are all statements of erotic partiality — e.g., "more sweet," "prefer them," "dearer far" — "masculine love" as understood by Heywood here is a larger, more general, sexual orientation, though in this case he presents it in a specific, limited, form (i.e., age-asymmetrical).

My final examples of "masculine love" in Renaissance writing, which I can only mention briefly because of limits of space, come from continental sources. The first appears in the continuous diary and scrapbook of contemporary documents that the Parisian court official Pierre de L'Estoile kept from Henri III's accession to the throne in 1574 until his own death in 1612, two years after the assassination of Henri IV; this extensive work was not published in its entirety until 1875, in a twelve-volume edition with the collective title of L'Estoile's *Mémoires-Journaux*. Long recognized by scholars as an invaluable record of French social history of the High Renaissance, the *Mémoires-Journaux* would also reward close study from a gay perspective, for it contains many telling depictions of Henri III's homosexuality, chiefly in the form of anonymous public broadsides attacking Henri III and his "mignons" that were distributed widely in Paris in the 1570s by either public posting or hand-to-hand circulation. In one of these, a verse dialogue of January 1579 by an unidentified member of the upper house of the Paris Parliament attacking the king's inauguration of an Order of the Knights of the Holy Spirit from among his followers, one of the speakers calls the sexuality between the king and his male entourage "l'amour viril," or "masculine love" (L'Estoile 224).[22]

My other continental Renaissance example of "masculine love" comes from the pen of Michelangelo's grandnephew, known as Michelangelo the Younger, as he prepared his granduncle's poems for their first collected, posthumous, edition in 1623. As some readers know, in that edition Michelangelo the Younger altered all his granduncle's romantic poems to other men to make them appear heterosexual instead; for example, he changed the "he"'s to "she"'s in all of Michelangelo's poems that show an obvious passionate attraction to other men.[23] (The parallel here to John Benson's editorial falsifying of Shakespeare's *Sonnets*, which occurred seventeen years later, is of course striking and, since neither editor could have been inspired in his bowdlerizing by the other, suggests how widespread hostility to male-male attraction was in the age.) In a remark written in the margin of the manuscript — a remark that he clearly never intended to be published and that indeed was not brought to light until 1863, when Cesare Gausti included it in his introduction to his first full and accurate edition of Michelangelo's

*Rime* — Michelangelo the Younger noted to himself that his grand-uncle's poems to other men must not appear in their original form because of the "amor . . . virile" ("masculine love") expressed in them (Gausti xlv).

The four Renaissance references to "masculine love" discussed here cover a wide range of cultures, times, and sorts of texts — from France in the High Renaissance to Italy and England toward the end of the age, from texts that were never intended to be published to works written expressly for public consumption, and from social or private writings to conscious literature. Furthermore, only limited possibilities existed for borrowing among them — the French and Italian remarks were not even published until the nineteenth century, though Bacon might have seen the attack on Henri III's "masculine love" (as mentioned, he was in the employ of the English ambassador to the French court at the time) and the *New Atlantis* was in print by the time Heywood was writing his *Pleasant Dialogues*. The fact that the same "masculine love" appears in these texts despite these diverse features and conditions strongly suggests that the term was entrenched and pervasive in Renaissance culture as a designation for what we would now call "a male homosexual orientation," at least among audiences that were free and willing to discuss the subject frankly; it also predicts that "masculine love" will appear in other Renaissance writings that have not yet been explored from this perspective.

Of course, a widespread Renaissance recognition of "masculine love" is also expressed in microcosm by the fact and manner of the term's appearance in my two English sources. For instance, the *New Atlantis* is a didactic utopian work and as such had to use well-established cultural concepts and terms as contrasting points of reference for its preferred agenda. Otherwise, its social program would have been lost on its audience, and "masculine love" clearly seems to be one such concept and term in the book. Bacon's "casual" style as he mentions the subject also supports the same point. Recall that he offers no elaboration of "masculine love" in his text, but simply evokes the phrase and then moves on. In part this procedure simply indicates that Bacon, like Bensalem, wants to be seen as having "no touch" of "masculine love," but at the same time the success of Bacon's strategy and point depends on the fact that his readers are already quite familiar with what he means. (For the presumed minority among its readers who might have missed "masculine love" in their social or personal experiences, a widely-read and influential work like the *New Atlantis* would also, of course, have helped to inform them of it.) In Heywood, too, "masculine love" is invoked without any elaboration, mentioned by both author and character as though the audience would immediately recognize the subject. And the familiarity of "masculine love" to Renaissance audiences is indicated much more blatantly in Heywood than it is in Bacon. In Juno's protest to Jupiter that "masculine love" is "much hated," we seem to have a clear reflection of the fact that it was also "much known about" in Heywood's world.

### 3.

Important as "masculine love" was in the Renaissance sexual vocabulary, according to my research on earlier homosexuality it was but one of several public languages for a distinct homosexuality/distinct homosexuals that existed in the eras before new-inventionism says homosexuality was "invented." [The same data also show, incidentally, that the life of "masculine love" extended well beyond the Renaissance—there are, for instance, Herder's 1787 discussion of "the masculine love of the Greeks" ("die männliche Liebe der Griechen," 540); Whitman's cognate "manly love" in his 1860 *Calamus* poems (127); the prevalence of the term throughout John Addington Symonds' work, especially in his 1889-93 *Memoirs* (e.g., "All my poems were composed upon the subject of masculine love," 165); and E. M. Forster's 1914 description of the relationship between Maurice and Alec as "masculine love" in *Maurice* (221).] Typically used concurrently in the same period or culture and sometimes even within the same text, these several languages constitute what I would call the characteristically "variegated" pattern into which the denotation of homosexuality fell in earlier ages (i.e., in contrast to our twentieth-century situation, where our public language for same-sex attraction has tended to be narrow and monolithic, dominated by only two terms, "homosexual" and "gay"). All the different kinds of possible languages for homosexuality that I defined in starting could be found in this variegated earlier pattern, as exemplified in the L'Estoile *Mémoires-Journaux* materials that I mentioned above, where typically premodern terms like "the art of . . . Ganymede," "sodomy," and "masculine love" are all used contemporaneously to denote what we would now call "male homosexuality"/"homosexuality."[24]

The presence of these languages does not of course mean that earlier homosexuality can be understood in all the same ways as twentieth-century homosexuality. But they clearly show that one key shift in recent Western sexual history has not been from the "non-existence" to the "existence" of homosexuality. Rather, among the most significant developments in the homosexual situation over that time (developments that either occurred or accelerated at the points when new-inventionism claims homosexuality was in fact "invented") were moves from more "local" or tacit acknowledgements of homosexuality and homosexuals to more universal and frank admissions of their existence (jumps of this kind occurred in both the eighteenth and nineteenth centuries) and a shift from a more affective, descriptive, variegated language for homosexuality/ homosexuals to a more "scientistic," non-visual, monolithic terminology for them (this was consolidated in the turn from the nineteenth to twentieth centuries).[25]

The difference between new-inventionism's and my views of homosexual history might at first seem simply to stem from our different methodologies. As reflected in my work on "masculine love" here, my research on earlier homosexuality has been chiefly based on a close reading of primary sources where same-sex attraction is the specific or manifest subject, sources drawn from a diverse body of materials covering a broad cultural range — e.g., a culture's mainstream literature, its informed social commentary (such as its historical writings and its equivalent of journalism), its personal writings (e.g., essays, memoirs, diaries) and, of course, its gay literature. In contrast, new-inventionism's argument about earlier homosexuality is founded on a few general dominant-culture sources in which homosexuality may not be the specific subject and which it tends simply to describe or otherwise take at face value. By far the chief of these are the ecclesiastical and, later, civil laws about sexuality in the earlier West (and police and trial records for violations of those laws, where available), laws that indeed did not literally and exclusively focus on same-sex sexuality, but on a technically broader "sodomy," i.e., any sexuality, heterosexual or homosexual, that could not be biologically procreative.[26] Foucault's comment that "What was taken into account in the civil and religious jurisdictions alike was a general unlawfulness [i.e., rather than a specifically homosexual one]" (38) and Weeks' observation that "[Sodomy] was not a specifically homosexual offense. . . . There was no concept of the homosexual in law" (*Coming Out* 11-12) illustrate the decisive role this legal evidence plays in new-inventionism's outlook.

But this difference really does not amount to an explanation. The more pertinent question is why commentators of the distinction of some new-inventionists would embrace this inappropriate kind of methodology in the first place. For example, law codes are a markedly unreliable measure of actual social experience and understanding. The fact that a culture's laws do not differentiate a discrete homosexuality does not mean that that culture has no awareness and language for homosexuality, as new-inventionism implicitly claims. Our culture today is obviously aware that homosexuality exists, but most contemporary laws proscribing homosexuality are still general "sodomy" laws, and if we applied the same methodology to the present that new-inventionism applies to eras like the Renaissance, we would have to conclude that "there is no homosexuality" now either. Relatedly, a term's meaning in law does not necessarily dictate its popular meaning, another implicit new-inventionist assumption (as in the L'Estoile examples I just mentioned, I have found that "sodomy" still often referred only to homosexuality in earlier popular cultural commentary, despite the term's broader technical, legal, meaning then). Similarly, the linchpin of the new-inventionist argument that earlier eras did not recognize the phenomenon of sexual orientation is the fact that the language of "act" and "behavior" is used in law to refer to sexuality. But this aspect of new-inventionism's procedure is only an achievement in circular reasoning — since in the Western tradition laws are directed only against acts and not against feelings, laws by definition only speak about sexuality as "act" or "behavior" and not as emotion or orientation.

This predominant dependence on law, and literalist reading of it, may be new-inventionism's most obvious methodological problem, but it is only one among several. Also puzzling is new-inventionism's willingness to work from a concept that is so nebulously defined. As I alluded to in starting, there is no overall clarity and consistency to what new-inventionism means by "the invention of homosexuality"; new-inventionism is especially vague about whether it is referring to the existence of actual, de facto, homosexuality or only to awareness of the phenomenon (and, within that, whether to large-scale or individual awareness, and chiefly in the dominant society or among homosexuals themselves). Another concern is new-inventionism's implicit belief that homosexuality can only be said to "exist" in a culture if that culture has a language for it. Jonathan Goldberg's claim that "There were no discrete terms for homosexual behavior" in the Renaissance, which I quoted in starting, assumes this dependency, as does Alan Bray's contention that homosexuality in the Renaissance remained "largely unrecognized and unformed" because of "means" that were "largely nominal — a question of giving or withholding a name" (79-80); Jeffrey Weeks states the underlying point baldly when he declares that "Nothing is sexual . . . but naming makes it so" (*Sexuality* 25). But surely the presence of highly circumscribed forms of homosexuality in a culture — e.g., the official age-asymmetrical homosexuality of ancient Greece, the institutionalized effeminate berdache figure of "primitive" societies — forms that seem designed to keep homosexuality under effective social control and constrained within the framework of a dominant "heterosexual model," would indicate a definite awareness of a discrete homosexuality in that culture, whether or not that homosexuality is ever named.[27]

A fuller discussion of new-inventionism's methodological problems must wait for future studies, however. Let me end simply by noting some of the most worrisome intellectual and social implications of new-inventionism. First, new-inventionism can have a repressive effect on gay studies. Inherently concerned as it is with the setting of a boundary before which homosexuality "did not exist," new-inventionism can effectively stifle inquiry into eras and materials before that dividing line (except, that is, for further demonstrations of homosexuality's "non-existence" in them) and leave entire potential sources of knowledge in this field unrecovered or untouched. This prospect would continue to be true even if new-inventionism were to keep pushing back the moment of homosexuality's "invention" — as seems to be happening, for example, with the recent shift in focus from the nineteenth to the eighteenth centuries among some new-inventionists — since, for the force of its argument to hold, new-inventionism will always require that there be a period when "there was no" homosexuality.

New-inventionism can also extend, if unintentionally, a helping hand to homophobia, as evidenced by an essay by Marjorie Rosenberg entitled "Inventing the Homosexual" that appeared in the December 1987 *Commentary*. Indicating the widespread audience new-inventionism has already won, Rosenberg proclaims that "in the late 19th century . . . a new kind of creature was born — 'the homosexual'" (36) and then goes on to use the vocabulary of new-inventionism to argue against social and civil rights for homosexuals, that is, since homosexuality is only an "invention" in the first place. New-inventionism can be inimical to the situation of contemporary gay people in a broader sense as well. Its implicit critique of the experiential category of homosexuality can of course work to undermine gay people's relatively recent gains in positive self-understanding, openness of expression, and social freedom. It certainly seems noteworthy that a movement among academics and intellectuals to proclaim the "non-existence" of homosexuality should arise so soon after gay people, for the first time in history (as far as we now know), began to insist publicly on their presence in humanity, society, and culture, and on a worldwide scale. New-inventionism has made some significant contributions to the study of gay history — e.g., the accomplishments of some of its scholars in primary-source research, its implicit caution against making simplistic connections between present and past homosexuality. Even the ultimate new-inventionist idea that a de facto homosexual orientation might in itself be a historical "invention" is not, in principle, unthinkable. But my materials and analysis here suggest that the powerful move to new-inventionism among many commentators now is based in something other than careful thought about the issues involved in that notion.

## NOTES

1. The words "homosexual" and "heterosexual" were not coined until 1868, when they appeared in a May 6th draft letter to Karl Heinrich Ulrichs by Károly Mária Kertbeny, a German-Hungarian writer and translator who was originally called Benkert and is sometimes still referred to by that name in the scholarly literature. In the next year, the words "homosexuality" and "homosexuals" appeared in print for the first time, in two pamphlets Kertbeny published anonymously in Berlin to protest the harsh laws against male homosexuality that the North German Confederation was in the process of adopting from the Prussian Penal Code. The word "heterosexuality" seems to have been used in print for the first time in 1880, by the German zoologist and anthropologist Gustav Jaeger, in the second edition of his *Die Entdeckung der Seele* (*The Discovery of the Soul*). For more on Kertbeny, Jaeger, and "homosexuality"/"heterosexuality," see Herzer (1985, 1990); I am grateful to Hubert Kennedy for referring me to Herzer's important work. Though "homosexuality" was used in the new sexological literature at the end of the century (e.g., Krafft-Ebing, Ellis and Symonds' *Sexual Inversion*), the term seems not to have achieved the hegemony it now has until the 1920s, when what I refer to later as the predominantly "variegated" pattern of denoting homosexuality in the West seems definitely to have ended. At present, the course of "heterosexuality"'s use and acceptance is much less clear. It may be noteworthy that Krafft-Ebing uses "heterosexual" in our contemporary sense by the sixth edition of *Psychopathia Sexualis* (1891), the first edition that was available to me after the first (1886), but does not use the term in his first edition. In the sixth edition, Krafft-Ebing refers, for instance, to "the normal heterosexual love" ("der normalen heterosexualen Liebe," 143) and "the heterosexual instinct,. . . the sexual instinct toward the opposite sex" ("Die heterosexuale Empfindung,. . . Die sexuellen Empfindung gegenber dem anderen Geschlect," 127).

2. Trumbach ("London's") appeared simultaneously with Weeks and before the English translation of Foucault and advances a similar view. Some important later discussions that to one degree or another follow the argument in Foucault and Weeks about the late nineteenth century (other than those already cited in the text) are: the essays by Padgug, Hansen, and Weeks in *Radical History Review*; Plummer; Hilliard; D'Emilio; Katz (*Gay/Lesbian Almanac*); Goldberg; Lynch;

Sedgwick (*Between Men*); Brown; and Cohen. [This essay was substantially completed in mid 1988 and covers the published scholarship on this issue only up until that time. Later publications indicate how even more dominant new-inventionist views have become in gay studies: e.g., Greenberg; the essays by Boon, van der Meer, Rousseau, Trumbach, and Hekma in Gerard and Hekma; the essays by Orgel, Sedgwick, Goldberg, and Cohen in *South Atlantic Quarterly*; and Halperin. Dall'Orto's essay in Gerard and Hekma offers evidence for a view of the Renaissance similar to mine here.]

3. McIntosh's pioneering article initiated this argument, though her eighteenth-century emphasis was not immediately picked up and she has frequently been cited in support of the late nineteenth-century interpretation (e.g., Weeks, *Coming Out* 4). Trumbach ("Sodomitical") summarizes recent research supporting an eighteenth-century "beginning" to homosexuality and states his agreement with McIntosh now (as opposed to his implicit emphasis on the late nineteenth century in his earlier "London's," e.g., 9). Bray's book is the most developed statement so far of this view, though he carefully acknowledges his affinity with the spirit of Foucault's and Weeks' work (134-37).

4. The reference to male homosexuality that is perhaps best-known to readers of English Renaissance literature at present is E. K.'s mention of "paederastice" ("pederasty") in his gloss about the Colin-Hobbinol relationship in the "January" eclogue of Spenser's *Shepherd's Calendar* (1579). In contrast to the direct and frank references to "masculine love" that I analyze in this essay, however, E. K.'s mention of "paederastice" remains equivocal, in what seems patently a defense against acknowledging male-male attraction openly and plainly. E. K. first says that "paederastice" has "some savor of disorderly love," clearly hinting that he means male-male sexuality. But he then undercuts this point by implying that "paederastice" refers only to an intensely spiritual male-male attachment, interpreting the Socrates-Alcibiades relationship in Plato as a love of the "soul" only and proclaiming that "no man [should] think . . . I stand . . . in defense of execrable and horrible sins of forbidden and unlawful fleshliness" (422-23).

5. New-inventionism tends to portray "sodomy" as an impenetrable concept in earlier discussions of sexuality outside of the law, as reflected in Foucault's influential characterization of it as "that utterly confused category" (101). In contrast, I have found "sodomy" to have no more than two or three meanings in earlier legal or popular commentary — any sexuality (heterosexual or homosexual) that could not be biologically procreative; homosexuality only; and, occasionally, bestiality. I have also found that it is almost always possible to tell which meaning of "sodomy" is intended in earlier writing from a knowledge of context and a close reading of the text. For more on the place of "sodomy" in new-inventionism's argument, see my concluding section.

6. Examples of the first kind of designation would be "masculine love" and a phrase like "the art of . . . Ganymede" (from the L'Estoile materials that I discuss later); "sodomy"/"sodomite" and "pederasty"/"pederast" would be examples of the second; and examples of the third, from eighteenth-century writing about homosexuality, would be Smollett's mention of a man with "a passion

for his own sex'' (312) and Gibbon's reference to ''the lovers of their own sex'' (536). See my succeeding discussion for more on the first two kinds of language as they functioned in the Renaissance.

7. The extent to which one must qualify the terms ''social constructionism'' and ''essentialism'' before they can have any meaningful connection to lived gay experience is well-illustrated in Epstein.

8. D'Ewes does not actually say here what Bacon's ''sin'' is, but its declared ''unmentionableness'' (a centuries-old code term for homosexuality) strongly suggests it is homosexuality, as does a process of elimination from the passage as a whole—for instance, D'Ewes does mention the greatest scandal in Bacon's life that already was public knowledge, his calamitous prosecution for taking bribes.

9. The sketches that make up the *Brief Lives* were probably composed between 1665 and 1690, but were not first published in book form until 1813. ''Pederasty''/''pederast'' technically mean ''love of youths''/''boy-lover'' and were sometimes used only in that strict sense in earlier periods. But, as suggested by E. K.'s use of ''paederastice'' in connection with the peer relationship of Colin and Hobbinol in *The Shepherd's Calendar* (see note 4), ''pederasty''/''pederast'' were often simply used as equivalent to a generic ''homosexuality''/''homosexual'' in earlier eras as well. That is what Aubrey is doing here.

10. For Anthony Bacon's homosexuality, including his little-discussed arrest for same-sex sodomy in France in 1586, see duMaurier (49-55, 231).

11. I discuss the convention of ''friendship'' as a language for homosexual attachment in gay male writing in ''*Drum-Taps*'' (53-54).

12. Many contemporary documents about the homosexuality of Henri III and his favorites, including some that Bacon could have read or heard, are preserved in the L'Estoile materials that I discuss later in the essay.

13. Another distinctly different way of representing reality that was common in the Renaissance and appeared in the age's depictions of homosexuality was the practice of figurative denotation, in which metaphors or symbols (usually from sources in classical or ''exotic'' cultures) were seriously and straightforwardly used as labels for contemporary phenomena. An example of this custom in Renaissance writing about homosexuality is the phrase ''the art of . . . Ganymede,'' a term equivalent to ''male homosexuality'' in the L'Estoile materials I discuss later. Both these affective and figurative ways of denoting homosexuality continued well into the next two centuries, and a good example of the critical misconception I mentioned above is Coward's dismissal of ''chevaliers de la manchette,'' a common eighteenth-century French term for male homosexuals, as euphemistic, in an otherwise informative article (''Attitudes'' 233).

14. An example of such misreading occurs in Sedgwick's *Between Men*, where, in criticizing John Addington Symonds, she cites the view that '''Manly love' . . . is *always* correlated [with] the degradation of women'' (209, emphasis mine). Sedgwick is quoting Havelock Ellis' essay on Whitman in his *The New Spirit* (108), so her remark is technically a repetition of an earlier misreading, but the view seems clearly to be her own as well. Sedgwick herself provides no historical background for the term ''manly love'' or structural analysis of it.

15. For "stew" as a common early English term for a male-female brothel, see *Shorter OED* 2017. The exclusively heterosexual meaning of this word in the Renaissance is further supported by the fact that authors who wanted to designate male homosexual brothels had to add the adjective "male," or variations on it, to "stews," in a construction similar to the addition of "masculine" to the word "love" to indicate male homosexuality in the age. See, for instance, Marston's reference to "male stews" in his 1598 *The Scourge of Villainy* (112) and Drayton's mention of "malekind stews" in his 1627 *The Moon-Calf* (174). I was led to these extremely interesting references by Bray's mention of them in *Homosexuality*; he does not, however, examine them as I do.

16. One common way in which homophobic critics deny the homosexual content of earlier texts is to claim that earlier ages often blurred the distinction between sexuality and non-sexual attachment and correspondingly used the language of eroticism simply to express friendship. Perhaps the greatest focus of this particular brand of critical denial has been Shakespeare in the *Sonnets*. See, for example, Hubler's remark that "It must be remembered that the meanings of words shift with the years. . . . To Shakespeare and his contemporaries the words 'love' and 'lover' as used between men did mean 'friendship' and 'friend'"(153). Bacon's distinction between "masculine love" and "friendship" here clearly gives the lie to such claims and suggests that the Renaissance was quite aware of a difference between eroticism and friendship. For further support for this point, from a knowledgeable commentator who lived closer to the Renaissance, see Jeremy Bentham's remark in his draft essay on "Paederasty" (c. 1785) that "the Greeks knew the difference between love and friendship as well as we" (393). A detailed criticism of Hubler's argument appears in Pequigney (75-76).

17. Perhaps the best-known reflection of this Renaissance attitude is Montaigne's essay "Of Friendship" (1572-76, 1578-80), written in praise of his late friend Etienne de La Boétie. Holding to an unfortunate male-supremacist outlook, Montaigne writes, for example, that "the ordinary sufficiency of women cannot answer this conference and communication" (199). For present purposes the pertinent point here is not Montaigne's lesser opinion of women, but the broader implication that male-female relationships do not properly fit in the category of "friendship."

18. I have modernized Heywood's spelling and punctuation in my discussion.

19. This episode is traced in Clark 57-61, 91-98. Swetnam's tract and some of the contemporary responses to it (though not Heywood's) are excerpted in Goreau.

20. Boswell, *Christianity*, especially chapter 9. Furthermore, for Ganymede as a symbol for male homosexuality in Renaissance painting and sculpture, see Saslow.

21. For a recent summary of Benson's tampering, see Pequigney 2-3.

22. The dialogue in which this phrase appears is one of the several L'Estoile scrapbook materials that were originally written in Latin but that are translated and presented only in French by his modern editors. I have not seen the original manuscript, which is available only in the Bibliothèque Nationale, but, because of the

many echoes between it and other Renaissance writings about homosexuality, I accept the translation as accurate.

23. For a frank and thorough, if somewhat contradictory, discussion of Michelangelo's homosexual poems, see Clements, especially chapters 6 and 10.

24. An anonymous ballad attacking Henri III's mignons, dated 25 July 1576 and ironically entitled "The Virtues and Other Good Qualities of the Mignons" ("Les vertus et propriétés des mignons"), describes them as "practicing among themselves the art of . . . Ganymede" ("entre eux ils pratiquent l'art/ De . . . Ganimède," 134). Another anonymous document of January 1579 attacking the king's inauguration of the Order of the Knights of the Holy Spirit (i.e., besides the verse dialogue I discussed above in which "masculine love" appears) is a poem addressing the king and his entourage as "princes of Sodom" ("princes de Sodome," 225).

25. This shift in the breadth and type of language for homosexuality suggests one interesting question that could be raised about the differences between earlier and modern homosexuality—i.e., would the experience of an earlier "male homosexual" who understood himself through the imagistic vividness and emotional frankness of the language of "ganymedes" and "masculine love" actually have a different texture from that of a modern one who knew himself through the abstractness and impersonality of our contemporary vocabulary of "homosexual"/"homosexuality"?

26. Some new-inventionists (e.g., McIntosh; Trumbach "London's") cite anthropological studies of "primitive" cultures in support of their argument as well. But by their very nature these are secondary sources that, screened as they are through the consciousnesses of their observer-authors, keep us at a remove from the raw material of their subject matter; this problem is then only compounded by the fact that new-inventionist commentators typically summarize these studies in a few sentences. Bray is unusual in citing literary sources for his views as well. But he, too, usually only summarizes these materials and when he does feature an author he sometimes misrepresents him. For example, Bray's claim that Richard Barnfield was really heterosexual rests on Barnfield's Isham MS, which Bray says is "entirely heterosexual" and which he portrays as a suppressed "commonplace book" that Barnfield "never intended for publication" (61). The Isham MS actually contains only two poems that could be read heterosexually (several others treat diverse non-sexual topics) and, according to Barnfield's editor, was simply a manuscript that happened to go unpublished in Barnfield's lifetime (that is, for no ulterior reason). Bray also omits any mention of the sequence of twenty homosexual sonnets in Barnfield's 1595 *Cynthia, with Certain Sonnets, and the Legend of Cassandra*. See Barnfield xiii, xxxiii-xxxiv, 77-96, 198-220. In any case, Bray's chief materials for his argument remain legal ones—e.g., his use of sodomy trial records, where he assumes (incorrectly, I think) that witnesses were telling the court the truth when they registered incomprehension about what was happening (68-69, 76-77).

27. In a similar vein, questioning what he calls the "nominalist" strain in the current study of sex in history, John Boswell remarks that "Lack of terminology for the homosexual/heterosexual dichotomy should not be taken as a sign of igno-

rance of it'' (''Revolutions'' 102). This essay is a sustained critique of the same viewpoint I am examining here, though it focuses on a different range of materials, is based on a different, philosophical, perspective, and uses different critical terms.

# REFERENCES

Aubrey, John. *Aubrey's Brief Lives*. Ed. Oliver Lawson Dick. Ann Arbor: U of Michigan P, 1957.

Bacon, Francis. *Essays and New Atlantis*. Ed. Gordon S. Haight. Roslyn, NY: Walter J. Black, 1942.

Barnfield, Richard. *The Complete Poems of Richard Barnfield*. Ed. Alexander B. Grosart. London: Nichols, 1876.

Bentham, Jeremy. ''Offenses Against One's Self: Paederasty. Part 1.'' C. 1785. Ed. Louis Crompton. *Journal of Homosexuality* 3 (1978): 389-405.

Boswell, John. *Christianity, Social Tolerance, and Homosexuality: Gay People in Western Europe from the Beginning of the Christian Era to the Fourteenth Century*. Chicago: U of Chicago P, 1980.

————. ''Revolutions, Universals and Sexual Categories.'' *Salmagundi* 58-59 (Fall 1982-Winter 1983): 89-113.

Bray, Alan. *Homosexuality in Renaissance England*. London: Gay Men's P, 1982.

Brooke, Tucker. ''The Renaissance (1500-1660).'' *A Literary History of England*. Ed. Albert C. Baugh. New York: Appleton, 1948. 315-696.

Brown, Judith. *Immodest Acts: The Life of a Lesbian Nun in Renaissance Italy*. New York: Oxford UP, 1986.

Cady, Joseph. *''Drum-Taps* and Nineteenth-Century Male Homosexual Literature.'' *Walt Whitman: Here and Now*. Ed. Joann P. Krieg. Westport, CT: Greenwood, 1985. 49-59.

Cohen, Ed. ''Writing Gone Wilde: Homoerotic Desire in the Closet of Representation.'' *PMLA* 102 (1987): 801-12.

Clark, Arthur Melville. *Thomas Heywood: Playwright and Miscellanist*. Oxford: Blackwell, 1931.

Clements, Robert J. *The Poetry of Michelangelo*. New York: NYU P, 1965.

Coward, D. A. ''Attitudes to Homosexuality in Eighteenth-Century France.'' *Journal of European Studies* 10 (1980): 231-55.

D'Emilio, John. *Sexual Politics, Sexual Communities: The Making of a Homosexual Minority in the United States, 1940-1970*. Chicago: U of Chicago P, 1983.

D'Ewes, Sir Simonds. *The Autobiography and Correspondence of Sir Simonds D'Ewes*. Ed. James Orchard Halliwell. Vol. 1. London: Bentley, 1845.

Drayton, Michael. *The Works of Michael Drayton*. Ed. J. William Hebel. Vol. 3. Oxford: Blackwell, 1932.

duMaurier, Daphne. *Golden Lads: Sir Francis Bacon, Anthony Bacon and their Friends*. Garden City, NY: Doubleday, 1975.

Ellis, Havelock. *The New Spirit*. 1890. 3rd ed. London: Walter Scott, 1892.

Epstein, Steven. "Gay Politics, Ethnic Identity: The Limits of Social Constructionism." *Socialist Review* 17.3-4 (1987): 9-54.

Farrington, Benjamin. *The Philosophy of Francis Bacon: An Essay on Its Development from 1603 to 1609 with New Translations of Fundamental Texts*. Chicago: U of Chicago P, 1966.

Forster, E. M. *Maurice*. London: Edward Arnold, 1971.

Foucault, Michel. *The History of Sexuality. Volume I: An Introduction*. Trans. Robert Hurley. New York: Pantheon, 1978.

Gausti, Cesare. Introduction. *Le Rime di Michelangelo Buonarroti*. Firenze: Felice Le Monnier, 1863.

Gerard, Kent, and Gert Hekma, Eds. *The Pursuit of Sodomy: Male Homosexuality in Renaissance and Enlightenment Europe*. New York: Harrington Park, 1989. Simultaneously issued as *Journal of Homosexuality* 16.1-2 (1988).

Gibbon, Edward. *The History of the Decline and Fall of the Roman Empire*. Vol. 4. 1788. 6 vols. 1776-88. Ed. J. B. Bury. Vol. 4. London: Methuen, 1909.

Goldberg, Jonathan. "Sodomy and Society: The Case of Christopher Marlowe." *Southwest Review* 69 (1984): 371-78.

Goreau, Angeline. *The Whole Duty of a Woman: Female Writers in Seventeenth-Century England*. Garden City, NY: Dial, 1985.

Greenberg, David F. *The Construction of Homosexuality*. Chicago: U of Chicago P, 1988.

Halperin, David M. *One Hundred Years of Homosexuality*. New York: Routledge, 1990.

Herder, Johann Gottfried. *Ideen zur Philosophie der Geschichte der Menschheit*. Vol. 3. 1787. 4 vols. 1784-91. Frankfurt: Deutscher Klassiker, 1989.

Herzer, Manfred. "Kertbeny and the Nameless Love." *Journal of Homosexuality* 12 (1985): 1-25.

———. "Kertbeny, Károly Mária (Karl Maria Benkert; 1824-1882)." *Encyclopedia of Homosexuality*. Ed. Wayne R. Dynes. Vol. 1. New York: Garland, 1990.

Heywood, Thomas. *Pleasant Dialogues and Dramma's von Tho. Heywood nach der Octavausgabe 1637*. Ed. W. Bang. Vol. 3 of *Materialien zur Kunde des lteren Englischen Dramas*. Ed. W. Bang et al. Louvain: A. Uystpruyst, 1903.

Hilliard, David. "Unenglish and Unmanly: Anglo-Catholicism and Homosexuality." *Victorian Studies* 25 (1982): 181-210.

Hubler, Edward. *The Sense of Shakespeare's Sonnets*. Princeton: Princeton UP, 1952.

Katz, Jonathan. *Gay American History: Lesbians and Gay Men in the U.S.A.* New York: Crowell, 1976.

———. *Gay/Lesbian Almanac: A New Documentary*. New York: Harper & Row, 1983.

Krafft-Ebing, Richard von. *Psychopathia Sexualis, mit besonderer Bercksichtigung der Contrren Sexualempfindung: Eine klinisch-forensische Studie*. 6th ed. Stuttgart: Ferdinand Enke, 1891.

L'Estoile, Pierre de. *Journal de L'Estoile pour le Règne de Henri III (1574-1589)*. Ed. Louis-Raymond Lefèvre. 2nd ed. Paris: Gallimard, 1943.

Lynch, Michael. "'Here Is Adhesiveness': From Friendship to Homosexuality." *Victorian Studies* 29 (1985): 67-96.

Marston, John. *The Poems of John Marston*. Ed. Arnold Davenport. Liverpool: Liverpool UP, 1961.

McIntosh, Mary. "The Homosexual Role." *Social Problems* 16 (1968): 182-92.

Montaigne, Michel de. *The Essayes of Michael Lord of Montaigne*. Trans. John Florio. 1603. Vol. 1. London: Dent, 1910.

Pequigney, Joseph. *Such Is My Love: A Study of Shakespeare's Sonnets*. Chicago: U of Chicago P, 1985.

Plummer, Kenneth, Ed. *The Making of the Modern Homosexual*. London: Hutchinson, 1981.

*Radical History Review* 20 (Spring/Summer 1979). Special Issue on "Sexuality in History."

Rosenberg, Marjorie. "Inventing the Homosexual." *Commentary* Dec. 1987: 36-40.

Saslow, James M. *Ganymede in the Renaissance: Homosexuality in Art and Society*. New Haven: Yale UP, 1986.

Sedgwick, Eve K. *Between Men: English Literature and Male Homosocial Desire*. New York: Columbia UP, 1985.

_____. "Comments" on Karen Swann's essay, "Harassing the Muse." *Berkshire Review* 21 (1986): 104-09.

*Shorter Oxford English Dictionary*. 3rd ed., rev. Oxford: Clarendon P, 1969.

Smollett, Tobias. *The Adventures of Roderick Random*. 1748. Ed. Paul-Gabriel Boucé. Oxford: Oxford UP, 1979.

*South Atlantic Quarterly* 88.1 (1989). "Displacing Homophobia" Issue.

Spedding, James, Ed. *The Letters and the Life of Francis Bacon*. Vol. 1. London: Longman, 1861.

Spenser, Edmund. *The Poetical Works of Edmund Spenser*. Ed. J. C. Smith and E. De Selincourt. London: Oxford UP, 1912.

Symonds, John Addington. *The Memoirs of John Addington Symonds*. Ed. Phyllis Grosskurth. New York: Random House, 1984.

Trumbach, Randolph. "London's Sodomites: Homosexual Behavior and Western Culture in the 18th Century." *Journal of Social History* 11 (1977): 1-33.

_____. "Sodomitical Subcultures, Sodomitical Roles, and the Gender Revolution of the Eighteenth Century: The Recent Historiography." *Eighteenth-Century Life* 9.3 (1985): 109-21.

Weeks, Jeffrey. *Coming Out: Homosexual Politics in Britain, from the Nineteenth Century to the Present*. London: Quartet, 1977.

_____. "Havelock Ellis: Sexuality as Knowledge." Rev. of *Havelock Ellis: A Biography*, by Phyllis Grosskurth. *Body Politic* Oct. 1980: 33.

_____. *Sexuality*. Chichester: Ellis Horwood; London: Tavistock, 1986.

Whitman, Walt. *Leaves of Grass*. Ed. Sculley Bradley and Harold W. Blodgett. New York: Norton, 1973.

# Tradition and the Individual Sodomite: Barnfield, Shakespeare, and Subjective Desire

Gregory W. Bredbeck, PhD

University of California, Riverside

**SUMMARY.** This article compares Shakespeare's sonnets with those written by Richard Barnfield in order to examine the possibility of homoerotic subjectivity in early Renaissance England. Social constructionist debates about sexual subjectivity have convincingly argued that "the homosexual"—the person defined by homosexuality—did not exist before the Enlightenment. The sequences of Shakespeare and Barnfield, both of which deal with homoerotic desire, suggest that homoerotic desire could indeed play a role in defining the individuated subject prior to the Enlightenment. However, the ways in which they use homoeroticism also suggest that subjectivity was defined in radically different ways during the period.

Can we speak of the sodomite? The question is far more complex than it may appear. Indeed, the question has in many ways led to a paralysis in the theorization of gay history, a sort of selective blindness in which we become so paranoid over the difficulties of determining the sodomite—that is, the person whose subjectivity is de-

Gregory W. Bredbeck is Associate Professor of English at the University of California, Riverside.

Research for this essay was supported by a University of Pennsylvania Penn-In-London Fellowship, a University of Pennsylvania Dean's Fellowship, and field and intramural research funds from the University of California. Earlier versions of this essay were read by Rebecca Bushnell, Stuart Curran, George Haggerty and Phyllis Rackin. The author wishes to thank them for their helpful comments.

Correspondence may be addressed to the author at Department of English—40, University of California, Riverside, CA 92521-0323.

*41*

termined by, at least in part, a male-male sexual preference — that we ignore him altogether; the impulse is to decline to recognize the sodomite behind (or perhaps in front of) the sodomy, and label the discourse "subject-less." This is the approach Alan Bray finally adopts in *Homosexuality in Renaissance England*:

> It was not tolerance; it was rather a reluctance to recognize homosexual behaviour, a sluggishness in accepting that what was being seen was indeed the fearful sin of sodomy. It was this that made it possible for the individual to avoid the psychological problems of a homosexual relationship or a homosexual encounter, by keeping the experience merely casual and undefined: readily expressed and widely shared though the prevalent attitude to homosexuality was, it was kept at a distance from the great bulk of homosexual behaviour by an unwillingness to link the two.(76)

For Bray, the rhetoric of the stigmatized sodomite is fully inscriptive, fully able to mark and identify the *tabula rasa* of the sexual subject, and hence every English subject necessarily thinks of male-male sexual behavior as the mark of subjective erasure, as a movement from the "rational" world of social subjectivity to the "irrational world" of the *contra naturam*. Bray's belief in the ability of sodomy to signify *in one way* in turn backs him into a corner, and he finds himself forced to define the subject of sodomy as a "subject on the run," an individual only able to maintain a sexual identity by dodging the inscriptive abilities that he posits in the rhetoric of Renaissance sodomy. Subjectivity, then, becomes possible only in the rupture of the subjecting ability of language — a formulation that turns the sodomite into a sort of free-wheeling or sublinguistic subject who exists *despite* the society — and language — around him.

As easy as it is to criticize Bray's formulation, it is perhaps even easier to empathize with it. Bray's statement is produced by the dynamics of a specific critical moment, one in which the "responsibility" of the critic is defined in relation to precepts of constructionism and of epistemological discontinuity.[1] Hence, we are told, we must only speak of homosexual*ities*,[2] we must recognize homosexuality only as it is played out along the dominant axes of race, class, and gender,[3] and we must not speak of homosexuality in the past —

for "the homosexual" is not something that existed much before the end of the seventeenth century.[4] All of these formulations, which in the aggregate have gone far toward undermining the tyranny of the bourgeois criticism that has dominated the academy, have, on the other hand, also left us with no place to go if we are searching for the sodomite. Oozing into the plural and constantly on the brink of a historical aporia, the sodomite becomes someone who is no one, a chimera, and we are made to feel slightly ridiculous that we would even ask, can we speak of the sodomite?

In all of these formulations there is, I will claim, an implicit logocentrism and, paradoxically, a nostalgia for the present. For they all begin with the assumption that unless we can find the subject *as he is inscribed in our own language*, then we cannot find him at all. In my argument I hope both to problematize our notion of how we can read the sodomite, and also to find a place for the sodomite within (rather than around, behind or beneath) the linguistic practices of the culture of early modern England. I will do so by comparing the *potentiality* for the sodomite present in the sonnet sequences of Richard Barnfield and William Shakespeare. Ironically, my strategy will entail arguing that these poems, which are some of the few from the Renaissance that have been canonized as "gay," are not concerned at all with articulating the sodomite, but rather "place" the sodomite in relation to broader purposes of subject construction.[5] However, erasing the sodomite from our understanding of these sequences will, I hope, create a better understanding of the possible ways in which the rhetoric of Renaissance sodomy was subjectively inscriptive.

Although my primary concern here is reading the sodomite, my argument necessarily entails some critical assumptions that need to be outlined briefly. Throughout my analyses I will be suggesting that we can posit an analogy between subjective sodomy in these poems and the possibility of the sodomite in Renaissance society. The correlation between textual subjectivity and social subjectivity is far too complicated to analyze fully in my argument. However, current critical practice has provided terms that empower my analogy. Traditionally the process of reading is thought of as identification or decoding. A reader *decodes* a text, unravels it and assimilates it, and, typically, achieves an empathy or identification with ideas expressed *in* the text. In this schema the reader is neutral, and the text acts as a contained unit transporting fixed ideas. However, contemporary Marxist criticism has foregrounded reading as a process in which a textual consumer is forced into a position of subjectivity posited by the text — a position from which the frequently disparate elements of a text achieve meaning or comprehensibility.[6] As Frederic Jameson has noted, interpretation is "an essentially allegorical act, which consists in rewriting a given text in terms of a particular interpretive master code"(10). The reader is not a consumer, but rather a builder, and the act of reading consists of assuming a position of subjectivity that rectifies the determinants of meaning in the text with the determinants of meaning — the master codes — that constitute the reader as a social subject. As such, meaning is neither in the text nor the reader, but rather is in the new position achieved by the dialectical confrontation of text *and* reader.

Jameson's formulation is, of course, an amplification and recasting of Althusser's famous formulation of literature as "ideological state apparatus"(*Lenin and Philosophy* 121-173) — which is to say that literature from a specific culture creates structures that engage the basic assumptions or ideologies that empower the social formations of that culture. Jameson has not been alone in contesting the viability of Althusser's formulation, but the point here is not to engage the active debate on Marxist criticism, but rather to recognize that in both formulations textual and social subjectivity, while not identical, are at least reciprocally interactive. In the texts of Barnfield and Shakespeare, as I will demonstrate, homoeroticism is a *textual determinant*, a "quasi-material transmission point" (Jameson 154) that aids in the reciprocal mediation of textual and social subjectivity. Crudely put, readers of the poems must "read" sodomy, and hence sodomy becomes a part of who they are as readers. And while this potentiality happens in a literary milieu that is patently *not* the same as the material considerations of social subjectivity, if we accept, along with Althusser and Jameson, that textual subjectivity and social subjectivity are engaged with each other, then we can also assume that the presence of the sodomite in literature indicates the *possibility* of the sodomite in society. What we can find in the poems of Barnfield and Shakespeare, then, is not the *actual* sodomite, but rather a delineation of the *conditions* for his existence. Recovering the material subject is, perhaps, impossible. However, recovering historically specific textual subjectivities allows us to begin to sketch a spectrum of the possible determinants constituting the subject at a given historical moment. Such a sketch will be the goal of my readings of Barnfield and Shakespeare.

## BARNFIELD: FOLDING SODOMY

Barnfield's earliest publication, *The Affectionate Shepheard*, provides a means of deciphering the problematic of the sodomite through an engagement of that most sexually problematic of all genres, the pastoral.[7] Daphnis, the male singer of the eclogues, articulates his plea in the familiar rhetoric of pastoral seduction:

> If thou wilt come and dwell with me at home;
> My sheep-cote shall be strowd with new greene rushes:
> Weele haunt the trembling Prickets as they rome
> About the fields, along the hauthorne bushes
>      I have a pie-bald Curre to hunt the Hare:
>      So we will liue with daintie forrest fare.(11)

However, these familiar words, which for many may evoke Marlowe's "The Passionate Shepherd," are resituated in relation to the typical heteroerotic expectations of the genre by a dramatic contextualization:

> Scarce had the morning Starre hid from the light
> Heauens crimson Canopie with stars bespangled,
> But I began to rue th'vnhappy sight
> Of that faire Boy that had my hart intangled;
>      Cursing the Time, the Place, the sense, the sin;
>      I came, I saw, I viewd, I slipped in.

> If it be sinne to loue a sweet-fac'd Boy,
> (Whose amber locks trust vp in golden tramels
> Dangle adowne his louely cheekes with ioy,
> When pearle and flowers his faire haire enamels)
>      If it be sinne to loue a louely Lad;
>      Oh then sinne I, for whom my soule is sad.(6)

The dynamics of heteroeroticism implicit in seduction are here overturned by a specification of a pederastic dynamic. This is a homoerotic plea from man to boy, with intimations of sodomy encoded in the punning Caesarian allusion, "I came, I saw, I viewd, *I slipped in*."

The establishment of a homoerotic voice is clear and purposeful in Barnfield's poem. Not only does the continued stress on "sinne" align the speaker's voice with the common Renaissance legal rhetoric of sodomy, but the narrative of the eclogue also undermines the lucidity of heteroerotic meaning. The erotic complication in the poem is that Daphnis loves Ganimede, but Ganimede loves the nymph queen, Guendolen. Guendolen, however, is enamoured with a dead youth and pursued by an old man. In describing how this chain of diverted passions formed, Daphnis recounts how

> . . . Death and *Cupid* met
> Upon a time at swilling *Bacchus* house,
> Where daintie cates vpon the Board were set,
> And Goblets full of wine to drinke carouse:
> > Where Loue and Death did loue the licor so
> > That out they fall and to the fray they goe.(6)

In the drunken revelry Death and Cupid confuse their arrows and bring death to the boy meant to love Guendolen, and love to the old man meant to die. The passion of Daphnis may be *contra naturam*, but it certainly makes more sense than the heteroerotic love in the poem, which is explained in terms of slapstick mishaps, deathly misfires, and divine mistakes. The pederastic seduction, then, is part of a wholesale effort at constructing a system of meaning outside of the mytho-erotics of man-woman sexuality; it is one difference within a set of differences that, together, *make* homoerotic *sense*.

Barnfield's poem is particularly important for examining the implied social subjectivity behind textual subjectivity, for the subsequent publication of *Cynthia. With Certain Sonnets, and the Legend of Cassandra* indicates, first, that the reading audience of the time recognized the potentiality of the sodomite within Barnfield's eclogues, and, second, that homoerotic subjectivity was something that could be both expressed and controlled textually. In the epistle to the volume, Barnfield alludes to a controversy that intersects the textual and social precisely at the point of "the sodomite":

> Some there were, that did interpret *The affectionate Shepheard*, otherwise then (in truth) I meant, touching the subiect thereof, to wit, the loue of a Shepheard to a boy; a fault, the which I will not excuse, because I neuer made. Onely this, I will vnshaddow my conceit: being nothing else, but an imitation of *Virgill*, in the second Eglogue of *Alexis*.(4)

Barnfield's defense succinctly encapsulates many of the problems of speaking of the sodomite. On the one hand, it indicates that his reading public recognized themselves as subjects to a homoerotic discourse. They were forced to make sense of homoeroticism, and were displeased. But, on the other, it also demonstrates how Barnfield could also disengage his authorial subjectivity from his text through a simple act of disavowal: I may have *said* it, but I did not *mean* it. Exactly what we can read from this text, then, is up for grabs. But what is not up for grabs is the fact that, as Barnfield acknowledges, one thing that could (and can) be read is the sodomite. And the possibly coy disavowal also indicates that at least some of Barnfield's reading public interpolated a link between the textual subject of sodomy and Barnfield's own social subjectivity.

While this exposure of a transaction between the textual and the social is in and of itself interesting, the volume is even more fascinating because of the tacit belief presented in it that the sodomite (that is, the potentiality for homoerotic subjectivity) can be both expressed and controlled. The twenty "certain Sonnets" included in the volume ironically reinvoke the homoeroticism that the epistle has disavowed:

> Sporting at fancie, setting light by loue,
>> There came a theefe, and stole away my heart,
>> (And therefore robd me of my chiefest part)
> Yet cannot Reason him a felon proue.
> For why his beauty (me hearts thiefe) affirmeth,
>> Piercing no skin (the bodies sensiue wall)
>> And hauing leaue, and free consent withall,
> Himselfe not guilty, from loue guilty tearmeth,
> Conscience the Iudge, twelue Reasons are the Iurie,

> They finde mine eies the beutie t'haue let in,
> And on this verdict giuen, agreed they bin,
> Wherefore, because his beauty did allure yee,
> Your Doome is this: in teares still to be drowned,
> When his faire forehead with disdain is frowned.
>
> (I.ll.1-14)

Like Daphnis's pastoral lament, this sonnet includes gendered textual determinants — determinants that *constitute* a homoerotic discourse. The poem genders the "theefe" as "him" (l. 4) and "Him-
selfe" (l. 8), and mentions *his* physical allure three times (ll. 5, 12,
14). Moreover, while the poem does not determine the gender of
the speaker — the "I" — the volume as a whole has already twice
gendered the "I" as male, once in the male speaker of "Cynthia,"
and once in the "I" of the epistle, the author himself.

The homoerotic subjectivity of the sequence is further entrenched
both intertextually and vernacularly through the sustained use of the
name Ganymede. Sonnet IIII introduces the term by stating "Two
stars there are in one faire firmament, / (Of some intitled *Ganymedes* sweet face . . . )" (ll. 1-2). The use of the name establishes a
web of connections between the sequence and, on the one hand, the
social rhetoric of sodomy, and on the other, Barnfield's own canon.
Not only does the term carry with it vernacular associations of sodomy,[8] but the possible neo-platonic or "desexualizing" traditions[9]
sometimes ascribed to the term are removed from the sequence by
sonnet III, an extended rumination on philosophical traditions that
claims that "The Stoicks thinke . . . / That vertue is the chiefest
good of all, / The Academicks on *Idea* call" (ll. 1-3).[10] These traditions, which might construe "Ganymede" as a typological em-
blem, are contradistinct to the poetry at hand for, as the couplet
says, "My chiefest good, my chiefe felicity,/ Is to be gazing on my
loues faire eie" (ll. 13-14). Moreover, the sequence frequently ex-
ploits the conflation of mythological and vernacular meanings. Sonnet X begins with "Thus was my loue, thus was my *Ganymed*"
(l. 1), which seems to draw on the vernacular analogy of male lover
and Ganymede, but then also imports the myth of Venus creating
"faire *Ganymede*" from "pure blood in whitest snow yshed" (ll.
4-7). Sonnet XV likewise begins with the personal/sexual address

"Ah fairest *Ganymede*," but then reinscribes this address within the pastoral tradition from whence it derives by stating, "Though silly Sheepeheard I, presume to loue thee, . . . / Yet to thy beauty is my loue no blot" (ll. 1-4). The recourse to pastoral also completes an intertextual loop, returning us to the pastorals of *The Affectionate Shepheard* and a recognition that Ganymede is also the name of Daphnis's love in that condemned eclogue cycle. Unlike the epistle, then, which distances "the sodomite" from the pastorals and Barnfield from sodomy, this sequence shatters these established distances of decorum, and places the sodomite in the volume.

The web of meanings invoked in both these texts and the author's apologia demonstrates that the rhetoric of sodomy and the potentiality of the subject do, indeed, intersect. However the sonnets, untitled and curiously placed after a chivalrous romantic poem — "Cynthia" — also pose a textual dilemma; indeed, they would seem more at home as a conclusive coda to Barnfield's pastoral volume than they are in this volume which, after all, disavows homoerotic intentionality. However, the purpose of the sequence becomes apparent in relation to the structure of the volume as a whole. Immediately after the sequence comes an ode, titled simply "Ode," that is another speech by Daphnis, the central speaker of *The Affectionate Shepheard*. But the poem reverses the plot of the eclogues, for it recounts how

> Love I did faire *Ganymed*;
> (*Venus* darling, beauties bed:)
> Him I thought the fairest creature;
> Him the quintessence of Nature:
> But yet (alas) I was deceiu'd,
> (Love of reason is bereau'd)
> For since then I saw a Lasse
> (Lasse) that did in beauty passe,
> (Passe) faire *Ganymede* as farre
> As *Phoebus* doth the smallest starre. (ll. 51-60)

The ode fully rewrites the lament of Daphnis as a conventional lament for an unobtainable woman, complete with a frustrated epithalamion:

> Her it is, for whom I mourne;
> Her, for whom my life I scorne;
> Her, for whom I weepe all day;
> Her, for whom I sigh, and say,
> Either She, or else no creature,
> Shall enjoy my Loue: whose feature
> Though I neuer can obtaine,
> Yet shall my true loue remaine:
> Till (my body turn'd to clay)
> My poore soule must passe away,
> To the heauens. . . . (ll. 73-83)

Read as the conclusion to the sonnet sequence, the ode serves to make the volume a mimetic enactment of Barnfield's epistle. If *The Affectionate Shepheard* confronted readers with the sodomite, then the sonnets reinvoke this position and the ode subsequently separates Barnfield from it by casting the sodomite as one distinct subject position which is disavowed in favor of "normal" heteroerotic subjectivity.

The process of disavowing homoerotic subjectivity is further stressed in the ode by a manipulation of poetic voice. While the eclogues and sonnets speak in the first person, the ode prefaces Daphnis's speech with a lengthy narrative introduction that establishes a distinctive difference between the poet and the shepherd. The "I" of the poem wanders through a pastoral glade where "Nights were short, and daies were long" (l. 1), and sees

> By a well of Marble-stone
> A Shepheard lying all alone.
> Weepe he did; and his weeping
> Made the fading flowers spring.
> *Daphnis* was his name (I weene)
> Youngest Swaine of Summers Queene. (ll. 11-16)

The conflation of author/"I"/Daphnis present in the eclogues and sonnets is replaced by a clear division between author/"I" and Daphnis. And while the ode's Daphnis is troubled by a conflict between Love's command to love the Lasse, and Fancy's command to "not remoue/ My affection from" Ganymede (ll. 61-63), the author/"I" sees nothing in the scene but a clear dictate to adopt the heteroerotic norm—a norm made all the more normative by the invocation of the traditional tribute to "Eliza":

> Scarce had he [Daphnis] these last words spoken,
> But me thought his heart was broken;
> With great griefe that did abound,
> (Cares and griefe the heart confound)
> In whose heart (thus riu'd in three)
> ELIZA written I might see:
> In caracters of crimson blood,
> (Whose meaning well I vnderstood.)
> Which, for my heart might not behold,
> I hyed me home my sheep to folde. (ll. 87-96)

With this return to the fold, the poem is folded back into the preface.[11] The homoerotic subject constructed in the sonnets reconstructs the subject of the eclogues, but this entire subject is then relabeled as the "fancy" of a fictional shepherd; the "I" of the ode becomes a distanced spectator fully concordant with the orthodox author of the volume's preface. The strategy was evidently successful, for the preface to Barnfield's next volume, *The Enconium of Lady Pecunia: or The Praise of Money*, recalls the favorable acceptance of *Cynthia*: "Gentlemen, being incouraged through your gentle acceptance of my *Cynthia*, I have once more aduentured on your Curtesies: hoping to finde you (as I haue done heretofore) friendly"(83).

Regardless of how it is adjudicated, homoeroticism in all of these poems is recognized as a specific nexus of intersecting meanings that, in the aggregate, make "sense." And hence sodomy is more than a universal sign of unintelligibility; sodomy, here, *is* the sodomite. The daemonized sodomite of orthodox ideology—the "anti-subject" existing only in an implied space outside of meaning—here becomes a character *within* the language of subjective possibility. Importantly, Barnfield's canon as a whole also begins to suggest some of the myriad issues we must keep in mind when discussing any subjectivity during the period, for it indicates the ways in which *the* subject fractures into *many* subjects. My discussion has not stressed the point, but I have been dealing with several different subjects: the subject *in* Barnfield's text—the position designated as intelligible for various characters by the codes of meaning within the poetry; the subject *of* Barnfield's texts—the position a reader finds her- or himself in when reading the text; the narrating subject—the position of the speaking voice determined by the intersection of systems of meaning it is bringing to its topic, as well as its nebulous relation to the author; the writing subject, or author—a seemingly monolithic concept that immediately disintegrates when we realize the difference between how Barnfield was interpreted by his reading audience and how he constructs his own intentions. There are, of course, deciding differences between all of these subjects. However, as Jameson suggests and as Barnfield's epistle bears out, these subjects, though all different, are neither mutually exclusive nor unrelated. But what is of central importance to my argument is the fact that all of these positions in relation to Barnfield's texts are contingent on a *subjective* comprehension of homoeroticism. If, in the world of the text, sodomy can make a sodomite, should we believe it is *necessarily* different in the "real" world?

## SHAKESPEARE: UNFOLDING SODOMY

The ability to find "the sodomite" within the subjective rhetoric of Barnfield's canon also, ironically, problematizes our ability to read *any* subjects. For while Barnfield's texts are an effort to construct the sodomite, they are also equally an effort to construct Barnfield. And in this latter subjective effort a space opens up that confounds the subjecting ability of language: for Barnfield creates himself only by creating what he is not. There is, therefore, an implicit exceeding of language, an idea that Barnfield him*self* exists in some sort of *de facto* sense, and that his poetic self-representation is simply an effort to toss aside the chaff of opinion. There is here, to borrow Stephen Greenblatt's famous formulation, a very strong idea that "there [are] both selves and a sense that they [can] be fashioned" (1). However, this "self"—what we might think of in heterocentric humanist terms as the "real" self—ironically comes to occupy a space analogous to Bray's sodomite, for it is a self that Barnfield fashions only from a rupture in signification, from an ability to place his "self" in the negatively contingent space implied by the subjective constitution of his sodomite. The sodomite becomes a determining other, for what Barnfield's canon as a whole says is: this is what *it* is, and I am that which *it* is *not*. This structure is even more fully exploited in Shakespeare's sequence in a way that confuses both how we can read the sodomite and how criticism has read these famous lyrics.

The history of commentary on Shakespeare's sonnets is also the history of how to read humanistically.[12] Questions of the identity of the dark lady, the rival poet, the boy; debates on the identity of W.H.;[13] biographical arguments over what is sexual, what is platonic, and what was Shakespeare's sexual preference:[14] these questions, which form the bulk of criticism about the sonnets, all presuppose that the importance of the text is in its ability to act as a conduit of atemporal human emotions — the sort of basic drives that, in a humanist criticism, transcend time and become the key to all mythologies (cf. Belsey 1-36). Even very recent criticism tends to adopt hybrid forms of this methodology. Hence Joseph Pequigney, in *Such Is My Love: A Study of Shakespeare's Sonnets*, takes as his aim "a searching and persuasive exposition of Shakespeare's Sonnets, one elucidative of their aesthetic coherence, their moral values, and their psychological depths" (4-5). The presupposition is that the sonnets necessarily function as expressions of an authorial psyche — or, in a more simplistic form, of Shakespeare himself — and that the purpose of reading them is to explicate the *man* behind them and expressed through them.[15]

Such a program of reading inherently betrays the epistemology of sonnets, for, as is obvious in Barnfield's canon, the subjectivity within sequences typically is designed only to imply through difference the space occupied by the poet. A more appropriate program of reading has been proposed by Joel Fineman, who finds in the sonnets "the internally divided, post-idealist subject of a 'perjur'd eye'" (29). Through the "using up" of epideictic conventions, Fineman claims, the sequence severs poetics from the poet and establishes a space of true poetic subjectivity for the authorial figure. Ironically, while Fineman's argument short-circuits the humanist assumptions underpinning criticism of the poems, it also accepts without question the sexual subjectivity of them; that is, Fineman accepts, in accordance with tradition, that the first one hundred and twenty-six sonnets are an erotic address to a boy from a male, and that this pattern of desire is then reconfigured into heteroerotic lust for the fabled "dark lady." I would like to put into play the variable of sexual difference that Fineman takes as a given, and argue that in order to understand the sexual subjectivity of the sequence we must abandon our belief in the ability of language to subjugate, at least directly. The purpose of the "boy sonnets," as they have come to be known, is not erotic, but linguistic. These poems actually take as their project the task of frustrating the ability to read erotic meaning in general. If Barnfield's sodomite is a means of achieving subjectivity through the control of sexual meaning, the Shakespearian sodomite procures the poet's subjectivity at the expense of sexual meaning.

The process I am suggesting can be best explicated through an analysis of the first twenty sonnets. Fineman claims these poems as a sub-sequence that "equates the true poetry and true love that goes with the young man" (75). Fineman is not alone in his assumptions; the beginning sonnets of the 1609 quarto are generally accepted as a self-contained unit, one that "give[s] expression to one compelling case, that of saving from time and wrack the rare and ravishing beauty of the youth addressed" (Pequigney 7). However, the boy who is so prominent in these readings seems to me to be much more difficult to find in the poems themselves, for the gendering of this "subsequence" continually diffuses along an axial of ambiguous and mutually exclusive possibilities. The familiar opening of the first sonnet outlines the difficulty:

> From fairest creatures we desire increase,
> That thereby beauties *Rose* might never die,
> But as the riper should by time decease,
> His tender heire might beare his memory. . . . (1.ll.1-4)

There is, I will claim, no way to "make sense" of these lines. The thematic insistence on *husband*ry might imply that the receiver of this advice is male. However, in *All's Well That Ends Well*, Parolles offers advice to a female, Helena, claiming "loss of virginity is rational increase, and there was never virgin got till virginity was first lost" (I.i.125-127). This biological exhortation, then, is not inherently gendered as a male-male language. The gendering of this quatrain fully inscribes itself within a web of punning multiplicity. As Stephen Booth has noted, the coordinating conjunction "but" carries the possible meanings of "and" and "except" (135). Hence the "decease" of the "riper" imports the momentary possibility of undermining the immortality of "beauties Rose." Moreover, line four incorporates two cognate puns, "heir/air" and "bear/bare": the heir of a father who carries on the memory of patrilineal lineage is also at the same time something vaporous that strips away that memory.

Nothing in this sonnet conveys a single meaning, let alone a single gender or sexuality. The narcissistic person "contracted" or tithed to "thine owne bright eyes" (1.1.5) is also potentially a person "contracted" or reduced to "bright eyes." In the first case the person is belligerently irreverent; in the second the person is stereotypically inscribed in the language of the sonnet and blason genres. And when this person (person—but as yet not specified as male or female) is said to "within thine owne bud buriest thy content" (1.1.10), the derision may be toward either masturbation or monogamy, since "owne" and "one" are Renaissance cognates. We could be confronting here a man who masturbates, a woman who masturbates, or a man who satisfies himself with only one vagina. Moreover, the sexual charges here are fully complicated by Renaissance idiomatics: "buriest" foreshadows the "graue" of the final couplet, and implies death and the demise of "beauties Rose"; death, however, also implies orgasm and "increase"; and the image of a flower also recalls the Renaissance euphemism for menstruation. What is happening here is hard to tell—and this, more than likely, is not the problem but the point.

The strategy involved in this sonnet can be clarified if we again return to the idea of the first twenty sonnets as a subsequence. The unity of these poems is frequently taken to be an effect of Shakespeare's extended use as a source of Erasmus's "Epistle to Persuade a Young Gentleman to Marriage" as reprinted in Thomas Wilson's *The Arte of Rhetorique*. This argument, which has been scrupulously analyzed by Katherine Wilson in *Shakespeare's Sugared Sonnets* (146-167), usually accepts Wilson's example of Erasmus as a *thematic* inspiration for Shakespeare's poems. However, if we consider the epistle's context a more interesting set of possibilities arise. Erasmus's epistle is included in the *Rhetorique* as an example of persuasive oration, and it in many ways can be viewed as an exemplum that works within the specific textual dynamics of seduction present in Barnfield's eclogues. Persuasion, like seduction, is a highly motivated discourse that seeks specific ends. Wilson's use of Erasmus then, in the simplest form, can be thought of as an example of how to make language *work*. The first sonnet of the Shakespearian sequence, in contrast, is an example of how to *stop* language from working. And it achieves this end by deceptively simple means: it erases the gendered determinants present in the title of Erasmus's epistle. What is a conservative effort to assure the continuance of the patrilineal line in Wilson's *Rhetorique* becomes, in the Shakespearian poetic, a way to stop making sense. And hence the link between the text and source, while involving thematic issues, might best be formulated on the theoretical level: both the *Rhetorique* and the *Sonnets* are extended ruminations on the significatory propriety of language.

To a certain extent the multiplicity of the first sonnet might be dismissed as the effect of the inherent polysemy of any language, and particularly of the unregularized English of the Renaissance. However, this slipperiness of sexual meaning is consistently exploited throughout the first twenty sonnets in a way that indicates more than accidental multivalence. Each sonnet in this sequence constructs a pattern that demands a gendered reading, but then frustrates attempts to find the determinants that would make such a reading possible. The second sonnet, for example, begins with traditional imagery of warfare —

> When fortie Winters shall besiege thy brow,
> And digge deep trenches in thy beauties field,
> Thy youthes proud liuery so gaz'd on now,
> Wil be a totter'd weed of smal worth held. . . . (2.ll.1-4)

— but this imagery, which is usually associated with the female, is only a further complication of the man to son expectations brought to bear on the text by its relation to Erasmus's epistle. Furthermore, the poem can be read in (at least) two entirely independent ways. In the Erasmian tradition, it works coherently as an exhortation to a young man to breed. In the tradition of Parolles, it might be a demand to a woman to surrender her virginity. The two possibilities exist coterminously because there is no convenient "Stella" in the title to gender the sequence; there is only "Shake-speares Sonnets Neuer before Imprinted."

The process of interpretation demanded by these opening sonnets is metaphorically redacted in sonnet 8, when music is used to describe that "speechlesse song being many, seeming one" (8.1.13). Like a concord sounded in unison, third, fifth and sixth, these poems, which appear as one sequence, continually break into constituent parts. But unlike a chord that achieves a "mutuall ordering" (8.1.10), the poems create a disordering of the assumptions that must precede the meaningfulness of gendered language. This interpretive frustration can be traced throughout the first eighteen sonnets. The couplet of sonnet 13 seems to imply that the receiver is male, for it suggests "You had a Father, let your Son say so" (13.1.14); but then we realize that this patrilineal order affords two positions between grandfather and grandson: son and daughter. Sonnet 9 seems to specify a similar gendering, for the couplet claims "No loue toward others in that bosome sits / That on him-selfe such murdrous shame commits" (9.11.13-14). But a backward glance reveals that this sentiment does not refer to the receiver of the sonnets, but rather to a hypothetical "vnthrift" (9.1.9); the gender of the receiver remains a mystery. The ambiguity of these sonnets shows forth especially in comparison to Barnfield's; if Barnfield's demonstrate how to "make" a sodomite, Shakespeare's encode the *possibility* of the sodomite, but only as one of many that, in the aggregate, *un*make the possibility of any *one* coherent subject. All of which, of course, can be seen as a means of creating a greater subjective space for the poet. The poet in Barnfield's sequence is he who orders our experience of and differs from the sodomite; the poet in Shakespeare's is he who unorders all gendered experience, and hence is he who differs from all the (poetically) conventional strategies of making gendered sense.

We can therefore extend Fineman's analysis of the *Sonnets'* use of poetic tradition to their use of sexuality, and specifically to their use of the sodomite. For, as with the instance of epideictic tradition, these sonnets "use up" sexual rhetoric—expend its subjecting ability through an "embarassment of riches" and excessive meanings. The importance of the Shakesperian sodomite within this hermeneutic becomes apparent in sonnet 19, when the sustained neutrality of gender is pointedly suspended. The speaker implores time to

> carve not with thy howers my loues faire brow,
> Nor draw noe lines there with antique pen,
> Him in thy course vntainted doe allow,
> For beauties patterne to succeeding men. (19.ll.9-12)

There is no possible referent for "Him" other than "my loue." The effect of this specificity genders the sequence retroactively and makes us aware that what we have been reading is, indeed, "the sodomite." However, the delay in this specification is as important as its arrival, for the solidification of gender makes us also aware of its indeterminacy in the preceding poems. We become aware, in short, that we have not been dealing in textual truths, but rather have been importing our own assumptions—either hetero-, homo-, or otherwise erotic. And in the process it also stresses the inability of conventionalized language to restrict the expression of desire.

That the critique of language and not the construction of the sodomite is the topic of these poems seems certain, for the sequence follows the specification of gender with a poem that is a tour-de-force and condensation of the obfuscational strategies deployed throughout the preceding poems. Although sonnet 20 is one of the most famous of the cycle, its centrality to the sequence—and my argument—makes it worth presenting *in toto*.

> A Womans face with natures owne hand painted,
> Hast thou the Master Mistris of my passion,
> A womans gentle hart but not acquainted
> With shifting change as is false womens fashion,
> An eye more bright then theirs, lesse false in rowling:
> Gilding the object where-vpon it gazeth,
> A man in hew all *Hews* in his controwling,
> Which steales mens eyes and womens soules amaseth,
> And for a woman wert thou first created,

Till nature as she wrought thee fell a dotinge,
And by addition me of thee defeated
By adding one thing to my purpose nothing.
　　But since she prickt thee out for womens pleasure,
　　Mine be thy loue and thy loues vse their treasure.

　　　　　　　　　　　　　　　　　　　　(20.11.1-14)

The poem creates a perfectly androgynous — or perhaps more appropriately hermaphroditic — reading experience, for it is equally gendered as both male and female. This perfect duplicity is amply displayed in the famous crux of the poem, the coinage of "Master Mistris": is this a man (master) who is used as a mistress would be, or a mistress who holds a primary (master) position in the speaker's mind?[16] The overt hermaphroditism of this phrase is punningly and subtly sustained throughout the entire sonnet. The first explication of the "Master Mistris" seems to gender the receiver of the poems as female (20.ll.3-6), but this possibility is juxtaposed to the equal possibility that the receiver is male (20.ll.6-8). As in many of the sonnets there is almost an infinity of meanings here, two of which are particularly telling. One possibility is that the speaker is addressing a woman who surpasses the "fashion" of other women, and through her chaste gentility "gilds" (i.e., renders worthy or priceless) the man on whom she "gazeth" ("A man . . . " in this case being an appositive for "object"). Yet there is also the possibility that the speaker addresses a man, and that "A womans gentle heart" is a metaphor for the unique beauty of the male. As Stephen Booth has noted, "acquainted" carries with it a pun on the noun "quaint," a slang term for the pudendum (163). With this meaning in place, an apt paraphrase of the lines might be, "a woman emotionally, but not physically, a man capable of entrancing both men and women." And in either case, the symmetrical placement of masculine and feminine metaphoric referents frustrates attempts to decide between them.

　　The overabundance of possible meanings continues throughout the poem as a nemesis to interpretation. The sonnet maintains that "And for a woman wert thou first created," a seemingly straightforward line that, nonetheless, fragments into varied possibilities: "you were first created *as* a woman"; "you were first created for

sexual pleasure with women [but now shall have it with men]";
"you were first created for your mother [but now should take a
wife]." And when the sonnet "sexualizes" the rhetoric with the
famous phrase "nature . . . me of thee defeated, / By adding one
thing to my purpose nothing," the gendering is still not stabilized.
The juxtaposition of "one thing" and "nothing" visually captures
on the page a yoking of phallic and vaginal imagery. Additionally,
the "one thing," which is so frequently taken to be the penis, might
just as easily refer to the problematic self-entrancement that keeps
the receiver from marrying. There is, in short, no possible way to
determine the meaning, for these lines all mean *too much*. Indeed,
this conflation (and hence nullification) of meanings is perfectly
demonstrated in the couplet: "But since she prickt thee out for
womens pleasure, / Mine be thy loue and thy loues vse their treasure" (20.11.13-14). Here the speaker says, "Since you were created with a penis to pleasure women, I will love you platonically
and women will use you sexually." But he also at the same time
says, "Since you were created to be used as a woman (i.e., penetrated), I will be your lover, and others (presumably women) will
have to masturbate ('vse' of 'treasure' playing within the metaphors
of usury associated with onanism)."

Like Erasmus's epistle, this sonnet is also an exemplum of persuasive rhetoric, but what we are persuaded of is that this is a poet
unfettered by the strictures of gendered and sexualized rhetoric that
are generically indicative of his medium. Every effort to read these
poems continually reminds us that here is a poet who has created a
text that constantly recoils when we touch it. When we find one
meaning, it is only at the expense of the many. The importance of
the punning play within sonnet 20 cannot be overstated, for the
sonnet also sets up a system of obfuscation that implicates the entire
cycle. The speaker's description of "A Womans face with natures
owne hand painted" (20.1.2) incorporates the cognate pun on one/
own already seen in the first sonnet, and thereby immediately establishes the poem as a janus-like statement. If painted by nature's
"own" hand, the receiver's allure is validated as natural. But if
painted by nature's "one" hand, it remains that nature's *other* hand
may soon grab a brush and paint again. In the first instance sexual
allure is naturally or platonically absolute; in the second it is part of

a continual flux of possibilities. This latter instability implicates the entire sequence, for it is indeed true that nature's other hand surfaces:

> For since each hand hath put on Natures power,
> Fairing the foule with Arts faulse borrow'd face,
> Sweet beauty hath no name no holy bourse,
> But is prophan'd, if not liues in disgrace. (127.ll.5-8)

One hundred and six sonnets separate nature's own/one hand from this other that surfaces in the first of the so-called dark lady sonnets. But the resurfacing of the hands of nature collapses the linearity of the cycle and draws us back to the "master mistris" even as it pushes us ahead to the "mistress." Although "each hand" is, in the poem's own syntax, a metonymy for the work of other poets, it is also a macro-device within the sequence that, as the poems turn from homo- to heteroerotics, also returns us to the hermaphroditism of sonnet 20. The rhetorical point is clear: nature does not dictate *one* course of desire; desire is, rather, multifaceted, and is always subject to repainting by the strokes of a powerful but deferred other hand.

The ordering of the 1609 quarto does much to support such a polymorphously perverse interpretation.[17] Sonnet 126, which can be considered the envoy to "my louely Boy" (126.l.1), ends with a missing couplet, as if to imply that the passion of the first one hundred and twenty-six sonnets never ends, but rather exists coterminously with the passion presented in the dark lady poems. Yet even without the questionable support of textual order, one thing remains certain: these poems punningly intermingle virtually every sexual subjectivity, and all to the ends of serving a greater subject, the poet himself. In Shakespeare's poems, the sodomite destroys or uses up language, and thereby establishes a space different from language for the poet. Barnfield's poems fold both the poet and the sodomite into the economy of orthodox meaning; Shakespeare's poems unfold this economy and mark its edges and impotencies. For by continually intermingling the tropics of hetero- and homoerotic desire, the sequence creates an experience wherein we are continually able to read the sodomite, but are never quite sure if we should. The

Shakespearian sodomite, then, might best be thought of in the poet's own words: it is "one thing," but to the poet's purpose, "no thing."

## TRADITION AND THE INDIVIDUAL SODOMITE

Although there is a decided difference between *how* the sodomite functions in Barnfield and Shakespeare, the more important point is that he is *present* in both cycles. For each cycle depends on the *inscription* of the sodomite in order to enact its own rhetorical ends. The sodomite within these texts derives neither from an anomoly nor a mistake. Rather, the ability of the text to dictate the sodomite is concordant with the basically conservative views of language implicit in the very tradition of the sonnet. In the dedication to the Earl of Derby that prefaces *Cynthia*, Barnfield outlines an androcentric project that typifies the sonnet genre:

> Small is the gift, but great is my good-will; the which, by how much lesse I am able to expresse it, by so much the more it is infinite. Liue long: and inherit your Predecessors vertues, as you doe their dignitie and estate. This is my wish: the which your honorable excellent giftes doe promise me to obtaine: and whereof these few rude and unpollished lines, are a true (though an undeserving) testimony. If my ability were better, the signes should be greater; but being as it is, your honour must take me as I am, not as I should be. (43)

The dedication is obviously informed by certain proprieties of patronage, but it also indicates the extent to which poetry and patrilinearity intersect: Barnfield's poems are a "testimony" to the progenital conformity of the Earl's masculine lineage. Although the preface is, perhaps, as much a convention as it is anything else, it also intersects with the basic assumptions underpinning sonneteering in general. Giles Fletcher, who provides one of the most sophisticated manifestos about sonneteering in his preface to *Licia*, succinctly outlines the dynastic (and patriotic) assumptions carried with the task of the sonneteer:

> Peruse but the writings of former times, and you shall see not onely in other countreyes, as *Italie* and *France*, men of learning, and great parts to have written Poems and Sonnets of Love; but even amongst us, men of best nobilitie, and chiefest families, to be the greatest Scholler and most renowned in this kind. (4)

For Fletcher, this patrilineal heritage is intricately linked with the propriety of language, for he takes as the task of his sequence the purification of English:

> . . . if aniething be odious amongst us, it is the exile of our olde maners: and some base-borne phrases stuft up with such newe tearmes as a man may sooner feele us to flatter by our incrouching eloquence than suspect from the eare. (8)

The critical assumption of both Fletcher and Barnfield is clear: great men write sonnets in a language that, in turn, expresses the greatness of men.[18] The ability of Barnfield to express the sodomite, then, becomes part of the "natural" ability of poetry to express, delineate, and control meaning in general — an ability tacit within and necessary to the continuance of the patrilineal power manifest within his culture and implicit within language itself. And if Shakespeare's poems seem to differ, they still inherently bear out the point that implicit in the ability to control the (textual) self is the need to control *everything* — the sodomite, included. And hence the sodomite is fully returned to us *not* as the exception, but as a part of the very conditions of meaning within the Renaissance culture.

Although the sequences of Barnfield and Shakespeare differ in their strategies, on the broadest level they are both *negotiating* the sodomite, deploying the possibility of homoerotic subjectivity strategically and with a measured economy designed to gain other meanings at a calculated expense. There is, in other words, a general acknowledgment in the sequences that one can speak of the sodomite, but to the end of saying something else altogether. In this manner the sodomite becomes something more than a mutant or deviant. He becomes a redaction of the very jousts of self and other, of being and nothingness, of all and none, of meaning and rupture, that characterize both sonneteering and subjectivity itself. While I have sketched this problematic in the sometimes cumbersome terms of current critical theory, Shakespeare's sonnets make it pithy and eloquent, for as the speaker tells us, "To giue away your selfe, keeps your selfe still" (16.14). "Still" — the cotermineity of all and nothing that marks both the poet and the sodomite: still — continuous and transitive through time; still — static and atemporal; still — to distill and reduce to an essence; still — a trace of stell, perhaps: the pen that traces the traces of presence . . . still.

## NOTES

1. For a discussion of these precepts, as well as how they relate to issues of race, class, and gender, see Fuss.

2. The actual formulation is from Roland Barthes; for an overview of its impact see Marks and Stambolian.

3. For an extremely important discussion of the problematics that this axial view of sexual difference entails see Sedgwick.

4. The idea originated with McIntosh's famous article. Although Foucault does not acknowledge a debt to McIntosh, his work has widely popularized a similar idea in current critical practice.

5. The extent of this "gay" canonization is witnessed by the appearance of both sequences in gay literary anthologies by Coote and Fone.

6. The major texts that have paved the way for this formulation are Althusser (*For Marx*) and Eagleton. Strong proponents of Althusser and Eagleton have argued that the subjective reformulation of Marxist textuality subordinates the materiality of "art" and exalts the position of the Freudian psyche; I prefer, however, to recognize that a "work" is specifically designed as a consumer object, and therefore its "materiality" cannot be analyzed apart from its potentiality for "consumption." Belsey provides a cogent if somewhat schematic overview of the debates and trends that are at play in the current debate on the neo-Marxist textual/social subject (56-102, 125-146).

7. For a full discussion of the relationship between pastoral and sodomy in the Renaissance see Bredbeck.

8. Throughout the Renaissance "Ganymede" functioned much as the modern terms "homosexual" or "faggot" do in our own culture. Cooper, for example, defines "Ganimede" as "a Trojan chylde, which feigned to bee ravyshed of Jupiter, and made his butlar" (Iiiii4v), and Blount defines him as "any Boy, loved for carnal abuse, or hired to be used contrary to Naturem to commit the detestable sin of *Sodomy*," and lists the cross-references of ingle, buggerer, and catamite (92-93).

9. Berchorius devotes book 15, chapter 1, to a Christian typologization of Ovid entitled *Metamorphosis Ovidian Moraliter*, which refigures Jupiter as a type of the Christian God and Ganymede as a figure of the transcendent soul. This

pattern also proliferated in the Renaissance, as in Landino's Christian glosses, which are discussed by Panofsky (179, 214), and Golding's influential and common English translations. For a full discussion of this tradition, see Saslow (41, 1-62 passim).

10. The allusion to "Idea" obviously encodes an attack on Drayton, whose sonnet cycle, "Idea's Mirrour," would have been in wide circulation by the time Barnfield composed his (cf. Westling).

11. The use of the ode as a closure or rewriting of the sonnets is not entirely atypical; Neely examines several examples of sequences that "diffuse . . . the conflicts into other poetic modes" (360). Neely's essay is the most encompassing study of the generic qualities of the Elizabethan sonnet cycle; however, I differ with it on several points, the key one being that Neely claims that "most of the English sequences conclude unresolved, but all make gestures toward closure" (360). This claim results from Neely's dependence on thematic and narrative analyses. I claim that the project of the sequences is to clear a subjective space for the poet, and as such the unresolved plots are actually fully operative strategies with this greater project.

12. For an excellent overview of Shakespearian criticism and the question of humanism, though not specifically on the sonnets, see Drakakis (1-25).

13. This problem has been masterfully put to rest by Foster, who convincingly argues that W.H. is a misprint for W.Sh., i.e., William Shakespeare.

14. The most astute comment on this subject to date comes from Booth, who wryly notes that "William Shakespeare was almost certainly homosexual, bisexual, or heterosexual" (548). All of the critical issues mentioned here are objectively anatomized in Appendix I of Booth's edition, and rather than accumulate a lengthy bibliographic note I refer readers to this excellent resource.

15. The role of this "Authentic Shakespeare," as Orgel would call him—the assumed figure of authority validating our interpretive practice—has been explored inventively in relation to debates of authorship of the plays by Garber (122-146), and in relation to performance and editing problems by Orgel (1-26).

16. Few critics have actually recognized this famous phrase as one that in and of itself indicates androgyny. Most begin with the assumption that the phrase is masculine (cf. Winny and Neely 366-367). This tendency is also demonstrated in Fineman's work. He sees sonnet twenty as "the *locus classicus*" in a debate that presupposes homoerotic rhetorical intents: "Given the poet's love for the young man, and the young man sonnets surely give it frequently enough, the question that remains is just what it is the young man's poet wants" (272). Such statements, I think, insert a critical determinism into Fineman's argument that betrays its overall destabilizing intentions.

17. Scholarship has generally come to a point where it accepts the 1609 ordering (cf. Pequigney and Booth). The most important point in the argument is that alternative orderings are always, at best, as unauthorized as that of the 1609 quarto. For example, Sterling's massive effort at recollating the poems on the basis of thematic links ultimately becomes nothing more than assertion of how Sterling thinks the sonnets should read. The sonnets are, indeed, in a received

order, one that is certainly the same as the order they were in when buyers in 1609 purchased their copies. As such, the 1609 order most assuredly supplies to us the same process of reading and the same status of textual authority that was present during the Renaissance. Authenticity, then, becomes a problem only when the sonnets are viewed as an example of *Shakespeare's* mind rather than as a Renaissance printed text.

Neely makes a point that is central to this argument. Using the examples of the *Canzoniere* manuscripts and the several revised editions of Drayton's *Idea*, she claims, "An examination of its development shows that Drayton's sequence, like Petrarch's, was a structured yet elastic work which could expand, contract, and regenerate itself without altering its fundamental characteristics" (362). This point is important, for it suggests that the structure of sequences in general is not one that relies on linear narration, but is rather a retrospective process that puts the poems into an almost iconic form designed to convey a total "sense" or "experience." The suggestion of cycles as a form of retrospective ordering implies that whoever decided on the order of the 1609 quarto did so from the perspective of a Renaissance subject creating iconic sense from the individual poems, and hence the 1609 order, regardless of its "authority," becomes the "valid" order.

18. The assumed conductivity of language present here also has literary roots deep within the sonnet tradition. The transparency of language forms the basis of most western cultures ("in the beginning was the Word . . ." [John, 1.1]), and also strongly informs Petrarch's early and influential work in the sonnet genre (see Freccero 20-32).

# REFERENCES

Althusser, Louis. *For Marx*. Trans. by Ben Brewster. Harmondsworth: Penguin, 1970.

———. *Lenin and Philosophy and Other Essays*. Trans. Ben Brewster. London: New Left Books, 1977.

Barnfield, Richard. *Cynthia. With certain Sonnets, and the Legend of Cassandra*. London: Humfrey Lownes, 1595.

———. *The Affectionate Shepheard. Containing the Complaint of Daphnis for the loue of Ganymede*. London: Iohn Danter, 1594.

———. *The Enconium of Lady Pecunia*. London: G.S., 1598.

Belsey, Catherine. *Critical Practice*. London: Methuen, 1980.

Berchorius, Petrus. *Metamorphosis Ovidiana Moraliter a Magistro Thomas Walleys Anglico de Professione Praedicatorium Sub Sanctissimo Patre Dominico*. . . . Utrecht: Instituut voor Laat Latijn der Rijksuniversiteit, 1906.

Blount, Thomas. *Glossographia: Or a Dictionary Interpreting the Hard Words of Whatsoever Language, Now Used in our Refined English Tongue*. London: John Martyr, 1670.

Booth, Stephen, Ed. *Shakespeare's Sonnets*. New Haven: Yale UP, 1977.

Bray, Alan. *Homosexuality in Renaissance England*. London: Gay Men's Press, 1982.

Bredbeck, Gregory W. "Milton's Ganymede: Negotiations of Homoerotic Tradition in *Paradise Regained.*" *PMLA* 106(1991): 262-276.

Cooper, Thomas. *Bibliotheca Eliotae*. London: n.p., 1552.

Coote, Stephen, Ed. *The Penguin Book of Homosexual Verse*. Harmondsworth: Penguin, 1983.

Drakakis, John, Ed. *Alternative Shakespeares*. London: Methuen, 1985.

Eagleton, Terry. *Criticism and Ideology*. London: Verso, 1976.

Fineman, Joel. *Shakespeare's Perjur'd Eye: The Invention of Poetic Subjectivity in the Sonnets*. Berkeley: U California P, 1986.

Fletcher, Giles. *Licia*. London: n.p., n.d.

Fone, Byrne R.S., Ed. *Hidden Heritage: History and the Gay Imagination: An Anthology*. New York: Avocation Publishers, Inc., 1980.

Foster, Donald W. "Master W.H., R.I.P." *PMLA* 102 (1987): 42-54.

Foucault, Michel. *The History of Sexuality, Volume I: An Introduction*. New York: Random House, 1980.

Freccero, John. "The Fig Tree and the Laurel: Petrarch's Poetics." *Literary Theory/Renaissance Texts*. Ed. Patricia Parker and David Quint. Baltimore: Johns Hopkins UP, 1986. 20-32.

Fuss, Diana. *Essentially Speaking: Nature, Feminism, Difference*. London: Routledge, 1989.

Garber, Marjorie. "Shakespeare's Ghost Writers." *Cannibals, Witches and Divorce: Estranging the Renaissance*. Ed. Marjorie Garber. Baltimore: Johns Hopkins UP, 1987. 122-146.

Greenblatt, Stephen. *Renaissance Self-Fashioning from More to Shakespeare*. Chicago: U Chicago P, 1980.

Jameson, Frederic. *The Political Unconscious: Narrative as a Socially Symbolic Act*. Ithaca: Cornell UP, 1981.

Marks, Elaine, and George Stambolian, Eds. *Homosexualities and French Literature: Cultural Contexts/Critical Texts*. Ithaca: Cornell UP, 1979.

McIntosh, Mary. "The Homosexual Role." *Social Problems* 16, no. 2 (1968): 183-92. Rpt. in *The Making of the Modern Homosexual*. Ed. Kenneth Plummer. London: Hutchinson, 1981. 30-44.

Neely, Carol Thomas. "The Structure of English Renaissance Sonnet Sequences." *ELH* 45 (1978): 359-389.

Orgel, Stephen. "The Authentic Shakespeare." *Representations* 21 (1988): 1-26.

Panofsky, Erwin. *Studies in Iconology: Humanistic Themes in the Art of the Renaissance*. Oxford: Oxford UP, 1939.

Pequigney, Joseph. *Such is My Love: A Study of Shakespeare's Sonnets*. Chicago: U Chicago P, 1987.

Saslow, James. *Ganymede in the Renaissance: Homosexuality in Art and Society*. New Haven: Yale UP, 1986.

Sedgwick, Eve Kosofsky. "Across Gender, Across Sexuality: Willa Cather and Others." *Displacing Homophobia: Gay Male Perspectives in Literature and*

*Culture*. Ed. Ronald R. Butters, John M. Clum, and Michael Moon. Durham: Duke UP, 1989. 53-72.

Sterling, Brents. *The Shakespeare Sonnet Order: Poems and Groups*. Berkeley: U California P, 1968.

Westling, Louise Hutchings. *The Evolution of Michael Drayton's Idea*. Salzburg: Institut für Englische Sprache und Literatur, 1974.

Wilson, Katherine M. *Shakespeare's Sugared Sonnets*. New York: Barnes and Noble, 1974.

Wilson, Thomas. *The Arte of Rhetorique*. Ed. G.H. Mair. Oxford: Clarendon Press, 1909.

Winny, James. *The Master-Mistress: A Study of Shakespeare's Sonnets*. New York: Barnes and Noble, 1969.

# Body, Costume, and Desire
# in Christopher Marlowe

Gregory Woods, PhD

Nottingham Polytechnic, England

**SUMMARY.** All the desired youths in Marlowe come clothed in favors, the tokens of older and richer men's yearning. These bribes and rewards, often feminine or effeminate ornaments, not only beautify the already gorgeous bodies of young men, but also label and augment their value and their power. The moment of virility's blooming, in adolescence, is seen as a time when boys can negotiate favorable terms of entry into the realms of manhood by the seductive use of their glamor. For their part, desirous men are distracted from the affairs and cares of state by their nostalgic encounters with girlish boys, at worst, to the extent that their own patriarchal power is compromised by sodomitic dalliance. Marlowe's involvement in these plots is iterative and committed.

Our familiarity with Marlowe starts, in the anthologies, with a simple lyric of amorous invitation: "Come live with me, and be my love." Like so much English pastoral and elegy, "The Passionate Shepherd to His Love" is shaped by Virgil's second Eclogue, one of the most influential of all homo-erotic poems. In Virgil's poem, Corydon tries to persuade the boy he loves, Alexis, to come and live with him, by promising him gifts: equal share in his livestock and the milk they produce, a set of pan-pipes, two young deer,

---

Gregory Woods teaches at Nottingham Polytechnic, England. He is the author of *Articulate Flesh: Male Homo-Eroticism and Modern Poetry* (Yale University Press, 1987). His first book of poems, *We Have the Melon,* will be published by Carcanet in 1992. Correspondence may be addressed to the author at: Faculty of Humanities, Nottingham Polytechnic, Clifton Lane, Nottingham, NG11 8NS, England.

flowers gathered by the nymphs, ripe fruit gathered by Corydon himself, fragrant cuttings to wear. But Alexis is not impressed and does not respond. It may be that these riches are altogether too bucolic for his tastes.

Marlowe, in his turn, was fascinated by the figure of the gilded boy, the boy lacking in shame, who demands to be spoilt by a rich and indulgent patron; in short, the boy who—even if his price is high—can be bought. Before a man can strip such a boy he must first adorn him with signs of admiration, deck him out with jewels. In the famous lyric, the passionate shepherd promises his love (ungendered, but generally and logically assumed to be female, at any rate since Walter Ralegh wrote "The Nymphs Reply") a cap, a "kirtle" (smock/coat), a woolen gown, a pair of lined slippers with gold buckles, a belt decorated with coral and amber. Clinching the offer, he concludes:

> And if these pleasures may thee move,
> Come live with me, and be my love

thereby returning to the proposition with which he started. Ralegh's nymph is not taken in by the promise of such gifts: she dismisses them as ephemera.

Marlowe's boys, on the other hand, tend to be as dazzled by promises of such wealth as he by the boys themselves. An adorned boy is one who likes to attract the eye. He is a narcissistic flirt. He dresses, not to hide his nakedness, but to draw attention to it. A richly costumed boy proclaims the success of his own beauty, proving it with the wealth that some besotted patron has spent on him. The more florid, the more feminine his apparel, the more Marlowe seems to feel a boy is amenable to being undressed. Such boys fancy themselves in jewels and want more of them.

In the opening lines of *Dido, Queen of Carthage,* Jupiter tries to secure the continuing love of Ganymede by offering to feather his nest. The god promises the boy feathers from Juno's peacock and Venus' swans, and actually plucks him a feather from the wings of the sleeping Hermes. Perhaps this is a cunning way of getting the boy to think of feather beds and what goes on in them; it is certainly, also, a threatening reminder of the ornithological manner of his rape. Jupiter then gives him jewels which Juno wore at her wedding, urging him to "trick thy arms and shoulders with my theft." For his part, Ganymede, without a word of thanks, takes the jewels and asks for more:

> I would have a jewel for mine ear,
> And a fine brooch to put in my hat,
> And then I'll hug with you an hundred times. (I.i.46-8)

The sale is blatant: affection costs gifts. Jupiter does not haggle, but agrees to Ganymede's price at once, in words which echo those of the passionate shepherd: "And shall have, Ganymede, if thou wilt be my love."[1]

When Venus enters and finds Jupiter cuddling the boy in his lap, she refers scornfully to Ganymede as "that female wanton boy." There are several reasons for this. Firstly, of course, she calls him female because of his implied sexual role as passive partner to Jupiter's activities. But she is also alluding to the effeminacy of his appearance, bejewelled as he already must be in recognition of services rendered. Partial to feathers and gems, the boy is, to all intents and purposes, in drag. His feminine ornaments are the outward signs—the bridal jewels—of the gender role he adopts in relation to Jupiter. Venus is also, implicitly, contrasting this "female" boy with Aeneas, the beautiful and unequivocally manly hero whose champion she is. It is a contrast that Marlowe reinforces later on, when Dido adorns Aeneas with her crown and sceptre. Neither toyboy nor queen, heroic Aeneas is not tempted by such finery. He says firmly:

> A burgonet of steel, and not a crown,
> A sword, and not a sceptre, fits Aeneas. (IV. iv. 42-3)

(A "burgonet" is a helmet.) That Dido ignores this protest and likens his kingly appearance to Jupiter's serves to underline the contrast with Ganymede. Indeed, she calls for a mere Ganymede to be this new king's cup-bearer. She sees in Aeneas' very manliness a divinity that could do for her what Jupiter did for Ganymede:

For in his looks I see eternity,
And he'll make me immortal with a kiss. (IV. iv. 122-3)

In the purity of his virile physique lies all the spirit she considers she requires for an eternity of bliss. She seems to believe that Ganymede's effeminacy is wanton, trivial and ephemeral by contrast. The beauty of her Aeneas requires no decoration, since it shows itself to best effect in the exertion of heroic deeds.

Love, also, has the effect of augmenting physical beauty. Marlowe sees love itself as an adornment, a kind of cross-dressing in the aptness of the loved one's garb. In *Hero and Leander,* after the lovers' first night together, Leander heads for home, quite incapable of hiding his love: for he is wearing it.

With Cupid's myrtle was his bonnet crowned,
About his arms the purple riband wound
Wherewith she wreathed her largely spreading hair;
Nor could the youth abstain, but he must wear
The sacred ring wherewith she was endowed
When first religious chastity she vowed[.] (II.105-110)

As well as being a literal adornment, this ring is Marlowe's representation of the rupture of Hero's maidenhead. Leander wears her hymen on his penis; they are wed.[2] All the more disruptive, then, is the virtual adultery of the famous sequence (which follows some 40 lines later) when Neptune mistakes the naked Leander for Ganymede and almost drowns him while caressing him. The god tries to woo the youth, in a typically Marlovian scene, by putting Helle's bracelet on his arm and giving him "gaudy toys to please his eye." But Leander is not seduced, and says to Neptune, rather primly, "You are deceived, I am no woman, I" (II.192). Evidently used to dealing with this error ("Some swore he was a maid in man's attire, / For in his looks were all that men desire" — 1.83-4), Leander is polite but firm. Not for him the glittering finery of Ganymede, effeminized by acquisitiveness.

Even naked, though, Leander is clad. His body is a prime locus for mythology. For sheer richness, his uncut hair rivals the Golden Fleece (I.55-8). Cynthia, or the moon goddess Diana, yearns to be held in his arms, as she yearned, also, for Endymion (59-60). His body itself is "as straight as Circe's wand," a bewitching instrument of seduction (61). Jove could, dog-like, lap nectar from Leander's hand, as though from Ganymede's most lavish and shapely receptacle (62). Leander's shoulder is as white as the ivory in which Hermes fashioned a new shoulder for Pelops, yet as tasty as Pelops' original flesh, which Demeter ate (63-5). The "immortal fingers" of an unnamed god have left their imprint on his spine, the "heavenly path" that leads directly to the paradise of his behind (65-9). His eyes, cheeks and lips are lovelier than those of Narcissus (72-6). Even the celibate Hippolytus could not have resisted falling in love with him (77-8). None of him is his own. All has been prefigured in Greek myth and its Roman revisions. All Leander can do is outdo immortal beauty, but for all too mortal a span.

This proliferation of myth is unsurprising, coming from the pen of so devoted a fan of Ovid as Marlowe was. The body of his Leander is no blank sheet: it is fully inscribed with the text of *Metamorphoses*.[3] The boy himself has none of the privilege or understanding of authorship; nor has he even chosen, as though ordering tattoos, the myths to which his body will refer. Only those who desire him can read him, and he is no Narcissus. He is innocent of his own beauty.

Others in Marlowe are, as we have seen, far more aware, even in literal economic terms, of their erotic worth. Gaveston, in *Edward II*, is typical of Marlowe's gilded boys, as spoilt by Edward as Ganymede by Jove. (In fact, Gaveston was a year older than Edward.) Edward proves his love by dishing out, not jewels, but political honours (though there are, indeed, bejewelled insignia that go with some of these). The younger Spenser receives similar, if less lavish, treatment later on.

Critical responses to the Edward-Gaveston relationship have been unsurprisingly negative. Typically faint in its praise is John E. Cunningham's remark: "If we can overcome the repugnance most of us feel for the whole subject [of homosexuality], the parting between Edward and Gaveston is a truly moving one" (44). That dates from 1965. It is depressing that this kind of view continues to be expressed, as in the following—albeit more sinuous—version, from Judith Cook, published in 1986: "*Edward II* is not often performed today . . . and it is not too difficult to see why. . . . We have to accept in Marlowe's world that the Edward who has been shown as so unsympathetic in the first half of the play becomes sympathetic to us in the second in spite of his proclivities and his weaknesses, but there is no logical link to show us how this comes about" (107). We know what is meant by "proclivities" and can see how, like Cunningham, Cook tries to recruit all contemporary audiences into her homophobic "us." Just as wrong-headed is the apparent assumption that a tragic hero's "weaknesses" militate against an audience's sympathy. Perhaps Cook has never seen *Hamlet* or *Othello* or *King Lear*.

Occasionally, however, we find a more measured response, such as Harry Levin's remark that "Gaveston is more and less than a friend to Edward, who devotes to him an overt warmth which Marlowe never displays toward the female sex" (116).[4] There is in the relationship a degree of emotional balance which could not have been established if Gaveston were merely a gold digger. He has an eye for the main chance, to be sure, and is seeking both advancement and wealth; but he also, crucially, loves the king. For all its fragility, their balance has its effect on audience response. As A.L. Rowse has written, "Marlowe's sympathy is distributed between Gaveston and the king, his interest is in the relationship between the two; and so the most memorable scenes of the play are those that depict the king's infatuation, and those of his downfall and end" (134). But it is the "end" that is most likely to stay with the audience when they go home.

If Gaveston is the love of Edward's life, in comparison with whom young Spenser is a pale but much needed imitation, the king's nemesis appears in the gorgeous and frightful shape of one last lover, Lightborn, the love of Edward's death. In even the most restrained production, Lightborn is—has to be—the last man Edward sees, speaks to and touches. He is the last lover to penetrate the king.

In Gerard Murphy's 1990 production for the Royal Shakespeare Company at Stratford-upon-Avon, the assassination scene was fully played as a seduction, with a leather-clad Lightborn (George Anton) lying with the king (Simon Russell Beale) and embracing him before stripping him naked for the rapacious murder. Murphy insisted on the full physicality of the action, arguing that "The physical can only happen when Edward is bereft of all political and regal power. In my eyes, the play primarily questions the price you have to pay for kingship, fame, power, success." Simon Russell Beale said of his interpretation of the scene: "It's a love scene. It's the first time someone treats Edward with apparent affection and the first time we see any sexual thrill on stage" (Stephenson).[5]

Like all the other sexy men and boys in Marlowe, Lightborn is an inscribed text. His face gives away his purpose, even while he is acting out such false kindness as "Lie on this bed, and rest yourself awhile" (74). As he leads Edward to bed, Edward says "I see my tragedy written in thy brows" (76), as if the whole play were tattooed thereon. But Edward's need for a last moment of love is even stronger than his terror, and for a fleeting moment his incorrigible sugar-daddy instincts reassert themselves: he offers the seducer the last of his jewels. This gesture is an attempt at a bribe—

> O, if thou harbour'st murder in thy heart,
> Let this gift change thy mind, and save thy soul! (89-90)

—but also, inevitably, calls to mind all those earlier gifts the king showered on his lovers. Lightborn's response, "lie down and rest," is apt to either reading of the giving of the jewel. This is the reply of the paid hustler, about to do what he was paid for, but also, since the bed is to be the scene of the crime, a cynical enticement into a deadly trap. As it happens, however, Lightborn is less in control of the sequence of events than he imagines, and his seduction of the king results in death that is mutual.

It is illuminating to compare Lightborn with another seductive figure who appears at a play's tragic climax in intimate connection with the downfall of its hero. I am thinking of Helen of Troy in *Doctor Faustus.* The two scenes are similarly bare of detail. They do not work well on paper—they are, after all, written for the stage. In both scenes, language defers to action, or at least to visual representation. The main consequence of this shift from the spoken is a concentration on physicality: the violation of Edward, the beauty of Helen. By this point in each play, temporal life asserts itself in a last brief spurt of carnality (in which mortality is implicit), before the question of the survival of the soul is re-established as pre-eminent.

Critics often discuss Helen as a theatrical problem, hardly less extreme than that of enacting Edward's assassination on stage. John E. Cunningham describes Marlowe's stratagem as follows: "Marlowe was faced with the problem of presenting an adolescent boy on the stage in full daylight, and persuading the audience that they were seeing the most beautiful woman who ever lived. He therefore reduced the actor's movements to a minimum, gave him no speech at all, and put all the beauty into Faustus' lines" (48).[6]

In this scene Marlowe's use of boy actors as women does, indeed, become risky and reflexive. The boy actor must be seen as the devil in the flesh. Paradoxically, the evil spirit who plays the role of Helen, like the actor who plays him playing her, is more substantial than the womanly flesh he adopts as his disguise. This is not a virtuous beauty, but suggestive and subversive: vice cross-dressed, all the more vicious for being in drag, at once visibly sinful and deceptively innocent. It is the *boy* in "Helen" that Dr Faustus desires. Boyishness signifies the sins of the flesh, since to Marlowe that is what boys meant. It is as natural to Faustus to lust after this "Helen" as it might have been to Marlowe himself.

Modern attempts to solve the scene's potential problem have veered between extremes, of which two are worth mentioning here. In Clifford Williams's production for the Royal Shakespeare Company at Stratford-upon-Avon in 1968, Maggie Wright played Helen completely naked, and therefore unquestionably female in her beauty. On the other hand, in Christopher Fettes's 1980 London production (at the Lyric Theatre, Hammersmith, and then the Fortune Theatre), Helen was played by a boy. Critical accounts of the latter version are varied. William Tydeman says this male Helen was "controversial but effective": she "achieved an extraordinary erotic rapport with Faustus" (76). But Michael Scott is less positive: "Wearing a white linen trouser costume with gold fastenings around the ankles and the back slit to the waist, this Helen was exquisitely decadent. . . . Faustus was a slave to her but the audience was far from convinced of her beauty and was rightly uneasy at her appearance" (30).[7]

Looking at the text—from which Helen, as Cunningham suggested, is virtually absent, since she has nothing to say—one notices that Faustus never comments on her body. What little he says about her is located above the neck: "Was this the face . . ." and "heaven is in those lips." As far as the hero's concentration is concerned, then, hers is an ungendered beauty. Boys, too, have faces and lips; there is no reason why a boy should not convey this much of her attractiveness. It does not take a naked actress to do the trick.

Echoing *Dido, Queen of Carthage* — indeed, "quoting" Dido's words precisely, as though expressly making a classical reference to shape his lips to the times from which Helen has been summoned — Faustus begs Helen to "make me immortal with a kiss."[8] What follows, although expressed in metaphysical terms, is strangely puerile:

> Her lips suck forth my soul: see where it flies.
> Come, Helen, come, give me my soul again.
> Here will I dwell, for heaven is in those lips,
> And all is dross that is not Helena.(V.i. 100-103)

This reminds me, anachronistically, of a distinctly adolescent erotic mode: the passing of chewing gum from mouth to mouth. There is as much spittle as soul in these kisses. Faustus is deceived, by the taste of a devil's tongue, into believing that his soul is being sucked to heaven, when it is actually on its way to hell. Kissing the "dross" that he does not see within "Helen," Faustus ejaculates his spirit into damnation. Unable to tell woman from boy, angel from devil, heaven from hell, and spirit from physique, he sets the seal on his own fate.

Marlowe's texts, and the characters within them, are continually establishing cross-references to each other. Faustus "quotes" Dido, Gaveston likens himself to Leander (I. i.8); Neptune mistakes Leander for Ganymede (II.157-8); Isabella likens Edward and Gaveston to Jove and Ganymede (I.iv.181), Lancaster says Gaveston is "like the Greekish strumpet," Helen of Troy (II.v.15). One begins to see in such references the threads of Marlowe's interests and the purposeful, if somewhat enclosed, nature of his learning. His texts seem to conjoin, self-consciously, as an oeuvre. One gets into the habit of following the connections between them. So when Faustus, having kissed Helen, embarks on his fantasy of re-enacting the Trojan wars in Wittenberg, and mentions Achilles, I immediately start turning pages until I come to the reference to him in *Edward II* (II.i.396).[9]

After the initial burst of eroticism there follows a macho tirade in which Faustus's motives are shown to be, rather than heterosexual, homosocial. His attempt to impress Helen with the strength of his desire relies on homosocial proofs: he will relate to the woman via the men in her life. He will take the part and place of Paris. He will fight "weak Menelaus" — not a very impressive promise, this, if his opponent's weakness is a foregone conclusion. And he will "wound Achilles in the heel" — again, not much of a promise, since he *knows* that Achilles's weak point is his heel — for which heroic act he will expect Helen to reward him with a kiss. It may be useful to recall the reference in *Edward II*. Marlowe knew of Achilles as a homosexual lover: he is one of the men brought up to justify the Edward-Gaveston relationship. Perhaps one of Faustus's thrills, here, is to be that of queer-bashing. As a last affirmation of the doctor's heterosexuality — that is to say, of his desire for women and not for men — the Helen scene does not truly involve an exchange of spirit. Faustus uses his desire for Helen to place himself above other men, a distinctly worldly maneuver. That Helen is a mere illusion — spirit, indeed — is beyond Faustus's understanding. He is interested only in the apparently physical surface: the look of her, the feel of her. He is completely unaware of, even if attracted to, the youthful devil within.

Joseph A. Porter has spoken of how, in the world of Marlowe's imagination, "the human body of either gender is the most insistently corporeal of objects: it realizes with peculiar provocativeness the renascent and newly problematic (because newly secular) appreciation of the body that had come up from the Italy of Botticelli and Michelangelo to an England comparatively starved for pictures and statues of nudes" (128).[10] Marlowe's classical references, coming as they do against a lush background of Mediterranean pastoral set in temperate weather, solidify this impression of the visibility and erotic abundance of flesh. And, by constantly voicing such classical allusions, many of his characters become involved in the same welcoming of Greek and Italian sunshine into northern European life. For instance, as Claude J. Summers has said, in *Edward II* "Gaves-

ton conceives elaborate, Italianate spectacles designed to translate
the dour English court into a homoerotic theatre in which pages
become nymphs and men satyrs'' (231). There is a real cultural
frisson of horror in his being exiled to Ireland (I.iv) so soon after he
has returned to England from France.

But there is a far deeper horror to be borne as the play reaches its
climax. Physicality taken to extremes can, no doubt, become intolerable. This, at any rate, is what happens to Edward. With all the
signs and comforts of his status confiscated, his lover killed, and his
body defeated by humiliation and unaccustomed hardship, he is vis-
ited in the castle cistern by an apparent angel of mercy. More wary
than Faustus with Helen — and for good reason — Edward suspects
that Lightborn is truly a devil; but he clearly wants him to be an
angel, lover and liberator. Lightborn plays on this desire, like an
importunate lover, in order to gain access to the king's anus. He is
meticulous in his choice of an ''apt'' death for the sodomite, a
deadly rape to be carried out in the place of excrement: cistern and
rectum. The king is expected to consent to his own death as if to the
loving intercourse he craves.

Remember what W.B. Yeats's Crazy Jane said to the Bishop:
''Love has pitched his mansion in the place of excrement.'' In the
finest of recent revivals of *Edward II* — Nicholas Hytner's 1986 production at the Royal Exchange Theatre, Manchester — the excre-
mental version of sodomy was made all the more explicit by a set
designed by Tom Cairns. The early court scenes were performed in
an arena of dry dust on which bootprints were immediately obliterated by the sweep of the king's long, scarlet robes. But as the play
progressed and the joy of Edward's love turned inevitably to its
tragedy of sodomitic degradation, the dust turned to sludge — the
more so after Edward, being dethroned, was humiliated under a
running faucet and left to crawl about through the mud in wet un-
derwear. Thus the lavish court turns into the stinking castle cistern
of the closing scenes. The king is assassinated in a pit of excrement
that is used by his captors to represent his physique.

There have been some curiously muted responses to the assassination scene's representation of violent homophobia. Referring to
reactions in Marlowe's day to the red-hot poker, Harry Levin
writes: ''The sight of the instrument would have been enough to

raise an excruciating shudder in the audience; and subtler minds may have perceived, as does William Empson, an ironic parody of Edward's vice'' (124). In a more recent essay, Alan Bray is similarly tentative; he speaks of ''the hideous murder of Edward at the play's end, whose form seems to ape his sexual sin.'' Surely the issue is more clear-cut than this would suggest. Lightborn is delivering Edward's come-uppance for everything he has done with Gaveston. While it may be true that the noblemen show little overt homophobia during the play, it is not they who choose the manner of the king's death; it is Lightborn. He dispatches Edward with a queerbasher's mockery. His violent erotic imagination is no more inventive than the kind that, these days, produces violently anti-gay graffiti. He pretends to seduce the faggot king, and then gives him what every faggot needs: a red-hot poker up the arse. It no more takes ''subtler minds'' to read such signs than it does to scrawl them in the first place.

Marlowe does not allow this awful scene to be diluted. Take away the essential action, and there is virtually nothing left. He has, and is, determined to portray the crude violence to which the alliance between virility and political skulduggery is liable to lead. In a convincing reading of the linked themes of manliness and sodomy in Marlowe's work, Simon Shepherd has characterised these texts as ''problematising the male and masculinity'' (179). This goes against a more general, and reductive, critical trend, which Shepherd outlines succinctly as follows: ''The association between masculinity and violence is regarded by most commentators not as a critique but as a personal kink of Marlowe's deriving from his homosexuality'' (198).

In *Edward II,* there is no choice so straightforward as that between jewels (Ganymede) and armor (Aeneas), which we saw in *Dido, Queen of Carthage.* Edward's court is no safe haven for sybarites. It is located in fortresses; its luxuries are heavily defended. If there are pretty boys here, most will be soldiers, too. For all its beauty, the male body is a fighting machine. Even a lad as young as the king's son is practised at arms, and knows already how to gird himself in masculinity.[11] Nor is it only bodies that can be bought with jewels; it is also swords. (Or, for that matter, a red-hot poker.) Power and passion are inextricably confused. There is no clear opposition between dressing and undressing: one can just as well dress for love and undress for combat as put on armor and strip for bed.

Although in one of his translations of Ovid's elegies Marlowe writes that "Love is a naked boy" (X.15), in most of his work this is not strictly true. His boys are generally seen in either fancy dress or drag, and it is this adornment that shows they are either beloved already, or available to be loved. Cupid may go naked, but mortal boys are heavily clad. Their trinkets are the coinage of desire's transactions.

There is, however, a peculiar exception to this in *Edward II;* we receive it from the lips of Gaveston. The "Italian masques" he is planning for the king's delight include the following:

> Sometime a lovely boy in Dian's shape,
> With hair that gilds the water as it glides,
> Crownets of pearl about his naked arms,
> And in his sportful hands an olive-tree,
> To hide those parts which men delight to see,
> Shall bathe him in a spring[.] (I.i.61-66)

This is a fascinating paradox—a naked boy in drag. Blond, he is either long-haired or wearing a wig. His arms are bejewelled in a feminine, or effeminate, manner. But there can be no doubt that this is a boy. His genitals can hardly be properly concealed by a mere olive branch—the leaves of the olive, unlike those of the fig, are unsuited to the purposes of modesty— still less by such a branch in teasing, "sportful hands." This "lovely boy" is "in Dian's shape" only by the most sophisticated, symbolic criterion. At least the boy playing Isabella is fully clothed and, perhaps, strategically padded. But this Diana is in drag only insofar as he is being signalled as an object of male desire. The reference to "those parts which men delight to see" is a succinct celebration of universal bisexuality: it refers to both Diana's and the boy's "parts" with equal gusto. Whether the boy's genitals are visible, and so self-evidently male, or momentarily concealed by olive fronds, and so presumably female, the fact remains that they are being offered as a focus for powerful men's desire. More sportful hands than his/her own are assumed to be reaching out towards them. This Diana is a huntress eminently huntable.

This boy marks a crucial spot in Marlowe's erotic geography, equidistant between devilry and innocence, pastoral and decadence. He is caught, in the moment of Gaveston's dreaming him up, in that quintessentially Ovidian moment of metamorphosis, between one state and another. On the cusp of adolescence, he is neither child nor man; unmistakably male when his loins are exposed, but otherwise as girlish as any but the most choosy Humbert Humbert could wish. He is on the verge of becoming something plainer, less equivocal. He will probably be a soldier. By the time he comes to desire as well as to be desired, he will have embarked on manhood proper. But for now he is held in a state of imaginary suspension between real boyhood and apparent girlhood, boyhood past and manhood to come. He is there to be desired. That is what his adolescence means.

Age, therefore, is a crucial signifier, not only in these texts — as in the classical literature to which they incessantly refer — but also in their performance. The majority of the desired used to be played by adolescent boys or very young men; most desirers were men in the prime of manhood. Before and after these come, respectively, pre-pubertal boys and old men, virtual spectators around the arena of the erotic. They have had, or are still waiting, their turn.

There is no plain love-making in this dramatic vision. Every embrace is a cultural sign and involves an assertion or adjustment of power relations. Just as Edward II's last bedchamber, which he shares with the glamorous Lightborn, is "the sink / Wherein the filth of all the castle falls," so, too, do all bedchambers — and, indeed, the nether regions of all human bodies — become the conduits of mortality. No aspect of the lives of lovers does not pass through these narrow, foetid spaces in which bliss finds its cradle. Money, power, status, violence; even, at times, love itself.

## NOTES

1. For another echo of these words, see *The Jew of Malta* IV. ii.106-116.

2. This usage of "ring" reverberates throughout the last scene of Shakespeare's *The Merchant of Venice:* Bassanio and Gratiano have given away Portia and Nerissa's respective rings to the doctor and the clerk — who were Portia and Nerissa themselves, cross-dressed as men. All of the play's themes relating to the price of flesh culminate, here, in a cascade of bawdy jokes which depend on the double meaning in "ring," a word which Shakespeare places at the ends of lines

193-7 and 199-202 by way of comic, ringing emphasis. The main joke is about men who turn from the sacred, conjugal bed to homosexual intercourse. Heterosexual order is restored, however, in the play's closing line, when Gratiano pledges himself once more to the pleasurable duty of "keeping safe Nerissa's ring."

3. Once the body is scripted — whether with public declamation or the introspection of soliloquy — love, too, grows loud with significance. Marlowe's versions of love invariably involve (as whose do not?) a measure of discourse. Like heart and genitals, the tongue is an organ convulsed by desire. As he writes in *Hero and Leander,* "Love always makes those eloquent that have it" (II.72). This does not necessarily contradict what he has already said — "True love is mute, and oft amazed stands" — since even the silences of lovers are gushingly expressive. Lovers can speak with "dumb signs," a kind of unspoken speech, just as Hero and Leander "parled by the touch of hands" (I.185-7).

4. But this shift, by sleight-of-hand, from Edward to Marlowe, needs to be regarded with a degree of skepticism.

5. Beale's last remark is not strictly true of this production, since Act II Scene i began with Baldock and young Spenser getting out of bed, apparently having just made love while spectacularly, if anachronistically, clad in Calvin Klein knickers.

6. This seems to be a modern and heterosexual reading of the "problem." Shakespeare, after all, seems to have had no significant difficulty in presenting on stage a Cleopatra who, although likewise played by a boy (if, perhaps, pre-adolescent rather than adolescent), was allowed both movement and speech, and still seemed devastatingly beautiful. However, for a modern audience of unreconstructed heterosexual men, Cunningham's point may, indeed, be apt.

7. The worry here is Scott's claim to read a whole audience's — or, rather, a whole *series* of audiences' — reactions, and the hint of moralizing in his use of the word "rightly." But might the unease (if that is what it was) not simply have been the reaction of an audience unused to a convention taken for granted in Marlowe's theatre, rather than unconvinced that a boy could be sufficiently beautiful to impersonate Helen of Troy? In any case, if the audience were to be left *at ease* by this scene, could the production really be said to have succeeded at all?

8. This instance of Marlowe's quoting himself is of changeable significance, according to whether we believe *Dido* precedes *Faustus* — as I am assuming here — or vice versa.

9. Edward, too, has a fantasy of re-enacting the Trojan wars, when he is forced to send Gaveston into exile. In a soliloquy he threatens Rome: "I'll fire thy crazed buildings, and enforce / The papal towers to kiss the lowly ground" (I.iv.101-2).

10. This is, of course, a much simplified version of the spread of Italian Renaissance images and ideas; but Porter's point about Marlowe's post-medieval carnality is, nonetheless, worth considering.

11. Purvis E. Boyette has said, in relation to the play's closing scenes, "From the King's bowels, a new king is born" (47-48). The boy was, of course, born of woman (albeit a woman played by an older boy), and the young warrior and

statesman has been shaped by the constraints of courtly machismo; but the new king emerges in the moment of Edward's horrendous scream, as it reverberates through the bowels of the castle and beyond. The new king is the offspring of his father's tragedy, which itself stemmed from Edward's love of Gaveston.

## REFERENCES

Boyette, Purvis E. "Wanton Humour and Wanton Poets: Homosexuality in Marlowe's *Edward II.*" *Tulane Studies in English* 12 (1977): 33-50.

Bray, Alan. "Lovers or just good friends?" *The Guardian* 6 July 1990: 37.

Cook, Judith. *At the Sign of the Swan: An Introduction to Shakespeare's Contemporaries.* London: Harrap, 1986.

Cunningham, John E. *Elizabethan and Early Stuart Drama.* London: Evans Brothers, 1965.

Levin, Harry. *Christopher Marlowe: The Overreacher.* London: Faber, 1961.

Porter, Joseph A. "Marlowe, Shakespeare, and the Canonization of Heterosexuality." *Displacing Homophobia: Gay Male Perspectives in Literature and Culture.* Ed. Ronald R. Butters, John M. Clum, and Michael Moon. Durham, NC: Duke University Press, 1989. 127-147.

Rowse, A. L. *Christopher Marlowe: A Biography.* London: Macmillan, 1964.

Scott, Michael. *Renaissance Drama and a Modern Audience.* London: Macmillan, 1982.

Shepherd, Simon. *Marlowe and the Politics of Elizabethan Theatre.* Brighton: Harvester, 1986.

Stephenson, Terence Michael. "Sweet Lies." *Gay Times* August 1990: 36.

Summers, Claude J. "Sex, Politics, and Self-realization in *Edward II.*" *"A Poet and a filthy Play-maker": New Essays on Christopher Marlowe.* Ed. Kenneth Friedenreich, Roma Gill, and Constance B. Kuriyama. New York: AMS Press, 1988. 221-240.

Tydeman, William. *Doctor Faustus: Text and Performance.* London: Macmillan, 1984.

# Verse Letters to T.W.
# from John Donne:
# "By You My Love Is Sent"

George Klawitter, PhD

Viterbo College

**SUMMARY.** Relying on an audience of one for their impact, the verse letters of John Donne are closer to autobiography than anything else in his poetry. Among the most tender of these lyrics are the verse letters written to a young man named Thomas Woodward, whose older brother was one of Donne's closest friends. Using sexual metaphors, the poems reflect a homoerotic undercurrent and demonstrate affection that most readers of Donne associate only with his heterosexual love poems.

John Donne enjoys the reputation of being a man who sowed wild oats in his youth but lived to repent, father twelve children, and die a holy priest. Few biographers have speculated on Donne's "wild oats," contenting themselves with Sir Richard Baker's epithet for him, "a great visiter of Ladies" (II, 156). Since Baker was Henry Wotton's roommate at Oxford and knew Donne, both having enrolled at Hart Hall the same day, Donne probably was a ladies' man; but to extrapolate from some of the amatory verse, as Le

George Klawitter is Associate Professor at Viterbo College, where he chairs the English Department. He has edited the poetry of Richard Barnfield for Susquehanna University Press and has published articles on medieval and Renaissance literature in *Hartford Studies*, *Comparative Drama*, *Mediaevalia*, and the *George Herbert Journal*. An abbreviated version of this essay was presented at the John Donne Society Conference (Gulfport, MS) in 1990. Correspondence may be addressed to the author at: Department of English, Viterbo College, La Crosse, WI 54601.

Comte does, that "women were the *sine qua non* of Jack Donne's poetry" ("Jack Donne" 9) seems too sweeping an endorsement of facile readings. Donne was probably no more promiscuous than other young men of the time: "None of Donne's contemporaries seems to have been sufficiently impressed by profligacy on his part to have recorded the crime" (Sprott 338). He was, in other words, a man of his times, acted no worse than his fellow students, and did not publicly repent of his "spirit of fornication," in an All Saints Day Sermon (Le Comte, *Grace* 56), until he had to earn a living articulating morality from a pulpit. But to conclude that John Donne's affections were spent entirely on young ladies is to ignore those verses that demonstrate very tender feelings for several of his male friends. As we read the lyric pieces of John Donne, we should be able to keep ourselves open to their dealing with sexual liaisons of many varieties, not concluding that Donne lived out any of the fantasies that may exist in the verse, but willing to understand that, given the homosocial context of the Inns of Court, we can interpret the ambiguities on different levels, one of them homoerotic.

A few critics have defended autobiography in Donne's poems, but they have been reluctant to read anything into the poems more than they can confirm from Donne's prose letters and a handful of contemporary references to him. Donne had a few friends who no doubt knew of his love affairs, but only the receptor of individual poems knew the depth of the intimacy that lay behind each one. To claim that all of the poems were *jeux d'esprit* Donne wrote for a coterie to exhibit his facility in lyric poetry ignores in some of the verses a tone too personal to be indicative of literary exercises, a tone especially true in the verse letters.[1] The nature of Donne's relationship to both men and women may be illuminated by the following observations: there are no early letters to ladies; he is openly affectionate to young men; and when he does finally begin addressing verse epistles to ladies ("That unripe side of earth" to the Countess of Huntingdon), he is at a distance from them, tamed by his marriage, and he treats of virtuous love and honor. Among the three dozen letters that Donne penned in verse to friends between 1592 and 1618, the earliest, dated 1592-1594 by R.C. Bald (283), were written to men when Donne was between twenty and twenty-two years old and enjoying student life at Lincoln's Inn.

One of his correspondents was a Mr. T.W., whom most critics identify as Thomas Woodward, younger brother of Rowland Woodward and eighteen years old in 1594.

The first of the Donne poems to T.W., "All haile, sweet Poet," elicited a warning from Sir Herbert Grierson, Donne's first important twentieth-century editor, that the "'sweet Poet' must not be taken too seriously: Donne and his friends were corresponding with one another in verse, and complimenting each other in the polite fashion of the day" (II, 165), but I think we should take the matter seriously. In "All haile sweet Poet" Donne seems anxious and tender in an opening stanza conventional enough in its hyperbole but difficult to accept today since Donne subordinates himself effusively to someone who lived, more or less, without developing his poetic talent:

> All haile sweet Poet, more full of more strong fire,
>> Then hath or shall enkindle any spirit,
>> I lov'd what nature gave thee, but this merit
> Of wit and Art I love not but admire;
> Who have before or shall write after thee,
> Their workes, though toughly laboured, will bee
>> Like infancie or age to mans firme stay,
>> Or earely and late twilights to mid-day.[2]

We get the impression that both poets were just beginning to master poetic technique, but the narrator recognizes enough "strong fire" in Woodward's verse to warrant his praising "what nature gave thee." Born with poetic gifts, Woodward has succeeded, says the speaker, in perfecting them with "wit and Art" so that no matter how hard any other living, dead, or future poet would labor, all poems will be weak compared to Woodward's. A double metaphor carries the idea: all other poets' works are as weak as an infant or old man; they are as weak as twilight in the morning or evening. Woodward's, on the other hand, are as strong as man in his prime or as light at noon. The narrator is not content to denigrate himself as a poet; he has to downgrade all poets before and after the young Woodward, excluding no one.

In the second stanza the speaker elaborates his envy of the younger man's powers and begs for pity:

> Men say, and truly, that they better be
>> Which be envyed then pittied: therefore I,
>> Because I wish thee best, doe thee envie:
> O wouldst thou, by like reason, pitty mee,
> But care not for mee: I, that ever was
> In Natures, and in fortunes gifts, (alas,
>> Before thy grace got in the Muses Schoole)
>> A monster and a begger, am a foole.

Although he wants to be pitied, Donne does not want Woodward to fret over him ("care not for mee") because Donne realizes he is making a fool of himself for Woodward. Formerly "a monster and a begger," he now realizes that by comparison to Woodward's poetic talents, which Woodward learned in "the Muses Schoole," his own talents are lackluster; he is foolish to believe he could ever write as well as Woodward. "Fool," of course, carries connotations of love as well: being a fool in love, Donne carries himself deep into self-abnegation, despairing ever of having either Woodward's talents or his affection. The bleakness of Donne's self-image seems more than poetic hyperbole. By calling himself a monster in nature's gifts, he denigrates his physical attractiveness, and by naming himself a beggar in fortune's gifts, he is calling attention to his lack of money. Before knowing Woodward to be an excellent poet, Donne imagined himself ugly and poor, two strikes against his being able to attract a lover. Now, in addition, he is foolishly in love with a man who is beyond his own beauty, wealth, and talent.

The material in this stanza which appears variously parenthetical in Milgate and Shawcross (I have followed Milgate) appears without parentheses in the Westmoreland manuscript, a reading which Grierson did not follow in his "(Before thy grace got in the Muses Schoole / A monster and a begger)." If "was / In" be read as a phrasal verb meaning "had," then Grierson's parentheses (adopted by Shawcross) make the following sense of the passage: "I that had gifts am now a fool." With Milgate's parentheses, however, the narrator is saying that he always was a monster and a beggar even before Woodward started writing verses in the muses' school. Now, seeing how good Woodward is, the narrator is a fool in addition to being a monster and a beggar. The word "got" within the parentheses can mean more than "received into" the muses' school: it is a sexually charged word which Woodward, as we shall see later, picked up for his poetic reply to this letter.

Stanza three contains more poetic hyperbole, alleging that the only fit subject for a poem written by Woodward is Woodward himself. We ask, "Can the speaker be serious?" The answer is maybe, just as lovesick youths are ever serious in the outpourings of their tender hearts. Donne encourages his young friend to write a poem about himself because Woodward is the best subject matter for great verse:

> Oh how I grieve, that late borne modesty
> > Hath got such root in easie waxen hearts,
> > That men may not themselves, their owne good parts
> Extoll, without suspect of surquedrie,
> For, but thy selfe, no subject can be found
> Worthy thy quill, nor any quill resound
> > Thy worth but thine: how good it were to see
> > A Poem in thy praise, and writ by thee.

Within the stanza may be some punning: it is difficult to read "owne good parts" without understanding a reference to sexual organs. The speaker thus puns when he singles out Woodward's "quill" for special praise: "no subject can be found / Worthy thy quill."[3] The mixture of tones to include a humorous mode is not untypical of Donne who can within one poem be both silly and serious (e.g., "The Flea"). 

In the final stanza the speaker regrets the harshness of his own rhyme, a flavor of Donne's verse for which the poet would be excoriated by Jonson and Dryden:

> Now if this song be too'harsh for rime, yet, as
> > The Painters bad god made a good devill,
> > 'Twill be good prose, although the verse be evill,
> If thou forget the rime as thou dost passe.

This "song" refers to the narrator's present verses, seemingly too "harsh" to be good poetry, but adequate to be called "prose," much as a second-rate painter's attempt at painting God could turn out to be a rather good picture of a devil. As he began, the speaker ends by putting the younger poet on a pedestal, volunteering to be his "ape" if Woodward would only consent to send him more verses to imitate:

> Then write, that I may follow, and so bee
> Thy debter, thy'eccho, thy foyle, thy zanee.
>> I shall be thought, if mine like thine I shape,
>> All the worlds Lyon, though I be thy Ape.

It is pleasant stuff, certainly warm, and not intended for a general public. If there are poets who like to air their loves abroad because it increases the chances that their beloved will understand how totally exclusive and honest the admiration must really be to risk letting everyone know, Donne was not one of them. His personal verse letters read as if they were intended for individuals only. There is an anxiety in this first poem to T.W. that we best accept as genuine. The intent of the poem is to praise the friend, to further their intimacy, and perhaps most importantly, to request a response.

There was a response: Woodward wrote to Donne the poem "Thou sendst me prose," which few editions of Donne reprint (Grierson and Milgate have it in their notes). I include it here transcribed from the Westmoreland manuscript, with expanded abbreviations:

> To. Mr J.D.
>> Thou sendst me prose and rimes, I send for those
> Lynes, which beeing nether, seeme or verse or prose.
> They'are lame and harsh, and have no heat at all
> But what thy liberall beams on them let fall.
> The nimble fyer which in thy brayne doth dwell
> Is it that fyre of heaven or that of hell.
> It doth beget and comfort like hevens ey
> And like hells fyer it burnes eternally.
> And those whom in thy fury and iudgment

Thy verse shall skourge like hell it will torment.
Have mercy on me and my sinfull Muse
Which rub'd and tickled with thyne could not chuse
But spend some of her pithe and yeild to bee
One in that chaste and mistique tribadree.
Bassaes adultery no fruit did leave,
Nor theirs which their swolne thighs did nimbly weave,
And with new armes and mouthes embrace and kis
Though they had issue was not like to this.
Thy Muse, Oh strange and holy Lecheree
Beeing a Mayd still, gott this Song on mee.

Picking up on Donne's own concern over the inability to write valid rhyme, T.W. begins with a humility equal to Donne's: in return for prose and rhyme, Woodward sends Donne lines which are neither. Since the opening couplet is misleading if read with enjambment, it is helpful if I supply omitted elements:

Thou sendst me prose and rimes, I send for those [lines]
[These] Lynes, which beeing nether, seeme or verse or prose.

Woodward thus lowers himself to the same level as Donne by claiming his verse is lame and harsh, but Donne has let his "liberall beams" fall on Woodward's verse and has exalted it higher than it should be. As Woodward continues, he plays with Donne's intentions: is Donne's fire from heaven or hell, virtuous or evil? It both burns eternally and comforts, so Woodward begs for mercy for himself and his "sinfull Muse." What it is that the muse has done sinfully is not spelled out, but it might be that she has let his verses become harsh and lame because they have associated with Donne's: "rub'd and tickled with thyne." Such language is impishly sexual although Woodward attempts to ameliorate the reference by claiming the association is one of "chaste and mistique tribadree," an oxymoron of the most striking variety, linking chastity with homosexual coupling. "Tribadree" comes from the Greek word "to rub" and has 1610 as its earliest reference in the OED (Ben Jonson). The word exists today as "tribadism," a lesbian practice which attempts to simulate heterosexual intercourse. Woodward could simply mean that his muse and Donne's have been engaging in a kind of mystical tribadism, but there is an undercurrent in the lines. The imagery is violent. First of all, rubbing and tickling are sensations of sexual abrasion between "muses" who in this context lose control over their sexual emissions ("could not chuse but spend"). The activity results in a climax and loss of seed because Woodward's sinful muse has had to "yeild" and ejaculate "some of her pithe" (semen). These lines seem to be talking about more than the exchange of poems.

To reinforce the image of homosexual coupling, Woodward refers in line 15 to Bassa whose "adultery no fruit did leave," an allusion to a Martial epigram (I, 90) in which Bassa is described as committing "adultery" with other women and bearing no offspring: "I never saw you intimate with men, and that no scandal assigned you a lover, but every office a throng of your own sex round you performed without the approach of man." The Martial reference strengthens the imagery of same-sex coupling that metaphorically takes place as Donne entices the younger poet into writing this poem. Martial's horror at Bassa's conduct is not the reason Woodward selected the epigram to flavor his poem: his purpose is not moral, but simply referential. Poor Bassa's energies went for naught while Woodward's have miraculously conceived this poem.

In addition to the fruitless adultery of Bassa, there is copulation between those with "swolne thighs" and "new arms and mouthes," a copulation which does result in some kind of issue, but issue very much unlike the poem Woodward says he is writing in response to "All haile sweet Poet." This allusion may be to Aristophanes' explanation (in Plato's *Symposium*) for the origin of the human race, first composed of three sexes (male, female, androgyne). Each person had four hands, four feet, two faces, but aspiring to rival the gods, all persons were cut in two by Zeus as punishment. They then spent all their time clinging to the severed half, and when one half died, the living half looked for a replacement of the same kind. Zeus saw their desperation, invented sexual intercourse for them, and they adjusted themselves to male-male, female-female, and male-female sexual matters. According to Halperin,

One consequence of the myth is to make the sexual desire of every human being *formally identical* to that of every other: we are all looking for the same thing in a sexual partner, according to Plato's Aristophanes — namely, a symbolic substitute for an originary object once loved and subsequently lost in an archaic trauma. (20)

Woodward thus moves his classical allusion from an exclusively lesbian context to one inclusive of homosexual men by reference to those Aristophanic creatures. Some others embrace with "new armes and mouthes" to produce new offspring, but a difference lies in progeny: their "issue was not like to this [poem]." Woodward does not identify which pairing of sexes he prefers, but his imagery is fecund since there is matter born of his coupling with Donne's muse. In other words, he has the best of both worlds: intimate with Donne, he enjoys metaphoric tribadism through conjunction of their respective muses, and intimate with Donne's muse, he is the mother of a new poem.

For the final line Woodward picked up "Gott this Song on mee" as an image from the second stanza of Donne's "All haile sweet Poet" in which Donne had said that the younger poet was begetting things in the "Muses Schoole." Although Woodward's poem depends for its momentum on lesbian coupling between Donne's muse and Woodward's, the final lines imply a paradoxical inversion of fertility roles. "Thy Muse . . . gott this Song on mee" could mean, of course, the muse "gott this Song [from] mee," but that would make little sense since muses traditionally inspire and are not inspired by poets. "Gott this Song [into] mee" rather means Donne's muse impregnated Woodward making Woodward female, a passive receptor (in Renaissance sexual psychology). Identifying Donne with Donne's muse ("Thy Muse") creates a female Woodward who submits to a female muse capable of something that lesbian coupling is incapable of (procreation) and thus is potently male. Donne becomes Woodward's inseminator. Each poet sees himself as subservient to the other: Donne for learning from Woodward, Woodward for being inspired by Donne. In either case the female submits to the strong male, but in a "chaste" submission because it is, for all we know, an intercourse of minds only. Assuming the egalitarian sexual role through the two muses, however, is not humble enough for Woodward's purposes: he must submit to the insertive power of Donne via the muse and become the passive partner in a hierarchical relationship for which he is here claiming to be the lower person, just as Donne had taken the female-passive role in "All haile sweet Poet." The imagery is strange, but not unlike the bawdy talk teenage boys bandy about among themselves.

Woodward's entire poem, being the ploy of a young man surprised at the discovery of his own poetic talents but who recognizes that they may be overpraised by another man, must explain away somehow his poetic harshness in an age that prized smooth, golden verses. Since the whole point of Woodward's poem is that the verses issuing from his poetic, cross-fertilized tribadism are harsh, Woodward intends to denigrate contrastive issue, Petrarchan, courtly poems, the very kind he and Donne were not writing. He is intent to put himself on the same poetic level as his correspondent and to express rapture ("Oh strange and holy Lecheree") at the process by which he has been enabled to produce such forceful verses, remarkably strong, we must admit, for a sixteen year old.

In response to "Thou sendst me prose," Donne wrote "Hast thee harsh verse," a poem addressed to the poem itself (the "you" and "thee" in the poem). Beginning again with a reference to his own "harsh verse" technique, Donne does not bother to apologize for lack of smoothness but simply enjoins the lines to carry his message and puns about the inadequacies of the "weake feet" (ll. 3, 4) in his poetic meter:

> Hast thee harsh verse as fast as thy lame measure
>> Will give thee leave, to him; My pain, and pleasure.
> I have given thee, and yet thou art too weake,
>> Feete, and a reasoning soule and tongue to speake.
> Plead for me, and so by thine and my labour
>> I am thy Creator, thou my Saviour.
> Tell him, all questions, which men have defended
>> Both of the place and paines of hell, are ended;
> And 'tis decreed our hell is but privation

Of him, at least in this earths habitation:
And 'tis where I am, where in every street
Infections follow, overtake, and meete:
Live I or die, by you my love is sent,
And you'are my pawnes, or else my Testament.

The poem attempts to intensify the relationship, trying to seduce the younger man in terms even stronger than Donne had used in "All haile sweet Poet." The ruse of simply wanting more verse from the young Woodward is gone from this poem: the speaker wants the man's love, not his poetry ("And 'tis decreed our hell is but privation / Of him, at least in this earths habitation"). The game of soliciting verses from T.W. so that Donne may become a better poet by imitation has dropped into the background, and a firmer resolve at a personal relationship has risen to the surface. In effect, Donne works on the presumption: "I will not bother to smooth out my harsh lines because expediency is necessary if I hope to enkindle our friendship."

Struggling with his emotions, Donne senses a mixture of pain and pleasure in the relationship: joy at knowing Woodward, emptiness at being away from him. The question of hell's location, debated by theologians, is irrelevant to Donne, he says, because hell on earth for him is lack of Woodward's company. For Donne, living in a London ravaged by plague (the "infections" of line 12), the only torture is life without Woodward, and its only reprieve, temporary at best, is the sending of this letter-poem which conjures up for the writer the image of his beloved. He calls the letter "my Saviour," sent as it is by him, God the Father ("I am thy Creator"), to carry a message of love to Woodward. This is the traditional division of Trinitarian labors (creation, mission, infusion by love) parcelled out in dogma to Father, Son, and Holy Spirit, application of which to the Donne-Woodward liaison may have raised eyebrows what with its insouciant adaptation of sacred matter to an ordinary relationship.[4] If there was a kind of whimsical selection of images for Donne's earlier letter ("monster," "zany," "ape"), carrying with it a tone of playfulness, there is in "Hast thee harsh verse" a fretful urgency that indicates Donne is restless with the slow pace of this love relationship. The poignancy of "Live I or die" connotes an acute indifference to matters beyond the parameters of their friendship, an obsession with the loved one that expects and demands a reciprocity as fervent as the passionate fires of the letter writer. Such a writer does not care if he stoops to blasphemy or not.

Donne's next letter begins with an image of pregnancy that may be a reaction to Woodward's imagery of sexual coupling:

> Pregnant again with th'old twins Hope, and Feare,
> Oft have I askt for thee, both how and where
> Thou wert, and what my hopes of letters were;
>
> As in our streets sly beggers narrowly
> Watch motions of the givers hand and eye,
> And evermore conceive some hope thereby.
>
> And now thy Almes is given, thy letter'is read,
> And body risen againe, the which was dead,
> And thy poore starveling bountifully fed.
>
> After this banquet my Soule doth say grace,
> And praise thee for'it, and zealously imbrace
> Thy love, though I thinke thy love in this case
> > To be as gluttons, which say 'midst their meat,
> > They love that best of which they most do eat.

This letter lacks the passion of "Hast thee harsh verse." Donne, asking friends frequently about Woodward and the chances of getting a letter from him, compares himself to a beggar (again) who watches pedestrians carefully in hope of a handout. The letter from Woodward becomes the resuscitating handout which nourishes Donne, the "poor starveling." After eating, Donne says grace (a curious twist on the time for table prayers) and determines that Woodward's love for him is dependent upon the number of letters he posts to Woodward. Donne awkwardly compares love from Woodward to gluttons who love whatever they eat the most of but only, says Donne, because it is the most available. Woodward's love is gauged by the frequency of Donne's own infatuated letter writing, whereas the "banquet of [Donne's] soule" is Woodward's letter which Donne reads over and over again, letting it form the solitary basis for his love-meal. I do not agree with Milgate that "Woodward's love is killing Donne" (213). The implication is rather that Woodward would love whatever is most frequently encountered. Donne hopes T.W. loves him but also fears that T.W. loves him only because Donne writes to him more often than anyone else does. Sexual imagery throughout the poem ("pregnant" balancing "Conceive," and "body risen againe" preparing Donne sexually for a "zealous embrace") point up even more strongly the predominant emotion of the poem, which is neither hope nor fear but rather the frustration born of the soul's being pulled between hope and fear. It is this impasse that leads Donne, I believe, to write the letter in the first place: his sincere desire for T.W. to move the relationship in either direction, to give Donne, that is, grounds for hope or grounds for despair, either state being a relief from the tenterhooks of frustration.

We may be missing a letter from Thomas Woodward to Donne which may belong between "Hast thee harsh verse" and "Pregnant again with th'old twins" because in his next poem Donne explains his continued interest in T.W. with a kind of pressing need: "Oft have I askt for thee, both how and where / Thou wert, and what my hopes of letters were." The use of the plural "letters" should not be construed, however, to mean a furious correspondence has taken place between the two men: it is, after all, Donne's "hopes of letters" that move the poem, not the reception of actual letters. The love-struck person is rarely content with one love token, especially when a relationship begins, and requires a stream of reminders that reciprocity exists. The interminable telephone conversations of today's lovers have replaced the billet-doux of times past but serve the same purpose of researching and strengthening a burgeoning relationship. Moreover, when Donne remarks in line 7 "Thy Almes is given, thy letter'is read," he is probably referring to Woodward's earlier letter "Thou sendst me prose and rimes" which we know, by synchronization of theme and imagery, Donne had elicited between his own two verse letters "All haile sweet Poet" and "Hast thee harsh verse." I make this point only to assuage fears that we have surely lost a verse letter from T.W. to Donne. In fact, the existence of only one letter from T.W. may help to explain the despair that enters "Pregnant again with th'old twins" and the resignation that flavors the final poem to T.W., "At once, from hence."

Donne's final letter to T.W. is riddled with sadness, with a sense that the relationship Donne had such strong hopes for is evaporating:

> At once, from hence, my lines and I depart,
> I to my soft still walks, they to my Heart;
> I to the Nurse, they to the child of Art.
>
> Yet as a firme house, though the Carpenter
> Perish, doth stand: as an Embassadour
> Lyes safe, how e'r his king be in danger:
>
> So, though I languish, prest with Melancholy,
> My verse, the strict Map of my misery,
> Shall live to see that, for whose want I dye.
>
> Therefore I envie them, and doe repent,
> That from unhappy mee, things happy'are sent;
> Yet as a Picture, or bare Sacrament,
>> Accept these lines, and if in them there be
>> Merit of love, bestow that love on mee.

This poem is a valediction. Donne has recognized that the verses to Thomas have gotten nowhere: they are buried in his heart as a "strict Map of my misery," and they will pass to Thomas, the "child of Art," who, Donne had noted in "All haile sweet Poet," welded "Wit and Art" together. But the envy Donne feels for his own verses is that they will see Woodward, whereas he cannot, and he repents that he must send happy lines when he is so miserable. Well, they are not all that happy. They are downright melancholic. As a "Sacrament" (l. 12), Donne says, they are a symbol of what he would like to be, i.e., in their place, close to Woodward. If they spark love in Woodward, Donne says ultimately (l. 14), he wishes the young man would not love the verses but transfer the love to Donne. It is a final attempt for love and executed with little of the

vigorous passion that highlighted earlier correspondence. Donne
has set himself up as a museum piece, a map of misery, and his last
wish is that some scrap of love be given him. He no longer has the
hope of a letter and does not press for one. He has moved into the
realm of memory and good wishes. In no other group of verses by
Donne can we follow so meteoric a path from hot to cool, light to
dark, headiness to sobriety. The naughty sexual punning has
calmed into the blandness of ordinary metaphors: "things happy'are sent; / Yet as a Picture, or bare Sacrament." No wild con-
ceits in these images, the delirious joy of first love has been replaced by cold facts.

Of the four poems Donne wrote to T.W., three contain fourteen
lines each, a pattern which suggests a kind of sonnet sequence,
reminiscent of *Astrophil and Stella* and Shakespeare's sequence;
but the Donne sequence is decidedly less ambitious than either Sidney's or Shakespeare's. It has, however, a momentum that carries
the author through a change of emotions suggesting a story line.
The tone of "All haile sweet Poet" is exuberant and brash: the poet
is testing the waters, flattering T.W., soliciting a response-poem.
"Hast thee harsh verse" continues the precipitious motion with
quasi-blasphemous metaphors and an almost giddy tone indicative
of the euphoria Donne experienced on reception of T.W.'s erotic
letter-poem "Thou sendst me prose and rimes." Donne is aggres-
sively confident the relationship is moving forward. With "Pregnant again" the tone changes to anxiety because of "the'old twins
Hope, and Feare." Donne, expecting letters, has been asking after
T.W. In the final poem "At once from hence," Donne languishes
in melancholy, with a grudging acceptance of T.W.'s lack of interest. Donne's final half-hearted plea for love rings hollow to the
reader. Gone are the earlier excitement and anticipation. The imagery of this final poem is tame as Donne backs off and resigns himself to the reality of a cooled friendship. Interestingly, the language
is as sexual as that in his other three letters to T.W.: the "firme
house" which "doth stand" is penile, and "lyes safe," "prest,"
and "for whose want I die" are very suggestive of love-making.
"Dying" in Elizabethan poetry was a standard metaphor for orgasm.

Few critics have taken the time to study the early verse letters of

John Donne closely, and those who have are careful to avoid letting any taint of affection for male friends tarnish Donne's courtier-turned-priest image. William Empson dared touch the untouchable possibilities, but even he failed to follow through with scrutiny of the verses themselves:

> It turns out that when Donne was twenty he wrote several of them [letters] to Woodward's younger brother Tom, aged eighteen, threatening to die for love of him and such like. . . It would leave a scandalmonger in no doubt that the two lads had been up to something together, and also it insinuated that the wit of Donne's poetry or the intent of his conversation perhaps derived from secret heretical opinions . . . one way or another, Donne would find this a peculiarly exasperating corpse to emerge from the glacier. (132)

But the corpse is there. For too long have critics hoped these poems express nothing more than very strong affection between the two young men, but the feelings expressed are more affectionately intense than what most Renaissance poets admitted in their verses to men. It is time that we face these early Donne poems freed from heterosexual expectations and let the words speak for themselves. If we find in the verse letters to T.W. a highly charged homoeroticism, we should not let the "exclusive promotion of adult marital sexuality" (Foucault I, 115), which straight-jackets Western civilizations in the twentieth century, obfuscate our ability to read Renaissance language as language. I love you still means I love you.

## NOTES

1. Allen Barry Cameron has demonstrated that Donne's letter-poems could be at once both compliment to a specific person and a deliberation upon a moral subject (380). He stresses the need to read Donne's verse letters as non-public poetry, a context that affords them more credibility as autobiographical material than lyric verse. Cameron does not focus, however, upon the intense personalism of Donne's early verse letters to T.W., letters which raise questions as to their sexual implications. Similarly, Pebworth and Summers have explored those exchanged by Donne with Sir Henry Wotton, and many of the Pebworth/Summers insights on the immediacy and dynamism of verse letters as personal communica-

tion are applicable to the Donne-T.W. exchange as well, but what is most striking about the verse letters between Donne and T.W. is their intense familiarity. They contain, for example, none of the court gossip that is contained in the letter to Sir Henry Wotton, "Here's no more newes," which Marotti explains as containing a veiled reflection on the boxing of Essex's ears by the queen (122). Such hidden agendas distract from an "I-you" message whereas the intimacy between the correspondents in the Donne-T.W. letters gives the impression of one heart speaking to another, undistracted by the greater world of college and court.

2. All quotations from the poems, except where noted, come from the Shawcross edition.

3. Marvell also played on the image of quill as penis in "The Kings Vowes": "I will have two fine Secretaryes pisse thro one Quill" (l. 36).

4. In the Westmoreland manuscript, written in Rowland Woodward's hand, certain lines in Donne's verse letters to Thomas Woodward have been crossed out. It is impossible to say whether these were obliterated by a brother sensitive to possible criticism of his younger brother, or if they were tampered with by a later hand, but the lines affected are among the most compromising in the letters.

## REFERENCES

Baker, Sir Richard. *Chronicle of the Kings of England*. London: 1643.

Bald, R.C. "Donne's Early Verse Letters." *Huntington Library Quarterly* 15 (1952):283-9.

Cameron, Allen B. "Donne's Deliberative Verse Epistles." *English Literary Renaissance* 6 (1976):364-403.

Empson, William. "Rescuing Donne." *Just So Much Honor*. Ed. Peter A. Fiore. University Park: Pennsylvania State University Press, 1972. 95-148.

Foucault, Michel. *The History of Sexuality*. 3 vols. Trans. Robert Hurley. New York: Pantheon Books, 1978.

Grierson, Herbert J., Ed. *Poems*. By John Donne. 2 vols. Oxford: Oxford University Press, 1912.

Halperin, David M. *One Hundred Years of Homosexuality*. New York: Routledge, 1990.

Le Comte, Edward. *Grace to a Witty Sinner: A Life of Donne*. New York: Walker, 1965.

———. "Jack Donne: From Rake to Husband." *Just So Much Honor*. Ed. Peter A. Fiore. University Park: Pennsylvania State University Press, 1972. 9-32.

Marotti, Arthur F. *John Donne: Coterie Poet*. Madison: University of Wisconsin Press, 1986.

Martial. *Epigrams*. Trans. Walter G.A. Ker. New York: G.P. Putnam's Sons, 1919.

Marvell, Andrew. *Complete Poems*. Ed. Elizabeth Story Donno. New York: St. Martin's Press, 1974.

Milgate, W., Ed. *Satires, Epigrams and Verse Letters*. By John Donne. Oxford: Clarendon Press, 1967.

Pebworth, Ted-Larry, and Claude J. Summers. " 'Thus Friends Absent Speake': The Exchange of Verse Letters between John Donne and Henry Wotton." *Modern Philology* 81 (1984):361-377.

Shawcross, John T., Ed. *Complete Poems of John Donne*. Garden City: Anchor, 1967.

Sprott, S. Ernest. "The Legend of Jack Donne the Libertine." *University of Toronto Quarterly* 19 (1950):335-353.

# Lesbian Erotics:
# The Utopian Trope
# of Donne's "Sapho to Philaenis"

Janel Mueller, PhD

University of Chicago

**SUMMARY.** Famous for its self-assertive masculinity, John Donne's love poetry nonetheless includes a verse elegy which stands alone not only in his work but also in the entire literary production of the Renaissance for its celebration and defense of a passionate lesbian relation binding the two women of its title. No editorial grounds exist for denying Donne's authorship of "Sapho to Philaenis"; rather the interpretive task is to reconstitute the poem's significance in period terms. The task is complicated by Donne's penchant for flouting literary and social convention as he successively overturns Ovid's influential portrayal of Sappho as an aging

Janel Mueller is a professor of English and Humanities at the University of Chicago, and the editor of *Modern Philology*, a journal for historically contextualized studies in medieval and modern literature. Publications on Donne's poetry and prose span her career to date; she has also published on early modern women authors in English (Margery Kempe, Queen Katherine Parr), on Milton's poetry and prose, and on the development of early modern English as a literary medium in *The Native Tongue and the Word: Developments in English Prose Style, 1380-1580* (Chicago: U of Chicago P, 1984). The present essay—virtually identical with a plenary address delivered at the 1990 meeting of the John Donne Society—greatly compresses and variously recasts material from "Troping Utopia: Donne's Brief for Lesbianism in 'Sapho to Philaenis'," to appear in *Sexuality and Gender in Early Modern Europe: Institutions, Texts, Images*, ed. James Grantham Turner (Cambridge: Cambridge UP, 1992). Grateful acknowledgment is made to members of the John Donne Society—Diana Benet, Kate Frost, George Klawitter, Ted-Larry Pebworth, Michael Schoenfeldt, Jeanne Shami, Gary Stringer, Ernest Sullivan, II, and, especially, Claude Summers—for helpful questions, references, and discussion. Correspondence may be addressed to the author at The University of Chicago, 1050 East 59th Street, Chicago, IL 60637.

voluptuary reclaimed for heterosexuality, the virulent homophobia of Renaissance humanists, and the coy idealizations and transient evocation given to lesbian affectivity by the very few Renaissance writers (including Shakespeare) who touched on the subject at all. When "Sapho to Philaenis" is set in the context of Donne's other love elegies in verse as productions by a young intellectual moving in sophisticated London circles and writing for a coterie audience, lesbianism looks like a master trope for positively resolving a dilemma that confounded Montaigne and many other authors of the age. Could the perfections of love and friendship be united in a relation of equality between two persons? Gender hierarchy and separate socialization precluded a heterosexual construction of any such equality in the Renaissance, and the greater opprobrium cast on male homosexuality in this era must have influenced Donne's decision to figure his equal lovers and friends as a lesbian couple. Yet the disclosive power of "Sapho to Philaenis" goes far beyond the entailments of a specific choice of poetic representation. Donne really undertakes to imagine the pleasures, sustenance, and ideological implications by which lesbianism, as a mode of loving and being, resists patriarchal disposition and diminution of women. Donne anticipates the advances of twentieth-century feminists (Colette, Kofman, Irigaray) as he poetically articulates possibilities and knowledge that were otherwise denied expression by Renaissance culture and its exponents.

Donne's reputation has lately sustained frontal attacks on what for modern readers is its central terrain—the love poetry. Not only has his rhetorical extravagance been faulted for a phallocentrism that too eagerly embraces and enforces male dominance (Bueler, Mueller).[1] An implied authorial psyche that speaks at points in the elegies, songs, and sonnets—a world-eclipsing ego recognizing only the rule of its own desires—has seemed locked in arrested development or in some other pathology. Thus Stanley Fish has diagnosed Donne as "bulimic" (233) in his repeated ingestion and disgorgings of a rhetoric of gendered power, while Christopher Ricks decries a pattern of lyric closure in Donne that works as if by reflex to "debase, demean, and degrade . . . the poetic act and the sexual act" (38-39).[2] For certain passages in certain poems, there is truth in these charges.[3] But as William Kerrigan has recently warned, we severely limit our appreciation of the constitutive concerns in Donne's poetry if we read him either piecemeal or too programmatically:

> It is not yet clear what my generation . . . will make of the secular Donne. . . . Once one moves away from the unit of the particular lyric, Donne becomes notoriously difficult to talk about. . . . The ultimate locus of sensible discourse about these poems is the subject of love. I would not mind calling it the 'question' of love. . . . I would not even mind calling it the 'ideology' of love, if by ideology were meant an assembly of values that we should make choices about. (2-3)

Such cautionary notes are timely.[4] Critical approaches currently being applied to the poems — moralizing humanism, psychobiography, deconstruction, feminism, new historicism — appear inadequate in varying degrees to the challenge of coping with the "what if" imaginings of the desiring subject in Donne's writings.[5] There are many examples of what I mean by "what if" imaginings: the intuition in the libertine love lyrics that promiscuity rather than constancy grounds human sexual nature, the sense in the valediction poems that the test and guarantee of true mutual love is absence and not physical intimacy, the attempted defense of suicide from within a Christian context in *Biathanatos*, the recurrent attraction to envisioning great imponderables — the sight of God, the resurrection of the body, the modes of moving, sensing, and knowing that a disembodied soul might experience — in the divine poems and *Anniversaries*, and at still greater length in the sermons. In a now classic essay Thomas Greene argued for seeing "the flexibility of the self" as one of the most productive formations of Renaissance literature. Greene, however, made no mention of Donne, possibly because Donne often conflates and thus confounds the axial coordinates that framed Greene's discussion. These coordinates comprise a "vertical" series through which human nature ranges from animality to angelhood or divinity, and a "horizontal" series, the gamut of social and sexual roles by which an individual life takes on a "multiplicity of . . . existences," a "multiplication of possibilities" (250, 241, 248). Yet, as Donne again and again negotiates the passage from the imaginary to the symbolic in his writing, he proves one of

the era's most telling witnesses to human malleability, to the polymorphous self actuated in and by desire. We have long been charting through the songs, sonnets, and elegies the "hee and shee"
aspects of a utopian sexuality that is continually sought and fleet-
ingly articulated. In this paper, however, I address an all but ignored dimension of the erotics of the gendered body in Donne.[6] My
discussion centers on his one known poem in which lesbianism becomes a master trope for utopian sexuality in its existential—and
even, at some telling points, its societal—implications.

In the corpus of Donne's love poetry one item stands out as neither elegy nor song nor sonnet. Grierson's 1912 edition printed it to
follow the elegies, notating with the heading "Heroical Epistle"
Donne's sole entry in a once-modish category of vernacular imitations of Ovid's *Heroides* written in rhymed pentameter couplets
(I:xvii, 124; II:91). Here I can merely sketch the connection that
Donne's poem, "Sapho to Philaenis," makes with a strain of Ovi-
dianism that is otherwise familiar from a variety of realizations in
the literary history of the English Renaissance (Turberville, Lyly,
Drayton). Ovid's "Sappho to Phaon" is the fifteenth and last of the
single verse epistles—that is, unanswered letters—which comprise
the bulk of the *Heroides*. These histrionic productions in elegiac
couplets work variations on a stock situation: in each an abandoned
female pleads with her faithless male lover to return to her. Significantly, all of Ovid's abandoned heroines in the *Heroides* are mythological—Phaedra, Medea, Ariadne, Dido—with the exception of
Sappho. Yet she seems to have figured with Ovid as virtually mythological, ready to be made so. He certainly took a strong, fictional-
izing hand in depicting her, as both Linda Kauffman and Joan De-
Jean have recently discussed at some length (Kauffman 30-33,
50-61; DeJean 7-84).[7] In *Heroides* 15 Ovid downplayed Sappho's
poetic remains and instead worked selectively with the body of traditions and reports about her—her so-called doxography.[8] Ovid's
Sappho is an aging ex-lesbian crazed by the desertion of her boy-
friend, Phaon the ferryman, whom Venus has made magically irre-
sistible to women. Lovemaking with Phaon has brought Ovid's
Sappho to renounce her lesbian past, for he, she assures him, out-
classes all her previous sexual partners. She is desperately aware of
her fading physical charms and her waning poetical gifts, but stri-

dently assertive all the same. She can still recite her superb lyrics; she still knows the tricks and postures in which she and Phaon took such intense mutual pleasure even in outdoor lovemaking in the meadow and forest. Surges of desire and memory break over Ovid's Sappho as she writes, spinning her verse epistle out of her control and into involuntary hopelessness. She will leap from the cliff—the lovers' leap—at the far end of the island of Leucas and immolate herself along with her love, she tells Phaon, if he does not return soon. Are these wild words a threat or a promise? muses the reader swept up in Ovid's imperious poetic fiction. This study of psychosexual hysteria with its implicit tragic plot conforms Sappho to regnant social and cultural norms by confirming her as a "has-been" poet and lesbian.

Donne's intervention in the series of *Heroides* imitations respects the poetic and epistolary form of its prototype, but breaks with Ovid's portrayal of an aging, desperate, suicidal Sappho who yearns for the sexual attentions of a young man. Both the character and the implicit plot are thoroughly recast. Donne's Sapho is an ardent, active lesbian in full experiential and emotional career. Expressly comparing her love for Phaon and Philaenis, she declares for Philaenis, for always: "Such was my *Phao*' awhile, but shall be never / As thou wast, art, and, oh, maist be ever."[9] In "Sapho to Philaenis" one woman first confronts the trauma of separation from her beloved, another woman, and then passionately recalls for them both the erotic bliss they have experienced together. They are one another's ideal complement, two selves made one through the reciprocal identity of their knowing, desiring, and pleasuring. Donne's Sapho is, to be sure, both obsessed with desire and separated from her Philaenis—the convention of a verse epistle could scarcely make sense otherwise—but she looks forward unswervingly to the fullness of life and (re)union, not to a death that alone can vacate the devastation of a romantic, heterosexual betrayal.[10]

Does any reader escape surprise at finding Donne exchanging his vaunted "masculine persuasive force" for sapphic fire in order to body forth a conjoint image and argument for perfected sexuality? The denial of Donne's authorship by Helen Gardner, the ranking editor of his poems after Grierson, was perhaps an understandable reflex, but her misgivings had no textual warrant at all. On the evidence of the best manuscripts recorded in Gardner's own critical apparatus, the authenticity of "Sapho to Philaenis" is as well supported as that of "The Comparison," "The Computation," "The Paradox," and "The Dissolution," and it is better supported than that of "A Jeat Ring sent," "Negative love," "Farewell to love," and "A Nocturnall upon S. Lucies Day"—all poems that no one has dreamed of detaching from Donne's canon.[11] In editions of the poetry in 1967, 1971, and 1985 respectively, John Shawcross, A. J. Smith, and C. A. Patrides restored "Sapho to Philaenis" to the roll of canonical works, printing it at the end of the twenty elegies (Shawcross, Smith, Patrides). The editorial crisis met, the interpretive challenge remains: to engage and probe the Donnean trope that casts lesbian love as the supreme erotic fiction.

Donne's "what if" in "Sapho to Philaenis" does not—and, indeed, could not—pursue its utopianism of the gendered, sexually active body by fleeing beyond reach of a Renaissance network of literary associations in which Sappho distinctly, and Philaenis a good deal more obscurely, figured as women poets with contested identities and reputations. Donne worked for the most part by oppositional refashioning of his inherited materials to his own expressive ends.[12] In shaping "Sapho to Philaenis" as an antitype to Ovid's "Sappho to Phaon," Donne drew on extra-Ovidian sources for conceptions of Sappho, of women poets, and of lesbian erotics; the figure of Philaenis alone is proof of this. Here a contextual excursus is in order.

By the end of the sixteenth century a whole fund of material on women poets and lesbian erotics had built up around the name of Sappho in humanist scholarship. To illustrate with respected names of the era, this material starts manageably enough in Politian's notes for a lecture series on the *Heroides* at the Florentine Academy (1481), grows to middle size in Guy Morillon's annotations on "Sappho to Phaon" that were printed to accompany several editions of the *Heroides* including the London one of 1594, and becomes massive in Lelio Gregorio Giraldi's *Historia poetarum graecorum et latinorum* (1545), a veritable encyclopedia of poets' doxographies and commentary on memorable works and lines. Donne's contemporary, Thomas Heywood, borrowed extensively from Giraldi for accounts of women poets in his *Gunaikeion: Or,*

*Nine Bookes of Various History Concerninge Women* (1624).[13] The chief points to note about this humanist scholarship are its strident homophobia and its rigidly conventional notions of gender roles and proprieties — especially for females. What Donne makes whole and affirmative, humanist scholars divide and anathematize.

In the treatments of Sappho there is a powerful tendency, clearest in Giraldi's doxography, to bifurcate her distinguishing attributes — lyricism and lesbianism — and to embody them in two historical women. This splitting process can be traced back at least as far as Aelian's *Natural History*, a work of the late second century. We are given, on the one hand, a matchless and immortal lyric poet — in Plato's famous phrase for Sappho, "the tenth Muse" — who was also a sexually respectable and conventional noblewoman, wife, and mother.[14] On the other, we are given to believe, there was a libertine prostitute of the same name who got confused with her noble poetic predecessor. Besides the doxography stressed by humanist scholars, an additional and direct though scanty source for Renaissance knowledge of Sappho as poet and lesbian was provided by sixteenth-century printings of her poetic fragments. Henri and Robert Estienne (or Stephanus) published a two-page appendix to editions of Anacreon in 1554 and 1556; in the second edition, Sappho's only two lyrics in sapphic stanzas to survive to the Renaissance from antiquity in a nearly complete state were accompanied by Latin translations and by a handful of much briefer fragments (single lines or phrases).[15] One of the lyrics in sapphics was Sappho's hymn to Aphrodite preserved by quotation in Dionysius of Halicarnassus; the other, the famous stanzas anatomizing lesbian longing — the play of flames along her veins, the failed speech, sweating, faintness, and abjection that overtake Sappho when she sees her beloved in intimate conversation with a young man — that had been admiringly quoted and thus preserved both by the author of *On the Sublime* (long known as Longinus) and by Plutarch in his dialogue *The Lover*.[16]

Because the latter lyric supplies the core of original material in the Renaissance conception of Sappho as a surpassing poetic delineator of her own erotic experience and emotions, I offer a literal if prosaic translation that will at least serve the purposes of the present discussion: "He seems to me equal to the gods, the someone who sits closely facing you, and listens to your sweet tones of speech, your pleasurable laughter, which make the heart in my rib-cage beat so fast and high. As I look at you, Brochea, my voice goes to nothing, my tongue is broken, and subtle fire runs in courses through my body; my eyes see nothing, my ears ring; sweat pours from me as trembling seizes me completely; I become green, like grass, and death seems to me only a little way off. But impoverished now, I must dare all'' [alternatively reconstructing a textual lacuna: "I must be contented withall''].[17] I will be referring to this poem of Sappho's as *"Phainetai moi"* (its opening words in the Greek), since editors' numberings of her fragments vary.

For her part, Philaenis — always identified as Philaenis of Leucas, the island that provided the setting for Ovid's Sappho's death leap — emerges in poetic tradition and doxography as a shadowy, disreputable figure of uncertain date, though certainly later than Sappho. While not a line of Philaenis's work was known to survive, she is repeatedly represented as a poet. In the so-called *Greek* (or *Palatine*) *Anthology* that devolved from classical times and spurred a vogue of Renaissance imitations, there are two epigrams protesting in general terms the scandalous imputations attached to Philaenis's name.[18] The language from which the *Greek Anthology* took its name found most humanists far less proficient than they were in Latin. Except in Donne, I have found no Renaissance traces of a positive conception of Philaenis. The sole occurrences of Philaenis's name that I have found in classical Latin are in Martial's two savagely obscene epigrams (Book 7, nos. 67 and 70) which address a woman of that name and reprehend her practice of cunnilingus.[19] Giraldi's compilation (2: 1710) reports Philaenis of Leucas's reputation for promiscuity and pornographic poetry — verses on the postures and techniques of lovemaking. As far as I have been able to determine, it was Donne who defied chronology but respected geography when he devised an intersecting course for the figures of these two women poets on the island of Leucas and invented their lesbian love.[20] He also defied all the currents of classical doxography and Renaissance scholarship in making their lesbian love positive. The implicit narrative line of his "what if" imaginings in "Sapho to Philaenis" effectively turns inside out the inherited materials of literary tradition.

Thus, as we focus our attention on Donne's more immediate literary and experiential context — the London of the 1590s (if we sustain the linkage with the elegies observed in all of the most recent editions of Donne's poetry) — his location of a subject in lesbian love at first looks *sui generis*, as inaccessible to our understanding as it remained to Helen Gardner's. There is, first, the thunderous silence on the subject of lesbianism — in English, especially — that Donne broke. Lillian Faderman's pioneering research (Faderman, chaps. 1-2), reinforced by Holstun's recent article on the "lesbian elegy" and DeJean's more recent study of Sappho's reception history in France (DeJean 53-60), indicates the virtual absence of lesbianism as a vernacular literary subject in the Renaissance before the middle decades of the seventeenth century.[21] At that time, libertine obscenity modeled on Martial made sporadic appearances, especially in France (according to Faderman's examples). I have two English additions to this general picture of a paucity of literary references to lesbianism.[22] As early as 1601 an English poetic miscellany printed an epigram by Ben Jonson, Donne's friend and contemporary, which begins "Must I sing?"; it hews closely to the humanist line of viewing female homoerotics with disgust. Surveying possible companions with whom Venus might be found inventing "new sports," Jonson brands the Graces, no less, as a "Tribade trine" — thus naturalizing in English the classical term for lesbians, derived from the Greek verb *tribein* (meaning to rub, to draw along or across). Jonson's later "Epigram on the Court Pucell," Cecilia Bulstrode (before 1609), denigrates Bulstrode's poetry-writing as lesbian rape: "What though with Tribade lust she force a Muse?"[23]

But Donne, as I am stressing, treats lesbianism positively. Is he altogether alone in this? Prior to his "Sapho to Philaenis" I have been able to find a mere two instances of what I call lesbian affectivity, since erotics is too strong a term for the reticent locutions, hyperbolic compliments, and thwarted yearnings that mark these non-Donnean verses. One instance is a later sixteenth-century Scots protestation in stanzaic verse. A speaker salutes a certain lady in high-flown terms and proceeds to claim for their "freindschip reciproc" a devotion more selfless than that of David to Jonathan or Ruth to Naomi. Suddenly the speaker reveals her gender as she has an Ovidian brainstorm. If only mighty Jove would "metamorphos" her into his own sex, she could end her "smart" and unite with her beloved in the "band of hymen." The imagined bliss of sexual union that would attend on her sex-change carries the speaker to one further height: a vision of herself and her lady exalted for their "perfyte amitie" to a place among the stars, like Castor and Pollux. But this Scots poem ends with a forlorn return to earth and earthbound possibilities. The best future that the speaker can envisage is a constant friendship, which she urges the lady to sustain with her. This poem of unknown authorship was copied into the manuscript known as the Maitland Quarto for (and possibly by) its owner, Mary Maitland, about 1586; the Maitland Quarto was first printed in 1920.[24] The other instance in my category of lesbian affectivity is a composition from the Pléiade circle: Pontus de Tyard's "Elégie pour une dame enamourée d'une autre dame," published in his *Oeuvres complètes* (1573) and subsequently anthologized by Louis Perceau in his series, *Le Cabinet secret du Parnasse*. Tyard's elegy celebrates in heroic couplets the moral superiority of a lesbian attachment for an honorable gentlewoman who abhors the low designs constantly made upon her person by the gentlemen with whom her rank obliges her to associate at court. Yet despite the rectitude of the lyric speaker, her lesbian longings are altogether checked in the implied plot. Her beloved lady is disdainful and unresponsive. The elegy ends in hopeless, vengeful imaginings that the beloved lady will bestow her love on some base person and know the pain of rejection in turn (Perceau, *Ronsard et la Pléiade* 182-87).

I have no stake in arguing that Donne knew Tyard's poem, but I do think that its revelation of *mentalité* — a well-born woman's refusal to submit to the contemporary sexual mores of courtiers — gives us an initial bearing on Donne's exploration of a lesbian erotics. What was Donne's own situation in London in the 1590s, the commonly assumed date of "Sapho to Philaenis"?[25] It has recently been delineated by Arthur Marotti in these terms:

> The Inns-of-Court amorist is a stock figure in the literature of late Elizabethan England. If not love itself — in its most sophisticated forms — then the composition of love poetry was regarded as properly a gentleman's occupation, a sign of so-

cial status either within or outside the court. . . . Donne expected his sophisticated readers to understand the literary-historical vicissitudes of various genres and modes and to appreciate his inventive reformulation of them in ways that called into question both familiar conventions and their usual ideological and social affiliations. (Marotti, *John Donne, Coterie Poet* 67, 70)[26]

In my view, the period touches of Petrarchism that mingle with the speaker's analysis of the bodily sensations of the throes of passion in the opening lines of "Sapho to Philaenis" offer clear testimony that Donne looked to the Sappho of *"Phainetai moi"* (in some version) as a source of renewal for the well-worn conventions of Renaissance love poetry. At least I take her surpassing reputation as a poet of *eros* to have attracted his interest to her as he sought to engage with other gentlemen of the London Inns of Court in writing vernacular coterie verse. If a cultural ambiance now begins to come into focus around the Donne of the elegies, there remains the far more teasing question of his affirmative treatment of lesbian erotics, for which the figure of Sappho provided the vehicle. This question returns me to the cultural issues underlying the expressions of lesbian affectivity – in Tyard and the Maitland Quarto – that I have just surveyed.

As I bring "Sapho to Philaenis" into focus under a period lens, I see Donne conducting a thought experiment, one of his "what ifs" engendered in desire. At this era, as his friend and contemporary Sir Richard Baker later recalled, "Mr. *John Donne* . . . lived at the *Innes of Court*, not dissolute, but very neat; a great visiter of Ladies, a great frequenter of Playes, a great writer of conceited Verses."[27] Donne registers the stepped-up valuations both of marriage and of single-sex friendship in his day, together with the relation of incessant conflict between the two that was then fueling scores of plots for stage comedies and tragedies alike (Mills 214-304). A highly pertinent example – although it looks, to our present understandings, to be ten or fifteen years later than Donne's poem – is provided by Shakespeare and Fletcher's *Two Noble Kinsmen* (ca. 1613; 1st ed. 1634). In an early speech (Act 1, Scene 3) from Shakespeare's hand, the heroine Emilia celebrates her adolescent attachment to a certain Flavina. Emilia recalls how her soul wholly agreed with Flavina's in likes and dislikes, and how they decked themselves out for and with each other: "The flower that I would pluck / And put between my breasts, oh (then but beginning / To swell about the blossom) she would long / Till she had such another, and commit it / To the like innocent Cradle." Emilia ends her speech by voicing her conviction that "the true love 'tween Maid, and Maid, may be / More than in sex individual," and she concludes the scene with this announcement: "I'm sure I shall not . . . Love any that's call'd Man" (Waller 9: 303-04). Notwithstanding her declared homoerotic fidelity, in this stage adaptation of Chaucer's *Knight's Tale* Emilia is married off in due course to her surviving suitor, Palamon. Lesbian attachment and a woman's resolve never to marry can find dramatic expression from Shakespeare only as transient states falsified by the play's ending, which confirms anew the force of social convention.

Donne in "Sapho to Philaenis" resolutely refuses to pull just such punches. A principal aspect of his "what if" runs like this: "What if we try to synthesize the unitive perfections of marriage and friendship between equals? What would the resulting relation look like?" The abstract answer to this abstract question was nonetheless mediated by historically specific social concretions of gender and rank in Donne's day. Since gender was bound in hierarchical relations, men and women could not be equals. Hence, men and women could not be friends in the then specially charged and specially regarded sense of friendship. Separate socialization and education for the two sexes both set and reinforced limits on how human equality and mutuality could be conceived. The relation that remained available in the Renaissance for figuring the synthesis of friendship and marriage as a relation between equals was homoerotics. As a homoerotic alternative, lesbianism could figure this synthesis much more acceptably than male homosexuality because, according to longstanding theological traditions, the former involved relatively venial pollution—the rubbing of tribades, one might say in period terminology—whereas the latter incurred the mortal sin of disposing what was held to be the most vital element in human reproduction, the semen, in what were claimed to be unnatural ways (Bullough 78-79, 331-41, 353-61, 379-81, 444-46, 450;

Goodich 427-34; Boswell 322). In Europe by the fourteenth century at the latest, on John Boswell's account, these traditions had attained an all but hegemonic cultural grip within both learned and popular thought (Boswell 163, 202-03, 288-93, 295, 303-04). A contributory consideration predisposing Donne to a lesbian representation may have been the inequality of age and rank that remained a conspicuous feature of classical Greek homosexual love and its type figures — an older male lover of superior social standing and a youthful male beloved whose social standing was yet in formation.[28] Donne's project and projections required equality. It appears, then, that in Donne's time and circumstances only a marriage-friendship synthesis gendered female could have run the risk of representation, even by a "coterie poet" with the sophisticated acquaintanceship that Marotti details.

Let us now more closely consider this poem, "Sapho to Philaenis," in which I find Donne keeping his interrogation of cultural givens and biases steadily to the fore. As already suggested, his design of undoing the central portrayal in "Sappho to Phaon" shows perhaps most clearly in his revisions of Ovid's implicit narrative. On arrival in Leucas, Donne's Sapho does not end her life in thwarted lust for Phaon. Instead, she meets the libertine love poet Philaenis and falls so deeply in love with her that Phaon becomes a relic of Sapho's past. The moment of Donnean composition — the writing of his heroical epistle — ensues upon Sapho's separation from Philaenis, not Phaon. Having fixed this non-Ovidian point of departure, Donne next repudiates the humanist emphasis on doxography that left scant attention for the surviving fragments of Sappho's poetry.

Donne begins his verse epistle by ringing changes on the passionate formulations of Sappho's sapphics on lesbian desire in *"Phainetai moi,"* the poem quoted by Longinus and Plutarch, but the changes leave the original still recognizable in outline. The opening of Donne's poem inverts Sappho's sequence of images to begin with his Sapho's speechlessness and burning and to climax in the comparison with the gods. This comparison, moreover, is doubly refashioned: first, to pivot not on a male rival, but on Sapho's female beloved; then to make her beloved, not the gods, the standard of divinity. By way of update, finally, Donne's Sapho puts some

Petrarchan retouchings on the physiological symptoms of sexual passion:

> Have my teares quench'd my old *Poetique* fire;
>> Why quench'd they not as well, that of *desire*?
>> \*    \*    \*
> Onely thine image, in my heart, doth sit,
>> But that is waxe, and fires environ it.
> My fires have driven, thine have drawne it hence;
>> And I am rob'd of *Picture*, *Heart*, and *Sense*.
> Dwells with me still mine irksome *Memory*,
>> Which both to keepe, and lose, grieves equally.
> That tells me'how faire thou art: Thou art so faire,
>> As, *gods*, when *gods* to thee I doe compare,
> Are grac'd thereby. . . . (ll. 5-6, 9-16)

Thus far I have been reading the text of the poem as if breaking with the conceptual and cultural hold exercised by Ovid's Sappho and the homophobic reinforcements of humanist scholarship were project enough for Donne in "Sapho to Philaenis." But this can by no means be the whole story. Donne's thematics call into larger question the conventions of heterosexuality that ruled love poetry, erotic behavior, and social arrangements in his day. What can be said in this regard of the design of this verse epistle and its implications for a Renaissance readership?

"Sapho to Philaenis" demonstrably trades on a Renaissance understanding of friendship: a relation between two persons so alike in age, means, education and upbringing, interests, tastes, and values that they bond in mutual joy and constancy at finding another self with whom to share both experience and intimacy. The prime period source for this understanding is Montaigne's celebration of his relation with Étienne de La Boétie in his essay "Of Friendship." Montaigne memorably evokes "mindes . . . that have with so fervent an affection considered of each other, and with like affection so discovered and sounded, even to the very bottome of each others heart, that I did . . . know his, as well as mine owne. . . . It is I wot not what kinde of quintessence, of all this commixture, which having seized all my will, induced the same to plunge and lose it selfe in his, which likewise having seized all his will, brought it to lose and plunge it selfe in mine." Severed by death from his friend, Montaigne continues: "All things were with us at halfes. . . . I was so accustomed to be ever two, and so enured to be never single, that me thinks I am but halfe my selfe" (Montaigne 150, 149, 153-54). Donne's Sapho's repeated reciprocals and assertions of "like-nesse" (ll. 47, 51) sustain by similar means the key motifs of this intense mutuality, even merger, of identities: "Me, in my glasse, I call thee" (l. 55). Sapho can also be found conflating a still larger literature of friendship within a single couplet: "O cure this loving madnesse, and restore / Me to mee; thee, my halfe, my all, my more" (ll. 57-58). In the *Confessions* Augustine had called his friend half of his soul,[29] and in "Of Friendship" (1625 version) Bacon declares: "It will appeare that it was a Sparing Speech of the Ancients to say, That a Frend is another Himself: For that a Frend is farre more than Himselfe" (Arber 181).

While evident enough in all this language of union and mutuality, it is perhaps worth emphasizing that "Sapho to Philaenis" does not question the Renaissance construction of gender implicit in the stress on friends as equals. Donne accepts the single-sex definition of the friendship literature.[30] Just as crucially, however, he accepts neither the male chauvinism nor the compulsory heterosexuality that bedevil Montaigne's weighing of friendship against marriage:

> The ordinary sufficiency of women, cannot answer this con-ference and communication, the nurse of this sacred bond [of friendship]; nor seeme their mindes strong enough to endure . . . a knot so hard, so fast, and durable. Truly, if . . . such a genuine and voluntarie acquaintance might be contracted, where not only mindes had this entire jovissance, but also bodies, . . . and a man might wholly be engaged: it is certaine, that friendship would thereby be more compleat and full: But this sex [that is, females] could never yet by any example at-taine unto it, and is by ancient schooles rejected thence. (Mon-taigne 147)

Montaigne leaves himself with a negative dichotomy, a *je ne sais quoi*, as he struggles to articulate the character of his relationship with La Boétie. Such perfect friendship is not marriage; but it is even more emphatically not "that Greeke licence . . . justly abhorred by our customes" (147).[31] Donne's "what if" in "Sapho to Philaenis," by contrast, consists precisely in closing Montaigne's negative dichotomy and uniting friendship and marriage through homoerotics — the "truly . . . more compleat and full" engagement of bodies as well as souls. Homoerotics in turn translates as lesbianism under the theologically originating taboos that we have already noted to be in force in Donne's day. In stating this, however, I do not want to be understood as implying that Donne treated lesbianism merely as a trope dealt to him by the limits set in his age on how unitive perfection might be figured between two lover-friends. Through the personages of Sapho and Philaenis Donne, in my reading, really undertook to explore how utopian erotics might be gendered all-female. The recognitions articulated by his Sapho differentiate "Sapho and Philaenis" sharply from the renunciatory speakers in the Maitland Quarto stanzas and in Tyard's "Elégie." They view lesbian affectivity only as tragic impossibility in a world they must inhabit while yearning, futilely, to escape. Donne both intensifies lesbian affectivity into erotics and gives the erotics an altogether positive representation. His further projection of some economic implications reaffirms his positive portrayal.

Tyard's "Elégie" becomes most suggestive by comparison with Donne's "Sapho to Philaenis" in fugitive moments when its proto-feminist speaker declares that the sexual predation of courtiers can be met by a full-scale alternative of being and loving. This alternative is the logic of lesbianism, but there are, in Tyard's poem, no takers for it beyond the speaker herself. Donne tallies with Tyard in several particulars of the case for lesbianism, but he articulates their argumentative content much more fully and also imbues them with much more circumstantial and rhetorical force. While resolving opposition between women's love and women's honor is a primary motive with the speaker in Tyard's elegy, she nevertheless just barely deals with avoiding the scandal and danger of pregnancy as she exalts, in a passing remark, a love whose sweetness leaves honor unscathed and beauty unimpaired: "Amour . . . jamais plus mollement . . . car l'honneur non blessé . . . sa beauté nullement entamée" (Perceau, *Ronsard et la Pléiade* 165). Heightened by the images of robbing and being robbed, the issues of honor, sexual pleasure, and the threat to honor posed by pregnancy are brought into fully articulated conjunction by Donne's Sappho as an argument, specifically, for lesbian erotics. The images of the movement of fishes and birds through the water and air that are their natural elements also work to undermine the powerful contrary-to-nature associations with single-sex love in the Renaissance (and long before and after):

> Men leave behinde them that which their sin showes,
>> And are, as theeves trac'd, which rob when it snows.
> But of our dallyance no more signes there are,
>> Then fishes leave in streames, or Birds in aire. (ll. 39-42)

Tyard's elegy, moreover, registers only obliquely—in the same passing remark that has just been quoted—the superiority of the softness of a woman's body as a site of erotic pleasure ("Amour . . . jamais plus mollement"). Donne, however, intensifies this pleasurability and its attendant bodily sensations thrice over: through contrast with the scratchiness of a man's beard, through a brief, eroticized Renaissance reflection on mutability and permanence (youths' bodies lose the softness that female bodies always retain),[32] and, above all, through what becomes a dominant tactile motif, the redoubled pleasure in softness that accrues from two lovers' bodies alike in their softness:

> Plaies some soft boy with thee, oh there wants yet
>> A mutuall feeling which should sweeten it.
> His chinne, a thorny hairy unevennesse
>> Doth threaten, and some daily change possess.

*   *   *

> Such was my *Phao'* awhile, but shall be never,
> As thou, wast, art, and, oh, maist be ever.

*   *   *

> My two lips, eyes, thighs, differ from thy two,
>> But so, as thine from one another doe;
> And, oh, no more; the likenesse being such,
>> Why should they not alike in all parts touch?
>>>> (ll. 31-34, 25-26, 45-48)

The qualitative difference, however, between Donne's Sapho and her poetic counterparts in Tyard and the Maitland Quarto does not reduce simply to differences in explicitness or reticence or to the degree of success attained in affirming lesbian love. The quantum leap that Donne, and only Donne, is found making occurs on the plane of love theory. Donne theorizes lesbianism as an *ars erotica* — that unattested genre in Western society, according to Foucault, where *scientia sexualis* has held discursive sway at least since the sixteenth century. Not expecting fellow Westerners to be able to recognize an *ars erotica*, Foucault supplies a characterization: "In the erotic art, truth is drawn from pleasure itself, understood as a practice and accumulated as experience; pleasure is considered . . . first and foremost in relation to itself; it is experienced as pleasure, evaluated in terms of its intensity, its specific quality, its duration, its reverberations in the body and the soul. Moreover, this knowledge must be deflected back into the sexual practice itself, in order to shape it as though from within and amplify its effects. In this way, there is formed a knowledge" (Foucault 57). Donne's *ars erotica* addresses the truth about female sexual pleasure. This has scarcely been an unvexed historical question, as no post-Freudian needs to be told.

Only a decade ago Sarah Kofman broached her critique of Freud's theory that a young female recognizes herself in lack, as a deficient male. Kofman detects in the formulations of the female castration complex and penis envy an attempted reprisal on women for their resistance to male desire on male terms, "for having known how to safeguard their narcissism, their independence, their nonchalance, and their high self-esteem by repelling everything that might be capable of depreciating them." Hence she construes a woman's "taking of narcissistic pleasure in herself" not "as a compensation for a natural deficiency, but rather as a compensation for social injuries" that accordingly comes to constitute "the ground of all desire" (Kofman 37-38). The erotic pleasures catalogued by Donne's Sapho can seem strikingly knowledgeable in the arts of female sexual gratification, even to late twentieth-century readers. She knows the self-empowering pleasures of narcissism, of autoeroticism, of mirror-gazing, as means by which an acculturated female invests her body and her psyche with a sense of worth and gains the confidence to be a subject, not merely an object of desire.

Donne's Sapho confides to Philaenis the "strange selfe flatterie" of "Me, in my glasse" and of "touching my selfe": "My selfe I embrace, and mine owne hands I kisse, / And amorously thanke my selfe for this" (ll. 51-55). By further implication, in these same lines on the autoerotic play of hands for which she amorously thanks herself and with which she fails to compensate for Philaenis's absence, Sapho's is a self-cognizant clitoral sexuality.

Donne's Sapho, moreover, knows the asymmetry between male and female orgasm in the closeness of their respective ties to the mechanics of reproduction. She argues from the facts of female bodies to her lesbian *ars erotica*. It is not necessary to get pregnant or even to risk getting pregnant in order to experience climactic pleasure, as she assures Philaenis: "And betweene us all sweetnesse may be had; / All, all that Nature yields, or Art can adde" (ll. 43-44). Focused tactility figures prominently in exhortations that their body contact and caresses be sustained to an implied climax: "And oh, . . . the likeness being such, / Why should they not alike in all parts touch?/ Hand to strange hand, lip to lip none denies; / Why should they breast to breast, or thighs to thighs?" (ll. 48-50). Gender difference, moreover, makes a whole world of difference in this Donnean *ars erotica*. Sapho declares that knowledge of female sexual pleasure can best be transmitted experientially to a woman from a woman, who inhabits and experiences just such a body.[33] Again, the link between female knowing and female pleasuring is very clearly articulated. Emphasis is laid repeatedly on "touch" and "touching" (ll. 48, 51) and on prolongation of actions and effects: " As thou, wast, art, and, oh, maist be ever," "And so be change, and sicknesse, farre from thee, / As thou by comming neere, keep'st them from me" (ll. 26, 65). Most emphatically, in this lesbian erotics, the joy of binariness figures as primary in pleasure ("two lips, eyes, thighs" – l. 45).

In the process of its articulation this female *ars erotica* is invested with overtly utopian dimensions:

> Thy body is a naturall *Paradise*,
>     In whose selfe, unmanur'd, all pleasure lies
> Nor needs *perfection*; why shouldst thou than
>     Admit the tillage of a harsh rough man? (ll. 35-38)

Sapho's expostulation to Philaenis not only repudiates the "phallo-centric confidence" in the sexual indispensability of males to fe-males that is commonly taken to identify Donne as a love poet. It goes far beyond this to offer a primal, Edenic image of woman's body as a plenum of life and pleasure. Donne's utopian "what if" cuts through the cumulative shroudings of cultural repression to ut-ter the unspoken and unspeakable knowledge of total female com-petency in female sexual pleasure. It is preposterous or naive to suppose that the clitoral site of orgasm was known only to women as historical subjects.[34] Men too surely knew—and among them I do not hesitate to number that subtle amorist, Donne. He joins his Sapho to speak as a lover of women. What sets him apart is no secret erotic knowledge, but what he could imagine and image as yet-to-be-realized possibility in the erotic knowledge that he had.

Accordingly, on the cultural plane, "Sapho to Philaenis" regis-ters a great prolepsis through its multiple points of accord with the utterances of twentieth-century lesbian feminism. Consider what Donne's Sapho knows and writes in the light of this passage from Colette's *Ces Plaisirs* (1932): "It is not sensuality that ensures the fidelity of two women but a kind of blood kinship. . . . I have written kinship where I should have said identity. Their close re-semblance guarantees similarity in *volupté*. The lover takes courage in her certainty of caressing a body whose secrets she knows, whose preferences her own body has taught her" (translated and cited in Foster 124; cf. Wittig). Perhaps most striking in their lyrical affini-ties with Donne's Sapho are Luce Irigaray's celebrations of touch and prolongation produced through the twoness of female anatomy and lesbian erotics. Here is one such passage from "This Sex Which Is Not One" (1977): "The *one* of form, of the individual, of the (male) sexual organ . . . suppplants, while separating and divid-ing that contact of *at least two* (lips) which keeps woman in touch with herself, but without any possibility of distinguishing what is touching from what is touched. . . . If woman takes pleasure pre-cisely from this incompleteness of form which allows her organ to touch itself over and over again, indefinitely, by itself, that pleasure is denied by a civilization that privileges phallomorphism." A sec-ond passage from "When Our Lips Speak Together" (1977) evokes the production of pleasure as knowledge to be articulated and transmitted by lesbian lovers: "I love you: our two lips cannot separate to let just *one* word pass. A single word would say 'you,' or 'me.' Or 'equals'; she who loves, she who is loved. Closed and open, neither ever excluding the other, they say they both love each other. . . . Aren't my hands, my eyes, my mouth, my lips, my body enough for you? Isn't what they are saying to you sufficient? . . . Together . . . we feel the same things at the same time. If we don't invent a language, if we don't find our body's language, it will have too few gestures to accompany our story. We shall . . . leave our desires unexpressed, unrealized" (Irigaray 26, 208, 214).

Remarkable enough as a utopian figuration on the erotic plane, Donne's Sapho's image of the paradisal plenitude of a female body refusing to "Admit the tillage of a harsh rough man" also carries utopian connotations onto an economic plane. Emotively this image works to ballast the connotations of feminine all-sufficiency that proliferate later in the poem: "All, all that Nature yields, or Art can adde," "thee, my *halfe*, my *all*, my *more*," "*Envy*'in all *women*, and in all *men*, *love*" (ll. 44, 58, 62). But the image also encapsulates a logical conversion of erotics into economics, by one of the inside-out turns of reasoning patterns that are so omnipresent in Donne's poetry. Here the reasoning pattern that Donne subverts is the prop to the phallicism that has traditionally secured the dependence and repression of females in patriarchal Western societies. Patriarchy argues thus: he who holds property and purse strings also effectively possesses the woman's body, whether sexually or by power of disposition. The woman with the body has to eat and be housed and clothed; she also has to find her social place in some fashion, by some means. Historically in all these matters she has been at the disposition of males.[35] Donne's Sapho, however, argues this way: the inhabitant of the woman's body effectively holds all that endows property and purse strings with their value and power to sustain life. "Thy body is a naturall *Paradise*, / . . . / Nor needs *perfection*; why shouldst thou than/ Admit the tillage of a . . . man?" she asks.

Page du Bois (26-27) has recently traced the earliest verbalization of the image of the paradisal female earth-body, unploughed and dewy, fecundating by its own energies in the moonlight, to one of Sappho's fragmentary sapphics addressed to Atthis. No Renaissance reader could have known this poem, however, for it was discovered at the end of the nineteenth century among the Oxyrhynchus papyrii in a hand of the second century A.D.[36] I can offer to account for Donne's argument-encapsulating image of the economically self-sustaining female body only in the way that I have: by tracing the effect of local inversions he performs on the traditional hierarchical construction of sexual difference. The effect is to free the other who has always been there — the female, actualized as Sapho — so that she can speak and thus figure as other than silence, preempted, yet tacitly essential to the male-dominant system. The effort of working such inversions within a resistant cultural context, however, is severe enough to leave discernible signs of strain within Donne's text. These recall the reader to a sense of its circumstances and date. There is, first, a lack of temporal or spatial concreteness in the envisaged final situation of the two lesbian lovers. Significantly, no present exists for Sapho's and Philaenis's perfect mutuality; all hangs in suspension between Sapho's memories of the past and anticipations of the future. Next, the imaging of Philaenis's "mighty,'amazing beauty" as the object of female envy and male love (ll. 61-62) recalls the conventional Petrarchan love-worship accorded the pair of heterosexual lovers in Donne's "The Canonization." This intertextual echo seems to relegate the pair of lesbian lovers to an indistinct locale as marginalized (albeit idolized) curiosities for a larger heterosexual world.

Yet the fact that economic aspects of lesbianism are addressed at all remains for me a compelling index to the rigor and seriousness of Donne's "what if" in "Sapho to Philaenis" — the attempt to imagine friendship and marriage as a conjoint relation of equality. But eventual complications in the elliptical handling of these economic aspects clash with the assured, even triumphant handling of the erotics. Sapho takes an enthymemic argument through a typical Donnean course in lines 58-64. In outline this argument holds that, once the lovers reunite and become "all" and "more" than all to each other, (1) Philaenis's "mighty,'amazing beauty" will be eternally self-sustaining ("So may thy cheekes red outweare scarlet dye, / And their white, whiteness of the *Galaxy*"); (2) her beauty will also become everyone's locus of erotic value ("So may thy mighty,'amazing beauty move / *Envy*'in all *women*, and in all *men*, *love*''), thus presumably legitimating the lesbian lovers' cohabitation as a social arrangement; and (3) that Sapho and Philaenis will be physically sustained as well by this secured and legitimated cohabitation (''And so be *change*, and *sicknesse*, farre from thee, / As thou by comming neere, keep'st them from me''). What typifies Donne in this poetic argument is the extension of a notion from one semantic field into another field with the specious implication that meaning has been preserved. The key notions here are greatness and sustenance. By the lines' implicit logic, what sustains great beauty must be great sustenance — great enough to sustain not only Philaenis but also the whole society's erotic economy, and Sapho too, and for always. My flat paraphrase voids the wit but exposes the unstable meanings of the synonyms for greatness (''my *all*, my *more*,'' ''mighty,'amazing,'' ''farre from'' in ll. 58, 61, 64) and for sustenance (''outweare,'' ''keep'' in ll. 59, 64). Sapphism as carried here to the economic plane thus appears to end in sophism. As the poem ends, common sense nags at the heels of the superbly hyperbolic logic. Who could draw life-sustenance from enduring beauty? What beauty, when it comes to that, is enduring? Thus, if we do print ''Sapho to Philaenis'' among Donne's works as a heroical epistle, using Grierson's heading, we might be advised to place it at no great distance from the youthful Donne's paradoxes as well. Nonetheless, when all necessary concessions are made, the power of a poetic representation that innovates by configuring self-sufficiency — economic as well as erotic — for a pair of lesbian lovers remains. Here Donne put in play intimations of experiential alternatives that we twentieth-century readers have only lately come to see actualized in any significant degree. The envisioning and defense that Donne offers of what had, perhaps, never been but might somehow, sometime be, projects the lesbianism of ''Sapho to Philaenis'' into a fully utopian moment for human possibility.

## NOTES

1. Roma Gill's prescient study broached some key features of later feminist critiques of Donne's poetry.

2. Fish's charge was first aired in a presentation at the Modern Language Association convention in 1987.

3. All this while, Donne has not lacked defenders on circumstantial or *ad*

*hominem* grounds. Empson remains the earliest and the most notable, while Flynn and Patterson stand out among more recent critics.

4. Cutting more deeply, Howard Felperin converts an irony to a problematics while considering how paradigm shifts have failed to diminish (or otherwise mitigate) hegemonic pretensions in the methodologies and practices that are now most favored in literary and cultural criticism.

5. Besides the foregoing references, see Carey, Goldberg (chapter 5), Marotti, and Novarr.

6. Two exceptions to date are essays by James Holstun and Elizabeth Harvey. Holstun sensitively complicates a reading of Donne's "Sapho to Philaenis" before aligning with the negative camp of critics of Donne's love poetry. He sums up his position as follows: "Though 'Sapho to Philaenis' does consider lesbian eroticism with considerable imaginative sympathy, it finally masters this eroticism by subordinating it to a patriarchal scheme of nature, history, and language"(838). Harvey likewise has a measure of sympathy for Donne's treatment of female authorship and female homoerotics, but she sees the relation of poet to subject in "Sapho to Philaenis" as an Ovidian battle of the sexes fought out on the male poet's own terrain. Harvey charges Donne with overmastering Sapho, assimilating her person to his persona and locking her in solipsism so as to explore and possess her through "a process . . . mediated both by ventriloquism and by voyeurism" (126). My reading locates Donne's "considerable imaginative sympathy" within a no less "patriarchal scheme" than Holstun and Harvey discover, but I reach diametrically opposed findings with respect to the erotic fiction that develops and reigns within "Sapho to Philaenis."

7. DeJean's book reworks and extends her "Fictions of Sappho," *Critical Inquiry* 13.4 (1987): 787-805, while also taking basic issue with a psychosocial explanation of the origins of female authorship first broached by Lipking.

8. This generalization is somewhat controversial. I would defend it on two grounds. (1) Although a number of scholars have expressed the view that Ovid was well versed in Sappho's poetry, only three vocabulary items in the 220 lines of Ovid's "Sappho Phaonis" are generally agreed to trace to her usage; see Jacobson, 281 n. (2) In ll. 3-4 of Ovid's poem, his Sappho says that she is inscribing her name into the lines she is writing, since she is so distracted that her verse cannot be recognized as hers. Here, as I read, Ovid puts in his Sappho's mouth a declaration of his freedom in handling her poetic corpus (Ovid 180).

9. "Sapho to Philaenis," ll. 24-25, in Shawcross. I reproduce the entire poem from this edition as an appendix. All further citations are from Shawcross's edition and appear as parenthecized line references in my text.

10. This psychological dynamic staged by Donne's Sapho has obvious affinities with the "what if" of the valediction poems, as sketched above, but just as obviously overgoes their thematic confines by envisioning the reunion beyond present-tense separation.

11. For relevant particulars and discussion, see Gardner xlvi, lxvii-lxxi, 119, 158, 160-61, 177, 212, 216, 218, 223.

12. See McEachern for a thoughtful statement of how source study can contribute to current critical and historical agendas.

13. See Heywood, sig. A4ᵛ (on his method of epitome and condensation, citing Aelian and Valerius Maximus as his classical antecedents), and 394-95 (for accounts of Sappho and Philaenis that accord in numerous specifics with Giraldi's).

14. Aelian's and Plato's pronouncements are collected in the Sappho doxography that precedes the texts of her poems and fragments in Edmonds, *Lyra Graeca* (1:147, 163).

15. Both editions bear the title *Anakreontos Tēiou Melē / Anacreontis Teii Odae;* Sappho's fragments are found in the first (Paris: Henricus Stephanus, 1554) on 62-63, 84, and in the second (Paris: Robertus Stephanus, 1556) on 50-52, 67-69.

16. The immediate contexts in which Dionysius, "Longinus," and Plutarch quote Sappho's famous stanzas are conveniently reproduced by Edmonds (1:183, 185-87, 169). Other sixteenth-century editions of Sappho are noted by DeJean (37). To her account, which is confined to France, should be added the superbly compendious, Greek-only gathering of Sappho's poetic remains in Fulvio Orsini's *Carmina novem illustrium feminarum* (7-17). For access to this volume I am grateful to Betsy Karlberg and Bret Baker of the rare book collection of the University of Illinois Library, Urbana.

17. I translate from the Greek text in Edmonds 1:186.

18. See *The Greek Anthology* 2:186-87, 244-47. Guss offers evidence of Donne's acqaintance with this compilation in "Donne and the Greek Anthology" (57-58).

19. Martial, *Epigrams* 1:468-71, with, however, Italian translations in the place of the expected English. English translations of the two epigrams are supplied in *Martial's Epigrams in Fifteen Books, Completely . . . Translated for the First Time,* an anonymously printed and circulated edition that identifies itself only by a date of 1921.

20. If Donne is not the originator of this plot, fuller research into humanist commentary will doubtless settle just how, when, and where Sappho and Philaenis came to be linked as lovers. Harriette Andreadis of Texas A & M University, in "Sappho in Early Modern England: A Study in Sexual Reputation" (unpublished paper), records a post-Donnean link in medical discourse. She cites (9) this remark regarding *"Confricatrices* Rubsters" from the Swedish anatomist, Thomas Bartholin, who in 1653 published a revised text of his father's 1633 Latin anatomy of the human body, in an English translation: "Which lascivious Practice is said to have been invented by Philaenis, and Sappho, the Greek Poetress, is reported to have practised the same." Every item here traces to the doxographic assemblages represented in my discussion by the works of Politian and Giraldi.

21. For dates approximating the earliness of Donne's (1572-1631), Faderman's only exhibit in the category of epigram is "Tribades seu Lesbia" by Frañois Mainard (1582-1646), printed in Perceau, *Malherbe et ses escholiers* 183. Similarly, for this date, there is only one homoerotically explicit passage involv-

ing women in a prose romance, the sophisticates at the court of Henri II who figure in the Premier Discours of *Les Dames Galantes* by Pierre de Bourdeille, Seigneur de Brantôme (1540-1614), first printed in 1665. Brantôme's typical array of classical references includes "Sapho de Lesbos . . . [et] son grand amy Faon" (Brantôme 123).

22. Unlike Faderman 32, 35, and Holstun 835-36, I define lesbian as cognizant female homoerotics and thus omit consideration of a convention that has some currency in Renaissance prose romances and dramas: the situation itself of Ovidian origin—the story of Iphis and Ianthe in bk. 9 of the *Metamorphoses*—where a woman falls in love with another woman who is disguised as a man. Constance Jordan 223-28 has recently suggested that such sexually ambiguous configurations might be read as evidence of a viable period concept of androgyny.

23. The quotations are, respectively, from "The Forrest," no. 10, and "The Under-wood," no. 49, in Jonson 8:107, 22. I thank Claude Summers for the latter reference. Jonson's editors note of the former, "Must I sing?," that the lines were first printed among the "Diverse Poetical Essaies" appended to Robert Chester's *Love's Martyr* (1601).

24. Item no. 49, with bracketed title "An Address of Friendship," in *The Maitland Quarto Ms.* 160-62.

25. There is an intriguing possibility that the Donne Variorum edition, currently in press with a first volume, may compel relocation of this poem in the chronology of Donne's writings. Gary Stringer has informed me (personal communication) that astronomical terms like "galaxy" do not appear in Donne's writings before 1613, unless, of course, l. 60 of "Sapho to Philaenis" is a rule-breaking counter-instance.

26. Smith's "The Metaphysic of Love" and Guss's *John Donne, Petrarchist* continue useful as accounts of Donne's Petrarchanism.

27. Sir Richard Baker, *Chronicle of the Kings of England,* 1st ed. (1643), Pt. 2:156, quoted in Bald 72.

28. See Dover's account, 42-68, 81-109, of the culturally formalized, unequal roles of *erastēs* (lover and superior) and *erōmenos* (beloved and subordinate).

29. Augustine's phrase, "dimidium animae suae" (*Confessions,* bk. 4, chapter 6) is itself an allusion to Horace, Odes, bk. 1, no. 3, l. 8.).

30. Mills 7-12 discusses Aristotle and Cicero as influential antecedents for the Renaissance stress on friendship as an equality relation.

31. References at this point to Plato's Academy, Achilles and Patroclus, Harmodius and Aristogeiton make it clear that Montaigne is repudiating male homosexuality—and specifically, perhaps, pederasty as a relation between unequals.

32. A comparable and, I think, a quite likely item of knowledge on Donne's part is a passage from (pseudo-)Lucian's *Erotics,* a work mentioned in Politian's lectures on *Heroides* 15. In this dialogue a defender of heterosexual love argues against a proponent of male homosexual love. The former heaps disapproval on the figure of the pederast, who may even be found making "attempts on a boy of twenty": "Then . . . the chins that once were soft are rough and covered with bristles, and the well-developed thighs are as it were sullied with hairs. . . . But

ever does her attractive skin give radiance to every part of a woman and . . . the rest of her person has not a hair growing on it and shines more pellucidly than amber, to quote the proverb" *(Lucian* 8:191). Lucian was one of the favorite authors of the Renaissance. If Donne did work off this Lucianic passage, he performed a characteristically bold and witty maneuver. Ignoring its homophobia entirely, he converted its attack on male homosexuality into a defense of female homosexuality—surely a consequence unintended by this speaker and by the author of the dialogue.

33. A contemporary classical scholar offers similar perceptions based on a considerably fuller acquaintance with Sappho's poetic remains than was available to Donne: "In contrast with the male poets [contemporary with her], Sappho imagines that either woman might initiate the relationship, for the two women must be equals, each understanding the other from insight into herself" (Stiger 53).

34. For references ranging from antiquity to (and beyond) the sixteenth century, see the index entry "Clitoris" in Laqueur 207.

35. Important literature on this important issue is vast. Major discussions include Part 2 of de Beauvoir's *The Second Sex*; Kathleen Gough, "The Origin of the Family," and Gayle Rubin, "The Traffic in Women: Notes on the 'Political Economy' of Sex," both in Reiter 51-76, 157-210; Roisin McDonough and Rachel Harrison, "Patriarchy and Relations of Production," and Annette Kuhn, "Structures of Patriarchy and Capital in the Family," both in Kuhn and Wolpe 11-41, 42-57; and MacKinnon 3-80.

36. For the Greek of Sappho's fragment and an English translation, see Edmonds, 1: 246-47.

## REFERENCES

Arber, Edward, Ed. *A Harmony of Lord Bacon's Essays.* Birmingham: English Reprints, 1871.

Bald, R. C. *John Donne: A Life.* New York: Oxford UP, 1970.

Boswell, John. *Christianity, Social Tolerance, and Homosexuality.* Chicago: U of Chicago P, 1980.

Brantôme, Pierre de Bourdeille, seigneur de. *Les Dames Galantes.* Ed. Maurice Rat. Paris: Garnier, 1960; reprint, 1965.

Bueler, Lois E. "The Failure of Sophistry in Donne's "Elegy VII." *Studies in English Literature* 25.1 (1985): 69-85.

Bullough, Vern. *Sexual Variance in Society and History.* Chicago: U of Chicago P, 1975.

Carey, John. *John Donne: Life, Mind and Art.* New York: Oxford University Press, 1981.

de Beauvoir, Simone. *Le deuxiéme sexe.* 2 vols. Paris: Gallimard, 1949. Abridged Eng. trans. by H. M. Parshley as *The Second Sex.* New York: Alfred A. Knopf, 1952.

DeJean, Joan. *Fictions of Sappho. 1546-1937.* Chicago: U of Chicago P, 1989.

Dover, K. J. *Greek Homosexuality.* Cambridge, Mass.: Harvard UP, 1977.

Drayton, Michael. *Works of Michael Drayton.* 5 vols. Ed. J. William Hebel. Oxford: Clarendon P, 1931-41.

du Bois, Page. *Sowing the Body: Psychoanalysis and Ancient Representations of Women.* Chicago: U of Chicago P, 1988.

Edmonds, J. E., Ed. *Lyra Graeca, Being the Remains of All the Greek Lyric Poets.* 2 vols. Loeb Classical Library. London: William Heinemann / Cambridge, Mass.: Harvard UP, 1922.

Empson, William. " 'There Is No Penance Due to Innocence' — An Exchange on Donne." *New York Review of Books* 29.3 (March 4, 1982): 42-50.

Faderman, Lillian. *Surpassing the Love of Men: Romantic Friendship and Love Between Women from the Renaissance to the Present.* New York: William Morrow, 1981.

Felperin, Howard. "Canonical Texts and Non-Canonical Interpretations: The Neohistoricist Reading of Donne." *Southern Review* (Australia) 18.3 (1985): 235-50.

Fish, Stanley. "Masculine Persuasive Force: Donne and Verbal Power." *Soliciting Interpretation.* Ed. Elizabeth D. Harvey and Katherine Eisaman Mu. Chicago: U of Chicago P, 1990. 223-52.

Flynn, Dennis. "Donne the Survivor." *The Eagle and the Dove: Reassessing John Donne.* Ed. Claude J. Summers and Ted-Larry Pebworth. Columbia: U of Missouri P, 1986. 15-74.

Foster, Jeanette H. *Sex Variant Women in Literature.* New York: Vantage Books, 1956; reprint Baltimore: Diana Press, 1975.

Foucault, Michel. *La Volonté de savoir.* Paris: Gallimard, 1976. English translation by Robert Hurley as *The History of Sexuality — Volume I: An Introduction.* New York: Vintage Books, 1980.

Gardner, Helen, Ed. *The Elegies and The Songs and Sonnets.* By John Donne. Oxford: Clarendon P, 1965.

Gill, Roma. *"Musa Iocosa Mea:* Thoughts on the *Elegies." John Donne: Essays in Celebration.* Ed. A. J. Smith. London: Methuen, 1972. 47-72.

Giraldi, Lelio [Lelius Gregorius Gyraldus]. *Poetarum historia, graecorum et latinorum.* 1st ed., 1545. Vol.2 of *Opera omnia.* 2 vols. Leyden: Hack, Boutesteyn, Vivie, Vander Aa, & Luchtmans, 1696.

Goldberg, Jonathan. *James I and the Politics of Literature.* Baltimore: Johns Hopkins UP, 1983.

Goodich, Michael. "Sodomy in Ecclesiastical Law and Theory." *Journal of Homosexuality* 1 (1976): 427-34.

*The Greek Anthology.* Ed. and trans. W. R. Paton. 5 vols. Loeb Classical Library. London: William Heinemann / Cambridge, Mass.: Harvard UP, 1916-20.

Greene, Thomas A. "The Flexibility of the Self in Renaissance Literature." *The Disciplines of Criticism: Essays in Literary Theory, Interpretation and History.* Ed. Peter Demetz, Thomas Greene, and Lowry Nelson, Jr. New Haven: Yale UP, 1968. 241-64.

Grierson, Herbert J. C., Ed. *The Poems of John Donne.* 2 vols. Oxford: Clarendon P, 1912.

Guss, Donald L. "Donne and the Greek Anthology." *Notes & Queries,* New Series, 10 (1963): 57-58.

_____. *John Donne, Petrarchist.* Detroit: Wayne State UP, 1966.

Harvey, Elizabeth D. "Ventriloquizing Sappho: Ovid, Donne, and the Erotics of the Feminine Voice." *Criticism* 31.2 (1989): 115-38.

Heywood, Thomas. *Gunaikeion: or, Nine Bookes of Various History concerninge Women: Inscribed by yᵉ names of yᵉ nine Muses.* London: Adam Islip, 1624.

Holstun, James. "'Will You Rent Our Ancient Love Asunder?': Lesbian Elegy in Donne, Marvell, and Milton." *ELH: A Journal of English Literary History* 54 (1987): 835-67.

Irigaray, Luce. *Ce Sexe qui n'en est pas un.* Paris: Minuit, 1977. English translation by Catherine Porter and Carolyn Burke as *This Sex Which Is Not One.* Ithaca: Cornell UP, 1985.

Jacobson, Howard. *Ovid's Heroides.* Princeton: Princeton UP, 1974.

Jonson, Ben. *Poems and Prose Works.* vol. 8 of *Ben Jonson.* Ed. C. H. Herford, Percy and Evelyn Simpson. 11 vols. Oxford: Clarendon P, 1925-52.

Jordan, Constance. *Renaissance Feminism: Literary Texts and Political Models.* Ithaca: Cornell UP, 1990.

Kauffman, Linda S. *Discourses of Desire: Gender, Genre, and Epistolary Fictions.* Ithaca: Cornell UP, 1986.

Kerrigan, William. "What Was Donne Doing?" *South Central Review* 4.1(1986): 2-15.

Kofman, Sarah. "The Narcissistic Woman: Freud and Girard," *Diacritics* 10 (1980), 36-45.

Kuhn, Annette, and Ann Marie Wolpe, Ed. *Feminism and Materialism: Women and Modes of Production.* London: Rutledge and Kegan Paul, 1978.

Laqueur, Thomas. *Making Sex: Body and Gender from the Greeks to Freud.* Cambridge, Mass.: Harvard UP, 1990.

Lipking, Lawrence. *Abandoned Women and Poetic Tradition.* Chicago: U of Chicago P, 1988.

*Lucian.* Ed. and trans. M. D. Macleod. 10 vols. Loeb Classical Library. London: William Heinemann / Cambridge, Mass.: Harvard UP, 1967.

Lyly, John. "Sapho and Phao." *Complete Works of John Lyly.* Ed. R. Warwick Bond. 3 vols. Oxford: Clarendon P, 1902; reprint, 1967. 2: 396-415.

MacKinnon, Catharine A. *Toward a Feminist Theory of the State.* Cambridge, Mass.: Harvard UP, 1989.

*The Maitland Quarto Manuscript.* Ed. W. A. Craigie. Publications of the Scottish Text Society, New Series, No. 9. Edinburgh, 1920.

Marotti, Arthur. "John Donne and the Rewards of Patronage." *Patronage in the Renaissance.* Ed. Guy Fitch Lytle and Stephen Orgel. Princeton: Princeton UP, 1981. 207-33.

_____. *John Donne, Coterie Poet.* Madison: U of Wisconsin P, 1986.

Martial [M. Valerius Martialis]. *Epigrams.* Ed. and trans. W. R. Paton. 2 vols.

Loeb Classical Library. London: William Heinemann / Cambridge, Mass.: Harvard UP, 1919.

McEachern, Claire. "Fathering Herself: A Source Study of Shakespeare's Feminism." *Shakespeare Quarterly* 39.3 (1988): 269-90.

Mills, Laurens J. *One Soul in Bodies Twain: Friendship in Tudor Literature and Stuart Drama.* Bloomington, Ind.: Principia P, 1937.

Montaigne, Michel de. *The Essayes of Montaigne: John Florio's [1603] Translation.* Ed. J. I. M. Stewart. New York: Modern Library, 1933.

Morillon, Guy. *P. Ovidii Nasonis Heroidum Epistolae . . . Guidonis Morilloni argumenta.* London: R. F[ield] and John Harrison, 1594.

Mueller, Janel M. "'This Dialogue of One': A Feminist Reading of Donne's 'Extasie'," *Association of Departments of English Bulletin* 81(1985): 39-42.

Novarr, David. *The Disinterred Muse: Donne's Texts and Contexts.* Ithaca: Cornell UP, 1980.

Orsini, Fulvio [Fulvius Orsinus]. *Carmina novem illustrium feminarum.* Antwerp: Christophe Plantin, 1568.

Ovid [P. Ovidius Naso]. *Heroides and Amores.* Ed. and trans. Grant Showerman. Loeb Classical Library. London: William Heinemann / Cambridge, MA: Harvard UP, 1925.

Patterson, Annabel. "Misinterpretable Donne: The Testimony of the Letters." *John Donne Journal* 1.1 (1982): 39-53.

Perceau, Louis, Ed. *Francois Malherbe et ses escholiers.* Vol. 3 of *Le Cabinet secret du Parnasse.* Paris: Au Cabinet du Livre, 1932.

———. Ed. *Pierre de Ronsard et la Pleiade.* Vol. 1 of *Le Cabinet secret du Parnasse.* Paris: Au Cabinet du Livre, 1928.

Poliziano, Angelo [Politian]. *Commento inedito all'Epistola Ovidiano di Saffo a Faone.* Ed. Elisabetta Lazzeri. Florence: Sansoni, 1971.

Reiter, Rayna R., Ed. *Toward an Anthropology of Women.* New York and London: Monthly Review P, 1975.

Ricks, Christopher. "Donne after Love." *Literature and the Body: Essays on Populations and Persons.* Ed. Elaine Scarry. Selected Papers from the English Institute, New Series, No. 12. Baltimore: Johns Hopkins UP, 1988. 33-69.

Smith, A. J. "The Metaphysic of Love." *Review of English Studies,* New Series, 9 (1966): 362-75.

Stiger, Eva Stehle. "Sappho's Private World." *Women's Studies* 8 (1981): 47-63.

Turberville, George. "Sappho to Phaon." *The Heroycall Epistles of the learned Poet Publius Ovidius Naso, In English Verse.* London: Henry Denham, 1570. Sigs. Piir-Qiiir.

Waller, A. E., Ed. *Two Noble Kinsmen.* In Arnold Glover and A. E. Waller, Ed. *Works of Francis Beaumont and John Fletcher.* 10 vols. Cambridge: Cambridge UP, 1905-12. 9: 290-377.

Wittig, Monique. *Le Corps lesbien.* Paris: Minuit, 1973. English translation by David Le Vay as *The Lesbian Body.* New York: William Morrow, 1975.

## APPENDIX

The following text of "Sapho to Philaenis" is that of John T. Shawcross in his *Complete Poetry of John Donne*. Three modern scholarly editions—Grierson's, Shawcross's, and Patrides's—retain the spelling, punctuation, and italics of the first (1633) edition of Donne's poems in printing this text. Across these three editions "Sapho to Philaenis" reads almost identically; all variants are non-substantive. The total comprises *are* for *art* (Patrides, ll. 15, 21), omitted apostrophes for marking elisions (Grierson and Patrides, l. 25; Grierson, l. 61), and an omitted comma (Patrides, l. 16, following *as*).

Where is that holy fire, which *Verse* is said
    To have? is that inchanting force decai'd?
*Verse* that drawes *Natures* workes, from *Natures* law,
    Thee, her best worke, to her worke cannot draw.
Have my teares quench'd my old *Poetique* fire;       5
    Why quench'd they not as well, that of *desire?*
Thoughts, my mindes creatures, often are with thee,
    But I, their maker, want their libertie.
Onely thine image, in my heart, doth sit,
    But that is waxe, and fires environ it.       10
My fires have driven, thine have drawne it hence;
    And I am rob'd of *Picture, Heart,* and *Sense.*
Dwells with me still mine irksome *Memory,*
    Which, both to keepe, and lose, grieves equally.
That tells me'how faire thou art: Thou art so faire,    15
    As, *gods,* when *gods* to thee I doe compare,
Are grac'd thereby; And to make blinde men see,
    What things *gods* are, I say they'are like to thee.
For, if we justly call each silly *man*
    A *litle world,* What shall we call thee than?    20
Thou art not soft, and cleare, and strait, and faire,
    As *Down,* as *Stars, Cedars,* and *Lillies* are,
But thy right hand, and cheek, and eye, only
    Are like thy other hand, and cheek, and eye.
Such was my *Phao'* awhile, but shall be never,    25
    As thou, wast, art, and, oh, maist be ever.
Here lovers sweare in their *Idolatrie,*
    That I am such; but *Griefe* discolors me.
And yet I grieve the lesse, least *Griefe* remove

My beauty, and make me'unworthy of thy love.                    30
Plaies some soft boy with thee, oh there wants yet
    A mutuall feeling which should sweeten it.
His chinne, a thorny hairy unevennesse
    Doth threaten, and some daily change possesse.
Thy body is a naturall *Paradise,*                              35
    In whose selfe, unmanur'd, all pleasure lies.
Nor needs *perfection*: why shouldst thou than
    Admit the tillage of a harsh rough man?
Men leave behinde them that which their sin showes,
    And are, as theeves trac'd, which rob when it snowes.    40
But of our dallyance no more signes there are,
    Then *fishes* leave in streames, or *Birds* in aire.
And betweene us all sweetnesse may be had,
    All, all that *Nature* yields, or *Art* can adde.
My two lips, eyes, thighs, differ from thy two,                 45
    But so, as thine from one another doe,
And, oh, no more; the likenesse being such,
    Why should they not alike in all parts touch?
Hand to strange hand, lippe to lippe none denies;
    Why should they brest to brest, or thighs to thighs?     50
Likenesse begets such strange selfe flatterie,
    That touching my selfe, all seemes done to thee.
My selfe I embrace, and mine owne hands I kisse,
    And amorously thanke my selfe for this.
Me, in my glasse, I call thee; But alas,                        55
    When I would kisse, teares dimme mine *eyes,* and *glasse.*
O cure this loving madnesse, and restore
    Me to mee; thee, my *halfe,* my *all,* my *more.*
So may thy cheekes red outweare scarlet dye,
    And their white, whitenesse of the *Galaxy.*              60
So may thy mighty,'amazing beauty move
    Envy'in all *women,* and in all *men, love,*
And so be *change,* and *sicknesse,* farre from thee,
    As thou by comming neere, keep'st them from me.

# Sodomy and Kingcraft in *Urania* and *Antony and Cleopatra*

Ellis Hanson, PhD (cand.)

Princeton University

**SUMMARY.** Despite his description of sodomy as a horrible crime that a king is "bound in conscience neuer to forgiue," James I pursued the affections of a string of young and handsome "favourites" on whom he lavished gifts, titles, and power. Relying on the evidence of the King's own letters and frank comments from his Puritan critics, most historians assume that his relations with some of these men were sexual. The King's friendship with Robert Carr (who was later made Earl of Somerset), coupled with his estrangement from Queen Anne, may have been an inspiration for at least two literary accounts of kingship confounded by sex: Lady Mary Wroth's *Urania* (1621) and Shakespeare's *Antony and Cleopatra* (1608). Wroth describes a duke who is made politically vulnerable by his love for a young man that leaves him "issue-les." The rise and fall of this disloyal companion closely resembles that of Somerset and would seem to indicate Wroth's belief that the King's relationship with the Earl was sexual. *Antony and Cleopatra* is in many ways a reflection of Jacobean court extravagance and decadence. Cleopatra, despite her sex, seems to fill the same role in political and sexual scandal as did Somerset; and Antony's vacillation between pleasure and duty recalls a certain Renaissance discourse on sodomy and "kingcraft."

So is there some horrible crimes that yee are bound in conscience neuer to forgiue: such as Witch-craft, willful murther, Incest, (especially within the degrees of Consanguinitie) Sodomie, poisoning, and false coine.

James I, *Basilikon Doron* (20)

---

Ellis Hanson is a doctoral candidate in English at Princeton University. Correspondence may be addressed to the author at the English Department, 22 McCosh Hall, Princeton University, Princeton, NJ 08540.

Of the possible union of England and Scotland, King James I said, "I hope, therefore, that no man will be so unreasonable as to think that I, that am a Christian King under the Gospel, should be a polygamist and husband to two wives; that I, being the head, should have a divided and monstrous body" (Bingham, *James I* 49). Such metaphors are ironic coming from a king whose queen, Anne of Denmark, was deposed by a string of male "favourites" on whom he publicly lavished affection in a manner not generally associated at the time with the Gospel (except, of course, by Marlowe). My intention here is to examine how "sodomy" and what has come to be seen as James's own divided and monstrous body became an issue in what he called "kingcraft." Furthermore, through a discussion of two literary texts, Lady Mary Wroth's *Urania* and Shakespeare's *Antony and Cleopatra,* both of which seem to refer to James's relationship with Robert Carr, I hope to come to a clearer understanding of the relationship of sodomy to the Jacobean conception of monarchy.

Contemporary accounts, some reliable and others less so, give the impression that, throughout his life, James demonstrated a passionate preference for handsome young men. The first of his favorites arrived in Scotland when James was thirteen: he was Esmé Stuart, a much older cousin, who came from France to further the interests of Mary, Queen of Scots, then in exile. His allegiance shifted to the young King, who demonstrated his affection publicly and enthusiastically, and the two probably became lovers. Esmé Stuart attained the rank of Duke of Lennox before he was driven from the country by the King's enemies, and he died soon thereafter in France. After his accession to the English throne, James took a similar interest in James Hay, whom he made Viscount Doncaster and then Earl of Carlisle, and Philip Herbert, whom he made Earl of Montgomery.

At the time *Antony and Cleopatra* appeared in the Stationers' Register in 1608, James was paying off Philip Herbert's considerable debts and had already engineered the swift rise of a former page, Robert Carr, who soon became Viscount Rochester and later Earl of Somerset. Judging from the degree of affection that James demonstrated toward Carr, many historians assume that their friendship was sexual. Carr was followed by George Villiers, who quickly became the Duke of Buckingham and whom James referred to as his "wife and child." Meanwhile, throughout her tenure as Queen of England, Anne's marriage was "one of an appearance of affection duly maintained by the King, punctuated by clashes and decisions to dwell apart as much as they decently could" (Akrigg, *Pageant* 265).[1] Apart from her role in the provision of heirs, Anne was cordially ignored.

After even so haphazard a sketch as the above, I find surprising James's prohibition against sodomy in *Basilikon Doron*. What do we make of a king who issues so apparently unequivocal a dictum, even though it would censure as unforgivable many of his own sexual practices since the age of thirteen? Caroline Bingham writes that the King, being rather pedantic, probably "convinced himself that other homosexual acts were not seriously blameworthy" (*James I* 80). This argument not only makes presumptions about what James did or did not do in private, but also lends to the word *sodomy* a precision of meaning that it never had. We would have to take into account English Renaissance notions of sodomy in relation to witchcraft and papism; moreover, we could follow the lead of Alan Bray in viewing Renaissance sodomy not as a sexuality in the modern sense but as a sign of debauchery, a temptation to everyone, a possibility for erotic chaos within a strict patriarchal structure.

James was clearly not in league with witches or popes, though he cultivated an interest in both; nor would he have deemed himself disruptive. Perhaps James simply did not recognize his behavior as "sodomy." A discrepancy is apparent between Renaissance English society's "extreme hostility to homosexuality which one comes across when homosexuality was being referred to in the abstract and its reluctance to recognise it in most concrete situations" (Bray, *Renaissance* 77). How could the King, whose virtues were exaggerated for him daily by his own sycophants, come to see himself as a disruption in the same natural order that was to view him as father, as head to the English and Scottish bodies? Alan Bray leaves us with the impression that any understanding of same-sex desire was so vague, panicked, and metaphysical, it is a wonder anyone ever recognized it at all. Indeed, the King fondled men with an unselfconsciousness unheard of in our own time: clearly, a Roman thought rarely struck him.

At the same time, however, I see in contemporary accounts of the King an anxiety over his erotic doubleness, the juxtaposition of masculinity and effeminacy, kingcraft and sodomy, in his own person. One of the more subtle and sympathetic of these depictions is a fictionalized account of Robert Carr's career in Wroth's romance, *Urania,* published in 1621. Although by that year Wroth had ceased to be a central figure at Court and was highly critical of Court life, she was during Carr's rise an intimate of Queen Anne, while her husband, Sir Robert Wroth, was a hunting companion of the King. She performed in sumptuous Court entertainments, such as *The Masque of Blackness* and *The Masque of Beauty.* She was a niece to Sir Philip Sidney and the Countess of Pembroke, and therefore also a cousin to the King's favorite, Philip Herbert. Wroth inscribed her *Urania* to Philip Herbert's wife, the Countess of Montgomery, and she had two illegitimate children from an adulterous and incestuous relationship with Herbert's brother William. In short, Wroth had an intimate acquaintance with the King's personal affairs and was especially sensitive, as both her life and her long romance suggest, to the trials of love and Court gossip.[2]

In a brief narrative of an unnamed Duke, his favorite, and the King of Morea, Wroth gives a veiled account of James's relationship with Carr. The Duke arrives home with a virtuous wife, but notes "yet so much was I besotted on a young man, whom I had unfortunately chosen for my companion, as at last all delights & pastimes were to me tedious and lothsome, if not liking, or begun by him." Furthermore, he adds, "Long time this continued, which continuance made me issue-les, wherefore I made him my heire, giving him all the present honor I could in my own power, or by the fauor of the king (who euer grac'd me much) procure him" (28). Wroth is describing a sexual relationship between the Duke and an undeserving favorite who keeps him from his wife. Although King James had fathered three heirs by the time he met Carr, he had ceased conjugal relations with Anne. Moreover, the considerable attention directed at Carr inspired much envy, and many felt that Carr, as a former page (and not a very bright one at that), did not deserve such favor.

Same-sex friendships in *Urania* are almost always an escape from the miseries of marriage and the inconstancy of love, but this narrative is an exception. The favorite betrays the Duke in a vicious intrigue in which he usurps the Duke's place. Like Carr and Anne, the favorite and the wife quarrel. Even after the betrayal, the Duke continues to demonstrate his affection for the young man: "Though hee had chang'd gratefulnesse to the contrary, and loue to hate, yet my affection could not so much alter it selfe as to hate where once so earnestly I affected" (27). These lines echo the sentiments of James who, even after Carr had begun to despise him and rail at him, maintained toward his favorite a widely recognized and curiously ineradicable affection: "God is my judge my love hath been infinite towards you; and only the strength of my affection towards you hath made me bear with these things in you and bridle my passions to the uttermost of my ability" (*Letters* 339).

Carr finally fell from James's favor in 1615, when he was found guilty along with his wife, the Countess of Essex, in the poisoning of Sir Thomas Overbury. Though condemned to die, they were granted pardons by the King and held in the Tower until January 1622. When Wroth published *Urania,* therefore, Carr was still in the Tower, no doubt fuming with the same sort of rage the King ascribed to him in his letters, those "strange streams of unquietness, passion, fury, and insolent pride" (336). In this context, it is ironic to see how the King of Morea intervenes on behalf of the Duke, degrading the favorite and "committing him to a strong Tower, whereinto he was walled vp, meate giuen him in at the windowe, and there to ende his dayes: which were not long, pride swelling him so with scorne of his fall, as he burst and dyed" (30).

Wroth's narrative is interesting not only for its suggestion of a sexual relationship between James and Carr, but also for the intervention of a third man, the King of Morea, who imprisons the favorite. It is as though Wroth thought it necessary to split the figure of King James in two: one a harmless but ineffectual sodomite "bewitch'd" by a young man, the other a manly King who disregards the Duke's affections and punishes the evil favorite. The suggestion here is that sodomy is incommensurate with kingcraft. King James embodied a contradiction: he was a symbol of both erotic disruption and patriarchal order. In Wroth's romance, the division perceived in the King's character is made literal.

For a less sympathetic view of this division between sodomy and kingcraft, we could look to the Puritan memoirists, who are proof in themselves that when a sodomite was criticized or actually prosecuted, generally a constellation of ulterior political motives hovered nearby. Many of the Puritan sketches of the King were either written or reprinted as anti-royalist propaganda during the Interregnum, which might explain their viciousness. We have Lucy Hutchinson, for example, fulminating at Papists and describing the change from James to Charles by noting the catamites "who did not abandon their debosheries" but had the decency to "retire into corners to practise them" (127-28). We have Anthony Weldon's notorious sketch of the King that notes his "eyes large, ever rowling after any stranger came in his presence," his weak legs attributable to "some foul play in his youth," his "ever leaning on other mens shoulders" and "fidling about his Codpiece" (165-66), all calculated to fill the reader with a distinctly sexual disgust for the effeminacy of the King. We have also Arthur Wilson, who compares James to Tiberius and writes that "Peace begot Plenty, and Plenty begot Ease and Wantonness, and Ease and Wantonness begot Poetry, and Poetry swelled to that Bulk in his time, that it begot strange Monstrous Satyrs against the King's own Person" (289-90). After the fashion of *Antony and Cleopatra*, peace and extravagance are strung together in a causal relationship with self-destructive, even demonic, sexual deviance in the criticism of a political leader.

Unfortunately, these dubious correlations between sexual politics and Court politics are reaffirmed by modern accounts of King James. Despite the availability of more enlightened perspectives on sex between men, many modern historians insist upon James's "vice" or attempt to locate obscure excuses for his sexual behavior. Such historians sometimes question the biases of the Puritans and yet still rely heavily on Puritan diatribes to describe James and the Court. One rarely hears the evidence of the King's own letters, nor does one see how the King's behavior was often taken as a matter of course at Court. Modern accounts lead me to believe that Puritan indignation toward sodomy, as opposed to the more general Renaissance blindness to it, is far more attractive to modern prejudices about sex and its consequences for the course of history.

One of the earliest interpretations in this century, though by far the least puritanical, belongs to Charles Williams (1934). No doubt still reeling from an acquaintance with Freud's work, Williams waxes poetic in describing James's love for Esmé Stuart as a narcissistic object-choice that confirmed the King's own Stuart character:

> He was the son of Mary of the leopards of France, and now, called by its French mate, the leopard in him began to stir and emerge from its spiritual lair. . . . [James] had been given himself. As he wandered with and talked with the stranger, he beheld in a mirror the image not of the clumsy youth but of the cultured, unscrupulous, and exquisite Majesty of France or Scotland. (31-32)

On the following page, Williams adds: "In an exquisite and thrilling union his submission and his supremacy were combined and flattered. The very man at whose feet he was ready to fall, fell humbly at his own."

Contrast Williams and his romantic daydream with David Mathew (1967) and Helen Georgia Stafford (1940), who would rather not talk about sex at all. Or much worse, Otto J. Scott's (1976) use of illness metaphors and terms like "faggotry" to describe sex between men. Or the scowling of William McElwee (1958), who sees fit to invent painful rebuffs from James's queen and children (who render him "lonely and starved of affection") in order to justify his grotesque and infantile condescension to dote on handsome men. D. Harris Willson (1936) is more sympathetic: it is not the "vice" itself that he finds shocking, so much as "the completeness of the King's surrender to it" (337). Then we have Robert Ashton (1969), who labels James a "pederast" and locates different excuses for James's sexual behavior at different stages of his life, moving from "lonely and deprived infancy in Scotland after the deposition of his mother" to "adolescent hero-worship" to "the need for some sort of family relationship which he was unable to obtain from his own children" (106-07). How convenient to have an alibi for every moment!

G.P.V. Akrigg (1962) is especially adept at the gay "red herring." He asserts that there is no evidence for James's "homosexuality," neglecting the fact that there is more evidence for James's "homosexuality" than for his "heterosexuality" (especially since noblemen tended to marry and father children no matter what their sexual tastes). Akrigg goes on, however, to cite instances of James's behavior that would seem very gay indeed. More recently, Alan Bray (1990) has put forward the provocative, though unlikely, argument that James's "sodomy" is a figment of modern imaginations and the vicious slant that the Puritans gave to his allegedly mundane demonstrations of friendship. And yet we also have Antonia Fraser (1974), fading with ennui as she says one might as well assume the obvious about James, and Caroline Bingham (1979 & 1981) doing just that.

Are these people talking about the same king? Even Bingham gives cause for alarm. Much of her discussion of James and sex appears in a chapter called "The Poisoned Fountain." Of James's love for Carr, she writes, "When the King, who was the cynosure of the nation, forgot his role as arbiter of morality, it was inevitable that his courtiers should feel that what was good enough for him was good enough for them" (*James I* 84). Sodomy takes on a contagious quality here. To follow Bingham's logic in this chapter is to arrive at the familiar Puritan causal relationship between sodomy and the worst excesses in personal dress on the part of the courtiers. We enter a whirlpool of metaphors, where desire gathers bizarre meanings, not to mention saffron ruffs, silk embroidered with seed-pearls, padding and farthingales, exotic plumage, and gowns cut to display the breasts. What more? Inflation of honors, an empty exchequer, a bitter gentry, mutinous guardsmen, and one very grumpy Queen Anne, all from the sex-poisoned fountainhead of James's audacious dalliance with his favorites. Could it be, as others have pointed out, that James's inability to remain solvent and his promotion of a viciously competitive and sycophantic court had less to do with sex than with his own limited understanding of politics and finance?

To return to the Puritans, I find most interesting a comment by Francis Osborne on the King's choice of favorites:

> Now as no other Reason appeared in favour of their choyce but handsomnesse, so the love the King shewed was as amorously convayed as if he had mistaken their Sex, and thought them Ladies. Which I have seen *Somerset* and *Buckingham* labour

to resemble, in the effeminatenesse of their dressings. Though in w— lookes and wanton gestures they exceeded any part of woman kind my Conversation did ever cope withall. Nor was his Love, or what else posterity will please to call it, (who must be the Judges of all that History shall informe) carried on with discretion sufficient to cover a lesse scandalous behaviour; for the Kings kissing them after so lascivious a mode in publick, and upon the Theater as it were of the world, prompted many to imagine some things done in the Tyringhouse, that exceed my expressions no less then they do my experience: And therefore left floting upon the waves of Conjecture, which hath in my hearing tossed them from one side to another. (127-28)

I quote at length not only because of Osborne's disgust with a transgression in gender rules, but also because he describes a key problem of modern historians. He leaves the judgment of the King's sexual behavior to posterity, and yet posterity relies on Osborne's account. The King's desire defies Osborne's expressions as it defies his experience and, like every historian to follow him, he is left "floting upon the waves of Conjecture." Of James's love for men, one account in this century, having ruled out anything "abnormal," claims that "these are subtleties which will continue to puzzle the minds of the most astute scholars in human behavior" (Steeholm and Steeholm 369). James's biographers, now as always, confront a long tradition of bizarre myths, prejudices, and prohibitions, all whirling about the same absent center: sodomy, the gay male unmentionable, what Foucault called "that utterly confused category" (101).

In his descriptions of the Court as "the Theater as it were of the world," Osborne aligns his attack on James with a tradition of Puritan anti-theatrical prejudice, recalling such outrageous diatribes as Prynne's *Histrio-Mastix* and Stubbes's *Anatomie of Abuses*.[3] The Puritan attack on theater was obsessed with effeminacy, lasciviousness, spectacle, and the blurring of gender and class categories — the same issues that obsessed Puritan attacks on James and the Court. Jonas Barish has related this prejudice against the theater (and by extension, I would argue, the Court) to the Puritan relationship with God. The Puritan fervently believes in fixed identity and the transcendent soul, ideals of stasis reflected by the emphasis on ritual repetitions. The excesses of Jacobean theater are in this context "a deeply disturbing temptation, which could only be dealt with by being disowned and converted into a passionate moral outrage" (Barish 113).

The theater makes an ostentatious display of the supposedly degenerate capacity for dissemblance, for the performance of the opposite gender and alternative identities. Furthermore, when Osborne writes that the King's favorites resemble ladies in their attire, he blurs the distinction between the false show of popular theater and the decadence of the Court. Jacobean pageantry and extravagance, intended as a reflection of the King's own power, is here summoned in the same breath as popular theater, which was already associated with sodomy and prostitution. In this way, the extravagance of the Court is reinterpreted not as glorious but as scandalous. In Osborne's view, Carr and Villiers symbolize the performance of erotic possibilities that, transplanted from the theater to Whitehall, have an almost supernatural power to threaten and transform an entire world-picture.

The Court becomes in this passage not a seat of authority but a false show. The King is other than what he ought to be. He demonstrates the stagey arbitrariness of roles rather than their conventional fixity. He is, in a sense, dishonest. Osborne is determined to reveal what Barish would call the "protean" aspect of the Court, a decadent and effeminate changeability that contrasts sharply with the more traditional, masculine and austere ideal of kingship. The notion of concealment and changeability is further emphasized by the dressing room, the "Tyring-house," where atrocious behavior may be indulged in out of view. Like the abominable stage that in Shakespeare's time called for boys to play women, the Court that permits Carr and Villiers to usurp the position of the Queen is to be condemned as false, heretical, and an invitation to chaos. In light of Osborne's attack, we can see how Shakespeare's summoning together the issues of kingcraft, theater, and sex in *Antony and Cleopatra* might find an ironic context in a performance at Court.[4]

After the fashion of G. P. V. Akrigg I will first toss out a red herring and note that I have no evidence whatsoever that Shakespeare intended his play to be performed at Court, or even that he had James in mind when he created Antony. But then I will point out that many of the plays of this period in his career, including *Hamlet, Macbeth,* and *The Tempest,* were performed at Court, and a few were specifically tailored to James's interests. In fact, in 1607 Samuel Daniel chose to revise his own *Cleopatra* from the previous decade, which leads me to suppose that this classical tale of decadence and political intrigue enjoyed considerable popularity at this time. The parallels that can be drawn between the Egyptian palace and Whitehall are far too interesting to ignore. In my view, James and Antony both concomitantly embodied a threat to the popular notion that there is a single austere male sexuality that is appropriate to kingship.

Shakespeare would certainly have been aware of the extravagance, even the riot of the Jacobean Court. While the image of the overdecked courtier may not quite approach the richness of Enobarbus's description of Cleopatra on her barge, such a spectacle, even in words, would have certainly appealed to Jacobean aspirations. Also, the "Eight wild boars roasted whole at a breakfast, and but twelve persons there" [II.ii.179-80] are reminiscent of James Hay's "Ante-Suppers," in which a table was presented with "the choycest and dearest viands sea or land could afford: And all this once seene having feasted the eyes of the Invited, was in a manner throwne away, and fresh set on to the same height, having only this advantage of the other, that it was hot" (Osborne 125). Extravagance takes on a debilitating, deviant sexual character in the play, though more in the imaginations of the austere Romans than in any proper demonstration: for example, Caesar says, "Let witchcraft join with beauty, lust with both, / Tie up the libertine in a field of feasts, / Keep his brain fuming; epicurean cooks / Sharpen with cloyless sauce his appetite" [II.i.22-25]. These lines demonstrate the association of witchcraft, sexual deviance, and excess that characterized the discourse on sodomy.

*Antony and Cleopatra* was probably written shortly after the visit of the Queen's brother, King Christian of Denmark, in the summer of 1606.[5] The spectacle of Cleopatra would have been standard fare as a theatrical reflection of the King's political power and is certainly equal to the expense and exoticism with which James entertained his Danish visitor. Sir John Harington, for example, describes festivities that recalled "Mahomet's paradise": during a representation of the story of Solomon and the Queen of Sheba, the drunken Lady playing the Queen delivered precious gifts to the two kings—though, when she tripped on the steps, the gifts landed in Christian's lap. The King, once drunk, had to be removed to another room, and a presentation of Faith, Hope, and Charity ended in the former two "sick and spewing in the lower hall" (127-29). The oriental metaphors here, not to mention the wild drinking, would suggest that the exoticism and excess of Cleopatra's world would have been more than welcome at Court. Furthermore, the drunken party aboard ship (II.vii) would recall the notorious behavior of the visiting Danes, which caused King Christian to appoint a special marshal to take control of his drunken countrymen by chaining their thumbs together and nailing the chain to a post.

The polarity between Egypt and Rome, Cleopatra and Octavia, which Shakespeare emphasizes with rapid scene changes back and forth, could suggest the division in James's own life between duty to the Queen and pleasure in his favorites. While Anne herself hardly resembled Octavia in her person, she was obliged to play the role of the largely forgotten wife, married more for political reasons than for love. Antony did not marry Fulvia for love, and clearly he marries Octavia in order to pacify Caesar. Similarly, James seems to have required little of Anne but heirs. His passion for Carr and the conclusion of his conjugal relations with Anne have been seen by more than one historian as the "severing of the bond of convention which had maintained the discipline of the English Court" (Bingham, *James I* 80).

One problem with comparing Cleopatra to James's favorites is, of course, the fact that she is a woman and they were men. Cleopatra is not, however, sufficiently womanly, nor were Carr and Villiers adequately manly to satisfy all critics on that rather fundamental issue. Moreover, Cleopatra was written to be played by a boy actor, a fact which she alludes to ironically in the final act. The issue of cross-dressing on the Renaissance stage has generated considerable critical interest recently; suffice it to say here that Shakespeare's self-conscious use of boy actors further complicates a play already preoccupied with the deconstruction of conventional gender roles.

Part of the attraction of Cleopatra's court is its mixture of sex and outrageous theatricality. Even her stagey suicide blends the language of sexual acts with that of theatrical performance. Cleopatra is surprisingly bawdy. She is as playful about lesbianism as about cross-dressing (II.v.5-7). As for her relationship with Antony, she is as enthusiastic in submission to him as in her domination of him, that is, when she puts her tires and mantles on him, whilst she wears his sword Phillipan (II.v.22-23). Antony "is not more manlike / Than Cleopatra; nor the queen of Ptolemy / More womanly than he" (I.iv.5-7). A decadent slippage in gender is suggested when Cleopatra is mistaken for Antony (I.ii.78) and is later mistaken for the soldier Eros (IV.xii.29); Antony is even compared with Mardian, when the eunuch appears just as Antony is shouting, "O thy vild lady! She has robb'd me of my sword" (IV.xiv.23). There is an absurd scene in which Cleopatra and Eros both try to dress the pathetic Antony in his armor (IV.i). Especially given the soldier's suggestive name, this new triumvirate is a peculiar one in a play where gender distinctions among the three characters seem to dissolve.

Antony's sexual crime, like that of sodomy, is a subversion of the natural (masculine) order, accompanied by the inevitable international conflicts. Even divine favor in the form of Hercules (clearly not the effeminized slave of Omphale here) is suffered to emigrate. Regarding Antony, Hélène Cixous writes, "Although he might have a hard time keeping up with Cleopatra in the realm of invention, he wins in another generosity—the one that for a man consists of daring to strip himself of power and glory and to love and admire a woman enough to take pride happily in rivaling with her in passion" (124). The link between masculinity and kingcraft makes its debut in the first scene of the play: "Take but good note, and you shall see in him / The triple pillar of the world transform'd / Into a strumpet's fool" (I.i.11-13). Such firm and phallic symbols of state as pillars, poles, and swords, are forever in decline throughout the play, just as the masculine order and the ascetic masculine self of Antony's stale-drinking days are constantly threatened with dissolution, melting like Egypt into Nile, melting like Rome into Tiber as the "crown o' th' earth doth melt," a narcissistic fusion of Antony into Cleopatra, her oblivion a very Antony and Antony none other than her oblivion. "Here I am Antony, / Yet cannot hold this visible shape. . . . " He stands like a child, uncertain of his identity, slipping from dragon to bear to citadel to promontory like the polymorphous vapor of a cloud. The enemy is triumphant. Naught is left but the collapse of his kingship, naught but the sound of a voice as it strikes at the mirror of its own narcissism, "Ourselves to end ourselves" (IV.xiv.2-22).[6] Even the act of suicide is not "well done."

Fortunately, Shakespeare complicates this conservative reading by making Caesar and Octavia sterile and dull and by locating sexual fertility entirely (though illegitimately) in Egypt. Cleopatra is the center around which fascination whirls. She attracts some of Shakespeare's most sensuous poetry. She and Antony do not fit the role of villain, as James did for the Puritans. Cleopatra in particular embodies riotous sexuality, but she does not alienate our affection. In her "infinite variety" she is, to borrow Barish's term, one of the "proteans" that the Puritans found intolerable in theater, a creature of cosmetics and costumes, erotically and dramatically unpredictable. She is the sensuous sign of self-abandon. She is the sign-as-absence, at once a presence and an oblivion, the most vital character but also the one most susceptible to frequent, highly eroticized "deaths." Antony's love for her, like James's love for his favorites, provides the exciting gap, the disruption in the social contract, the unspeakable whose eruption into culture loosens the foothold of the world. Shakespeare reproduces the conventional sexual narrative favored by the Puritans (that is, transgression and punishment), but at the same time he complicates the narrative by admitting his fascination and his sympathy for the fated pair.

Shakespeare is particularly ambivalent toward Antony. Antony is clearly defeated by his own actions, but he is frequently elegized in a manner that we want to believe is accurate. Lepidus says that

"His faults, in him, seem as the spots of heaven, / More fiery by night's blackness; hereditary, / Rather than purchas'd; what he cannot change, / Than what he chooses" (I.iv. 12-15). This subtle assertion that Antony is somehow more perfect than the element in which he functions is further suggested in Cleopatra's speech over Antony's body, "Young boys and girls / Are level now with men; the odds is gone, / And there is nothing left remarkable / Beneath the visiting moon" (IV.xv.65-68). Even in his desire for her, Antony was more a man in her opinion than all other men; he was, for her, the only remarkable one. "For his bounty," she says of him, "There was no winter in't; an autumn it was / That grew the more by reaping. His delights / Were dolphin-like, they show'd his back above / The element they liv'd in" (V.ii.86-90). Antony was for her the embodiment of mature yet inexhaustible pleasure, a sort of hard gem-like flame. But her reverie is interrupted by Dolabella. She asks, "Think you there was or might be such a man / As this I dreamt of?" and his answer is simply, "Gentle madam, no." Within the given construction of masculinity and kingship, such a man as Antony, whose legs bestrid not only the ocean but pleasure and duty as well, can only be a dream or a threat.

Especially in Cleopatra's dolphin speech, I am led to wonder about Shakespeare's sympathies toward the King for whom he was wont to write. If we presume that Shakespeare brought *Antony and Cleopatra* to Court, or at least conceived of Antony with James in mind, we can see the dramatist mining a familiar Puritan correlation between the stage, the Court, and sex (though with vastly different results). The issue of sodomy both in Shakespeare's work and in the King's life has already been examined, but what of the influence of James's life on the dramatist's work? Given that Shakespeare's most passionate emotional attachment was probably not to his wife but to a younger and more handsome man,[7] how did he view the King's favorites? Why this curious dream of a masculinity unthinkable within the context of his own culture? An impossible masculinity, and yet an idyllic reconciliation — "O well-divided disposition, O heavenly mingle" — of "masculine" and "feminine" roles estranged by the politics of gender.

## NOTES

1. Akrigg further theorizes that "feather-brained" Anne wished to be revenged on her husband's sexual "abnormalities," a presumption all his own.

2. For a more detailed biography of Wroth, see Roberts's introduction to The *Poems* (3-40).

3. For an overview of Puritan anti-theatrical commentary specifically relating to homosexuality and cross-dressing, see Sprengnether (192-96).

4. For a similar discussion of Villiers and *Coriolanus*, see Goldberg (141-46).

5. Davies has suggested that Antony is based on King Christian, though he denies any resemblance between Antony and James because of James's "homosexuality."

6. Dollimore arrives at a similar reading of this line: "*Virtus*, divorced from the power structure, has left to it only the assertion of a negative, inverted autonomy" (211).

7. See, for example, Akrigg, *Shakespeare and the Earl of Southampton*: "We have seen that Shakespeare's love for young Southampton may have been the greatest emotional experience of his life" (239).

## REFERENCES

Akrigg, G. P. V. *Jacobean Pageant, or The Court of King James I*. Cambridge: Harvard UP, 1962.

―――. *Shakespeare and the Earl of Southampton*. Cambridge: Harvard UP, 1968.

Ashton, Robert, Ed. *James I by his Contemporaries*. London: Hutchinson, 1969.

Barish, Jonas. *The Anti-theatrical Prejudice*. Berkeley and Los Angeles: U of California P, 1981.

Bingham, Caroline. *James VI of Scotland*. London: Weidenfeld & Nicolson, 1979.

―――. *James I of England*. London: Weidenfeld & Nicolson, 1981.

Bray, Alan. *Homosexuality in Renaissance England*. London: Gay Men's P, 1982.

―――. "Homosexuality and the Signs of Male Friendship in Elizabethan England." *History Workshop* 29 (1990): 1-19.

Cixous, Hélène, and Catherine Clément. *The Newly Born Woman*. Trans. Betsy Wing. Minneapolis: U of Minnesota P, 1986.

Davies, H. Neville. "Jacobean *Antony and Cleopatra*." *Shakespeare Studies* 17 (1985): 123-58.

Dollimore, Jonathan. *Radical Tragedy*. Sussex: Harvester, 1984.

Foucault, Michel. *History of Sexuality*. Vol. I. *An Introduction*. Trans. Robert Hurley. New York: Vintage, 1990.

Fraser, Antonia. *King James*. London: Weidenfeld & Nicolson, 1974.

Goldberg, Jonathan. *James I and the Politics of Literature.* Baltimore and London: The Johns Hopkins UP, 1983.

Harington, John. *Nugae Antiquae.* London, 1792.

Hutchinson, Lucy. *Memoirs of the Life of Colonel Hutchinson.* Vol. I. London, 1822.

James I. *Basilikon Doron.* In *The Political Works of James I.* Ed. Charles Howard McIlwain. Cambridge: Harvard UP, 1918.

_____. *Letters of King James VI & I.* Ed. G. P. V. Akrigg. Berkeley, Los Angeles, and London: U of California P, 1984.

Mathew, David. *James I.* London: Eyre & Spottiswoode, 1967.

McElwee, William. *The Wisest Fool in Christendom: The Reign of King James I and VI.* London: Faber and Faber, 1958.

Osborne, Francis. *Some Traditionall Memorialls on the Raigne of King James.* London, 1658.

Scott, Otto J. *James I.* New York: Mason/Charter, 1976.

Shakespeare, William. *Antony and Cleopatra.* In *The Riverside Shakespeare.* Ed. G. Blakemore Evans. Boston: Houghton, 1979.

Sprengnether, Madelon. "The Boy Actor and Femininity in *Antony and Cleopatra.*" *Shakespeare's Personality.* Eds. Norman N. Holland, Sidney Homan, and Bernard J. Paris. Berkeley: U of California P, 1989.

Stafford, Helen Georgia. *James VI of Scotland and the English Throne.* New York: D. Appleton-Century, 1940.

Steeholm, Clara, and Hardy Steeholm. *James I of England: The Wisest Fool in Christendom.* New York: Covici Friede Publishers, 1938.

Weldon, Anthony. *The Court and Character of King James.* London, 1651.

Williams, Charles. *James I.* London: Arthur Barker, 1934.

Willson, D. Harris. *King James VI and I.* New York: Henry Holt, 1956.

Wilson, Arthur. *The History of Great Britain, Being the Life and Reign of King James the First.* London, 1653.

Wroth, Lady Mary. *The Countesse of Mountgomeries Urania.* London, 1621.

_____. *The Poems of Lady Mary Wroth.* Ed. Josephine A. Roberts. Baton Rouge and London: Louisiana State UP, 1983.

# Not Since Sappho:
# The Erotic in Poems
# of Katherine Philips
# and Aphra Behn

Arlene Stiebel, PhD

California State University, Northridge

**SUMMARY.** The presentation of sexuality in poetry may be masked by the use of conventional literary devices that obscure as well as reveal the poems' erotic content. Traditional readings of Katherine Philips' and Aphra Behn's poetry have ignored or denied the lesbian aspects of their verse by dismissing them as asexual representations of well-known literary conventions. This paper argues for a recognition of the ways in which these poetic conventions present a complex and sophisticated lesbian sexuality and also comment on other taboo aspects of human sexual relations.

Despite polite acknowledgement of the newly credited importance of relationships among women, it is a commonplace of recent literary theory and criticism that lesbians do not exist. Critics tell us that there are women who were "autonomous," or unmarried; women who chose a "professional" or career mode rather than a familial allegiance; women who, because they were married, automatically qualify as heterosexual despite their primary emotional and erotic bonds with other women; and some anomalous women who had a hard time fitting in with societal expectations of their

Arlene Stiebel received her PhD from Columbia University with a specialization in Renaissance English and Comparative Literature. She currently teaches English and Women's Studies. Correspondence may be addressed to the author at: Department of English, California State University, Northridge, 18111 Nordhoff Street, Northridge, CA 91330.

time and so remained celibate. Only in a very few cases, and usually famous ones, such as that of Gertrude Stein, is it openly stated that literary women had sexual relations with other women and wrote about them. Most literary critics, even some who themselves are lesbians, collude in the polite fiction of obscurity that clouds lesbian literary lives. Bonnie Zimmerman confirms Marilyn Frye's analysis that, "we are considered to be both naturally and logically impossible" (62).

Indeed, the tradition of denial extends even to such distinguished works as Lillian Faderman's groundbreaking study and the most recent articles. Through various critical representations, emotionally intense relationships between women are asserted to be non-sexual.[1] Faderman insists not only that we do not or can not know whether these women had "genital sex," but that even if they did, it is unimportant because historically there was no such thing as a "lesbian." Although it is now fashionable to exploit this notion of the social construction of sexual identity, such semantic hairsplitting seems to beg important questions of sexuality in literature.[2] Historicizing lesbian identity ought not to deprive lesbianism of its sexuality.

Sandra M. Gilbert and Susan Gubar also relegate lesbians to the sexual sidelines. In their anthology of women's literature, they use every opportunity in footnotes, biographies, and glosses to explain away, where possible, evident same-sex choices in the lives and texts of lesbian authors. An example of how this bias works is evident in the way they distort Katherine Philips' clearly erotic poems. In their analysis (81), the eroticism is diffused through disembodied generalization into a sterile intellectual bonding. Their approach robs Philips' work of its emotional intensity. Surprisingly, their refusal to acknowledge the erotic in Philips' poems comes more than fifty years after Philip Webster Souers' standard biography, which carefully and clearly presents the succession of women to whom Philips was attached.

Harriette Andreadis, in an article in *Signs*, obscures the issue even further. She describes Philips' poetry as "desexualized — though passionate and eroticized" (39). In Andreadis' argument, eroticism is not sexual, so she can claim for Philips a type of lesbianism that maintains the social respectability she sees as an important aspect of Philips' reputation and life. Andreadis rehearses in detail some recent arguments dealing with gay and lesbian sexuality to attempt a definition of what is "lesbian." According to her definition, Philips had "a lesbian experience" and wrote "lesbian texts," but may not have "expressed her homoerotic feelings genitally" (59). Andreadis' definition does not include women's experiences of physical desire as a component of lesbianism. By writing sensuality out of lesbian literature, Andreadis maintains the tradition of denial, which is perpetuated in Dorothy Mermin's more recent article. Refusing to acknowledge a lesbian sexuality, Mermin picks up Andreadis' assertion that Philips' poems "did not give rise to scandal" and were therefore "asexual, respectable" (343). Mermin's characterization of "female homosexuality" as "unseemly" clearly indicates her approach to this literature.[3]

How can contemporary critics continue to overlook, if not deny outright the lesbian content of poems so clearly erotically charged with the love of women for women? The fact is that they can if they want to, because just as figurative language has the power to reveal more than it states, it can also conceal. When Muriel Rukeyser publicly wrote of her lesbianism, she noted in the content and title of her 1971 autobiographical poem, "The Poem as Mask,"[4] a technique that lesbian writers have used for centuries to express their love for women. Stein encoded her work, Amy Lowell sometimes changed pronouns to disguise her speaker's sex, and Willa Cather changed her protagonists' gender. Katherine Philips and Aphra Behn also used masking techniques based in the literary conventions of their time, but although they used the same conventions as their male counterparts did, the effects of their verses were radically different.

Evident in the poems of Philips and Behn is the use of literary conventions we take almost for granted—the courtly love address to the beloved and her response, the idealized pattern of Platonic same-sex friendship, and the hermaphroditic perfection of the beloved who incorporates the best of both sexes. The difference in the use of these conventions by the women poets lies in the significant fact that the voice of the lover is nowhere disguised nor intended to be understood as that of a male. Rather, Philips and Behn exploit the conventions to proclaim to all who would read their poems that the desire of a woman for a woman lover falls well within acceptable literary norms. The very transparency of their masking techniques is what makes them so fascinating.

Their contemporaries recognized the homosexual bias of the two authors. Both women were praised by other, male, poets as "sapphists," that is, women writers in the tradition of Sappho of Lesbos, whose verse fragments clearly celebrate the erotic attachments of women, lament their separation and loss, and generally become the first acknowledged model for female-identified love poems.

Katherine Philips (1632-1664) was known as "The Matchless Orinda" and "The English Sappho" of her day. Privately circulated in manuscript during her lifetime, her *Poems* were first published posthumously in 1664. That incomplete edition was superseded by the *Poems* in 1667, which became the basis for the subsequent edition of 1678. Of the collected poems, more than half deal with Orinda's love for other women. In addition to poems addressed to her beloved "Lucasia" (Anne Owen), there are poems by Philips to "Rosania" (Mary Aubrey), who preceded Lucasia in her affections, and to "Pastora," whose relationship with "Phillis" is celebrated by Lucasia after her own female lover has gone. In addition to these poems using the names Philips bestowed on members of her "Society of Friendship," which was "limited . . . to persons of the same sex" (Souers 41), Philips writes in her own historical voice openly to Anne Owen as well as "To the Lady E. Boyl" (*Poems* 1664, 149) with declarations of love.

Central to Philips' short life—she died of smallpox at thirty-one—was the romance with Anne Owen, and central to her poetry is the conventional representation of their involvement through the images of classical friendship and courtly love. "Orinda to Lucasia" (reproduced in the Appendix), in a traditional pastoral mode, illustrates the importance of the presence of the female beloved. Lucasia is the sun who will restore the light and energy of day (life) to Orinda, who cries for her "friend" to appear as the birds, flowers, and brooks call for their own renewal at a delayed sunrise. But Lucasia means *more* to Orinda than the sun to the world, and if Lucasia delays too long, she will come in time not to save Orinda, but to see her die. Conventional oxymoronic terminology permeates the verse—light versus dark, day versus night, presence and absence, life and death—while the elements of nature that reflect the lover's state of being are, in a reversal of the magnitude of traditional signification, portrayed microcosmically in relation to the macrocosm of Orinda's feelings. The true relationship between the lovers is clear, if we allow ourselves to read the text explicitly. But through the lens of customary literary metaphors, the relationship of the two women can be explained away as being only figuratively erotic—a clever reworking of the spiritualized romance tradition combined with idealized classical friendship to de-emphasize the sexual reality inherent in the concrete, physical terminology of the poem. But the mask should not be allowed to obscure the reality of sexual desire that the poem simultaneously reveals and cloaks.

The relationship between Lucasia and Orinda is further developed and clarified in "To My Excellent Lucasia, on Our Friendship" (also reproduced in the Appendix), for which the traditional soul/body dichotomy is the metaphorical basis. In this poem, Orinda's soul is not only given life by Lucasia, but Lucasia's soul actually *becomes* the animating force of her lover's body. They are united in one immortal soul, but their relationship, which grants to the speaker attributes similar to those of a "bridegroom" or "crown-conqueror," remains "innocent" because of their mutually female design. The echo of Donne's lines from "The Sun Rising," "She's all states, and all princes I / Nothing else is," forces the reader to regard their relationship as one of traditional courtly desire transformed into the sacramental union with a soul-mate through whose agency one participates in the heavenly. The speaker is careful to invoke both spirituality and innocent design as justifications for such language of excess, even though convention would allow her the license to claim another's soul as her own because of their affection alone. But, as female lovers, they need more than a mere statement rejecting what Donne characterizes in "A Valediction: Forbidding Mourning" as "Dull, sublunary lovers' love" to make their union acceptable. So Orinda's argument is that she and Lucasia are "innocent."

We may read this assertion as a refutation of the guilt surrounding accusations of unnatural love between women; as an outspoken declaration that lesbianism is not to be maligned. But I read it another way, in the time-honored tradition of irony that finds answers to bigotry in terms of the ignorance of prejudice itself. Orinda can maintain that love between women is "innocent" because, as Queen Victoria much later asked, what could women do? In a phallocentric culture that defines sexual behavior according to penile instrumentality, sex exclusive of men is not merely unthinkable, it is impossible. Which of us is unfamiliar with the characterization of "sex" as "going all the way," and what woman has not at one time or another been reassured that if it didn't go in "nothing happened"? In England, although male homosexuality was outlawed, women together could not commit a sexual crime. If the norm is androcentric, eroticism among women is illusionary, female "friendships" are merely spiritual bonds, and lesbians are non-existent.

As long as the definition of "the sex act" is inextricably linked to male anatomy and behavior, the question of what can women do is moot. So in order to address the question of sexuality in these poems, we must re-examine what we mean by erotic attraction and sexual activity. If we confuse ejaculation with orgasm, and both of these with sexual satisfaction, and deny the realities of varied sexual responses that are not centered actually or metaphorically in male anatomy, the true nature of lesbian relationships will remain masked. And to the extent that the bias of heterosexual denial and ignorance maintains that intercourse is the sexual norm, then, by definition, activity from which a penis is absent provides women with a love that is "innocent."[5]

What is interesting for readers of seventeenth-century English poetry is that the literature that documents most strikingly a man's inability to fulfill his anticipated role is by a woman who was herself publicly known for a preponderance of sexual activity with both women and men, and whose literary career was mediated by her social and sexual reputation. Aphra Behn (1640-1689) was known primarily as a scandalous playwright, although she also wrote incidental poems and what is perhaps the first real novel in English, *Love Letters Between A Nobleman And His Sister* (1682-5), which set the generic model (epistolary) and topic (courtship) for future lengthy prose works.[6] Behn's poem, "The Disappointment," is traditionally interpreted to be about impotence.[7] I would argue that it is also about rape, another kind of potency test, and presents a woman's point of view cloaked in the customary language of male physical license and sexual access to females. The woman's perspective of this poem provides the double vision that plays the conventional against the experiential.

The traditional interpretation of "The Disappointment" (reproduced in the Appendix) is that the female, Cloris, becomes so aroused and inflamed by the swain Lysander's advances that when he loses his erection and cannot manually stimulate himself, she, in her humiliation at being left wanting, flees from him and is ashamed. The disappointment, then, in this interpretation, is the result of his inability to please her sexually, and their frustration is based on their mutual deprivation of sexual satisfaction. But that is only one line of meaning in the poem. Embedded in the text is another version of their story, coded by diction, and clearly described by the speaker, who in the last of fourteen stanzas projects herself into the poem in identification with the young maid.

The story is this: One dark evening Lysander comes upon Cloris in obscure and isolated woods. They are already in love, and he makes sexual advances. She resists, and tells him to kill her if he must, but she will not give up her honor, even though she loves him. He persists. She swoons. He undresses her. She lies defenseless and fully exposed to him, but he cannot maintain an erection. He tries self-stimulation without success. She recovers consciousness, discovers his flaccid penis with her hand, recoils in confusion, and runs away with supernatural speed. He rages at the gods and circumstance, but mostly directs his anger at Cloris, blaming her for bewitching him to impotence.

Clearly, this story has more than one interpretation. First, it is the classic rape fantasy of the male, where every woman's sexual desires are denied or unexpressed although she really wants him to "take her." As a sexually passive female in the courtly love tradition, she must resist: "your lips tell me no, no, but there's yes, yes in your eyes." But he, as the lover of the cruel fair, must press his advances, believing she is merely playing the game with him, and as Scarlet O'Hara does in *Gone With The Wind,* she will wake up smiling in the morning. That is one way of looking at it, and the usual one. But it presupposes a male point of view about women that is not necessarily true.

Rape is a violent crime with sex as its instrument, and need not be limited to attacks by unknown assailants. A more usual sexual violation may be through coercion or enforcement of power in acquaintance or date rape, no less severe a violation than stranger rape, and perhaps even more of a betrayal for the female since her trust of another is traumatically compromised. If we look at Behn's poem in this light, the subtext becomes clear. Cloris is definite. She says leave me alone or kill me. For her, defloration is a fate worse than death, and she will not endure dishonor even for one she loves. He continues to force her "without Respect" until she lies "half dead" and shows "no signs of life" but breathing. Traditionally, her passion and breathlessness have been read as sexual arousal. But they might just as easily be read as signs of her futile struggle against Lysander, which exhausts her. Fainting is one reaction to shock and being overpowered. As soon as her struggle ends, he is "unable to perform." Although there are as many causes for impotence as there are cases, one well-documented circumstance is among rapists, who may be excited by their victim's struggles and rely on such resistance for arousal. Power and not sex is the crucial stimulant here; Henry Kissinger was voicing a well-worn concept when he maintained that "power is the ultimate aphrodisiac." It is not uncommon for a rapist to be impotent, unable to achieve penile penetration of his victim, and sexual assault may have many forms accordingly. In the poem, even though Cloris is out cold, Lysander tries to get it up, ostensibly to continue the attack. But Cloris awakens and takes the first opportunity she has to run away from her attacker as fast as she can.

Cloris' decision to flee may clearly be seen as an attempt to escape. When she sees the state of things, she shows no sympathy. Lysander's anger is greater than mere disappointment—he rants at the gods and the universe for his impotence, and accuses Cloris of witchcraft in a classic "blame the victim" syndrome. The extent of his rage is more easily explained as that of a thwarted assailant rather than an embarrassed lover. And the insertion of herself into the poem by the recognizably female speaker, who closes the narrative by identifying with Cloris to "well Imagine" and "Condole" the "Nymph's Resentments," completes the rape story. The usual interpretation of "The Disappointment" will stand in a conventional reading. But there is something else unconventional also going on here that adds another dimension to the presentation of topics such as impotence and rape that are frequently taboo in direct statement.

Behn was married and widowed early, and as a mature woman, her primary publicly acknowledged relationship was with a gay male, John Hoyle, himself the subject of much scandal. She celebrates gay male love between the allegorical Philander and Lycidas, as she describes her social circle in a poem called "Our Cabal." Her description of their "friendship" reflects the convention of androgyny, as it becomes the justification for "Tenderness . . . / Too Amorous for a Swain to a Swain."

Aphra Behn was herself apostrophized by her admirers for her androgynous characteristics, which were seen as the desirable reconciliation of her arguably masculine mind with her apparently feminine physique. This conventional reconciliation of sexual opposites was expressed in the dedicatory poems to her collection of 1684, *Poems Upon Several Occasions: With A Voyage To The Island Of Love.* But the most complex presentation of the hermaphroditic ideal is Behn's own. "To the fair Clarinda, who made Love to me, imagin'd more than Woman" (reproduced in the Appendix) explicitly states in the title the true relationship between the two women, and the poem develops the concept of a love that is "Innocent" into a full exploration of the safety in loving an androgynous female.

If Clarinda's "weak" and "feminine" characteristics are insufficiently noble to evoke the superlatives of praise which are more appropriately addressed to a "youth," then that very appellation lifts the constraints on a woman-loving female in pursuit of her courtship. The beloved's combination of masculine with feminine characteristics, the Maid and the Youth, the nymph and the swain, confers a sexual freedom on the lover, who can argue that friendship alone is addressed to the woman, while the erotic attraction is reserved for the masculine component of her beloved androgyne. This makes their love "innocent." Further, as we have seen, two women together can commit no "Crime," but *if* they can, Behn argues with sophistical Donnean wit, Clarinda's "Form excuses it." First, she is observably a female. Second, as the neo-platonic courtly beloved, her "Form" partakes of the ideal forms of the universe, desire for which refines the erotic to the highest plane of spiritual love, a morally acceptable transformation of mere physical attraction which might otherwise offend.

The serpent among the flowers imagery is reminiscent of that in "The Disappointment," a standard allusion to the phallic, with Edenic associations of sin. But the "different kind" who is the beloved in this poem clearly mitigates against any aspects of sinfulness by allowing the speaker (in a multi-layered and witty pun) to extend her love to Hermes, and her friendship to Aphrodite in a socially acceptable construction of their passionate attachment. We can read this poem as the speaker's justification of her own approach to a forbidden beloved. But Clarinda is no traditionally passive maiden fair. She is the one who, the title states, "made love" to the speaker, and, in the last quatrain, her "Manly part . . . wou'd plead" while her "Image of the Maid" tempts. Clarinda, therefore, may also be seen as the initiator of their sexual activity, with the speaker justifying her own response in reaction to the public sexual mores of her time. This reciprocal construction of the poem may suggest the mutuality of a lesbian relationship that rejects the domination and subordination patterns of traditional heterosexual roles.

The complexity of Behn's verse — its logical argument, pastoral and courtly conventions, biblical and classical allusions, and social comment — epitomizes the disguise that reveals meaning. Such eloquent masking allows the audience to go away satisfied that no breach of decorum has been made. It permits us to deny, dismiss or marginalize that which we do not wish to acknowledge, and exempts the poet from social condemnation while bestowing critical acclaim for her ingenuity. Just as in society the conventional polite fiction disguises true feeling, in literature conventional representations of friendship, courtly romance, and female androgyny may mask true meaning. In a male dominated society, with a male oriented literature, women authors who chose to write honestly about important issues in women's lives (and sexual issues may be at the core of these) needed to convey their experiences in ways that express meaning on more than one level simultaneously. By using conventions as maskings, invoking all the connotations of masquing as play, Katherine Philips and Aphra Behn present alternative views of sexuality around issues still considered taboo. It is time for us as readers at least to acknowledge the sexual content in these works by lesbian authors. The real question is not how innocent were they, but how innocent are we?

## NOTES

1. For some early examples of this critical approach, see Moers and Bernikow. For a contrary, and unique appreciation of lesbian writers and themes, see Rule.

2. For an example of how this current theory relates to the English Renaissance, see Bray. For a more woman-centered treatment of some similar ideas, see Cavin. In their introduction, Duberman, Vicinus, and Chauncey note that Faderman has been charged by other historians with denying the importance of sexual activity in lesbian women's lives (7).

3. Mermin also derogates Philips' poems for their lack of a particular kind of energy usually associated with heterosexual desire and not part of Philips' clearly lesbian tone: "Her celebrations of love usually lack, however, the dramatic tension between flesh and spirit that imparts nervous urgency to Donne's amatory verse" (343).

4. When I wrote of the women in their dances and wildness,
            it was a mask,
on their mountain, god-hunting, singing in orgy,
it was a mask; when I wrote of the god,
fragmented, exiled from himself, his life, the love
            gone down with song,
it was myself, split open, unable to speak, in exile
            from myself.
Quoted in Howe and Bass, (front.).

5. Much has been written recently by women about female sexuality. See, for example Hite and Loulan (1984, 1987).

6. Recent biographies of Behn by Duffy and Goreau supersede Sackville-West's interesting brief one. The standard edition of Behn's works is that edited by Montague Summers.

7. For example, Mermin's conventional assessment is that: "'The Disappointment' gleefully narrates the mortification of a youth and the indignation of his coy but willing mistress when seduction ends in impotence" (349).

## REFERENCES

Andreadis, Harriette. "The Sapphic-Platonics of Katherine Philips, 1632-1664." *Signs: Journal of Women in Culture and Society* 15.1 (1989): 34-60.

Behn, Aphra. *Poems Upon Several Occasions: With A Voyage To The Island Of Love.* London, 1684.

Bernikow, Louise. *Among Women.* New York: Harper, 1980.

Bray, Alan. *Homosexuality in Renaissance England.* London: Gay Men's Press, 1982.

Cavin, Susan. *Lesbian Origins.* San Francisco: Ism Press, 1985.

Duberman, Martin Bauml, Martha Vicinus, and George Chauncey, Jr. "Introduction." *Hidden from History: Reclaiming the Gay and Lesbian Past.* Ed. Duberman, Vicinus, and Chauncey. New York: New American Library, 1989.

Duffy, Maureen. *The Passionate Shepherdess.* London: Cape, 1977.

Faderman, Lillian. *Surpassing the Love of Men: Romantic Friendship and Love Between Women from the Renaissance to the Present.* New York: William Morrow & Co., 1981.

Gilbert, Sandra M., and Susan Gubar, Eds. *The Norton Anthology of Literature by Women.* New York: Norton, 1985.

Goreau, Angeline. *Reconstructing Aphra.* New York: Dial Press, 1980.

Hite, Shere. *The Hite Report: A Nationwide Study of Female Sexuality.* New York: Macmillan, 1976.

Howe, Florence, and Ellen Bass, Eds. *No More Masks: An Anthology of Poems by Women.* New York: Doubleday, 1973.

Loulan, Joann. *Lesbian Sex.* San Francisco: Spinsters, Ink, 1984.

———. *Lesbian Passion.* San Francisco: Spinsters/Aunt Lute, 1987.

Mermin, Dorothy. "Women Becoming Poets: Katherine Philips, Aphra Behn, Anne Finch." *English Literary History* 57.2 (1990): 335-56.

Moers, Ellen. *Literary Women.* New York: Doubleday, 1976.

Philips, Katherine. *Poems.* London, 1664.

———. *Poems.* London, 1667.

———. *Letters from Orinda.* London, 1705.

Rule, Jane. *Lesbian Images.* New York: Crossing Press, 1982.

Sackville-West, Vita. *The Incomparable Astrea.* London: Russell and Russell, 1927.

Souers, Philip Webster. *The Matchless Orinda.* Cambridge: Harvard UP, 1931.

Summers, Montague, Ed. *The Works of Aphra Behn.* London, 1915.

Zimmerman, Bonnie. *The Safe Sea of Women: Lesbian Fiction 1969-1989.* Boston: Beacon Press, 1990.

## APPENDIX: POETRY[1]

Katherine Philips. "Orinda to Lucasia"

> Observe the weary birds ere night be done,
> How they would fain call up the tardy sun,
>> With feathers hung with dew,
>> And trembling voices too.
> They court their glorious planet to appear,
> That they may find recruits of spirits there.
>> The drooping flowers hang their heads,
>> And languish down into their beds:
> While brooks more bold and fierce than they
>> Wanting those beams, from whence
>> All things drink influence,
> Openly murmur and demand the day.
>
> Thou my Lucasia are far more to me,
> Than he to all the under-world can be;
>> From thee I've heat and light,
>> Thy absence makes my night.
> But ah! my friend, it now grows very long;
> The sadness weighty, and the darkness strong:
>> My tears (its dew) dwell on my cheeks,
>> And still my heart thy dawning seeks,
> And to thee mournfully it cries,
>> That if too long I wait,
>> Ev'n thou may'st come too late,
>> And not restore my life, but close my eyes.

Katherine Philips. "To My Excellent Lucasia, On Our Friendship"

> I did not live until this time
>> Crown'd my felicity,
> When I could say without a crime,
>> I am not thine, but thee.

---

1. The texts of Philips' two poems are from *Poems* (1664). They are identical to those of the 1667 edition. The texts of Behn's two poems are from *Poems Upon Several Occasions: With A Voyage To The Island Of Love.* I consulted the editions of these works in the Henry E. Huntington Library, San Marino, CA.

This carcass breath'd, and walkt, and slept,
    So that the world believ'd
There was a soul the motions kept;
    But they all were deceiv'd.

For as a watch by art is wound
    To motion, such was mine:
But never had Orinda found
    A soul till she found thine;

Which now inspires, cures and supplies,
    And guides my darkned breast:
For thou art all that I can prize,
    My joy, my life, my rest.

No bridegroom's nor crown-conquerer's mirth
    To mine compar'd can be:
They have but pieces of the earth,
    I've all the world in thee.

Then let our flames still light and shine,
    And no false fear controul,
As innocent as our design,
    Immortal as our soul.

Aphra Behn. "To the fair Clarinda, who made Love to me, imagin'd
    more than Woman"

FAIR, lovely Maid, or if that Title be
Too weak, too Feminine for Nobler thee,
Permit a Name that more Approaches Truth:
And let me call thee, Lovely Charming Youth.
This last will justifie my soft complaint,
While that may serve to lessen my constraint;
And without Blushes I the Youth persue,
When so much beauteous Woman is in view.
Against thy Charms we struggle but in vain
With thy deluding Form thou giv'st us pain,
While the bright Nymph betrays us to the Swain.
In pity to our Sex sure thou wer't sent,
That we might Love, and yet be Innocent:

For no sure Crime with thee we can commit;
Or if we shou'd—thy Form excuses it.
For who, that gathers the fairest Flowers believes
A Snake lies hid beneath the Fragrant Leaves.
      Thou beauteous Wonder of a different kind,
Soft *Cloris* with the dear *Alexis* join'd;
When e'r the Manly part of thee, wou'd plead
Thou tempts us with the Image of the Maid,
While we the noblest Passions do extend
The love to *Hermes*, *Aphrodite* the friend.


Aphra Behn. "The Disappointment"

### I.

One day the Amorous *Lysander*,
By an impatient Passion sway'd
Surpriz'd fair *Cloris*, that lov'd Maid,
Who could defend her self no longer.
All things did with his Love conspire,
The gilded Planet of the Day,
In his gay Chariot drawn by Fire,
Was now descending to the Sea,
And left no Light to guide the World,
But what from *Cloris* Brighter Eyes was hurld.

### II.

In a lone Thicket made for Love,
Silent as yielding Maids Consent,
She with a Charming Languishment,
Permits his Force, yet gently strove;
Her Hands his Bosom softly meet,
But not to put him back design'd,
Rather to draw 'em on inclin'd:
Whilst he lay trembling at her Feet,
Resistance 'tis in vain to show:
She wants the pow'r to say—*Ah! What d'ye do?*

### III.

Her bright Eyes sweet, and yet severe,
Where Love and Shame confus'dly strive,
Fresh Vigor to *Lysander* give;
And breathing faintly in his Ear,

She cry'd — *Cease, Cease — your vain Desire,*
*Or I'll call out — What would you do?*
*My Dearer Honour ev'n to You*
*I cannot, must not give — Retire,*
*Or take this Life, whose chiefest part*
*I gave you with the Conquest of my Heart.*

### IV.

But he as much unus'd to Fear,
As he was capable of Love,
The blessed minutes to improve,
Kisses her Mouth, her Neck, her Hair;
Each Touch her new Desire Alarms,
His burning trembling Hand he prest
Upon her swelling Snowy Brest,
While she lay panting in his Arms.
All her Unguarded Beauties lie
The Spoils and Trophies of the Enemy.

### V.

And now without Respect or Fear,
He seeks the Object of his Vows,
(His Love no Modesty allows)
By swift degrees advancing — where
His daring Hand that Altar seiz'd,
Where Gods of Love do sacrifice:
That Awful Throne, that Paradice
Where Rage is calm'd, and Anger pleas'd;
That Fountain where Delight still flows,
And gives the Universal World Repose.

### VI.

Her Balmy Lips incountring his,
Their Bodies, as their Souls, are joyn'd;
Where both in Transport Unconfin'd
Extend themselves upon the Moss.
*Cloris* half dead and breathless lay;
Her soft Eyes cast a Humid Light
Such as divides the Day and Night;
Or falling Stars, whose Fires decay:
And now no signs of Life she shows,
But what in short-breath'd Sighs returns and goes.

## VII.

He saw how at her Length she lay;
He saw her rising Bosom bare;
Her loose thin Robes, through which appear
A Shape design'd for Love and Play;
Abandon'd by her Pride and Shame.
She does her softest Joys dispence,
Off'ring her Virgin-Innocence
A Victim to Loves Sacred Flame;
While the o'er-Ravish'd Shepherd lies
Unable to perform the Sacrifice.

## VIII.

Ready to taste a thousand Joys,
The too transported hapless Swain
Found the vast Pleasure turn'd to Pain;
Pleasure which too much Love destroys:
The willing Garments by he laid,
And Heaven all open'd to his view,
Mad to possess, himself he threw
On the Defenceless Lovely Maid.
But Oh what envying God conspires
To snatch his Power, yet leave him the Desire!

## IX.

*Nature's Support,* (without whose Aid
She can no Humane Being give)
It self now wants the Art to Live;
Faintness its slack'ned Nerves invade:
In vain th'inraged Youth essay'd
To call its fleeting Vigor back,
No motion 'twill from Motion take;
Excess of Love is Love betray'd:
In vain he Toils, in vain Commands,
The Insensible fell weeping in his Hand.

## X.

In this so Amorous Cruel Strife,
Where Love and Fate were too severe,
The poor *Lysander* in despair
Renounc'd his Reason with his Life:
Now all the brisk and active Fire

That should the Nobler Part inflame,
Serv'd to increase his Rage and Shame,
And left no Spark for New Desire:
Not all her Naked Charms cou'd move
Or calm that Rage that had debauch'd his Love.

### XI.

Cloris returning from the Trance
Which Love and soft Desire had bred,
Her timerous Hand she gently laid
(Or guided by Design or Chance)
Upon that Fabulous *Priapus*,
That Potent God, as Poets feign;
But never did young *Shepherdess*,
Gath'ring of Fern upon the Plain,
More nimbly draw her Fingers back,
Finding beneath the verdant Leaves a Snake:

### XII.

Than *Cloris* her fair Hand withdrew,
Finding that God of her Desires
Disarm'd of all his Awful Fires,
And Cold as Flow'rs bath'd in the Morning Dew.
Who can the *Nymph's* Confusion guess?
The Blood forsook the hinder Place,
And strew'd with Blushes all her Face,
Which both Disdain and Shame exprest:
And from *Lysander's* Arms she fled
Leaving him fainting on the Gloomy Bed.

### XIII.

Like Lightning through the Grove she hies,
Or *Daphne* from the *Delphick God*,
No Print upon the grassey Road
She leaves, t'instruct Pursuing Eyes.
The Wind that wanton'd in her Hair,
And with her Ruffled Garments plaid,
Discover'd in the Flying Maid
All that the Gods e'er made, if Fair.
So *Venus*, when her *Love* was slain,
With Fear and Haste flew o'er the Fatal Plain.

## XIV.

The *Nymph's* Resentments none but I
Can well Imagine or Condole:
But none can guess *Lysander's* Soul,
But those who sway'd his Destiny.
His silent Griefs swell up to Storms,
And not one God his Fury spares;
He curs'd his Birth, his Fate, his Stars;
But more the *Shepherdess's* Charms,
Whose soft bewitching Influence
Had Damn'd him to the *Hell* of Impotence.

# Seeing Sodomy:
# *Fanny Hill*'s Blinding Vision

Kevin Kopelson, PhD

University of Iowa

**SUMMARY.** One of the oddest and most erotic moments in Cleland's *Fanny Hill* occurs when Fanny is knocked "senseless" by a voyeuristic vision of two young men having anal intercourse. This sodomitical passage demonstrates a dominant culture's strong phobic attraction to a socially peripheral Other against which it defines itself. The passage also represents two types of transgression. On one level, it records an inversion of sex, gender, and class paradigms that structure bourgeois subjectivity. On another level, the passage also transgresses signification itself, exploding as well as inverting those paradigms, in a movement that recalls Barthes's distinction between the coded "studium" of the pornographic and the uncoded "punctum" of the erotic. This transgressive exemption from meaning might well be read, in a Barthesian sense, as true sexual enfranchisement in that, for Barthes, the liberation of sexuality requires the release of sexuality from meaning, and from transgression as meaning.

What is difficult is not to liberate sexuality according to a more or less libertarian project but to release it from meaning, including from transgression as meaning.
*Roland Barthes by Roland Barthes*

---

Kevin Kopelson is Assistant Professor of English at the University of Iowa. He has attended Yale University (BA 1979), Columbia University (JD 1982), and Brown University (PhD 1991). His doctoral dissertation, entitled "Love's Litany: The Writing of Modern Homoerotics," concerns ways in which nineteenth-century conceptions of romantic love inflect twentieth-century conceptions of homosexuality.

Correspondence may be addressed to the author at: 111 West 77th Street, New York, NY 10024.

*173*

Shortly before Fanny Hill, John Cleland's notorious "Woman of Pleasure," regains, in a transport of heterosexual bliss, both her beloved Charles and her modicum of bourgeois respectability, she witnesses an erotic congress she had thought physically impossible. Two not unattractive young men, one nineteen, one seventeen, enter the public house in which Fanny is temporarily lodged and occupy a bedroom separated from hers by a moveable partition. Fanny, prompted by her familiar "spirit of curiosity" (193), stands on a chair in order to cut a peep-hole in the top of the partition, and, from this precarious perch, watches as the youths romp and pull one another about in what appears to be "frolic and innocent play" (194). But matters soon take a serious turn:

> For presently the eldest unbuttoned the other's breeches, and removing the linen barrier, brought out to view a white shaft, middle-sized and scarce fledged, when, after handling and playing with it a little, with other dalliance, all received by the boy without other opposition than certain wayward coynesses, ten times more alluring than repulsive, he got him to turn round, with his face from him, to a chair that stood hard by; when knowing, I suppose, his office, the Ganymede now obsequiously leaned his head against the back of it, and projecting his body, made a fair mark, still covered with his shirt, as he thus stood in a side-view to me but fronting his companion, who, presently unmasking his battery, produced an engine that certainly deserved to be put to a better use, and very fit to confirm me in my disbelief of the possibility of things being pushed to odious extremities, which I had built upon the disproportion of parts. But this disbelief I was now to be cured of, as by my consent all young men should likewise be, that their innocence may not be betrayed into such snares, for want of knowing the extent of their danger; for nothing is more certain than that ignorance of a vice is by no means a guard against it.
>
> Slipping then aside the young lad's shirt, and tucking it up under his clothes behind, he showed to the open air those globular, fleshy eminences that compose the mount-pleasants of Rome, and which now, with all the narrow vale that intersects

them, stood displayed and exposed to his attack: nor could I, without a shudder, behold the dispositions he made for it. First then, moistening well with spittle his instrument, obviously to render it glib, he pointed, he introduced it, as I could plainly discern, not only from its direction and my losing sight of it, but by the writhing, twisting, and soft murmured complaints of the young sufferer. But, at length, the first straights of entrance being pretty well got through, everything seemed to move and go pretty currently on, as in a carpet-road, without much rub or resistance. And now, passing one hand round his minion's hips, he got hold of his red-topped ivory toy, that stood perfectly stiff, and showed that if he was like his mother behind he was like his father before; this he diverted himself with, whilst with the other he wantoned with his hair, and leaning forward over his back, drew his face, from which the boy shook the loose curls that fell over it in the posture he stood him in, and brought it towards his, so as to receive a long-breathed kiss, after which, renewing his driving, and thus continuing to harass his rear, the height of the fit came on with its usual symptoms, and dismissed the action. (194-95)[1]

Fanny is shocked and appalled. She hastens "to raise the house upon" these "criminal" sodomites, but jumps down from her chair "with such an unlucky impetuosity that some nail or other ruggedness in the floor" catches her foot and flings her on her face "with such violence that [she falls] senseless on the ground" (195-96). The young men, alerted by the noise of the fall, manage to escape, but, as Fanny's procuress subsequently reassures her, there is "no doubt of due vengeance one time or other overtaking these miscreants."

This sodomitical scene is anomalous—not because it doesn't "belong" in *Fanny Hill,* but because almost everything about it is singular. It is, for example, the only voyeuristic episode in the novel in which the voyeur unwittingly discovers herself, as well as the only such episode in which the voyeur is stationed in a position of instability or insecurity. It also denotes the only instance known to Fanny of successful anal penetration. And, not incidentally, it represents the only sexual act felt by Fanny to be morally outrageous.[2]

These and other aspects of the sodomitical scene are not only exceptional. They are remarkable. They disturb and fissure the unary representational framework Fanny so solicitously and perceptively articulates in her second epistle. "Madame," she writes,

> I imagined, indeed, that you would have been cloyed and tired with the uniformity of adventures and expressions, inseparable from a subject of this sort, whose bottom or groundwork being, in the nature of things, eternally one and the same, whatever variety of forms and modes the situations are susceptible of, there is no escaping a repetition of near the same images, the same figures, the same expressions. . . . (129)

It is true that the "figures" and "expressions" contained in the sodomitical passage are consistent with the rhetorical style of *Fanny Hill* as a whole — periodic, euphemistic, euphuistic, metaphoric, and inventive. However, as the narrative strains to emphasize, there is nothing about the "adventure" Fanny observes that is "uniform" in relation to the dominant structural paradigm of vaginal intercourse.

Nevertheless, it is the novel's *moral* paradigm that is most brutally violated by Fanny's "two young sparks" (194). As is the case with eighteenth-century whore biography in general, the moral framework constitutive of and ultimately celebrated by *Fanny Hill* is a simplistic opposition of Virtue, or chastity, on the one hand, and Vice, or impurity, on the other (see Richetti 35-41). What is unusual about Cleland's articulation of this moral paradigm is his heroine's "blandly rational tolerance" of even perverse or fetishist vice (Hollander 76). As Mrs. Cole, her procuress, reminds Fanny (who does not disagree with her), while ridicule may "vulgarly attend" the disposition of Mr. Barvile, their flagellant client:

> that, for her part, she considered pleasure of one sort or other as the universal port of destination, and every wind that blew thither a good one, provided it blew nobody any harm; that she rather compassionated than blamed those unhappy persons

who are under a subjection they cannot shake off to those arbitrary tastes that rule their appetites of pleasure with an unaccountable control; tastes, too, as infinitely diversified, as superior to and independent of all reasoning as the different relishes or palates of mankind in the viands; some delicate stomachs nauseating plain meats, and finding no favour but in high-seasoned, luxurious dishes; whilst others again pique themselves upon detesting them. (181)

And this broad-mindedness is not restricted to typically "English" vices like flagellation. Fanny describes lesbianism in morally neutral terms (as "one of those arbitrary tastes for which there is no accounting" [49], and as "this foolery from woman to woman" [71]), and heterosexual anality in morally neutral and *comic* terms (as "not going by the right door and knocking desperately at the wrong one" [178], and as involving a "double-way [presenting a] fair choice to him [who] was so fiercely set on a mis-direction as to give the girl no small alarms for fear of losing a maidenhead she had not dreamt of" [192]).

Fanny's buoyant broad-mindedness extends even to the aristocratic pederast who at first takes her friend Emily for a boy (she is disguised as a shepherd), and who, upon realizing his error, condescends to take her as a girl:

turning his steed's head, he drove him at length in the right road, in which, his imagination having probably made the most of those resemblances that flattered his taste, he got with much ado whip and spur to his journey's end. (192)

But Emily's would-be sodomite is exempt from Fanny's moral censure on two counts: he belongs to the nobility (against whose supposed depravity the bourgeois reader defined him- or herself), and he is at a masked ball (a carnivalesque locus of licit, containable transgression). Fanny's sodomites, on the other hand, only *appear* aristocratic ("two young gentlemen, for so they seemed" [193]), and they are not celebrating carnival.

This has something to do with why they practically leap out of Fanny's otherwise placid sexual/textual landscape. In a sense, the "immense disproportion" of parts (193) she imagines between the phallus and the (male) anus, and the "odious extremities" (195) to which she believes the penetrated anus must be pushed, function as tropes for the young sodomites themselves, who simply do not fit into her world-view. It is as if they are foreign objects crammed into and expulsed from her constrictive bourgeois image-repertoire. Vaginal intercourse, it goes without saying, poses no such problem. No penis in *Fanny Hill* is too large (and there are certainly some memorable ones) to be accommodated by some vagina. And even heterosexual sodomy is figured in a rather capacious manner: the female anus is both a possible "port in a storm" (178) and a "choice fair" of a "double-way" (192).

But if garden-variety homosexual sodomy is an un-fit sociosexual discourse, why does Cleland represent it graphically in a scene that arrests the reader's attention? And why does Fanny recommend that "all young men" (195) witness what Edward Coke had called, in a periphrastic figure typical of the period, the "detestable and abominable sin, amongst Christians not to be named" (Bray 61 [from Coke's *Institutes*])? "Ten times more alluring than repulsive," Fanny calls the willing Ganymede's "wayward coynesses" (194). This is also true of Fanny's furtive sodomitical vision in general; it is "ten times more alluring than repulsive." She, and perhaps even we, experience what Peter Stallybrass and Allon White call "phobic enchantment" (Stallybrass & White 124).

"Phobic enchantment" is the simultaneous repugnance and fascination attendant upon self-definition by a dominant culture whose political imperative to reject and eliminate a debased and debasing Other "conflicts powerfully and unpredictably with a desire for this Other" (Stallybrass & White 4). To cite Barbara Babcock's formulation, a socially peripheral Other is often symbolically central to the dominant culture that defines itself as not-Other (32). And because such a dominant culture usually includes its Other symbolically "as a primary eroticized constituent of its own fantasy life," an aversion/desire fusion is frequently integral to the construction of that culture's subjectivity (Stallybrass & White 5).

Others, then, can be essentially constitutive of the image-repertoires of dominant cultures. For *Fanny Hill* and her bourgeois readers, the homosexual sodomite is at once the Other one is not, the Other it is unthinkable to be, and the Other without whom one cannot be. He is represented at all because he embodies a devalued opposition that determines and valorizes bourgeois sexual identity. He should be seen by "all young men" in order that they may learn fully the lessons of resemblance and differentiation necessary to bourgeois subjectivity. And, because he is such an enthralling eccentric, his story is singularly compelling and remarkable.

But Fanny's "two young sparks," while appropriately central in a symbolic sense, are out of place socially. Not only are they not aristocratic and not seizing a fleeting carnivalesque moment, they are also having sex in a public house, in broad daylight, and, it bears emphasizing, in the same room as Fanny. In a word, they transgress.

What is the nature of their transgression? Clearly, these sodomites are doing what should not be done where it should not be done. But the sodomitical passage does not denote "symbolic inversion"[3] alone. It also denotes a kind of transgression that is unrelated to the mere infraction of binary structures.

Stallybrass and White suggest an alternative definition of "transgression" which they associate with extremist practices of modern art and philosophy: "movement into an absolutely negative space *beyond the structure of significance itself*" (Stallybrass & White 18, emphasis in original). I find that how the sodomitical passage transcends significance has everything to do with how unutterably erotic it is.

The pornographic is unary: banal, coded, and coherent. It is, in Fanny's words, the cloying, tiresome, and repetitive figuration of uniform "adventures and expressions . . . whose bottom or groundwork [is always] the same, whatever variety of forms and modes the situations are susceptible of" (129). The erotic, however, is ununary, and even un-binary. The erotic, to quote *Camera Lucida,* "is a pornographic that has been disturbed, fissured" (Barthes 41).

The erotic fissure is an unnameable disturbance, an uncoded addition to the pornographic (Barthes 51, 55). It is an overwhelming detail with an often metonymic power of expansion (Barthes 45, 49). It is an "odd contradiction: a floating flash" that illuminates an erotic blind spot (Barthes 53). In *Fanny Hill,* the floating flash is provided by the erotic transgression of the sodomitical "sparks."

For Fanny, the significance of sexual intercourse depends upon the confluence, correspondence, and stability of two oppositions: sexual difference (male/female) and gender difference (phallic penetration/phallic reception). The lesbian activity in *Fanny Hill* does not transcend significance: it violates sexual difference, but, because it does not involve phallic penetration, respects gender difference. Even the pederastic adventure signifies because Emily, after all, is "really" a girl. Homosexual sodomy, however, does not respect the coding of phallic penetration as "male" and phallic receptivity as "female," and, consequently, explodes the binary "bottom or groundwork" of sexual signification. It is erotically, transgressively, transcendently exempt from meaning.

This is why the young sodomites are figured, oxymoronically and non-sensically, as "unsexed male misses":

> [I]n fine, they [are] scarce less execrable than ridiculous in their monstrous inconsistency of loathing and condemning women, and all at the same time aping their manners, airs, lisp, skuttle, and, in general, all their little modes of affectation, which become them at least better than they do these *unsexed male misses*. (196, emphasis added)

An effeminate man may be a "male miss." But what on earth is an "*unsexed* male miss"? Fanny is simply unable to make "sense" of, to "figure" out, who the sodomites are and what they do, both of which are unknown to her text's linguistic, phenomenological paradigm. She has reached a significant in-significant impasse.

Of course, that is what is so perilous about paradigms. Non-meaning is always just beyond one's field of vision, always just on the other side of the partition. And if you dare to take just one little peek, you are likely to be dazzled, blinded, and, like Fanny, "flung . . . senseless on the ground" in a paroxysm of orgasmic dissemination. Because, it turns out, it is you who have transgressed, you who have surprised meaning in its hideout, you who have dis-covered what meaning is by glimpsing where it is not. And it is you who must pay the forfeit.

Fanny pays. She is so deafened by the explosion of meaning, so dumbstruck by the exemption from significance, that her text becomes, for a while, mesmerized by incoherence. "Good-natured

Dick," the simpleton whose amorous episode follows the sodomitical passage, is both uncomprehending and incomprehensible:

> he was not only a perfect changeling, or idiot, but stammered
> so that there was no understanding even those sounds that his
> half-a-dozen, at most, animal ideas prompted him to utter.
> (197)

But it is his phallus that, literally, cannot be taken. Even in relation
to its already somewhat oversized precursors, Good-natured Dick's
"man-machine" (200) is of ludicrous, unbelievable dimensions:

> In fine, it might have answered very well the making a show
> of: its enormous head seemed, in hue and size, not unlike a
> common sheep's heart; then you might have rolled dice se-
> curely along the broad back of the body of it; the length of it,
> too, was prodigious. (199)

This is no phallus; this is a table. And, to further confuse matters,
the phallus too large to be contained by any idea of it is also given a
diminutive Shakespearean designation: "the dearest morsel of the
earth" (201).

In a sense, the description of Good-natured Dick's heroic member poses a double riddle: when is a phallus not a phallus, and what
morsel is enormous? Two possible answers, "never" and "none,"
are, conveniently, transcendently transgressive insofar as they signify Stallybrass and White's "absolutely negative space beyond the
structure of significance itself." Yet there is a third puzzle embedded in Cleland's unattributed "morsel" citation, because it is the
tomb of Juliet which, according to Romeo, is "Gorg'd with the
dearest morsel of the earth."[4] The puzzle is why Fanny figures a
larger-than-life male phallus as a (seemingly) lifeless female form.
One solution is that, on some level, Fanny has not forgotten that
blinding flash in which she saw beyond the arbitrary binary coding
of phallic penetration as "male" and phallic receptivity as "female."

Some of us, unlike Fanny, get to see homosexual sodomy, if not
all the time, at least often enough. But even for us, there will always have been that first sighting in which it was not so much we

who discovered a new kind of sex, as a new kind of sex that saw, and showed us, who and what we had been, who and what we could no longer be. Because to envision sodomy turned out to mean our revision by sodomy. Alienated from our sense of who we were, alienated from "sense" in its larger sense, we suddenly became the Other we were not, our own significant Other—which is to say, insignificant. At least, that is, until we discovered the other Others who we, as "gays," were not.

Is it too bourgeois, too sentimental, to regret the lapsing of that senseless moment when, cast adrift from sexual significance, we felt we were everything, anything, and nothing?

## NOTES

1. There is some dispute as to whether this passage was included by Cleland in the first edition of *Fanny Hill* (1749) and subsequently excised under governmental pressure (see Epstein 183; Wagner 15; Foxon 61-62), or whether it was added by a bookseller named Drybutter in 1757 (see Quennell viii; Larsen).

2. *Fanny Hill* is neither the only nor the first work of its type to contemn homosexual sodomy. Anal intercourse had also been depicted and deplored in Nicolas Chorier's well-known *Aloisiae Sigeae Toletanae Satyra Sotadica de arcanis Amoris et Veneris* [a.k.a., *The Dialogues,* or *Satyra Sotadica,* published in France circa 1660 and in England (in an English translation of a French version) in 1745].

3. Babcock broadly defines "symbolic inversion" as "any act of expressive behavior which inverts, contradicts, abrogates, or in some fashion presents an alternative to commonly held cultural codes, values and norms be they linguistic, literary or artistic, religious, social and political" (14).

4.     Thou detestable maw, thou womb of death
       Gorg'd with the dearest morsel of the earth,
       Thus I enforce thy rotten jaws to open,
       And in despite I'll cram thee with more food.
                                              (Romeo and Juliet, V, iii, 45-48)

## REFERENCES

Babcock, Barbara. *The Reversible World: Symbolic Inversion in Art and Society.* Ithaca: Cornell UP, 1978.

Barthes, Roland. *Camera Lucida,* trans. Richard Howard. 1981. New York: Hill, 1987.

Bray, Alan. *Homosexuality in Renaissance England.* London: Gay Men's P, 1982.

Chorier, Nicolas. *Dialogues on the arcana of love and Venus / by Luisa Sigea Toletana,* trans. Donald A. McKenzie. Lawrence: Coronado, 1974.

Cleland, John. *Fanny Hill: Or Memoirs of a Woman of Pleasure,* Ed. Peter Wagner. Harmondsworth: Penguin, 1985.

Epstein, William H. *John Cleland: Images of a Life.* New York: Columbia UP, 1974.

Foxon, David. *Libertine Literature in England 1660-1745.* New York: Univ. Bks., 1965.

Hollander, John. "The Old Last Act: Some Observations on *Fanny Hill.*" *Encounter* 21 (1963): 69- 77.

Larsen, Poul Steen. "John Cleland's *Memoirs of a Woman of Pleasure:* A Bibliography of the Earliest Editions." Copenhagen, 1968. (Unpublished typescript.)

Quennell, Peter. Introduction. *Memoirs of a Woman of Pleasure.* By John Cleland. New York: Putnam, 1963. v-xiv.

Richetti, John J. *Popular Fiction Before Richardson: Narrative Patterns 1700-1739.* Oxford: Clarendon, 1969.

Stallybrass, Peter, and Allon White. *The Politics and Poetics of Transgression.* Ithaca: Cornell UP, 1986.

Wagner, Peter. Introduction. *Fanny Hill: Or Memoirs of a Woman of Pleasure.* By John Cleland. Harmondsworth: Penguin, 1985.

# The Sodomitical Muse:
# *Fanny Hill* and the Rhetoric
# of Crossdressing

## Donald H. Mengay, PhD

### Baruch College, CUNY

**SUMMARY.** Cleland's *Fanny Hill*, banned for centuries largely as a result of a passage depicting male sodomy, has been the focus of several critical approaches since it was republished in the United States in 1963. Critical readings by Nancy K. Miller and Randolph Trumbach in particular indicate that Fanny's persona itself is a "drag" act. While asserting this, no critic has traced the textual complexity of this persona, which is apparent in Cleland's use of figurative language and is accessible through close reading only.

The resurrection in the late 1980s of government's role as art censor and purveyor of morality serves as a reminder that legislative tolerance of overtly homosexual themes in art has traditionally been tenuous at best. The movement to suppress Robert Mapplethorpe's photographs echoes generations of official attempts to squash similar kinds of expression. Literary works of this century such as *The Young and the Evil*, *The Well of Loneliness*, and *Naked Lunch* come to mind. Prior to these one finds a paradigm in John Cleland's *Fanny Hill*, a novel whose checkered history mirrors that of beleaguered modern works that feature more overt and perhaps less ambiguous homosexual themes. A study of this text and the political and literary dynamics surrounding it indicates that governmental

---

Donald H. Mengay is Assistant Professor of English at Baruch College of the City University of New York. Correspondence may be addressed to him at: Baruch College, English Department, CUNY, 17 Lexington Ave., New York, NY 10010.

*185*

homophobia has lessened only slightly in post-eighteenth century England and America.

Cleland's text, riding a wave of French anticlerical and secular philosophy (Braudy 21-40; Wagner 227; Trumbach, "Mod. Prost." 69), broke all barriers of then proper English expression and, as a result, procured for him both official censorship and imprisonment. As Peter Wagner and Randolph Trumbach point out, the actions were brought to bear largely as a result of the male homosexual episode in Volume II (14 [citing Foxon 61]; "Mod. Prost." 74, respectively). This and the lesbian passages have fueled, directly or indirectly, much of the literary-critical controversy surrounding the book as well. As is true in the recent censorship debacle, politics and criticism conflate in a more general question — that of the "morality" of homosexuality in a vastly bourgeois, heterosexual social and literary context. The history of this criticism (i.e., since *Fanny Hill*'s U.S. publication in 1963) mirrors changes in sociosexual codes and merits some treatment here.

The sodomitical passage in *Fanny Hill* has as a rule been the touchstone for critics' readings of the book. Many have construed Fanny's meaning literally when she assails two male sodomites as "miscreants," "misogynists," and "monsters" (196) and alternately refers to sodomy itself as "a taste not only universally odious but absurd"; "not in nature"; "so disagreeable a subject" (193); and a "vice" (195). "The less said of it the better," she proclaims righteously and then diverts the narrative focus, "washing [her] hands of them [i.e., the sodomites]" (196). Reading these and other signs, critics like John Illo (20), Michael Shinagel (234) and Slepian and Morrissey (71) arrive at the conclusion that a primary purpose for Cleland's text is the affirmation of monogamous heterosexuality. Stephen Sossamon considers Cleland a "conservative novelist" (93), by which he means the author rejects "abuses" of sexuality (97) and sexual "excess" (98). Sossamon refers to "the horrors of intemperance and the supreme joys attainable only through the balancing of one's natural [i.e., heterosexual] sex drive" (105). Moreover, Raymond Whitley, citing Barry Ivker, speaks of *Fanny Hill* as a celebration "of relatively uncomplicated heterosexuality" (388).

These readings are fueled by Fanny's mere paragraph-long apology, her "tail-piece of morality" (223), that proceeds after the narration of over two hundred pages of extramarital behavior, both heterosexual and homosexual. She writes:

> [L]ooking back on the course of vice I had run, and comparing its infamous blandishments with the infinitely superior joys of innocence, I could not help pitying, even in point of taste, those who, immersed in a gross sensuality, are insensible to the so delicate charms of Virtue, than which even Pleasure has not a greater friend, nor Vice a greater enemy. Thus temperance makes men lords over those pleasures that intemperance enslaves them to: the one, parent of health, vigour, fertility, cheerfulness, and every other desirable good in life; the other, of diseases, debility, barrenness, self-loathing, with only every evil incident to human nature. (223)

Critics codify "gross sensuality" variously, but, again, frequently equate it in its most pejorative form with male homosexuality.

"Fanny, at a lovely fifteen," writes Illo, "is introduced to sexuality by a Sapphic encounter, not normal, perhaps, but not ugly, like male homosexuality, which is the only reprehended sexual behavior in the book" (21). Moreover, Shinagel argues that Fanny learns to reject all sorts of perversions through her experiences, "and most especially homosexuality" (222). Robert Markley agrees, asserting that "Lesbianism is discouraged ('not even the shadow,' Fanny tells us, 'of what I wanted') . . . [while] male homosexuality is positively abominated" (351). And so on.

Others, however, read Fanny's moral coda ironically, problematically. "Of course, it won't quite do," argues Malcolm Bradbury, "because it can be only an intellectual delight, a witty resolution, like some of Donne's. . . . Inevitably, then, it is the sexual *episodes* that dominate in the book" (275; emphasis in original). Stanley Solomon, too, posits that a straightforward moral stance is unlikely for Cleland (115), because of what he considers to be the author's ambivalence about accepted moral codes (108). According to Solomon, Fanny subverts the very (bourgeois) moral and literary conventions she insists she affirms.

Nancy K. Miller concurs with this view, referring to *Fanny Hill* as "a text of exposure" which "reveals what is covert in the more polite fiction of the period" ("Harlot's Progress" 53). In another place, Miller carries this notion a step further by identifying this covert nature as homoeroticism; in so doing she revolutionizes *Fanny Hill* criticism ("'I's' in Drag" 47-57). Speaking of Fanny as a female drag persona for a decidedly male implied narrator, she writes:

> [F]emale drag allows the male "I" not so much to please the Other—by subscribing or capitulating to women's "taste"—as to become the Other . . . the better to be admired by and for himself. By this I mean that the founding contract of the novel as it functions in the phallocentric (heterosexual) economies of representation is homoerotic: "woman" is the legal fiction, the present absence that allows the male bond of privilege and authority to constitute itself within the laws of proper circulation. ("'I's' in Drag" 49)

This exposure of a homoeroticized male "I" under Fanny's rhetorical make-up is a point well taken, even if Miller's insistence in equating homoeroticism with narcissism appears vastly overstated to the present day reader. (In the last paragraph of her article, Miller herself questions whether such a position need not be tempered. She suggests that social constraints—in essence, homophobia—and not necessarily narcissism forced Cleland to use a female persona to avoid a too blatant picture of inversion [57].)

Other critics have taken up her point, concurring with her (Markley 344; Trumbach, "Mod. Prost." 74). But none have expanded upon it or demonstrated in detail how Cleland achieves—intentionally or unintentionally—his portrait of this hypothetical he-Fanny. Given the rather subtle nature of the theme, any such portrait must be limned from an aggregate of textual elements, rather than from any one single part, such as the male sodomitical episode. In the broader context of the narrative, this episode appears to be merely one of several, and assumes no special importance. Viewed in the context of the more pervasive homoerotic subtext, though, the passage assumes a kind of structural and thematic centrality. I shall discuss four motifs in particular that serve as building blocks for this theme: the much-discussed phallocentrism of the text; its classical allusions; Fanny's self-referential phallic rhetoric; and the anxiety over penetration, especially anal intercourse.

Much has been said about the phallocentric nature of *Fanny Hill*, only the major points of which need to be repeated here (v. Bradbury 272; Markley 347; Quennell 15-16; Shinagel 225; Slepian and Morrissey 72-73; Taube 77). Comparing metaphorization of male with female genitalia Robert Scholes points out that the former "are described in considerable detail and are individualized by unique features as often as possible" while the latter "are described in a kind of soft focus . . . so that no details beyond hair color are reported" (135). What is important is this matter of "details," which is significant in a collective sense: the text generally is obsessed with the male member, far more than any other erotic fiction of the eighteenth century. Shinagel estimates there to be about fifty variations for the male—versus roughly *half* that for female—sex organs (225). In light of this, one can only find his comment that "Cleland is writing from a male point of view for a male audience" ironic, if Shinagel was referring to a heterosexual readership (225). If this were the case, one would expect the descriptive focus to be female, much in the way contemporary heterosexual erotica focuses on the woman as object-ideal. Or, as in the case of the erotic Chinese classic, *The Carnal Prayer Mat*, one would expect the preoccupation to be practical (one of Vesperus', the protagonist's major concerns is anxiety—and dismay—over a small phallic endowment [LiYu 97-109]). True, the hyperbolic, sometimes silly, metaphors pertain to the comic strain in eighteenth-century novels (a la Fielding and Sterne, for example [Shinagel 224-25; Slepian and Morrissey 72; Solomon 112]). But they serve another purpose as well. Fanny's longing to break through the metaphorical wall of "the same figures [and] the same expressions" (129), to find new ways of characterizing the phallus, exposes a narrative penis-longing and adulation that goes beyond mere authorial narcissism.

Besides signifying as narrative wish-fulfillment, the metaphors relate to a broader, more encompassing neoclassicism—i.e., a classical homosexual theme—in which the notions of beauty and form signify physically, literally, and not just literarily. With the exception of Mr. Crofts—who is 60, and whom Fanny calls a "monster" (58) and a "brute" (59)—and Mr. H, who is around 40, males depicted are young, hale, and well-endowed (67-68 [Polly's Italian lover]; 72, 75, 81-82 [Charles]; 106 [Will]; 136-37 [Emily's country lad]; 139 [Harriet's country lad]; and 146 [Louisa's country lad]). Fanny ascribes classical importance to these young men, referring to Charles, for example, as her Adonis (76, 90); Mr. Bovile as Bacchus (182); and the 17-year-old sodomite as Ganymede (194). Indeed, aside from the exceptions just noted, all of the male characters are Ganymedes of sorts, patterned after Zeus' catamite who was abducted, according to *The Oxford Companion to Classical Literature* "on account of his beauty." In contrast, about half of the women are older and their physical portraits much less flattering. (Fanny characterizes Mrs. Jones, the Chelsea landlady, for example, as a "harpy" [89]).

The narrator also reinforces the classical theme by alluding to statuary, speaking of the "smooth polish" of Will's penis (109), the "polished limbs" of Harriet's country lad (139) and the "harmony" of Fanny's limbs (83). She refers to the buttocks of the younger sodomite as "the mount-pleasants of Rome" (195), and in so doing situates not just the sodomites' behavior but the many statuesque, perfectly-formed bodies in a classical, homoerotic context. These allusions create the backdrop before which the implied narrator will undergo his unveiling.

Fanny doesn't cut the same mincing profile as the majority of eighteenth-century heroines, such as Richardson's Pamela and Clarissa, Fielding's Sophia or later figures such as Ann Radcliffe's Emily St. Aubert, Adeline, or Ellena. These paragons of literary sensibility capitulate to implicit literary/cultural dictates that a heroine be physically soft as well as submissive to men (Todd 17-21). The fact that Fanny fails to cut such a profile has been a source of debate among critics. Leo Braudy, for instance, interprets her atypical nature as a foreshadowing of modern feminism (37). But Miller dismisses this notion and asserts that Fanny is merely a pseudo-female who "supports the prerogatives of both class and masculinity" ("'I's' in Drag" 51). A third possibility derives from Trumbach's assertion of the establishment of a new sodomitical role. Although not addressing *Fanny Hill* specifically, his point nevertheless pertains when he claims that the new same-age, same-sex relationships of the eighteenth century "should be understood in the growing context of gender equality between men and women" ("Birth of the Queen" 129). In this way, Fanny fulfills a double role.

Her self-referential language, particularly during sex, is unmistakably masculine — phallic, to be exact. While she speaks of Charles's penis, for instance, as "stiff, horn-hard" (77), she in turn speaks of the "firm hard swell" of her breasts (76). She relates how she "throbbed" during sex with Mr. H (99) and in another episode tells how her breasts were "raised in flesh" (108). "They rose and fell in quick heaves under [Will's] touch," she writes (108). She places herself "with a jet" under Will (110) and the lad yields his "maiden tribute" to *her* (111). To emphasize her adoption of the male role, she portrays herself as the giver of sperm, observing that she "refunded a stream of pearly liquids, which flowed down my thighs" (112). Moreover, she apologizes for her descriptions which "flag" at times (129) and uses the same term later to refer to Mr. Barvile's penis, which also "flags" (180). She refers to her "cooked up" maidenhead (132). And, in the sadomasochistic scene with Mr. Barvile, she tells how she becomes "steeled to the sight by his stoutness" (184) after which she "resumes the rod" (184) — literally the switch, but metaphorically her own implied phallus — in order to bring Mr. Barvile to a climax. Finally, although the list goes on, Fanny, upon setting up house with Charles, cheerily declares, "thus, at length, I got snug into port" (223), a line which clearly establishes Fanny as the inserting "male" and Charles as receiver. The dynamic caused by the diction here metaphorically establishes Fanny as a masculine figure engaging in a sex act with another male. But this same-sex pairing in no way diminishes or even subordinates women. Instead, as a representative of a third-sex, Fanny affirms both homosexual and feminist roles: she is at once both male (implied narrator) and female (narrator proper) behaving on the whole as an egalitarian actor in relationships with other men.

This hermaphroditic side to Fanny is apparent also in her anxiety over penetration. In *The Carnal Prayer Mat*, Vesperus learns that after he has undergone an operation for a penis enlargement he will no longer be able to penetrate either young female virgins (vaginally) or boys (anally [LiYu 120-21]). "You will be killing every one of them that you sleep with," he is told by his physician. He enjoys both sexual experiences and laments their loss, telling his favorite catamite on the eve of the operation, "you and I won't be able to have sex again" and that he's come to say, by spending one last night with him, "farewell to your buttocks" (LiYu 121). Anal penetration of a boy and vaginal penetration of a girl are considered the same.

Cleland draws a similar parallel in *Fanny Hill*. There is a general apprehension and anxiety over first-time penetration and worry over the resulting pain. Fanny's penetration-anxiety grows as the experience proves more and more imminent. After being sexually aroused by a peep show of Mrs. Brown copulating with her paramour, Fanny rushes back to her room to masturbate and ponders a question of physics:

> At length, I resorted to the only present remedy [of achieving orgasm], that of vain attempts at digitation, where the smallness of the theater did not yet afford room enough for action, and where the pain my fingers gave me in striving for admission, though they procured me a slight satisfaction for the present, started an apprehension, which I could not be easy till I had communicated to Phoebe. (64)

She wonders how "the size of that enormous machine" will penetrate "the tender, small part of me" (65). But her fear isn't so much related to hymenal rupture as it is to the mere act of penetration itself. Although she understandably makes a great deal of the pain at the loss of her virginity, she nevertheless pairs the act of penetration alone with pain even after she in fact loses it. Speaking of Will, for instance, she relates:

I now felt such a mixture of pleasure and pain as there is no giving a definition of. I dreaded, alike, his splitting me farther up or his withdrawing: I could not bear either to keep or part with him: the sense of pain, however, prevailing, from his prodigious size and stiffness, acting upon me in those continued rapid thrusts with which he furiously pursued his penetration, made me cry out gently: "Oh, my dear, you hurt me!" (110)

In *The Carnal Prayer Mat* Vesperus explains to his catamite that women differ from boys "in preferring the large [penis] to the small" (LiYu 121), the seventeenth-century rationale being that women can accommodate or adjust to a large penis while males cannot. Indeed, this predilection for the smaller phallus in same-sex bonds existed in ancient Greece (Dover 127-28). It is also evident in *Fanny Hill* in that, unlike the heterosexual males in the book who as a rule sport oversized penises, the inserting sodomite features a "middle-sized" one (194). Fanny espouses the female role in admiring the large phallus, calling it "the amazing, pleasing object of all my wishes, all my dreams, all my love" and "king member" (147-148), but resembles the eighteenth-century sodomite in her inability to adjust to it. She fails to habituate over time to penetration by a large penis, as the episode with Will demonstrates.

In the sodomitical passage the reader finds the rhetoric of penetration strikingly similar to that of Fanny's heterosexual language. Having forgotten her own experience with Charles, in which her initial "narrowness" (84) adjusted *for the time* to his penis size, all of a sudden Fanny again ponders the mechanics of insertion. Posted behind the "very small opening" (194) of her peephole, a configuration foreshadowing that of the young sodomite and underscoring a more general anal preoccupation, she contemplates how the elder of the two will get his phallus into the other. When he does, her observations mimic closely her own experience:

The Ganymede now obsequiously leaned his head against the back of [a chair], and projecting his body, made a fair mark, still covered with his shirt, as he thus stood in a side-view to me but fronting his companion, who, presently unmasking his

> battery, produced an engine that certainly deserved to be put to
> a better use, and very fit to confirm me in my disbelief of the
> possibility of things being pushed to odious extremities, which
> I had built on the disproportion of parts. But this disbelief I
> was now to be cured of. . . . (195)

The younger sodomite undergoes "writhing, twisting" and "soft
murmured complaints" at penetration (195). And like Fanny's own
earlier experience, in which she "felt no more the smart of my
wounds below" (79), she notices after the initial pain that "at
length, the first straights of entrance being pretty well got through,
everything seemed to move and go pretty currently on" (195). The
pattern of temporary penetration-pain-habituation proves consistent
among the sodomite and Fanny.

By dint of the sociopolitical pressures bearing on Cleland, he
necessarily creates clear lines of demarcation between homosexual
and heterosexual experience, and to this end Fanny spews forth the
party line, inveighing against all she sees in the sodomitical passage. But not only is the rhetoric of homosexuality similar to that of
heterosexuality, a fact that undercuts Fanny's denouncements, one
sees in retrospect that the homoerotic more aptly informs the other.

This point appears all the more clearly when one considers the
series of anal near-misses in *Fanny Hill*. The text intimates anal
intercourse and even brings one character to the brink of it in its
build-up to the sodomitical passage. Speaking of Emily, for example, Fanny writes:

> Her spark then endeavoured, as she stood, by disclosing her
> thighs, to gain us a completer sight of that central charm of
> attraction, but not obtaining it so conveniently in that attitude,
> he led her to the foot of the couch, and bringing to it one of the
> pillows, gently inclined her head down, so that as she leaned
> with it over her lost hands, straddling with her thighs wide
> spread and jutting her body out, she presented a full back-view
> of her person, naked to her waist. Her posteriors, plump,
> smooth, and prominent, formed luxuriant tracts of animated
> snow that splendidly filled the eye, till it was commanded
> down the parting or separation of those exquisitely white

cliffs, by their narrow vale, and was there stopped, and attracted by the embowered bottom cavity. (156)

It is this "bottom cavity" in all its ambiguity, that receives Emily's lover's penis. It is in similarly vague language that Fanny describes penetration by her own "spark":

[A]nd softly turning up my petticoat and shift behind, opened himself the prospect of the back avenue to the genial seat of pleasure: where, as I lay at my side-length, inclining rather face downward, I appeared full fair and liable to be entered. (163)

Of course, the reader knows to what Fanny *should* be referring when she speaks of the "genial seat of pleasure," but based on the language alone, it is not entirely clear.

Fanny's flirtation with anal intercourse, though, comes close to the real thing during the episode in which Emily is crossdressed as a shepherd; a gentleman attempts to sodomize her:

[I]mpelling her to lean down, with her face against the bedside, [the stranger] placed her so that the double-way between the double rising behind presented the choice fair to him, and he was so fiercely set on a mis-direction as to give the girl no small alarms for fear of losing a maidenhead she had not dreamt of. (192)

Finally he finds "the right road" and Emily avoids a mishap.

It is not difficult to see that this talk about "right" and "wrong" roads is related to a conventional, even banal, morality, one that is threatened in the sodomitical passage, because the events therein appear so normal, despite Fanny's attempts to characterize them as unusual or obscene. Fanny has incrementally prepared the reader for the real thing through imagery, allusion, and language. When male anal penetration finally occurs after all of Fanny's narrative courtship of it, the reader is hardly surprised. Fanny unleashes a spate of invectives (193-95), but, it appears, does so only to offset the truth that the episode represents a narratological high point. Reaching its own climax, all real action in the narrative declines after the sodomitical episode.

This thematic falling off is mimicked by a more literal fall: Fanny's tripping over a nail and losing consciousness. After witnessing "so criminal a scene," Fanny marches straight off to the authorities to turn the sodomites in. She attributes her patience to tarry there and watch the entire scene to a desire to "gather more facts" (195), presumably with which to incriminate the two. But in perhaps the only true slapstick scene in the text, Fanny trips on a nail in her rage and indignation and is flung on her face "with such a violence that I fell senseless on the ground" (195-96). This motion that Fanny calls "unlucky" (195) heralds the equally "senseless" and predictable thematic and narratological resolution: Fanny's rediscovery of Charles; her subsequent union with him; and the perfunctory affirmation of the bourgeois ethos, monogamous heterosexuality. In Fanny's being knocked senseless Cleland mocks the high-handed moralizers of his day and calls into question their cock-sure condemnations, embodied, for instance, in the person of Mrs. Cole (196).

Purporting to shun the sodomites, Fanny writes: "But here washing my hands of them, I replunge into the stream of my history" (196). But in doing so she equates herself with the biblical figure Pilate, who renounces his conscience, and the sodomites with those "crucified" at the hands of the mindless mob, or society. Fanny's stumbling is a fall from individuality into a state of moral mindlessness. In this context, her "tail-piece of morality" is an awkward appendage that fails to fit the body of the text.

In the final analysis, *Fanny Hill* is not the straightforward celebration of the code of bourgeois heterosexuality that most critics claim it to be. Cleland subtly undercuts this notion at too many junctures in the text; if he doesn't *replace* it with a trenchant paradigm of homosexuality, or, more aptly, bisexuality, he certainly *juxtaposes* it next to the socially accepted one, offering it as a possibility. Behind Fanny's drag persona and the text's rhetorical apparatus lies the paradigm for a new social role and a new morality.

# REFERENCES

Bradbury, Malcolm. *"Fanny Hill* and the Comic Novel." *Critical Quarterly* 13 (1971): 263-275.

Braudy, Leo. *"Fanny Hill* and Materialism." *Eighteenth Century Studies* 4 (1970): 21-40.

Cleland, John. *Fanny Hill.* New York: Penguin, 1985.

Dover, K. J. *Greek Homosexuality.* Cambridge: Harvard University Press, 1978.

Foxon, David. *Libertine Literature in England, 1660-1745.* New Hyde Park: University Books, 1965.

Illo, John. "The Idyll of Unreproved Pleasures Free." *Carolina Quarterly* 17 (1965): 18-26.

LiYu. *The Carnal Prayer Mat.* Trans. Patrick Hanan. New York: Ballantine Books, 1990.

Markley, Robert. "Language, Power, and Sexuality in Cleland's *Fanny Hill.*" *Philological Quarterly* 63 (1984): 343-356.

Miller, Nancy K. *The Heroine's Text: Readings in the French and English Novel, 1722-1782.* New York: Columbia University Press, 1980.

_____ "'I's' in Drag: The Sex of Recollection." *The Eighteenth Century* 28 (1981): 47-57.

*Oxford Companion to Classical Literature.* Ed. Sir Paul Harvey. Oxford: Clarendon Press, 1980.

Quennell, Peter. Introduction. *Memoirs of a Woman of Pleasure.* By John Cleland. New York: Putnam and Sons, 1963, *v-xiv.*

Scholes, Robert. *Semiotics and Interpretation.* New Haven: Yale University Press, 1982.

Shinagel, Michael. *"Memoirs of a Woman of Pleasure*: Pornography and the Mid-Eighteenth-Century English Novel." *Studies in Change and Revolution: Aspects of English Intellectual History, 1640-1800.* Ed. Paul J. Korshin. Yorkshire: Menston, 1972.

Slepian, B., and L. J. Morrissey. "What is *Fanny Hill?*" *Essays in Criticism* 14 (1964): 65-75.

Solomon, Stanley. "Subverting Propriety as a Pattern of Irony in Three Eighteenth-Century Novels: *The Castle of Otranto*; *Vathek*; and *Fanny Hill.*" *Erasmus Review* 1 (1977): 107-116.

Sossamon, Stephen. "Sex, Love and Reason in the Novels of John Cleland." *Massachusetts Studies in English* 6 (1978): 93-106.

Taube, Myron. "Moll Flanders and Fanny Hill: A Comparison." *Ball State University Forum* 9 (1968): 76-80.

Todd, Janet. *Sensibility: An Introduction.* New York: Methuen, 1986.

Trumbach, Randolph. "The Birth of the Queen: Sodomy and the Emergence of Gender Equality in Modern Culture, 1660-1750." *Hidden from History: Reclaiming the Gay and Lesbian Past.* Ed. Martin Duberman, Martha Vicinus, and George Chauncey, Jr. New York: New American Library, 1989, 129-140.

_____. "Modern Prostitution and Gender in *Fanny Hill*: Libertine and Domesti-

cated Fantasy." *Sexual Worlds of the Enlightenment*. Ed. G. S. Rousseau and
  Roy Porter. Chapel Hill: University of North Carolina Press, 1988.
Wagner, Peter. Introduction. *Fanny Hill*. By John Cleland. New York: Penguin,
  1985, 7-30.
Whitley, Raymond. "The Libertine Hero and Heroine in the Novels of John Cle-
  land." *Studies in Eighteenth Century Culture* 9 (1979): 387-404.

# "The Voice of Nature" in Gray's *Elegy*

George E. Haggerty, PhD

University of California, Riverside

**SUMMARY.** Thomas Gray's "Elegy Written in a Country Churchyard" commemorates a problematic sexuality that traditional readings of the poem's "melancholy" usually ignore. By reconsidering the poem in light of theories of abjection, this essay uncovers the powerful poetic expression of a sexuality at odds with mid-century culture and shows how the poet's awareness of his own homosexuality shaped the familiar features of the most popular poem of the eighteenth century.

The homosexuality of a group of important mid- to late- eighteenth-century male writers has been the best kept secret of literary studies for some time. Only recently have critics addressed the sexuality of such writers as Mark Akenside, Horace Walpole, William Beckford, Matthew G. Lewis, Lord Byron, and, most importantly for our purposes here, Thomas Gray.[1] It is not very controversial these days to talk about Gray's relations with Horace Walpole and Richard West in sexual terms.[2] Even if, as George Rousseau explains, the question of definition is a strained one, there is hardly any basis for resisting the suggestion that Gray found members of his own sex attractive or that he animated his most intimate friend-

---

George E. Haggerty is Associate Professor of English at the University of California, Riverside. He is the author of *Gothic Fiction/Gothic Form* and a variety of essays on the literature of the eighteenth century. His *Body Language: Sensibility and Sexuality from Richardson to Austen* is forthcoming. "This essay is dedicated in memory of Thomas Stehling."

Correspondence may be addressed to the author at: Department of English-40, University of California, Riverside, CA 92521-0323.

ships with sexual tension. I am not myself interested in arguing the extent of Gray's sexual activity, but instead I would like to suggest ways in which his sense of his own sexuality helped to shape one of the best loved poems of his, or any, time, the "Elegy Written in a Country Churchyard."[3]

Rousseau has suggested a range of categories for discussing homosexual relations in the eighteenth century, and I think his ingenious "homoplatonic" offers us a place to start in discussing Gray's own circumscribed experience. But "homoplatonism," however useful as a descriptive category, suggests a poetic sublimation of desire which Gray's poetry belies. Gray's internal conflict is played out in each of his poems in vivid and at times painful ways, and "homoplatonism" becomes but another term for the closet in which Gray's poetry has been locked for generations. It is a closet that Gray himself knew well. His feelings about his own dark and troubling sexuality are everywhere apparent in his poetry, and in place of the traditional label "melancholy," which now obscures more than it reveals about private feeling, I would like to suggest that we consider the notion of abjection, which, in writing about a different figure in a different time, Julia Kristeva uses to describe a state very similar to that which concerns us here: "There looms, within abjection, one of those violent, dark revolts of being, directed against a threat that seems to emanate from an exorbitant outside or inside, ejected beyond the scope of the possible, the tolerable, the thinkable. It lies there, quite close, but it cannot be assimilated" (1). In his "Elegy Written in a Country Churchyard," Gray acts out such a "revolt of being," which behind the deceptive label "melancholy" harbors the sorts of ambiguities and anxieties that Kristeva describes.

We can best approach the "Elegy" by way of Gray's "Sonnet" on the death of Richard West. Gray and West were close friends from their years together at Eton College, where they formed part of the "Quadruple Alliance" with Horace Walpole and Thomas Ashton. Gray's feelings for West became increasingly intense in the months preceding West's death, when Gray was estranged from Walpole, and he lamented West's passing deeply.[4] West, with whom Gray shared the love and practice of poetry, died when both men were in their mid-twenties, and Gray's "Sonnet" expresses his loss in terms that are deceptive in their self-conscious artificiality. Beneath a veil of artifice, the poet struggles with brutal and unadorned emotion:

> In vain to me the smiling mornings shine,
> And reddening Phoebus lifts his golden fire:
> The birds in vain their amorous descant join,
> Or cheerful fields resume their green attire:
> These ears, alas! for other notes repine,
> A different object do these eyes require.
> My lonely anguish melts no heart but mine;
> And in my breast the imperfect joys expire.
> Yet morning smiles the busy race to cheer,
> And new-born pleasure brings to happier men:
> The fields to all their wonted tribute bear;
> To warm their little loves the birds complain.
> I fruitless mourn to him that cannot hear,
> And weep the more because I weep in vain.

Lonsdale astutely notices that "the diction is intended to evoke a Miltonic richness which contrasts with the barer language . . . used to describe the poet's barren spiritual condition. . . ." "[F]ruitful nature, in contrast with the poet's sterile, friendless solitude, is shown as actively harmonious and benevolent, giving, serving, sharing, and loving, all activities which emphasize the poet's condition and give added poignancy to the ironic paradox at the heart of the poem: that the poet is mourning the only friend who could have understood and shared such a grief" (66-67).

But the poet's "barren spiritual condition" is a physical ache as well. The first quatrain of the poem emphasizes the sights and sounds of a playful, passionate, and personal nature—"smiling mornings," "golden fire," "amorous descant," "green attire"—and the next answers with physical distress. "A different object do these eyes require" even suggests that reddening Phoebus burns in vain when there is no lover for the dawn or for the poet to woo. The poet's "anguish" is "lonely" because his "heart" "melts" alone; his "joys" are "imperfect" because they are not shared, and they "expire" because trapped in his own breast. Although easily translated into platonic longing, none of these complaints is primarily spiritual. They are instead vivid expressions of frustrated physical desire. It is perhaps no accident that Gray chose as his model a Petrarchan sonnet or that many of his images can be traced to a range of love poetry from Ovid to Thomson.

The sestet repeats the sense of the "In vain to me" of the opening: both the quality of the pain and the subjectivity of the feelings are reemphasized. "Pleasure" is for "happier men." Even the birds are able to "warm their little loves." But the poet is trapped in his own isolated response: "I fruitless mourn to him that cannot hear" is an odd usage, to be sure. That is, mourning is an intransitive and totally subjective activity, but the poet here sees it as an act of communion which is frustrated in death. Instead of mourning for West, he mourns to him. This underlines the personal loss — West is in the place of God here — and explains the loop of grief which the last line expresses and Gray in his life seems to have acted out. With West finally out of reach, Gray withdraws into his own misery. "I . . . weep the more because I weep in vain": Gray stops short of breaking through the language of grief to something (or someone) outside himself. "I" is the source of grief, that is, rather than "he" or "you."[5]

The poet begins the poem as an object on whom the world has ceased to assert itself ("In vain to *me*") and ends it as a doubly asserted subject of weeping ("I . . . weep the more . . . I weep in vain"). The poet has lost an object in the world but has refashioned it in his grief into nothing more than a heightened expression of subjectivity. Grief becomes the substitute for the friend and offers protection against the implications of desire. But at the same time it commemorates that desire, and perhaps its fulfillment, in conventional imagery that hides its personal intensity. Every line reveals as much as it conceals, and poetry itself, decorous and allusive, becomes the vehicle for private longing. Gray's abjection stems from the failure of the elegy to release him from the privacy of his emotion. A homoplatonic stance involves an internal contradiction and self-confrontation that West's death now makes inevitable. Homoplatonics, that is, are abject in their very conception.

Gray begins his "Elegy" with the oddly passive and objectified expression of his own presence in the poem. The "to me" with which the first quatrain ends is reminiscent of the opening of the

"Sonnet," but it also dramatizes a more complicated relation between subjective and objective experience than that found in Gray's earlier poems:

> The curfew tolls the knell of parting day,
> The lowing herd wind slowly o'er the lea,
> The ploughman homeward plods his weary way,
> And leaves the world to darkness and to me. (ll. 1-4)

The opening stanza displays none of the inflated diction for which Gray is famous, but instead expresses the scene in simple, neatly parallel subject/predicate statements. The final line, however, insinuates the subject of the poem, the Poet, as indirect object of the sentence, thereby implying the passivity of reflection and the solitude necessary to his ruminations. By refusing to articulate his subjectivity directly, the poet places himself in the scene and stands remote from—beside—himself.[6] The poet must establish his passivity as a way of avoiding the moral implications of self-assertion. But he is also establishing a quality of isolation and anxiety.

As the poem proceeds, this anxiety is given concrete form in the sounds of the night and the graveyard itself, "where heaves the turf in many a mouldering heap" (l. 14). The poet has an even more shadowy, self-effacing presence here, for the reasoned and precise observations of the countryside in the evening and the exceptions to the growing tranquility all ultimately focus on the absent object of the owl's complaint, wandering near her sacred bower and molesting her with his private ruminations. That object is of course the subjective presence which exists everywhere but nowhere (yet) in the poem, the poet himself:

> Now fades the glimmering landscape on the sight,
> And all the air a solemn stillness holds,
> Save where the beetle wheels his droning flight,
> And drowsy tinklings lull the distant folds;
>
> Save that from yonder ivy-mantled tower
> The moping owl does to the moon complain
> Of such as, wandering near her secret bower,
> Molest her ancient solitary reign.

> Beneath those rugged elms, that yew-tree's shade,
> Where heaves the turf in many a mouldering heap,
> Each in his narrow cell for ever laid,
> The rude forefathers of the hamlet sleep. (11. 5-16)

We take it for granted that a mid-century poet should depict himself wandering in a graveyard in the evening and that his stoicism will lead to pointed moralizing rather than to protogothicism. But by confusing the division between subject and object, as he does here, Gray creates a mood that emphasizes the impossibility of finding the object of his rambles even in these graves. The opening quatrains in fact repress the real desire behind this poem and postpone it in a delusion of identification and loss.

In the three stanzas that follow, the poet depicts what Lonsdale calls "the lives of the humble villagers" (114). It is their deaths, however, that oxymoronically suggest their lives to Gray, just as the neat regularity of the lines poeticizes what could only have been a far from poetic existence in the English countryside. Patricia Meyer Spacks says that "the psychic drama which unfolds through these scenes is surely more important than the scenes themselves . . ." (115). The psychic drama involves creating a world that is unavailable to the poet and then rejecting it, as he does subtly in the sixth stanza:

> For them no more the blazing hearth shall burn,
> Or busy housewife ply her evening care:
> No children run to lisp their sire's return,
> Or climb his knees the envied kiss to share. (11. 21-24)

This is not only a depiction of experience, but it is also a negation of experience. The structure of parallelism heightens the sense that this is a description of what is not. This implicit conflict between affirmation and negation is reflected as well in the terms of the description itself. For the very conventional nature of the lines renders them remote from experience. Perhaps the "doubtful" scribbled in Gray's manuscript next to "envied kiss" suggests his own discomfort with the idea as well as the image (Lonsdale 122). Gray narrates a tale the meaning of which lies in its impossibility.

Kristeva says that "narrative is, all in all, the most elaborate attempt . . . to situate a speaking being between his desires and their prohibitions, in short, within the Oedipal triangle'' (140). Gray enters the eerie geometric form of his unconscious by calling to mind his "rude forefathers" and depicting the scene of familial intimacy — an intimacy, by the way, which he never knew — and then negating them both, subtly but surely.[7] His desires lead him else-where.

The poet hints at the nature of his desire first in admonitory and even accusatory terms. The poem proceeds from "Let not Ambition mock their useful toil / Their homely joys and destiny obscure" (11. 29-30) to "Nor you, ye Proud, impute to these the fault, / If Memory o'er their tomb no trophies raise" (11. 37-38). Gray's tone shifts from the reflective to the judgmental, in part because he has articulated a social ideal in which he does not believe. Though "homely joys" are present in the poem, they are present as a result of their inaccessibility, to the dead and to the poet. This section of the poem turns on the aphorism "The paths of glory lead but to the grave" (36), a brutal reminder to those who are tempted to sneer, but also a suggestion of the abjection the poet feels and the utter uselessness of the usual patriarchal valuation of personal achievement.

The climactic stanza of this group directly articulates the object Death as a competing subject and seems for a moment to illumine the darker purpose of the poem:

> Can storied urn or animated bust
> Back to its mansion call the fleeting breath?
> Can Honour's voice provoke the silent dust,
> Or Flattery soothe the dull cold ear of Death? (11. 41-44)

This subtle personification enables the poet to express his sense of the finality of Death against the world of language and seeming. In other contexts, Honour could "provoke" or Flattery "soothe," but Gray seems to insist on the inability of the poetic personification of such abstractions to have any power in the real world of emotion and pain. Death, also personified, is for the moment the only possible subject and its "dull cold ear" is the most distinct physical feature yet observed in the poem. Personification, in other words, insists upon the force of Death to resist and to undermine the world of public value and the semblance of grandeur in favor of mere physical power.

Death has been hovering in the poem as a shadowy Other, but as he attains a physical presence here, it might seem that he is really the lover that the poet has been courting all along. The poet chooses Death as the only expression of a sexuality that terrifies him. This personified figure becomes the figure of abjection in the poem.[8] This poem begins with the morbid sexuality that a moralistic stance implies. The poet makes this choice because any other is fraught with the harrowing violence of what we would now call homophobia.

Sedgwick claims that the "Gothic novel crystallized for English audiences the terms of a dialectic between male homosexuality and homophobia" (92), and it would not be stretching the terms of her analysis to see homophobia already at work in a poem such as Gray's "Elegy." As Sedgwick states, building on the work of Alan Bray, "once the secularization of terms that Bray incisively traces began to make 'the homosexual' available as a descriptive category of lived experience, what had happened was not only that the terms of a newly effective minority oppression had been set, but that a new and immensely potent tool had become available for the manipulation of every form of power that was refracted through the gender system" (87).[9]

A vivid statement of this emerging homophobia can be found in tracts such as the mid-century masterpiece of panic, *Satan's Harvest Home* (1749). There, for instance, homosexuality is represented under the sign of abomination:

> 'Till of late Years, *Sodomy* was a *Sin*, in a manner unheard of in these Nations; and indeed, one would think where there are such *Angelic Women,* so foul a Sinshould never enter into Imagination: On the contrary, our *Sessions-Papers* are frequently stain'd with the *Crimes* of these *beastly Wretches;* and tho' many have been made Examples of, yet we have but too much Reason to fear, that there are Numbers yet undiscover'd, and that this *abominable Practice* gets Ground ev'ry Day.
>
> Instead of the *Pillory*, I would have the *Stake* be the Punish-

ment of those, who in Contradiction to the Laws of *God* and *Man*, to the Order and Course of *Nature,* and to the most simple Principles of *Reason,* preposterously *burn* for each other, and *leave* the *Fair*, the *charming Sex*, neglected. (52-53)

For someone like Gray, fastidious and anti-social in any case, such warnings may not have been necessary. The fear they instill, however, may be at the heart of his graveyard flirtation with Death.

But Gray goes on to express his own sexual frustration in terms that are both beautiful and haunting:

> Full many a gem of purest ray serene
> The dark unfathomed caves of ocean bear:
> Full many a flower is born to blush unseen
> And waste its sweetness on the desert air. (11. 53-56)

We hardly need a Freud to suggest that the "dark unfathomed caves of ocean" suggest Gray's fear of his own sexuality, and the "waste [of] sweetness," echoing as it does Shakespeare's "waste of shame," hints at the death-like masturbatory implications of the poet's lonely stance. In any case, these famous lines surely point to a disturbed and disturbing privacy.

Gray's letter to West (May 27, 1742) offers a helpful gloss to passages such as this:

> Mine, you are to know, is a white Melancholy, or rather Leucocholy for the most part; which though it seldom laughs or dances, nor ever amounts to what one calls Joy or Pleasure, yet it is a good easy sort of a state, and ça ne laisse que de s'amuser. The only fault of it is insipidity; which is apt now and then to give a sort of Ennui, which makes one form certain little wishes that signify nothing. But there is another sort, black indeed, which I have now and then felt, that has somewhat in it like Tertullian's rule of faith, Credo quia impossibile est; for it believes, nay, is sure of every thing that is unlikely, so it be but frightful; and on the other hand, excludes and shuts its eyes to the most possible hopes, and every thing that is pleasurable; from this the Lord deliver us! (*Correspondence* 1: 209)

Gray examines his own psychology as a way of answering ennui, fear, and desire. He personifies these humors as a way of giving them substance and understanding the most personal traits of his character. In the way Gray objectifies his emotion, he seems afraid to cross the boundary between external and internal, and he lapses into French and Latin as a way of avoiding the power of his own feeling. "Little wishes that signify nothing," "every thing that is unlikely": these phrases ring with the force of repression and the struggle to maintain it.

Gray's abjection has led him to this graveyard self-confrontation as a way of redirecting sexual desire and substituting an object—in this case death—for his own threatening melancholy. Of course, as his letter to West suggests, death is not the real object of Gray's desire, but at least it offers an alternative to his own self-involved sexuality. Death has the virtue as the ultimate Other of being in the grave indistinguishable from self. "Abjection then takes the place of the other, to the extent of affording him jouissance, often the only one for the borderline patient who, on that account, transforms the abject into the site of the Other" (Kristeva 54). For the moment, the site of the other is—simply—the silent grave.

Gray is trapped in a dance with death in the opening of the poem, and its first ending commemorates abjection:

> No more with Reason & thyself at strife;
> Give anxious Cares & endless Wishes room
> But thro' the cool sequester'd Vale of Life
> Pursue the silent Tenour of thy Doom.[10]

In this version, the poet steps back from the grave with the distance that a moralistic stance allows and steps into frigidity and silence, doomed to the knowledge of everything—of anything—but his own desire.

It is precisely this stance that the poet learns to move beyond in the course of revising the poem, a process which took several years, and which was for Gray a kind of reopening of the issues on which the poem is based.

In the final version, the tension surrounding the figure of Death is given voice. Gray pulls himself out of his moralizing closet and into confrontation with his own tormented sensibility:

> For who to dumb Forgetfulness a prey,
> This pleasing anxious being e'er resigned,
> Left the warm precincts of the cheerful day,
> Nor cast one longing lingering look behind? (11. 85-88)

This stanza takes us from a flirtation with the "dumb Forgetfulness" of Death to a crucial assertion of Gray's own subjectivity. "One longing lingering look" challenges the abjection that has brought the poet to the graveyard in the first place and begins to open up the possibility of a more honest recognition of his own desire:

> On some fond breast the parting soul relies,
> Some pious drops the closing eye requires;
> Ev'n from the tomb the voice of nature cries,
> Ev'n in our ashes live their wonted fires. (11. 89-92)

Here at last the real subject of the poem forces itself into view: not Death but the "fond breast" of companionship; not the silence of the tomb, but the "voice of nature"; not the "ashes," but the "fires." Kristeva says that abjection exists "at the crossroads of phobia, obsession, and perversion" and that language itself becomes a defense against desire (45). Gray places himself at this turning point between the forces of life and death in the poem as a way of confronting his own "perversion" and opening the language of the poem to the cry of nature that he earlier silenced.

Gray breaks out of his isolation in a way that hints at the dangers of the solitary stance that the poem at first celebrates. This process begins first with that odd shift in person, which creates an alter ego through which the poet can begin to talk about himself:

> For thee who, mindful of the unhonoured dead,
> Dost in these lines their artless tale relate;
> If chance, by lonely Contemplation led,
> Some kindred spirit shall inquire thy fate,
>
> Haply some hoary-headed swain may say, . . . (93-97)

If the lonely poem now becomes crowded with "spurious" egos —
what Kristeva calls "seeming egos that confront undesirable objects" (47) — they begin to lead the poet through abjection to an
attitude of tentative but meaningful self-assertion.

"Thee" refers of course to the poet himself — an earlier draft
reads, suggestively, "And thou, who mindful of the unhonour'd
Dead / Dost in these Notes *thy* artless Tale relate" (my italics) — but
it also suggests the presence of an idealized Other, a substitute for
Death, a friend, perhaps lost in death. At the very least we can say
that by addressing himself in terms of second-person intimacy,
Gray posits a soulmate who participates in and even in a sense creates his poetry. Lest we think this merely the private experience of
imagination, the "kindred spirit" suggests that there is a communion of such souls, bound together in the loneliness of contempla-
tion and drawn to a common fate. At the heart of privacy in the
poem is this unnamed other, more than kind but less than kin: a
lover. Our model of subjectivity is subtly undermined, if not ex-
ploded.

The "hoary-headed swain" multiplies egos further, but this time
the device offers an objective rather than a subjective view of the
poet:

'Oft have we seen him at the peep of dawn
'Brushing with hasty steps the dews away
'To meet the sun upon the upland lawn.

'There at the foot of yonder nodding beech
'That wreathes its old fantastic roots so high,
'His listless length at noontide would he stretch,
'And pore upon the brook that babbles by.

'Hard by yon wood, now smiling as in scorn,
'Muttering his wayward fancies he would rove,
'Now drooping, woeful wan, like one forlorn,
'Or crazed with care, or crossed in hopeless love.

'One morn I missed him on the customed hill,
'Along the heath and near his favourite tree;
'Another came; nor yet beside the rill,
'Nor up the lawn, nor at the wood was he;

'The next with dirges due in sad array
'Slow through the church-way path we saw him borne.
'Approach and read (for thou canst read) the lay,
'Graved on the stone beneath yon aged thorn.'' (11. 98 – 116)

Now we see the poet projected onto the scene of his wanderings, an object with supposed feelings, but feelings we can only imagine. Surely Gray chooses this "decorum" in order to hint at "truths" he dare not reveal.[11] For the "hoary-headed swain" cannot be expected to understand the real cause of this poet's unhappiness, nor would he dare to speak the name of the "wayward fancies" if he could. The "woeful" poet is lost in the frustration of a fully conscious but unattainable desire. "Love" is "hopeless" because unexpressed, or unexpressible. The suffering is more pointed than that earlier in the poem, but it is also more intense. The fear is vividly expressed in the poet's own corpse suddenly and shockingly produced.

The corpse itself carries the poem into a new range of possibility. For, as Kristeva says, "A decaying body, lifeless, completely turned into dejection, blurred between the inanimate and the inorganic, a transitional swarming, inseparable lining of a human nature whose life is undistinguishable from the symbolic — the corpse represents fundamental pollution" (109). Gray drags his own corpse into the poem and violates this fundamental taboo as a way of challenging the death-in-life that the early sections of the poem express. By seeing himself through death he rejects its power over him. His funeral becomes an odd celebration of life, and his corpse becomes the symbol of his physical desire, "inseparable lining of a human nature," and a sign of his triumph over the forces that were threatening to engulf him. Death cannot be proud because the poet finally flaunts the irrepressible desire that a culture's logic about death would repress.

The clearest statement of this "coming out" resides in the epitaph itself:

*Here rests his head upon the lap of earth*
*A youth to fortune and to fame unknown.*
*Fair Science frowned not on his humble birth,*
*And Melancholy marked him for her own.*

*Large was his bounty and his soul sincere,*
*Heaven did a recompence as largely send:*
*He gave to Misery all he had, a tear,*
*He gained from Heaven ('twas all he wished) a friend.*

*No farther seek his merits to disclose,*
*Or draw his frailties from their dread abode,*
*(There they alike in trembling hope repose)*
*The bosom of his Father and his God.* (11. 117-28)

The poem ends, as Hagstrum so eloquently suggests, in the anxiety of sexual fulfillment and "trembling" desire. "Hope trembles in the 'Elegy,'" he says, "because of guilt and the prospect of Judgement" (Hagstrum 10-11). Whether the "friend" was West or Walpole, or both, matters less than the fact that Gray recognizes the solace implicit in his unique wish. He expresses that solace in the "dread abode" with which the poem closes. "The bosom of his Father" both reverses the earlier negation of family and sexualizes the prospect of heavenly life. The abjection of this poem threatens literally to bury the ego, but also leads it through the bottom of its graveyard isolation in the merely contemplating self to possibly real (and possibly liberating) communion with the other, a "thee" of friendship and emotion. Beyond the power of death and repression, the poet comes alive to the possibility of intimacy in the world. He moves from the ignorance of abjection to at least the beginnings of self-knowledge. By inscribing his gay identity in stone, a gesture which generations of critics have questioned, Gray speaks at last with the voice of nature. And in positing a "kindred spirit" to read his words, he creates the life that might have been, or indeed might *be*.

## NOTES

1. See my essay on Walpole, Beckford, and Lewis ("Literature and Homosexuality in the Late Eighteenth Century"); see also the important studies by Crompton, Fothergill, Hagstrum, Marchand, Rousseau, Sedgwick, Trumbach, and Watson-Smyth.

2. Of all discussions of this kind, that by Hagstrum is the most imaginative and convincing.

3. The text of this and Gray's other poems is that of Lonsdale's Longman edition of *The Poems of Gray, Collins and Goldsmith.*

4. Lonsdale quotes Norton Nicholls, a close friend of Gray's in the 1760s, as remembering that "Whenever I mentioned Mr. West he [Gray] looked serious, & seemed to feel the affliction of a recent loss" (64). See also Hagstrum 15-16.

5. The Gray *Concordance* (Cook) lists twenty uses of "vain" — mostly in this sense of "in vain" — in Gray's poetry. It is not an exaggeration to call this mood typical.

6. For Kristeva, "passivation, which heralds the subject's ability to put himself in the place of the object, is a radical stage in the constitution of subjectivity" (39).

7. The cruelty of Gray's father is proverbial. For a useful account, see Hagstrum, 12.

8. Kristeva claims that "A certain sexuality . . . which does not even adorn itself with pleasure but with *sovereignty* and *knowledge*, is the equivalent of disease and death" (85).

9. See also Hocquenghem, *Homosexual Desire* 79-98.

10. For a discussion of the early version of the poem, see Lonsdale 130-31.

11. Much has been written about this feature of the poem. See, for instance, Brady, Bronson, and Jack.

## REFERENCES

Brady, Frank. "Structure and Meaning in Gray's *Elegy*." Hilles and Bloom. 177-89.

Bray, Alan. *Homosexuality in Renaissance England.* London: Gay Men's Press, 1982.

Bronson, Bertrand H. "On a Special Decorum in Gray's *Elegy*." Hilles and Bloom. 171-76.

Cook, Albert S., Ed. *A Concordance to the English Poems of Thomas Gray.* Folcroft, PA: The Folcroft Press, 1908; rpt. 1969.

Crompton, Louis. *Byron and Greek Love: Homophobia in Nineteenth-Century England.* Berkeley: University of California Press, 1985.

Fothergill, Brian. *Beckford of Fonthill.* London: Faber and Faber, 1979.

Gray, Thomas. *Correspondence of Thomas Gray.* Ed. Paget Toynbee and Leonard Whibley. 3 vols. Oxford: Oxford-Clarendon, 1935.

———. "The Poems of Thomas Gray." Lonsdale. 1-353.

Haggerty, George E. "Literature and Homosexuality in the Late Eighteenth Century: Walpole, Beckford, and Lewis." *Studies in the Novel* 18 (1986): 341-52.

Hagstrum, Jean. "Gray's Sensibility." *Fearful Joy: Papers from the Thomas Gray Bicentenary Conference at Carleton University.* Ed. J. Downey and B. Jones. Montreal: McGill-Queen's University, 1974. 6-19.

Hilles, Frederick W., and Harold Bloom, Eds. *From Sensibility to Romanticism: Essays Presented to Frederick A. Pottle.* London: Oxford University Press, 1965.

Hocquenghem, Guy. *Homosexual Desire.* Trans. Daniella Dangoor. London: Allison & Busby, 1978.

Jack, Ian. "Gray's *Elegy* Reconsidered." Hilles and Bloom. 139-69.

Kristeva, Julia. *Powers of Horror: An Essay on Abjection.* Trans. Leon S. Roudiez. New York: Columbia University Press, 1982.

Lonsdale, Roger. Notes and Headnotes. *The Poems of Gray, Collins and Goldsmith.* New York: Longman, 1969.

Marchand, Leslie. *Byron: A Biography.* 3 vols. New York: Alfred A. Knopf, 1957.

Rousseau. G. S. "The Pursuit of Homosexuality in the Eighteenth Century: 'Utterly Confused Category' and/or Rich Repository." *Eighteenth-Century Life* 9 (1985): 132-68.

*Satan's Harvest Home.* London, 1749; reprint New York: Garland, 1985.

Sedgwick, Eve Kosofsky. *Between Men: English Literature and Male Homosocial Desire.* New York: Columbia University Press, 1985.

Spacks, Patricia Meyer. *The Poetry of Vision: Five Eighteenth-Century Poets.* Cambridge, MA: Harvard University Press, 1967.

Trumbach, Randolph. "London's Sodomites: Homosexual Behavior and Western Culture in the 18th Century." *Journal of Social History* 11 (1977): 1-33.

Watson-Smyth, Peter. "On Gray's Elegy." *The Spectator* 31 July 1971: 171-74.

# Index

abjection, 199-214
"Address of Friendship, An"
    (anonymous), 111-12,113,
    118,120,128
*Advancement of Learning* (Bacon),
    15
Aelian, 109,127
*Aeneid, The* (Virgil), 22-23
*Affectionate Shepheard, The*
    (Barnfield), 45-52
Akenside, Mark, 199
Akrigg, G.P.V., 141-42,144,150
"All haile, sweet Poet" (Donne),
    87-90,93,95,97,98,99
*All's Well That Ends Well*
    (Shakespeare), 54-55,57
Althusser, Louis, 44,64
Anacreon, 109
*Anatomie of Abuses* (Stubbes), 143
Andreadis, Harriette, 127,154-155
Anne of Denmark, Queen of
    England, 135,136,137,138,
    139,141,142,144,146,150
*Anniversaries* (Donne), 105
Anton, George, 74
*Antony and Cleopatra*
    (Shakespeare), 5,83,135,136,
    140,144,145-49
Aristophanes, 92-93
Aristotle, 128
*Arraignment of Lewd, Idle,*
    *Froward, and Unconstant*
    *Women, The* (Swetnam), 22
*Arte of Rhetorique, The* (Wilson),
    55-56
Ashton, Robert, 141
Ashton, Thomas, 200
*Astrophil and Stella* (Sidney), 99

"At once, from hence" (Donne),
    97-99
Aubrey, John, 14,35
Aubrey, Mary, 156
Augustine of Hippo, Saint, 117,128
*Autobiography* (D'Ewes), 14

Babcock, Barbara, 178,182
Bacon, Lady Ann, 14
Bacon, Anthony, 14,35
Bacon, Sir Francis, 3,14-21,24,
    27-28,35,117
Baker, Sir Richard, 85,113,128
Bald, R.C., 86
Barish, Jonas, 143-44,148
Barnfield, Richard, 3-4,37,43,44,
    45-52,53,57,61,62,63,85
Barthes, Roland, 64,173,179
Bartholin, Thomas, 127
*Basilikon Doron* (James I), 135,137
Beale, Simon Russell, 74,75,83
Beauvoir, Simone de, 129
Beckford, William, 199,212
Behn, Aphra, 6,155-56,158-63,165,
    166-71
Belsey, Catherine, 64
Benet, Diana, 103
Benson, John, 24,26,36
Bentham, Jeremy, 36
Berchorius, Petrus, 64
Bernikow, Louise, 163
*Biathanatos* (Donne), 105
Bingham, Caroline, 137,142,146
Blount, Thomas, 64
Booth, Stephen, 55,59,65
Boswell, John, 22,36,37-38,115
Botticelli, 78
Boyette, Purvis, 83